FAIRYTALE CAVERNS.

A Novel by
Estelle Kennedy.

Shield Crest

© Copyright 2022 Estelle Kennedy

All rights reserved.

ISBN: 978-1-913839-60-4

MMXXII

A CIP catalogue record for this book
is available from the British Library.

Published by
ShieldCrest Publishing,
Boston, Lincolnshire,
PE20 3BT England
Tel: +44 (0) 333 8000 890
www.shieldcrest.co.uk

To the memory of my grandparents;

I find not a day passes by without remembering them in some way or other.

Contents

Chapter 1.

They say that in human life, it is quite possible to experience a sudden, often totally unexpected and unforgettable demarcation line or point. In fact, an experience so memorable that human life forever afterwards becomes somehow irrevocably changed or transmuted, categorised and compartmentalized into, 'before,' and 'after', the occurrence of the event. Nor need this demarcation line be restricted to a single event, it could be two, three, four or any number of events, but even the events themselves could then be subsequently classified or sub-divided according to the impact which they created on the recipient. Well, such was the case with Isabel.

Mid November, Wednesday evening, and the then nineteen-year-old Isabel Jackson had just begun university, a month previously. Down in the depths of the Blue Angel Night Club, she'd met Charles.

Charles Griffiths, six years her senior, complete with his newly acquired MB, ChB degree… The complete man of the world, on an evening out with colleagues after a medical banquet.

They had had two casual conversations, then proceeded to dance and dance, to in fact, almost all the hits that had risen to popularity earlier on during the year. Not devastatingly handsome, but perfectly presentable and obviously successful… And best of all, interested in Isabel, and quite captivated by her fair hair, piercing blue eyes and delicate frame.

The end of the evening approached, and over the microphone the disc jockey announced, 'Now to show your partner that you really love her…' The slow numbers were approaching.

'Will you?' Charles asked Isabel hesitantly.

'Yes, of course, Charles, darling.'

Charles held her close to him, and she snuggled into his welcoming, open arms. What a momentous year it had been! She had passed her 'A' levels with decent grades, started university at Liverchester, a good university by anyone's standards, settled in at university with any backward glances and longings for home now firmly relegated to the past. She was receiving good grades for her written work, finding new friends and of course, best of all, Charles, a successful 'Man of the World,' with prospects, was in love with her. The glitz, glamour and romance of the evening seemed to rise to the fore. This, this is your reward! Thought Isabel to herself... And in a way, it was...

A few years previously, the auspices had not seemed quite so positive, since the fifteen-year-old Isabel had suffered greatly from being bullied at school, grown up with a sense of inferiority and inadequacy, and yet nevertheless clung onto her dreams of knowing a world and a reality outside that of her hometown and of an intrinsic desire for self-improvement.

Consequently, she had beavered away at her 'A' level studies, and now of course, she was reaping the romantic benefits, and may be somewhere, somehow, in those intervening years, the 'ugly duckling,' had metamorphosed into a swan.

The 'Last Dance,' like music tinkled across the dance floor... How long this relationship was likely to last was anyone's guess, but one thing was absolutely certain in an uncertain world, Isabel was well and truly, 'spoken for' that night... An appropriate inauguration into up market, well-heeled, Liverchester society.

That night, Izzy had discovered the life of the world. She left the dance floor, and in fact, the night club with her mind reeling, and yet very happy.

On completion of her degree, Isabel was quite unsure of the next step to take. But in subsequent years, a definite, quite obvious pattern began to emerge and come to the fore in her life. Liverchester. She simply couldn't, and did not want to shake it off... 'It's a place to study that you never want to leave,' claimed advertising hoarding boards, marketing the city to would be students in subsequent years… So true… After a few brief attempts at living in other towns, Isabel returned to Liverchester, and the third time, permanently. The visceral and earthy town had reclaimed her. No more betrayals of Liverchester, it was her absolute home from home…

Over the course of a lifetime, things happen and occur to individuals… Very often for a reason, hence, maybe, in the long term, not altogether bad… At any rate, for years afterwards, as Isabel so lovingly liked to recall it, the rendezvous with Charles turned out to be, 'Demarcation Line, Number One,' and a truly momentous 'before' and 'after' at that.

Isabel retreated into the flat's kitchen, located the bottle of red wine, and refilled her glass.

Major 'Demarcation Line, Number Two.' Numerous minor demarcation points had also occurred during the interim years, but none so memorable as the one which at that instant next sprang to mind… Flirting with the beautiful, enigmatic, pony tailed, Ben Carroll lookalike, PhD student…

Totally sick of her cousin Oscar's stupid, immature and boring drivel, she attempted to detach herself from Oscar's group whilst casting the 'Pony Tail,' knowing looks… A tactically placed left hand up to smooth down her hair… No ring of any type on her wedding ring finger… 'I'm completely free for you!' was of course the subtle or not so subtle message…

'Oh, Isabel!!! You are fickle!' Her mother had responded with, noticing that maximum flirtation techniques appeared to be being employed for the general benefit of an individual a few feet away…

'…And why you, young lady, you're in your absolute element!' She had been too. Life demarcation point, number two completed.

The events leading up to demarcation point number three had resulted in her current predicament. Better to have in so many respects, 'let the proverbial sleeping dogs lie?' Or alternatively,

'…Lie low and say nothing?' Let the matter quietly and discreetly drop?' Events that occurred several years ago, would they have been better relegated to the past and safely left there?'

'Ghastly, simply awful man!!! I don't want our Izzy having anything to do with him!'

On this particular occasion, her grandma had been referring to Isabel's father, who she disliked intensely. Isabel had been twenty-five and spending a bit of time at her grandma's house, helping to entertain her cousin Oscar, then aged about six.

One afternoon, quite abruptly and with no warning whatsoever, Oscar suddenly piped up, '…Grandpa, where's Isabel's father?'

Isabel well knew her grandpa to be a man of his word, a man who firmly believed honesty to be quite literally the best policy, and best of all, who tried, wherever possible not to mince his words, and he answered Oscar eventually with, '…Well, that's a bit of a mystery!'

Oscar was rather an insensitive child, and half an hour later, totally undeterred, in the presence of their grandma, he tried again.

'Er…, grandma?' he bluntly enquired, 'Where's Isabel's father?'

At this, their grandma looked quite clearly and obviously embarrassed, and she said very hurriedly, as if trying to get that particular subject out of the way as soon as was physically possible, 'Oh, he, er… Died, quite some time ago.'

A few years later, in the aftermath of her grandma's death, Isabel learned what she had strongly suspected from that day onwards… Her father had not passed away… Well, certain factors had begun to render this totally implausible in the first instance… Isabel was only too aware from her legal training that for registration of a death and distribution of the contents of the deceased's estate to occur, a certified copy of the death certificate or grant of probate needed to be produced. She had spent an entire wet and drizzling afternoon sorting through a suitcase holding family certificates shortly after her grandma's death... Fruitlessly... No death certificate relating to Kenneth Jackson was found... And she'd scoured the entire case from top to bottom.

A few years after that, relieved at having got an examination out of the way, and after three glasses of wine, she'd found her father on none other than Facebook and by way of a few videos he had produced, and proudly displayed on the internet. Obviously, no sign of him having passed away... But supposing he ignored her? Or was not exactly the model father whom she had idealized?... 'I don't want to either see or ever speak to my father, ever again! Not after he tried to grope me!' She remembered reading of the woes of other individuals in a similar position... Certainly some of them had comprised singularly bad, negative and unfortunate experiences... But making contact simply had to be done! Well, what was better, making contact or spending the rest of her life, full of regrets and wishing she had dared to do it? As it so happened, this turned out to be the deciding factor...

Tentatively, she typed out a message, and sent Kenneth Jackson a friendship request, providing her mobile number as a contact point... She tapped on the send button... It had gone... Irretrievable... Well, Isabel reminded herself, after all, I am a woman of my word; if I say I'll do something, I don't just talk about it... I do it!

And of course, this, in turn had led to her current problem.

Subsequently, a few weeks later, Isabel learned that Kenneth had accepted her friendship request, and three or four days after that, they had talked on the 'phone much to the mutual satisfaction of both parties. Exchange of letters and general communication began to occur, and Isabel met her father and his second wife, a really nice and welcoming Polish woman, Agnieska, at a public house in North Yorkshire. The choice of Hawes, in North Yorkshire was a convenient meeting place for Kenneth, since he lived in Huddersfield… So far, so good… But now the major and almost insuperable problem had arisen…

Izzy's father seemed desperate for her to spend a few days at his house in Huddersfield, and at this stage, Isabel simply didn't want to do it. Isabel had made one excuse already. She now began to feel as if she was running out of excuses… Work commitments? No, she'd already played that card, and couldn't reuse it… Oh well, the can of worms was well and truly opened, for better or worse!

The next morning, Isabel wended her way down to her place of work in Liverchester City Centre. She was employed as a trainee solicitor at Brodie and Watson, and on the whole, quite enjoyed the work with a few exceptions. At exactly nine-thirty, she was checking through a list of buyer's requisitions[1], a small task allocated to Isabel by her supervisor, Mr Brodie, when she was interrupted by the firm's receptionist, a shallow, empty-headed girl named Tanya, who had no mind above perfectly manicured nails, invariably painted an improbable shade of purple. Tanya appeared to be a constant source of irritation to Mr Brodie, but he was far too much of a gentleman to even consider dispensing with her services.

'Miss Jackson-Talbot, I've got a man in to see you. He insists on seeing yourself… Says he's a regular client of this firm, and one of your next-door neighbours… And he's right worked up!'

'Well, please show him in,' Isabel answered calmly. Then she suddenly remembered she had best ask his identity. 'Oh, and incidentally, what's his name?'

'Oh, I forgot to ask…' At which a flicker of irritation crossed Isabel's countenance.

'Please ascertain it.'

---

[1] Requisitions – A series of questions and queries, usually made by the buyer, or buyer's solicitor.

Two minutes later, Tanya returned, 'Steven Webster,' she muttered.

'Yes, I'll see Mr Webster. Please show him in.' She knew Steven, he was a neighbour and worked as a chef at one of the top hotels in the city centre.

'…Oh, hello Steven, and please be seated and make yourself comfortable.' Isabel greeted him warmly. 'How can I help you?'

'It's Bertram.' Steven and Bertram owned the house next door but one to Isabel. The house was split into two flats. Bertram owned the top two floors, and Steven the lower two.

'It's Bertram… He's making my life an absolute misery!'

'Well that doesn't sound too good. Could you explain a bit more?'

'With me being a chef, I have to work at irregular times. Bertram's installing this noisy flooring and flippin' anti-social it is. Whenever I'm in my flat now, it's ghastly! I scarcely get a minute's peace… And of course, it's worse still now that I've met Angela, my new girlfriend, we can get no peace whatsoever in my flat… The only alternative is to go to her house.'

'Oh, I am sorry.'

Steven had a sheaf of paperwork with him. 'I'll leave this with you… This is my paperwork… And of course, this is a copy of his.'

'Steven, I know this is traumatic for you… But leave it with me, and I'll get back to you in the next three or four days. I can't say one way or the other at present but leave it with me. I hope that we can sort it.'

'Well, if you don't understand it, or can't do anything about it, it doesn't matter, it's just one of those things… I did launch legal proceedings before about a similar matter on a different property, and I lost the case, so don't worry.'

Isabel liked Steven. He was such a good, decent man that she obviously wanted to do her absolute best for him, and maintenance and adherence to rule 6 of the S.R.A[2], '…You must always, as a lawyer, do your best for your client…..' was not a problem to uphold, nevertheless, it was not currently her role to evaluate his chances of success or for that matter, failure, at this point.

'…Well, I hope you're successful… Just leave it with me for the time being.'

'Thank you. I know full well you'll do what you can.'

Isabel felt as though she had a rough inkling into the root of Steven's problem, she would simply need to thoroughly read the terms and conditions relating to his tenancy agreement.

She placed the tenancy agreement to one side. She would read it later in the afternoon, write up the advice and ask Mr Brodie to check it through in order to ascertain that Izzy's interpretation of the law was correct, and furthermore, that all eventualities were covered.

At approximately four o'clock, Isabel read through the terms and conditions of the tenancy agreement. The vast majority of the terms appeared to be fair and perfectly reasonable.

The terms were listed by points in alphabetical order, presently, Isabel located it, Bertram had broken term (n), '…not to allow or suffer to allow anything to grow or to become a nuisance… Or noise… To the tenant or tenants of the other flats…' According to further stipulations of the tenancy agreement, the tenant or landlord contravening the terms or conditions, these stipulations appearing in both the landlord and tenant's copy, entitled the injured party to a certain amount of compensation, in what exact amount or form, Isabel was uncertain. Nevertheless, she drew up her advice for Steven, which occupied a page and a half of what Izzy hoped was useful legal advice. All it now needed

---

[2] Solicitors' Regulation Authority.

was a thorough examination under the slightly myopic and pernickety scrutiny of Mr Brodie, Izzy's supervisor.

Uneasily, Isabel knocked on Mr Brodie's door at quarter to five, that afternoon.

'Mr Brodie, I'm really sorry to disturb you so late! Could you examine my advice for my neighbour? He is, incidentally one of our clients, also.'

'Not at all, not at all… And please, please, call me James!'

Mr Brodie came across as rather a sad, lonely character, who seemed to genuinely welcome Isabel's presence that early evening. A few minutes later, he said, 'That's exactly spot on, dear. You can now take it to your neighbour, I really do hope he wins his case.'

'Yes, I hope so too.' Isabel was just about to leave Mr Brodie's office, when he suddenly called after her, 'Could I have a brief word?'

Isabel's heart sank into her shoes. What had she done wrong?

'Have I done something wrong?' Once again, Isabel steeled herself for the absolute worst.

'No, not at all… In fact, I simply wanted to say you have the makings of an A1 solicitor… In fact, I was just thinking earlier on this afternoon how lucky I am to have you.'

'Oh, thank you, Mr Brrr-James!' Isabel quickly corrected herself. She felt rather uneasy calling her supervisor/manager James. In fact, it felt decidedly peculiar.

Anxious to change the conversation's subject Isabel said tentatively, 'I've no difficulty doing my best for this client, he's so nice and decent.'

'Yes, of course, dear,' Mr Brodie answered sympathetically. There was a moment's awkward, embarrassed silence, then James asked equally tentatively, 'Isabel, er, I was just wondering if you…' and then his voice abruptly trailed away, as though he felt too anxious to complete the question.

'Yes?' Isabel asked.

'Oh, it was nothing! Just me being stupid.'

Isabel began to feel a little awkward, and she began to generally catch Mr Brodie's drift. It sounded distinctly like the beginnings of, 'Isabel, I was just wondering if you would be able to meet me for supper one evening? Perhaps we could go to one of the Brazilian restaurants that you said you like so much, or maybe out for a Chinese meal?'

If Isabel were completely honest, she was not altogether overly keen on the prospect of a work-based romance. How did one maintain professionalism in the event of either a split in the relationship, or a continuation or development of it, for that matter? Surely, personal life was best kept out of the work environment? Furthermore, in addition to this problem fraught minefield, there was one other major issue. The age factor! Isabel was thirty-eight years old, and by contrast, Mr Brodie, kind, sensitive and a perfect gentleman though he may be was in his early sixties, at least! Old enough to be Izzy's father!! Of course, that reminded Izzy of someone else… Her father!!! Soon she would have to spend a few days holed up at his house in Huddersfield, yes, 'He who had to be obeyed!' As her mum, Edith,' had so aptly expressed it!! He who simply refused to take 'no' for an answer! Izzy began to feel anxious at the very thought of being closeted up with strangers and having to make forced, stilted, artificial conversation, she couldn't do it! No! No! The prospect was abhorrent!!

Unfortunately, Mr Brodie seemed to notice, and dropping his voice a tone, he said, 'Isabel, dear, is it something I've said?'

Another one who appeared to refuse to take 'no' for an answer!!

'Because if it is, I'm sorry… I shouldn't have been so presumptive.'

Isabel was still feeling anxious, and she decided possibly the best course of action was to try to be as honest and straightforward as possible.

'If you really want to know, I got in contact with my father back in February, after we'd had no contact for years. We've exchanged letters and talked a few times on the 'phone, and now he wants me to spend some time at his house in Huddersfield, and to express it bluntly, I just don't want to go.'

'Well then, simply don't go, you're under no obligation, tell him you're very much needed here, and your manager is unable to spare you.'

'I may have to go… After all, I created this problem… Hence, I need to sort it out.'

'Look, dear, I will back you whatever you decide to do.'

'Thank you, Mr Brodie.'

'Oh, please, call me James!'

'Sorry, James. Well, I think I'd better start to get myself homewards, my evening meal won't make itself.'

At this point, Isabel thought she detected a longing, rather wistful look on Mr Brodie's face, as if to say, '…How about me coming round, and you can make a meal for us both?'

Possibly she was wrong, but that was what she suspected. At any rate, he chose to remain silent on that particular subject.

'Well, I'll see you in the morning, dear… And get home safely.'

'Thank you, James.'

'…And please, remember what I've said… About your father, I mean. You're not under any obligation.'

'Yes, I'll bear that in mind. Anyway, I'd better shoot off now.' Isabel swept her legal advice to Steven into a carrier bag and beat rather a hasty retreat to the door. She then stepped out into the daylight of Dale Street… Relief!!! Out of James's way, for the time being at least!

Chapter 2.

Isabel returned to her first floor flat on Percy Street; a beautiful, Georgian terraced street, and began to put together a meal for herself. She had asked her supervisor to clarify a simple point of law, and he had effectively made a pass at her…!! Yes, and a pass which was decidedly not too welcome… Did she want or in any capacity need a work-based romance or relationship? No, Izzy thought not.

Her mind flicked back down the years and previous boyfriends flitted through her consciousness, in particular some of her late grandma's comments, nearly all of which were derogatory, of course… Surprise!! Surprise!!

'…Pete!! Not, a nice young man!! And similarly, 'That Charles!… Imagine, keeping a young lady, a young lady who's only just left home, keeping her out until three o'clock in the morning! Well, no good will come of that… There's absolutely no mystique about him, he's just after one thing!'

Isabel sipped the red wine she had just opened, as she finished her evening meal… And her grandma passing comment on Mr Brodie? Somehow, Isabel's intrinsic gut feeling seemed to tell her that her grandma's attitude towards James Brodie, partner solicitor and commissioner for oaths might quite possibly have been the entire reverse.

'Can't understand you, young lady! I think you've flipped!… This time, you have flipped, well and truly!… Nice, quiet, gentlemanly middle-aged man appears, a partner, and a solicitor and commissioner for oaths no less, and you're turning your nose up at him!'

'Grandma, he's old enough to be my father!' And at this point, Isabel thought briefly of that particular strange irony.

'Honestly, Isabel, these chances don't come along every day…'

'Yes, but when some of these chances do come along, they're not always appropriate – not in my book, at any rate.' How often Izzy carried on these imaginary dialogues in her head with her grandma these days!

Did Mr Brodie have a wife or girlfriend? Izzy suspected probably not. No, he did not come across as the cheating type. Perhaps the misguided type was far more likely. But did she really want or need a work-based relationship? Probably not. No, not probably, certainly and undoubtedly not. A really kind, decent man, but connected to her in a romantic capacity? Somehow, Isabel thought not.

Isabel had an unremarkable, average type morning, for the most part taking down clients' proofs of evidence in a personal injury matter. Mr Brodie left the office early at half past two in the afternoon since he needed to visit a client who was currently hospitalised and who wished to re-write his will. Before he left, James gave Isabel specific instructions to contact him on his mobile 'phone in the event that anything arose or occurred with which she felt unable to cope. In his absence, the other partner, Mr Watson, James's colleague, was to examine and supervise Isabel's allocated work.

'…Yes, that looks excellent to me!' said Mr Watson appreciatively, 'You know, young lady, you really do have a talent for this work!'

'Oh, thank you, Mr Watson! That's very kind of you to say that.'

Mr Watson, James's colleague and fellow partner, was the total antithesis of the sad and wistful Mr Brodie. A happily married man in his late fifties with two children, one of each and an extremely competent and capable partner and commissioner for oaths. This is not to say that James was incompetent, quite the reverse, but his style was entirely different.

'Not at all!' laughed Mr Watson casually, 'This is what we like to see in our trainees, carefulness and thoroughness. Oh, and incidentally, please call me Ben – why, Mr Watson sounds so formal!' Not another one who insisted on use of his Christian name!

Isabel was still feeling intrigued by the sad Mr Brodie. Never one to back-bite or tell tales, having herself suffered at the hands of others who both disliked and envied her, she was only too aware that this was not an attractive characteristic. Nevertheless, James fascinated her. Izzy found herself both wanting and needing to discover further information about him.

'I do like James. I've noticed especially lately he seems to be a bit of a sad character, almost as though something negative occurred in the past, and he well, er, never fully recovered.'

Ben looked casually up from the desk. 'A sad character? Yes, he is a bit. There was a singularly unfortunate episode, just over twenty years ago…' Ben's usually confident voice began to trail to a halt, and then he eventually finished the sentence by saying, '…With Alison.'

'Alison?' repeated Isabel. 'So, who is or was Alison?'

'James's then young lady… Or fiancée if you wish to be more precise. And what a woman!'

'How do you mean?'

'Alison Maitland, fresh out of law school in Leeds. Very go-getting and highly successful. She was a barrister who worked in Queen's Chambers further up Dale Street. If Alison couldn't successfully defend a person and fight their corner, then no-one could. She met James during her first few weeks of employment at the chambers, during an after-work bonding session. Alison was so bubbly outgoing and extrovert, the total opposite of James, who is just so quiet and shy. I don't think before the advent of Alison, James had ever had a girlfriend before. He'd always been so busy working before. Almost like chalk and cheese, those two were, you could say. Nevertheless, they seemed to get on like the proverbial, 'house on fire.' James said, of his own admission, 'Alison's so good for me!' They'd known each other for just over eighteen months and Alison at one stage had entertained plans for becoming a Q.C.[3], although as her relationship with James began to develop, her plans for professional development certainly began to take a back seat, and she began to entertain the prospect of only working three days per week.'

So, what had transpired to curtail these plans, thought Isabel to herself. Instead, she tentatively managed to ask, '... And then?'

'One Friday afternoon, Alison was due in court, and the case she was defending was particularly difficult. The general upshot of the afternoon was that she lost the case. Alison was absolutely devastated. She went back to her seat in the court room and sat with her head in her hands for at least half an hour. The court clerk witnessed her very visible trauma and distress and attempted to comfort her, 'Now come on love, this could have happened to anyone!' He was heard to mutter to her, 'Come on, darling! You pick yourself up, and you give it to them next time!' But poor Alison was inconsolable. I think, strictly between you and I, a lot of Alison's problems were rooted in her upbringing. She had to be succeeding all the time. She was very middle class. Nothing wrong with that, I am myself. I suppose you could say that Alison's parents were the epitome of middle-class respectability.

Her father was a bank manager and her mother was a dentist, so quite successful, oh, and there was a younger sister who had plans to go to Cambridge on completion of her 'A' levels. As the story goes, Alison stumbled out of the court room, tears streaming down her face, muttering to herself, 'Why am I stuck with this wretched job?' The stress and the pressures of the job were quite obviously taking their toll upon her. Now, as you are fully aware of the fact, in the barrister's world, once a case is concluded, the barrister needs to return to his chambers to pick up the next

---

[3] Queen's Council.

allocated brief. Alison abruptly left the courthouse and crossed the road at breakneck speed, she was so traumatised she didn't even bother to check the state of the traffic on Dale Street. Of course, the inevitable occurred. She was abruptly run over by a 'hit and run' driver coming in the opposite direction. Obviously, she was immediately taken to hospital, but died three or four days later as a result of severe head injuries. She had just turned twenty-four years old. Poor James never seemed quite the same again. For a while he became almost a complete recluse. He went back to live with his parents, and for a couple of years all he did was go to work, never went out on the town, drinking, clubbing or wine bar visiting with me and some of my friends.

About five years after the occurrence of this singularly unfortunate occurrence, James actually told me he had started to feel distinctly better, the previous five years had been little better than an existence to him, whereby he felt imprisoned in a meaningless cycle of work, eat, sleep and returning to work the morning after."

'Oh, poor Mr Brodie!' exclaimed Isabel.

'I would like this to remain strictly between us,' Ben also added quietly and calmly.

'Well, of course it will,' was Isabel's response.

'Yes, at the time, it seemed like such an awful waste of life… At any rate, just be aware that this has been a deciding factor in your supervisor's life.'

'Oh, I shall be, I shall be.' By now, Isabel was desperate to change the subject of conversation, so she tentatively asked Ben, 'Have you any plans for the weekend?'

'Well, Lilian and I thought we might go walking in North Yorkshire.'

Lilian was Ben's wife, a highly competent and capable nursing sister who was rapidly becoming bored and disillusioned with her job and now, after just over thirty years in the NHS was rather keen to transfer to private sector, part-time work. According to Ben, she was currently in the process of applying to become a practice nurse, and in the event of her application being unsuccessful, she was seriously considering becoming a bank nurse, largely due to the fact that employment as a bank nurse would mean having the freedom and flexibility to largely choose her own hours.

'I think you'd be best advised not to raise the subject of Alison with James,' Ben very wisely advised Isabel, 'Not, unless of course, he raises the subject first, as I suspect it's still a, how can I express it? A delicate area. At any rate, just be aware.'

Believing that the time was well and truly right to change the topic of conversation, Isabel casually enquired, 'So whereabouts are you going to in North Yorkshire?'

'Settle. We thought we might find a decent hotel. By decent hotel, I mean, hopefully two star, possibly three star, doesn't really matter provided it's comfortable, clean and the food's good.'

And at that point, Isabel strangely enough remembered another momentous demarcation point in her life. In those days, Isabel had lived with her grandparents only about thirty miles from Settle. She had been nine years old, and they went for a Sunday afternoon stroll on the hills which partly encircle the old market town of Settle. Isabel, being a sensitive and imaginative child, had been captivated by the walk up into the rocky limestone terrain, which as you progressed still further from the town began to develop into naturally and gently undulating hills, many of which were crowned with limestone outcrops. Yes, rocky limestone outcrops, almost like large, crumbling slabs of white Wensleydale cheese or icing.

Or, maybe something more than that. By this point, Isabel's imagination at the endless possibilities began to run absolute and total riot. The caverns. Beautiful, almost fairytale-like structures. A sort of shangrila, where one effortlessly obtained every human desire known to man. Beautiful country, so diverse and atmospheric in places. And to Isabel, north Yorkshire called to mind all the happy times she had spent walking and spending small, short holidays with her grandparents in that particular county. At the age of nine, she was beginning to develop an interest in photography, and thought she might request a small camera from her grandmother as a possible Christmas present. What glorious photographs she could have snapped of the fairytale caverns!

'If we're feeling strong enough, we might both attempt the Three Peaks walk[4]. Mind you, that's not to say we'll complete it, but we might make at least an attempt on one of the peaks,' said Ben casually, abruptly disrupting Isabel's train of thought.

Of course, Yorkshire reminded her of someone else. Her father! Yes, he who was so persistent and refused to take 'no' for an answer! And soon she was going to be holed up at his house in Huddersfield. Could she face the prospect? Well, she was going to have to.

'My father lives in Yorkshire, and sometime in the not too distant future, I'm going to have to spend a few days at his house… To be honest, I'm not really looking forward to it. But, well, there we are, it just has to be done, after all, father's so very keen that I spend some quality time with him!'

'Bit persistent, is he?' Ben asked sympathetically.

'Well, yes. That's one way you could describe him.'

Ben tried to look on the bright side. 'Well, you'll probably have a really good time. The days will very quickly pass, I'm sure.'

'Oh, I hope so.'

'And just imagine. The chance for you to share some quality time with your father for the first time in years! Quality father and daughter time! Helen and I enjoy quality time together almost every day, but sadly, that's all going to be disrupted because the University of Glasgow now seems to be calling, and she fancies the shops on

---

[4] The Three Peaks – Pen-y-Ghent, Ingleborough and Great Wernside, popular with walkers.

Sauchiehall Street! I do hope she's not going to get into horrendous debt.'

'Surely not. Your Helen's a good and very hard-working girl.' Helen was Ben's nineteen-year-old daughter, whom he appeared to get on with extremely well, which was more than could be said for the state of his current relationship with Helen's younger sibling, Jonathan, who had just turned fifteen. Ben himself looked sad for a few minutes, and as Isabel later on recalled, that particular day in question had seemed to be a day of baring souls and reminiscing generally on the past, Ben then quite suddenly and abruptly said, 'When I met Lilian she was a Staff Nurse on Ward 8B at the university hospital. I met her when I was having an appendicectomy, and she was looking after me. In the lead up to our wedding, would you believe it, she told me she'd somehow managed to bag the best looking man on the ward. I said no, surely not, I always thought that honour had been conferred upon Mr Seymour, the specialist; what could she possibly see in a dope like me? Her response was, 'Nonsense. He's an arrogant bastard. I wouldn't have him if his behind was studded with the proverbial diamonds. I spend all my working day among members of the medical profession, so I would prefer to spend the rest of my life with a man from a different profession. Quite understandable, I suppose. Yes, on the whole, we've been really happy. In fact, we've racked up twenty-seven happy years.'

'Good. I'm pleased to hear it.' Then, anxious at all costs to keep Ben away from the dreaded subject of her father, Isabel quickly added, 'And I hope you enjoy your walking in North Yorkshire, this weekend.'

'Oh, we shall, we shall,' answered Ben confidently.

Suddenly they both heard what sounded like the front door open. Isabel glanced at her watch. Exactly five past four.

'Sounds like James.' Ben said rather abstractedly, making a few last, final annotations to the client's proof of evidence. It was indeed James.

'Oh, hello, Izzy… Hello, Ben!' James greeted them both rather nervously and then added, 'You didn't have any problems, did you, Izzy?'

Ben answered the question for her. 'No, not at all, she did marvellously.'

'Do you know?' said James, rather absently and vaguely himself now, 'I think this young lady is going to be rather good… She will be when I've finished with her, at any rate.'

'How did you get on yourself, James?'

'As well as can be expected. Mr Pearson's re-written his will, it needed to be done in any event bearing in mind the fall out he had with his nephew. It all just needs to be committed to paper now, and Bernard now won't be receiving a penny. That's not too much of a pity since Bernard really is a useless good for nothing, who appears to believe that the world owes him a living.'

Isabel thought she would not attempt to take any sides at this particular point. Then she felt as though she ought maybe to clarify exactly what she was feeling relieved about. 'I mean, I'm relieved to hear that you were successful in your mission this afternoon.'

'Well, I have my ways!' laughed James. Again, Isabel thought she was aware of a slight sadness just dimly visible in James's eyes, but she was now fully aware of the reason for this.

'Oh, and incidentally, young lady, I have a whole new pile of requisitions to be thoroughly scrutinised in the morning, why, they will keep you going and happily occupied until lunchtime, at least! So don't say I never give you anything!' And again, James Brodie laughed uneasily.

'With pleasure, James. Consider them done.' Well, she now had plenty of work to keep her going tomorrow morning.

'James, did you know Isabel's going to be spending some of her time off at her father's in the depths of Yorkshire? Ben casually told his partner.

'Yes, I believe so. I was aware she was going to do that sometime… I don't think our Isabel's too keen on the prospect, are you, love?'

Mr Brodie, otherwise known as James had called her 'love'? Now Isabel well knew use of the word 'love' to be primarily a northern and midlands expression, but his use of the term, a term so frequently also used by her grandmother, seemed to imply familiarity, and a certain amount of, well, intimacy!

'Oh, I'm just, 'blanking out,' so to speak, for the time being at least,' answered Isabel, trying to appear casual and easily able to cope with the introduction of a new and entirely different set of family circumstances, '…I'm not thinking about it too much, to be honest… I just keep telling myself things will be alright on the night. Although whether they will be, of course, is at present, anyone's guess.' Yes, she currently had two weeks' breathing space. Then… And then, into the depths of Yorkshire for her ordeal.

'And I keep trying to tell her, the chances are, she'll probably enjoy it,' added Ben exuberantly, a little too exuberantly, with a touch of false jollity to his voice, Isabel could not fail to notice, 'And just imagine, you two can go walking in North Yorkshire, and why, you could spend a day in York, Lillian and I often have short breaks over to York, there's so much to look at, and why, Lilian loves the shops!'

That was quite a sensible idea, thought Isabel to herself. She had not spent any time in York for at least six years. That really would be a treat! Ashtons' department store, Zloggs, the Chemist, the innumerable jewellers' shops on Stonegate… The York souvenir shop on the corner by the Minster, the restaurant on 26, Coppergate famed for its' roast meats and mouth-watering puddings!!! MMMMMmmmmmm… Possibly a visit of a few days into Yorkshire was not going to be too bad after all!!! Yet again, she pushed the prospect from her mind. Temporarily, at least.

'… I just need to get through this,' Isabel thought readily to herself. Yes, get through this and out the right side of it.

22

'Let's express it this way,' Isabel answered with a sort of resigned dread in her voice, 'I shall feel much better when it's over and done with and I'm the right side of it, i.e. relegated to the past!'

At this particular point, James suddenly looked acutely worried. Was his beloved trainee being forced to stay closeted up with her father in Huddersfield, even though in reality, she would greatly prefer not to? Had Mr Jackson embarked on some peculiar ego trip in order to prove how extremely well he and his long-lost daughter bonded together? Was he the typical pompous, heavy-handed father who simply refused to take 'no' for an answer, to whom all other individuals capitulated for the sake of a modicum of peace? Instead, he managed to say hurriedly, 'Isabel, darling, if you can't face it, simply say that you're knee deep in work for the next month, at least!'

Isabel paled. This was rapidly becoming stranger and more bizarre by the moment. Now he had called her 'darling!' Well, in one way, this was very flattering; but did she really want or need the attentions of a man twenty-odd years her senior? Ben looked a touch embarrassed for a minute, or so, then he shot Isabel a slightly entertained and amused smile as if to say, 'Didn't I tell you so?'

'No, there's no if's or buts to it. I shall have to go... For three or four days... Absolute maximum.' Yes, for the time being at least, Isabel was in resigned mode.

'That seems to conclude matters, I think, on that particular subject for the time being,' Ben answered rather uneasily, 'And now, what time are we up to?' He glanced anxiously at his watch. 'Ten to five. Well, nearly time I wasn't here. I'll just go and collect my things and then I'm off home.' With that, he retreated rapidly to his back room.

Isabel was left standing uneasily facing James for a few minutes, which incidentally felt more like a lifetime, and an awkward, embarrassed silence appeared to have arisen between the partner and his trainee.

Eventually, James broke the silence by gingerly venturing, '…Isabel, just remember what I've said.' Oh my goodness! He said so many things! Then, seeing the expression of blankness on her face, he added hastily, 'About the being knee deep in work, I mean!'

'No… In two weeks' time I shall have to do it. I think it's rather a case of, 'bite the bullet!'

'Well,' answered James resignedly, 'As long as you're happy with this arrangement, dear.'

Now use of the word 'dear' was better, and she had heard him use this word before. Isabel felt able to cope with this term of endearment. Then he added, almost as an afterthought, 'If it makes you feel any better, I can 'phone you every night on your mobile.'

Well, that was just about the last thing Isabel felt as though she either wanted or needed!

Her supervisor checking up on her every evening! Suppose her father got the wrong impression? But if it made James feel better, then so be it! Instead, she managed to respond by saying, 'Well, that's very nice of you… Thank you for being so thoughtful.'

'Nonsense. The pleasure will all be my own,' answered James, in a slightly pompous manner, Isabel thought to herself.

At that precise moment, the 'phone sounded in the front office. The intellectually challenged Tanya answered it, and there was silence for a few minutes. Then she was heard to say, 'Mr Brodie's just about to leave, but I can get him to the 'phone before he leaves the office.'

Tanya shuffled into Isabel's room on skyscraper like high-heeled shoes.

'James! I've got Mrs Brodie on the 'phone.'

So, there was a Mrs Brodie! Then how dare James make a pass at her? Cheating on them both! Or did that no longer matter, now that he had attained the exalted rank of partner, and had occupied that role for the past sixteen or so years! Some form of mumbled conversation appeared to briefly pass between Mr and Mrs Brodie, and then James reappeared in Isabel's office, as she was picking up her belongings with a view to leaving work.

'That was my mother. She was most insistent that I do some food shopping at M and S for the evening meal.'

So that was who Mrs Brodie was! And no, James was not cheating! Perhaps she should stop being too fast to judge individuals, that was what her grandmother had once told Isabel, and maybe she was right… 'Give everyone a chance and give everyone the benefit of the doubt.' Isabel remembered her grandmother clearly and categorically telling her when Isabel was about nine. With that, she wished James and Tanya a good evening, and vanished once again out into the noisy depths of Dale Street.

Chapter 3.

That evening at seven thirty, Isabel began to put a meal together for herself. She had arranged to meet up with her friend, Francoise, a Frenchwoman, whose acquaintance she had made whilst living in her previous accommodation in Falkner Square, a little later on in the evening.

Isabel put her ready-made meal in the oven… Mentally reflected on what she would wear for her evening out with Francoise… A smart, pretty dress? No, too much bother and worry with where to store her cash and credit cards… The new black, relaxed fitting, floral embroidered jeans seemed somehow appropriate, together with one of her pretty blouses. Francoise! She really was a character!

Isabel poured herself a glass of red wine. At that particular juncture, she felt strongly as though she had just passed yet another major demarcation point in her life. Once again, her supervisor had made a pass at her, and the current situation reminded her briefly of a similar situation from the past. A few years after she had left university, she had been employed as a secretary for a building company. During her third or fourth month of employment at the company, the office manager/cum payroll clerk, then a man in his late fifties or early sixties, named Bert, saw fit to sexually harass her. Isabel had been twenty-five. He had groped her behind and tried to feel her breasts, talked dirty and was continually moaning to Isabel that his wife, Molly (who appeared to Isabel to be rather long suffering), of the past thirty-two years, did not understand him… No use in trying to report his revolting behaviour, since the construction manager was a totally unreasonable and singularly unpleasant character himself, with employees walking out almost daily being an only too regular occurrence and he would simply never have believed her for a start. No, all in all, that had been quite a difficult, taxing time.

Isabel carefully selected her clothes. Yes, the embroidered jeans and one of her pretty blouses seemed appropriate. She carefully applied her make-up. A brief, short squirt of perfume at both sides of her neck and on both wrists, and she was ready to go to meet Francoise.

'…Euh, I'm so glad you could meet me in 'Annah's Bar tonight!' Isabel's friend, Francoise greeted her with, in typical French tones.

'I'll be with you in a minute, I'll just go to the bar to get myself another glass of red wine!'

'Well, between you and me, you should really drink one of these!!!' And with that, Francoise held up her glass.

'What is it?' asked Isabel.

'A Superstar Martini Cocktail.'

'You know, you're leading me into very bad ways,' laughed Isabel, 'I think I'm a bit more of a strawberry or raspberry daiquiri woman myself. At any rate, I'm pleased you were able to come out tonight.'

'A'm almost always able to come out. And you know me, A'm a real party animal.'

'Oh, of that there's absolutely no doubt. Now, I can meet you one more time next week, work allowing, which I'm sure it will, and then I'm holed up at my father's in Huddersfield for at least three or four nights.... When did you last see your father, eh? That's what it ultimately boils down to. Well, a few months ago, but to be honest, before that? Oh, all of thirty something years ago!' At which Isabel laughed.

'You 'ave a good time with your father.'

'Well, I'll try,' answered Isabel resolutely. No, thought Isabel to herself, she was not, repeat not going to tell Francoise about the strange James Brodie, her supervisor. At least, not at this early stage, especially in view of the fact that nothing had yet transpired.

No, as an independent, professional, woman of the world, Izzy could fight her own battles and stand on her own feet.

'You know, I went back to Montpellier about a month ago, and it seemed good to be back for a few weeks, but then I started to miss Liverchester… 'A'm like so many people who spend time here, once they do, they can't leave,' said Francoise abruptly.

'So true,' was Isabel's response. 'I've spent nine and a half, almost ten years here and I just can't leave. At any rate, I don't think I can.'

'No… Good place to grow old and die in.'

'Too flippin' true.'

Francoise got up to get the next round. During her absence, Isabel sat back and relaxed.

Athough Francoise seemed an unlikely friend for Isabel, she couldn't help but like her. She really was such a character… She who called a spade a spade and pulled no punches whatsoever.

'To my mind,' said Francoise when she returned with the next round, 'This is the best city in the world…'

'My feelings entirely.'

'…And what do we do when we've been to all the clubs and bars in Liverchester worth going to?' asked Francoise.

'Simple,' laughed Isabel. 'We start again.'

'And maybe next, we go on to a party, because you know me? You know me?'

'Yes, I do know you,' answered Isabel unequivocally, 'Very well, in fact.'

'Yes, 'I'm a party animal!'

As it so transpired, they did not go to a party after completing the visit to Hannah's Bar. Instead, they paid a visit to Heebie Jeebies, where they downed a few further cocktails and fleetingly hit the dance floor for three quarters of an hour, before deciding to call it an evening.

'After all,' laughed Francoise 'I 'ave to go now… After all, I'm not nineteen any longer.'

'No,' answered Isabel, 'Neither am I.'

When Isabel returned to her first floor flat on Percy Street, she noticed she had an answerphone message. So, someone had attempted to call her when she was unavailable?

The big question was who? Her mum? No, Edith would have contacted her by way of Isabel's mobile just to check she was safely home, which incidentally she had already. Her long-lost father? No, it was far too late for him to call. He would, in all probability have long since gone to bed. Another friend? No. They would always contact Izzy by way of her mobile. Nevertheless, Izzy needed to ascertain who it was. She pressed the answerphone recorded messages button.

'You have one new message. Message One. Isabel. It's James. I was just hoping to speak to you tonight, but obviously, that's not possible. I've got the requisitions for you now. They shouldn't take too long in the morning, I'll speak soon, dear.'

Why had he 'phoned her to tell her that information? It was nothing that she didn't already know. Couldn't he simply have dumped the requisitions on her desk when she came in at nine o'clock the next morning? Izzy couldn't be bothered attempting to ascertain James's motives at that time of the night, and she collapsed into bed for a few hours rest and oblivion. Hardly surprising she didn't go clubbing every night, these days… Or even every week now, for that matter.

The next morning, Isabel duly breezed in at nine o'clock and sat down at her desk. No sign of the requisitions, whatsoever. She would wait for James to bring them in. Somewhere in the depths of the back office, Isabel was certain she heard raised, angry, irate voices. Not desiring to venture any further, or find herself drawn into the altercation, she sat down, her unease growing with every passing moment. At which point, Isabel had the misfortune to hear Ben's angry, raised voice abruptly announce, '…James! For goodness sake! Seriously, there's no fool like an old fool! And then a few minutes later, references to 'You filthy old man!' were made. What exactly was Benjamin Watson referring to?

Isabel's nerves were thoroughly on edge, when ten minutes later, who should erupt from James Brodie's office but Ben looking extremely red-faced and embarrassed, carrying a green folder which he placed on Isabel's desk.

'Here are the requisitions, Izzy, they shouldn't take you too long to complete.'

'Ben, are you O.K.?'

'Yes, I'm perfectly well. I'm going out to get some air!'

And with that, he slammed the front door, and vanished into the depths of Dale Street.

What had gone wrong between those two? 'James! For goodness' sake… There's no fool like an old fool!!!' and a little later, '… You dirty old man!' Isabel remembered her grandmother in particular using the, 'No fool like an old fool!' phrase, especially when she was invariably referring to an old or older man making passes at a considerably younger woman… And often unwanted passes at that… A sudden chill ran abruptly and without warning down Izzy's spine, and she found herself shivering, although the morning was anything but cold. And just then, Isabel remembered something she had read in a law magazine from a few years ago… 'When my supervisor realised I was gay, he started to make passes at me… I simply didn't and couldn't return his feelings, in fact, I was revolted by him. Yet what alternative did I have? If I refused to co-operate, he would refuse to sign off my articles contract, and I could be forced to look for another job which I might be unable to secure. There seemed only one solution to that situation, I had to endure it!!!

Yes, two years of complete revulsion and misery…' Well, nothing quite like that had yet transpired, nor was Izzy a lesbian. Hopefully, it would not. Resolutely, Isabel sat down to comb through the requisitions. She began to carefully note them down. A copy of June Price's marriage certificate was needed. A grant of probate for the property's previous owner, Mr Bernard Smith, as tangible proof of his death was also required. Had planning permission been granted for the extension to the kitchen? In the absence of a grant of planning permission, the entire extension could have to be demolished, and the entire property could ultimately become unsaleable. Additionally, the covenants referred to in the 1985 conveyance would need to be seen and closely scrutinised just to ascertain that no planning bye-laws had been interfered with or contravened. A second trustee needed to be appointed in order to overreach the beneficial interests of the trust. Once again, Isabel applied herself to listing the requisitions… Hopefully, this would keep her mind well away from both the prospect of being forced to spend time closeted up in Huddersfield at her father's house, and the very real prospect of possible unwelcome sexual advances in the workplace. Isabel scrutinised and re-scrutinised the requisitions.

'Those look to be sorted for the time being at least,' she muttered quietly to herself, and then casually glancing up, she almost leapt out of her skin at the sight of James Brodie, hovering over her and scrutinising Izzy intently. Yes, scrutinising her quite intently, with his short-sighted stare firmly in place. Izzy felt quite unnerved, and unnerved for two reasons now; (a) he had caught her talking to herself and might question her sanity, and (b) she did not relish the prospect of having her every move examined and watched… Who, why, who in his or her right mind possibly could?... My goodness! James was a bizarre man!!!

'I'm sorry if I unnerved you, young lady!' He eventually added in rather a pompous tone, 'No, that was not my intention.'

'Well, you did rather.' And then to Izzy's complete and total horror, he picked up her left hand, held it to his lips and kissed it. Unwanted and unwelcome kisses thought Izzy to herself that evening… A refined form of assault and battery[5].

Seeing Isabel's expression of absolute and utmost horror, James said casually, without the proverbial care in the world, 'Oh, I'm sorry! I'm being a bit premature 'aint I?'

Whatever was that supposed to mean? I have never given you, James Brodie, the remotest, slightest indication that I would like a personal relationship with you, be it in any shape or form! Isabel thought to herself, seething with embarrassment and mortification.

But instead, she managed to say in a reasonably calm and controlled way, 'I'm going out for lunch now. Perhaps you could have these requisitions checked through for me when I get back in an hour's time?'

Yes, she had to get out, for the time being at least, out from those claustrophobic chambers… And what did the, '…being a bit premature,' refer to or indicate? Did that mean that he was going to attempt to make further passes? Was this the shape of things to come regarding her employment at these chambers? If so, it was intolerable!!

Isabel stopped at Greggs bakery and bought a sausage roll, a sandwich and a bottle of fruit juice. She wandered past Liverchester One shopping centre and over to the nearest park to try to clear her head. She managed to eat the sandwich, but James's unwanted attentions seemed to have largely sapped her appetite. She was getting up to leave the park when who should she meet but Ben. He noticed her immediately.

'Oh, Isabel, hello there! I'm so sorry about what transpired this morning. I've been sitting here most of the day, so far!'

---

[5] Assault and battery – Unwelcome and unwanted kisses constitute a form of assault and battery.

'Dare I ask? What exactly happened?' asked Izzy.

'To put it bluntly, I had a small altercation with James. Again, this is strictly between ourselves, but I think James regards you as Alison's replacement. I was trying to tell him not to be so presumptive, and then it all began to get a little heated. There, I've said it.'

'To be honest,' answered Izzy in a matter-of-fact sort of tone, 'That's what I've been suspecting for quite a few weeks now.'

Ben looked genuinely worried. 'Do you think you can face this for another eighteen months? No- one could blame you if you couldn't. If you decide to leave, you could always give as your reason for leaving, 'A personality clash with my supervisor.' We all know these things happen. If you do decide to leave, there's no blame attached to or implicated in that. I'm quite happy to put in good words for you.'

Isabel tried to think quickly of what she should do, given the unfortunate circumstances. She, the professional, articulate, competent, capable woman of the world who was able to easily handle the vast majority of situations with easy, casual aplomb… Who said she would do or complete a task, and who was always, or almost always true to her word and was now baulking at the prospect of being sexually harassed by an older man? No, she would 'sit it out,' endure it, so to speak. She would only leave if the situation really did become well nigh intolerable.

'Ben,' said Isabel resolutely, 'I'm a woman of my word, I think it probably best if I try to, 'see it through,' for the time being, at any rate.'

'Well said, young lady! That's the spirit! And as I said before, I can only apologise for the singularly unfortunate events which occurred this morning. Don't get me wrong,' Ben continued, 'James is a good man, and so devoted to his eighty-eight year old mother… I do so hope he'll be able to manage when she passes away, but I think he's a little misguided.

'He was an only child, and his parents spoilt him to death… Then of course, he was always so busy working, he never somehow managed to find time to have a girlfriend, either steady or unsteady… Look, if James becomes really embarrassing, I can check through your allocated work, in future.'

'Oh, thank you Ben.'

'Not at all.'

'Is it time we were getting back?' Isabel asked tentatively.

'Probably. I don't exactly feel in the mood to rush back.'

When Isabel returned to the chambers, there was a short note left on her desk from James.

'The requisitions, dear, are excellent. I only found two errors in all, which I have corrected. So overall, I would give you at least 80%. That was extremely well and carefully done. J.'

'What's this?' Ben asked suspiciously and rather sarcastically added, 'Further communication from the demon lover?'

But there seemed to be additional communication added in the shape of a P.S. which read, 'I am working from home for the rest of the afternoon, since mother is not feeling too well.

Perhaps either Ben or yourself can lock up chambers at 5:00 p.m. When you're in Huddersfield next week, I'll call you on your mobile every early evening.'

'Can I look?' asked Ben uneasily. Isabel passed the note across to him, and he began to read it looking ever more critical. Silence for a couple of minutes, which Ben abruptly broke by saying, 'I know this sounds awful, but I suspect James is now feeling a little embarrassed… He probably couldn't face you this afternoon… But what's all this about him 'phoning you every evening next week in Huddersfield?'

'Oh, yes, that's what he's proposing to do,' answered Isabel, matter-of-factly.

A look of absolute distaste and revulsion crossed Ben's countenance, and he responded by saying, 'The silly old fool! Do you know? When we advertised for the new trainee, I had a feeling that if we appointed a woman to the post, James might make, er, sexual advances towards her. I just had this horrible, sinking feeling.'

For the first time in a long while, Isabel felt at an absolute and total loss for words. To her relief, Ben changed the subject by saying, 'Isabel, could you do some legal research for me?'

'Yes, with pleasure. It would be good for me to brush up on my legal research skills, and it's good practice.'

Isabel spent quite a happy and profitable afternoon completing Ben's legal research, and, after the unfortunate events of the morning she was well and truly ready to leave at 5:00 p.m. That evening, she packed her suitcase with clean clothes and the overnight essentials she would need to take with her for her stay in Huddersfield. Three or four changes of clothing, toothbrush, toothpaste, hairbrush, shower gel, soap, deodorant and moisturising cream. No, she had created this situation, so she had to see it through.

When Isabel arrived at the chambers the next morning, a long, in-depth conversation appeared to be taking place between James and Ben in Isabel's room. Just fortunately, the atmosphere did not appear to be particularly hostile or heated, and James greeted his trainee with, 'Ah, Izzy. Good morning. I've further requisitions for you… I'm sorry to keep burdening you with them, but you're so very good at them. They shouldn't take a capable, competent young lady like yourself very long.'

'Oh, how kind of you to say so, James,' answered Izzy. She had no idea whether James had some secret, hidden agenda somewhere up the depths of his sleeve, but all she required and needed from him was that he would remain reasonably civilised, not make unwanted sexual advances and sign off her articles' contract in eighteen months' time. That was all she needed.

'I'll leave these in your capable hands,' James said ingratiatingly, as Ben vanished to his room. Then he suddenly dropped his voice a tone, and added with a slightly conspiratorial air, 'Oh, I shan't half miss you next week when you're in Huddersfield… But don't worry at all or in the slightest, dear, since I shall 'phone you every evening!'

Oh my goodness! That was the absolute last thing Izzy either wanted or needed! Added to which, what impression was her long-lost father likely to receive? That James was her intended? Yes, that prospect too was rather abhorrent, seeing as James was easily old enough to be her father! No, and a definite 'no' to workplace romances… Too complex… Too many boxes which needed to be ticked… Too many problems which could inevitably arise in the event that not all boxes were ticked… Inevitable embarrassment and discomfort being the end result. And her mind again, flicked back down the years, to a conversation she once had had with her grandma… Yes, her grandma who said so much, and almost always had something to say on well nigh almost every single subject.

'…Everyone meets at work, these days!'

'Oh, really, grandma? It's first I've heard of it!'

And then, Izzy remembered a cousin who had once dated a work colleague. Of course, he later discovered that he and his would-be girlfriend were hopelessly incompatible, so a little later he ended the relationship, much to his enormous embarrassment and mortification, having to present himself for work for weeks after the termination of the liaison. Of course, the mighty James Brodie himself had once enjoyed a work-based relationship years ago, but that had been slightly different!

Alison had worked at an entirely different set of chambers, added to which, she had a slightly different job, hence, leading to a bit more variation… And in any event, thought Isabel to herself, she wanted to maintain an atmosphere of strict professionalism at all times during her employment at the chambers, and that could easily be compromised by sexual advances made to her by a colleague… In particular, a colleague old enough to be her father! No, that she could quite easily do without! And furthermore, she needed to get through the ordeal of the next few days.

Once again, she pushed the thought from her mind, and applied herself to completing the requisitions. She finished them in about average time, and was just getting up from her desk to go and get them checked through with either James or Ben, depending on which one was currently free, when who should appear in her office, walking purposely as usual, but Ben.

'Oh, just the man I need!' said Izzy, 'Ben, can you check these requisitions through for me?'

'Yes, with pleasure.' He sat down at Izzy's desk in the vacant client chair, and began to routinely examine Isabel's list. He was silent for a few minutes.

'Once again. Almost spot on. Just one amendment needed which I shall point out to you. Then, why you may, of course, publish and be damned!'

Isabel laughed secretly to herself. To be completely honest, she had quite enjoyed the morning and found she had learned some very valuable skills, and there had been no unwanted sexual advances from James, no, there was simply one unwanted burden hanging over her head like an albatross; the fact that now she had to spend a few days holed up at her father's house in Huddersfield. That, she could just do without, and as of this evening onwards, she would be incarcerated in the depths of Yorkshire being forced to make polite, fruity conversation with her long-lost father and his second wife, and yes, this time it had to be done.

Yet again, Ben abruptly cut through her thoughts, saying, 'Incidentally, young lady, James and I reserved a table up at Rigby's, just a way of giving you a small send-off before you descend into your Yorkshire sojourn for a few days. We neither of us like to drink at lunchtime as a rule, but we both wanted to do it this one time to let you know, how very much you're appreciated by us both.'

'Well that's very kind of you! I... I wasn't expecting anything!'

'Not at all. Why, you do so much of the routine day to day work for these chambers, I don't think either James or I could effectively run this partnership without you.'

'Well, thank you. That's so nice of you.'

When Ben and Isabel arrived at Rigby's, James and Tanya were already present in the bar, both looking acutely uneasy and quite obviously not enjoying each other's company in the slightest. Well, that was only really to be expected, since they had nothing in common whatsoever, at any rate, they both looked singularly relieved to see the other two appear.

'Well, I'll get the opening round,' said James, in a slightly uneasy tone, 'I'll have my customary pint of bitter, what will you have, Ben? Tanya?'

'Yes, I'll also have my customary bitter, a pint of course,' answered Ben.

'I'll have a Rigby's Orange Superstar, if you please,' replied the vacuous Tanya.

'And you, young lady?' James asked Isabel, as Isabel suspected, he was desperately trying to present to the outside world, a front of neutrality and indifference to his new trainee's charms.

'A small glass of red wine, please, James. Oh, don't get me wrong, I would love to have a large one, but I'm just bearing in mind that I have to do at least a modicum of work this afternoon, and then after work, get myself to Huddersfield by early this evening.'

'...Sounds as though our Isabel's going to be having a good time, these next few days,' said Ben airily. 'Surely your father will wine and dine you?'

'Well, I hope so,' answered Isabel hesitantly, a little uncertain as to whether or not this really would be the case.

At this point, James suddenly abruptly interjected by saying, rather in the manner of an elderly, doting father himself, 'It's going to be difficult for our Izzy, walking into a house full of strangers, but I'm sure she'll cope admirably. And what's more, I shall 'phone her early every evening to see how she's going on.'

Ben, Isabel and even Tanya looked acutely embarrassed. This was simply the last, absolutely the last thing Isabel wanted to hear at this particular point in time. After a silence of a couple of minutes, Isabel eventually managed to say, 'James, you really don't need to!'

'Oh, but I want to. After all, you're my trainee, and I feel responsible, at least partially, for your well-being.'

More embarrassment descended on the group, which Isabel eventually broke by saying, 'Well, let's face it, I shall be pleased to get back here, here in my spiritual home towards the end of next week.'

'Yes, and we'll be pleased to have you back, dear,' answered Ben, 'But I'm sure you'll enjoy it once you get there, you've simply got nothing more than the proverbial cold feet.'

'Let's hope so. Let's hope I successfully negotiate this major demarcation point in my life. Perhaps the most major demarcation point in my entire life so far.' Or was it in reality?

Had the rendezvous with Charles been the more momentous? Well, at any rate, it ranked extremely high up the list. And the episode with Charles? Possibly that was best left well and truly relegated to the past.

Lunch and further drinks were ordered, and a further agreeable and pleasant hour and a half was spent.

Three hours later, Isabel was on the train to Huddersfield, attempting to mentally blank out what was awaiting her for the next few days.

Chapter 4.

Sweeping wild moorland and shallow, verdant low-lying valleys began to confront Isabel, as she started to approach Huddersfield, still desperately blanking out how to cope with the immediate impact of meeting up, for so far only, the second rendezvous of her entire life with her so long absent father. She had told her papa she would arrive for early evening, which, in this case would be about seven p.m. So anxious to arrive on the first available train, Isabel suddenly realised she had changed trains too early, and taken a less direct train at Leeds, duly telephoning her father to inform him that she might be a little later than originally expected.

'Oh, hello, Isabel,' answered Agnieska, her father's second wife, on answering the 'phone call.

'Oh, hello, Agnieska. I'm really sorry, but I think I'm going to be a little later than we originally anticipated. I think I caught the wrong train in Leeds.'

'Oh, it's quite alright. I'll just tell your father to leave the house a little later. You would probably be best advised to get off that train at the next station, and board one which has Huddersfield as the end of the line.'

Isabel duly disembarked at the next station. What reception awaited her at Huddersfield, she was entirely uncertain of and uneasy about. Surely it would go well?

Presently, in fact all too soon, the train had arrived in Huddersfield. The train pulled in on platform two. Well, Isabel had negotiated her way there. And the meeting up with her father? Yes, this had to be successfully completed. No ifs or buts... it simply had to. Izzy pulled her suitcase and bag clear of the train. She walked through the station concourse, a faint, slight feeling of unease and dread slowly beginning to descend upon and envelop her.

She had almost reached the station's exit when who should she see sitting on a public bench, but an old man fast losing his hair, and the Eastern European looking, Agnieska.

Well, they at any rate had arrived on time, which was more than could be said for her.

'Welcome, my dear, welcome,' said Kenneth.

'Oh, hello, Izzy,' Agnieska greeted her warmly.

'Well, hello, you two. You're both looking very well,' Isabel replied, and then further added by way of explanation, 'I'm so sorry I'm a little late, but I didn't fully understand which train I needed to catch in Leeds.'

'Oh, that's quite alright, dear,' answered Agnieska welcomingly.

Kenneth took charge of Isabel's suitcase and wheeled it to a metallic green, middle-aged Ford car. Izzy piled into the back.

Suddenly her innate fear and inherent sense of dread appeared to slowly subside, possibly this was not going to be half as bad as she had hitherto been anticipating, and by now, feeling a touch more confident, she ventured to say, 'Well, as we came through on the train we passed through beautiful country, so open and wild, I loved the moorlands that we passed by.'

'Yes, there is some beautiful country here,' replied Agnieska, 'It's one of the things we're really lucky to have round here.'

Presently, Isabel's father piped up, commenting, 'Now, there is a fast route to reach our house, but I'll take you on the scenic drive, then you can have a real look at the town.

'Is it a large town?' asked Izzy.

'Well, about average, I think,' answered Kenneth, 'With a population of about forty thousand.'

'Oh, so quite large then. Not as large as Liverchester, but larger than my hometown.'

Eventually, they reached Isabel's father's house. Not half as grand as Izzy had imagined in her mind's eye, Mr Jackson stopped the car outside an unremarkable, red-brick, semi-detached house on an equally unremarkable, average street. Number thirty-five. Taking charge of Isabel's case, Kenneth led the way through a gloomy, depressing sombre looking hallway, and up an equally dingy, narrow, cramped staircase, with a singularly well-worn looking carpet. He turned left at the top and opened the nearest bedroom door.

Fortunately, Isabel's allocated bedroom was nothing like the gloomy hallway and staircase.

A double bed with wrought-iron bedstead and foot confronted Isabel, complete with a spotlessly clean blue and white patterned quilt. Off this led a small, compact ensuite bathroom.

'Well, I'll leave you to unpack. This, of course, is your little base in Huddersfield.' Which of course, was precisely what it was.

Isabel examined the room closely. In contrast to what she had so far seen of the rest of the house, this bedroom was not too bad at all. Strangely enough, it was the absolute, complete reverse of what she had so far seen of the house. Here, the overall message seemed to be one of brightness and cheer, light and optimism, rather like a small, positive oasis. Isabel unpacked a few overnight essentials, and the small token presents she had purchased for her father and stepmother. She used the ensuite facility... And now she had to face the point she had been really dreading for weeks, going down to speak and once again make contact with them... Well, it simply had to be done. Armed with the presents, she once again retraced her steps downstairs. Through a gloomy back room which later turned out to serve as the dining room, Isabel thought she heard her father saying, '...Now Isabel...'

'...Yes, Isabel's here,' Izzy replied.

'Ah, we were just talking about you…'

'Yes, I thought you must be.'

'Come and sit down, dear,' said Agnieska, 'And make yourself comfortable. Now, would you like a cup of tea or maybe something a little stronger, a glass of wine possibly?'

Izzy's mouth felt like the lower reaches of a parrot's cage, she really did feel in need of something strong to boost her flagging spirits, so she answered, 'Well, a glass of red wine would be very nice.'

'Yes, of course, I was just about to have one myself. I'll get it for you now… And what would you like, Kenny?'

'I'll just have a cup of tea.'

'Oh, I've got some little presents for both of you,' Isabel remembered the presents she had so lovingly bought that afternoon at Liverchester station and currently stashed into a Marks and Spencer carrier bag. Rather gingerly, she handed over a bottle of strong beer for her father, and a box of dark chocolate, cherry-filled liquour chocolates and a small tablet of carnation fragranced soap in a soap box for her stepmother.

'Oh, thank you, dear,' said Agnieska. 'Now, I shall have to hide these chocolates from Ella, otherwise she'll steal them.' Ella was eight, and the younger child of Izzy's half-brother, Christopher.

'I do hope you enjoy the carnation fragranced soap, it really does have a beautiful, subtle fragrance.'

'Oh, I'm sure I shall… It smells divine, in fact,' was Agnieska's response.

'Well, here's to us all meeting up again,' said Izzy.

'Yes, exactly,' answered her stepmother.

All three of them clinked glasses and cups together.

'Er, Kenny? Have you fed the cat yet? This is the cat we obtained a few months ago from Animal Rescue,' Agnieska explained, 'And you see, Ella who lives with us for much of the time so wanted a pet, and we thought a cat might be easier to manage than a dog, and according to the animal rescue centre, the previous owners of the poor cat had thrown it out, so we thought we'd try to provide her with a decent home.'

'My grandmother always said that was something she really couldn't bear, cruelty to animals, and nor can I for that matter,' answered Isabel, perhaps this small sojourn was not going to be half as bad as she had initially envisaged. She hoped so at any rate, and gaining a little more confidence she added, 'After all, as my grandmother always said, 'No-one's forced to have a pet! If you don't like animals, then don't have them!'

'No, exactly,' answered her stepmother.

The rest of the time passed quite easily and perfectly amicably, and Isabel helped her father to clear the supper dishes from the dining room table and into the dishwasher... My goodness! Izzy thought to herself as she sat in the gloomy back room which acted as a combined dining and sitting room area. This room, in her mind at any rate, could easily have been a room in which one could easily become extremely, seriously depressed, and the same applied to the kitchen which was little more than a small, dingy, cramped passage.

The three of them were just in the process of consuming a last glass of wine when Izzy's phone started to ring out. Who should bother to 'phone her at this time of night? Izzy suddenly remembered, James!

'I'll just take this call upstairs,' said Izzy. Happily, she retreated upstairs.

Her 'phone indicated, 'James calling.'

'Hello!'

'Oh, hello, dear! Did you safely reach your destination?'

James suddenly seemed like another world away.

'Yes, I did, thank you. I actually don't think it's going to be half as bad as I anticipated. I wouldn't want to live here all the time though.'

'No, of course not,' answered James in a kindly and benevolent tone.

'And how about you yourself?' asked Izzy. 'How are you spending this evening?'

'Well, mother and I are just enjoying a glass of wine each and mother's just put supper in the oven, so until supper is fully cooked, we'll enjoy putting the world to rights for the next three quarters of an hour, at least.'

'Oh, that sounds nice.' Isabel had never been to James and his mother's house, and furthermore, she didn't intend to, but at this exact, precise moment, in contrast to her current rather sombre immediate environment she imagined James's house as the absolute lap of palatial luxury, liberally adorned with brightly coloured soft cushions, discreet, soft-muted lamps and a cheerful, roaring log fire; a leather settee with carefully matching leather armchairs, a few tasteful pictures displayed on the elegant pale blue and white striped wallpaper and carefully contrasting, quality dusky pink curtains completed the luxurious overall effect of the imaginary dining room-cum lounge.

'Well, you enjoy it, if you can… And of course, don't let your father push you about.'

'Oh, don't worry, I shan't.'

There was silence for a few seconds at the other end of the 'phone which James eventually broke by saying, 'Oh, Izzy, dear… All I want is for you to be well and happy, and I know, I know for absolute certain from your work so far that… we…er, you have…er, have a future in law,' he finished off quickly.

Now there was embarrassed silence at Izzy's end of the line. That sounded as though what he really intended to say was, 'We have a future together, hence, the hasty correction and replacement of 'we' with 'you', and the rapid addition onto the end of the sentence of 'in law.'

'Well, that's very nice of you, James. And thank you for saying so.'

'Not at all, dear, not at all,' answered James pompously, 'So you don't think this stay at your papa's home is going to be as bad as you thought? I hope so, at any rate.'

'No.'

'Do you know? I really miss you. I shall be so pleased when you're back in Lancashire.'

Izzy tried to ignore the first part of the sentence, so in response she managed to say, 'Yes, I'll be relieved to get back to Lancashire too, back to familiarity.'

Oh to return to Liverchester, thought Izzy to herself! But she would be returning in a few days so there was no point in getting too worked up… Yes, soon back to James, and whatever he intended to throw at her, be it in the work or romantic department!

Izzy began to think it was possibly time that the conversation was brought to appropriate end, and she managed to say, 'Thank you for 'phoning tonight, James. I do appreciate it.'

'Not at all… Not at all, the pleasure was all my own,' James answered rather pompously.

'I shall have to get back downstairs now, father will wonder what's happened to me.'

'I'll let you go, why I think that mother's calling me!' was James's response.

Yes, thought Izzy to herself… Mrs Brodie, calling for her beloved James in sunny Woolton… Woolton, as Izzy had always so religiously believed from her own observations, the absolute and proverbial, 'back of beyond', yet somehow when compared to Huddersfield, the complete and total epitome of the lap of luxury, and not by any means an entirely unpleasant place to spend one's life!... No, not unpleasant by any means!

'Goodbye, James, and thank you for calling.'

'Not at all, dear, not at all, thank you. We'll speak again very soon.'

'Goodbye!' and with that, Izzy terminated the call.

'That was just a work colleague,' answered Izzy when she went downstairs.

'Was he checking? Checking to see that your old father was not leading you into really ghastly, reprehensible ways?' asked Izzy's father.

'I'm not exactly sure. He's rather a bizarre man… Certainly not my young man, at any rate, he hoped our meeting up was going well.'

'Which of course, it is,' answered her father. 'Er, incidentally, there's something on television which I would very much like to watch. Would you like to come and watch it with me?'

'Well, yes.' This didn't sound too bad a way to terminate the evening.

They ended the evening by watching a travel program in the front room, a neat, tidy, well-kept room, equipped with a comfortable settee and two comfortable armchairs. Two rather heavy, sombre paintings adorned the walls, but the overall effect of this room was reasonably bright, comfortable and cheerful and all in all, the total and complete antithesis of the back room, kitchen, hallway and stairs.

'Well,' said Kenny, as the evening began to draw to a close, 'I really need to show you my music and books room tomorrow, it's well worth seeing. But not now, it's too late at night. We'll leave that for the morning.'

'Yes, I would very much like to see it,' responded Izzy.

'Well, so far, so far… Why, it's going really well.'

'Yes, I think so too,' answered Izzy. Perhaps her stay was not going to be too bad after all.

She gave her father a hug, and began to make her way up to bed. 'I'll see you both in the morning.'

Well, thought Izzy as she got into bed that night, the day hadn't, in reality, been too bad and not too traumatic after all. If things could just remain in this vein then she could easily cope with her stay in Huddersfield. Long may that remain so. She then proceeded to sleep soundly.

'Well, your music and books room is glorious,' Izzy told her father when being shown the room in question, the next morning. The music and books room, like the lounge-cum-sitting room was not half as depressing, dingy and gloomy as the backroom, kitchen, hallway and staircase, being a bright, airy room which seemed to catch the morning sunlight, and was dominated by Izzy's father's piano and one wall which seemed to consist almost entirely of paperback books. Nevertheless, despite its' cluttered nature, this was a bright and attractive room.

'I was thinking that we could have a trip to York today,' said Kenny as they were consuming their morning coffee.

'Oh, I would love to go to York, why, I've not been to York for five or six years, at least.'

Later that morning, Izzy and her father set out for York. They spent a good two hours examining the minster, which Izzy thoroughly enjoyed, as there was so very much to look at, followed by a wander through the ancient streets. But here, Isabel found there was a small problem. Her father did not want to look at any of the shops… And he was a fast walker.

She found she had to walk at a constantly fast pace to keep up with him… Not too much fun… But of course, this had its' compensations… No danger of her exceeding her credit limit with the bank.

'And, why, I thought we could go for a curry at Wetherspoons… It's cut-price curry day today.' 'Yes, sounds good to me,' answered Izzy.

He led her to the nearest Wetherspoons at the end of Stonegate. Kenneth found a small table for two at the back of the public house.

They sat down. 'Well, this is very nice… And thank you for bringing me here,' said Izzy who was first to break the silence.

'Not at all… Why, the pleasure was all my own,' answered her father in a tone not altogether unlike that of James Brodie, and then he proceeded to add, '…You know, dear, you remind me so much of my late mother.'

Not having seen her other grandmother, Izzy thought to herself, she was entirely unable to express her own views on the subject, either way… But at that moment, something from one of her papa's letters stood out firmly and resolutely in her mind… 'I held you when you were two weeks old… You were just two weeks old and beautiful.'

'So, of course, that makes you extra special,' continued her father, '…And do you know?... Do you know? My mother, Jessica, also held you when you were a couple of weeks old and she said, '…There 'aint no doubt about it, this one's a Jackson!'

Isabel laughed.

'I'm so very pleased you managed to take the time out to come and see your old da,' added her father.

'Oh, this was the least I could do, the absolute least. And would you believe it? It's almost as though I've known you all my life already,' commented Izzy.

'Well, yes, it does appear a little like that, my dear,' was Mr Jackson's response, 'and it will seem still more like that when we've spent a few more days together.'

The two continued to converse for a further twenty minutes and then, quite abruptly, and a little to Izzy's surprise, without any further debate or conversation, her father went abruptly to the bar. On his return, he added almost as an afterthought, 'That's two Korma chicken curries I've just ordered.'

What? What? And Izzy had thought she might order the steak and ale pie! She had never made any reference whatsoever to requesting a Korma curry! Suddenly she did begin to realise what her mum had said about her father, '...Why, your father, he just gets one fixed idea in his head, and then does it... No reference to what anyone else might want or need!'

'Yes, I know what you mean, mother,' Izzy thought to herself, as the chicken Korma curry duly appeared at the table in due course... Oh well, best get on the right side of them, thought Izzy to herself. The curries and wine being consumed, they began to wind a desultory route back to the bus station... Oh well, money saved on Isabel's part!

'We went to the curry day at Wetherspoon's, dear,' said her father to Agnieska when they eventually returned to Huddersfield in the early evening, 'And of course, the minster was absolutely marvellous!'

'So, you enjoyed it?'

'Well yes,' answered Izzy emphatically, 'We felt as though we barely scratched the surface of what there was to look at in the minster!'

'Yes, there is a lot more to see,' answered her father.

'Would you like something to drink, Isabel?'

'Oh, yes please,' replied Izzy, by now, she was feeling well and truly ready for another glass of wine to perk up her rather frazzled spirits.

'And you, Kenny?'

'I'll just have my customary cup of strong tea.'

Agnieska went to get them. She had just returned with the tea and wine when Isabel's phone began to make its' presence felt in the trouser pocket of her jeans. No prizes for guessing who this was.

'Hello?' Izzy answered her phone.

'Oh, hello, dear.' James, and by the sound of his voice, he appeared to have consumed a little too much wine this evening, and was without doubt in ingratiating mode, '…Just your old supervisor, checking on his much valued, er… Hic… trainee…'

And now, there was no doubt about it whatsoever. Her supervisor, quite obviously and shamelessly the worse for intoxication… And at that instant, James let out another very pronounced hiccup,

'James,' said Izzy, 'You've been drinking!'

'Well, what if I have?' answered James airily.

'…I'll take this call upstairs!' Izzy muttered quickly. She needed some privacy, and she needed it fast. Up the dreary, dingy staircase to the comparative calm and sanity of her own bedroom. '…James! You've been drinking!' Izzy repeated ineffectually. If truth were known, she felt secretly rather irritated with James, after all, how could he embarrass her like this, especially at this rather difficult and awkward time?

James decided to conveniently ignore this comment, and his inebriation appeared to become worse, as he began to slur his words together, and at last he managed to articulate, 'So, have you been anywhere nice?'

'Well, yes. Today, we went to York.'

'Ah! York! Such a… Such a…' and then for a few moments, James appeared to be at a total loss for words, and then after what appeared to be a great effort, he managed to say, '…Beautiful place.'

'Yes, it is.'

'Of course, Alison and I used to spend much of our free time in York…Alison's parents, why, Eric and Susan lived just outside the town.'

So, at last, James had made reference to Alison!!! That paragon of womanhood whom he had somehow never managed to replace!

Somewhere, downstairs Izzy heard the front doorbell ring.

'Well,' continued James, '…Mother and I are just about to start our evening meal… I'm drunk as a… As a… As a lord… And I am sorry for that… Or am I?... Eat, drink and be merry… That's what I say!'

'Just remember that you have to go to work in the morning,' Isabel, ever the voice of reason, answered in comparatively sober tones from her end of the 'phone. Her supervisor, James Brodie, who she had always envisaged and imagined as the absolute and complete epitome of restraint, moderation and sobriety, actually telephoning her when he was as drunk as a lord! Matters were becoming still more bizarre by the moment!

'…How… How… How are you getting along at your father's?' James eventually managed to articulate through his drunken stupor.

Very well, thought Isabel, until you started to interfere! But instead, she managed to calmly and carefully respond by saying, 'We've had a really nice day today… I think we're due to go to Leeds tomorrow, and have a general wander round.'

'How nice… Well… The days will soon pass, oh, and now I think mother's calling me again, it's obviously… My supper time!'

'I'll let you go, James, you go and get some food into you, and thank you for calling me.'

Isabel, despite her initial irritation at his drunk as a lord 'phone conversation suddenly began to find herself beginning to warm to James's strange and outlandish ways.

'Not at all... Not... At all... The pleasure was... Was all my own. Goodbye, dear!'

'Goodbye, James!' And with that, Isabel terminated the call.

Isabel retraced her steps downstairs. Now she had to face her father once again.

'Everything alright with your supervisor?' Izzy's father asked casually, when Izzy returned to the dreary back room for the evening meal.

'Yes, and I'm sorry to say, he'd had a little too much to drink... He's a bit of a strange man is James.'

'Izzy,' answered her father, indicating a rather plump man in his mid-thirties and a girl of eight or nine, wearing a strange pink and white, all-in-one suit which appeared to sag round the crotch area.

'This is your half-brother, Christopher, and this is his little girl, Ella.'

Christopher and Isabel shook hands. Ella muttered a brief, fleeting and hurried 'hello', and rushed off in the direction of the bathroom upstairs.

'Now I've made pork chops for the evening meal,' said Agnieska.

'Sounds good to me,' answered Izzy. Come to think of it, she'd not eaten a pork chop for months and was feeling quite ready and in the mood for one.

'Christopher works for XYZ, the photographic company,' explained her father, 'But its' only part time, since he tries to fit his employment round caring for Ella.'

'So do you manage the XYZ Huddersfield branch, Christopher?'

'Oh no,' answered Christopher airily, 'I have worked as a manager in the past, but the responsibility ground me down. I couldn't cope with the responsibility. I currently work as a shop assistant, three days per week.'

Well, that was rather a turn-up for the book! Christopher was only a shop assistant, and to cap it all, only a part-time shop assistant, at that! The mystery deepened.

Presently, Ella returned from the bathroom, flung herself down on the settee in the back room and began to desultorily play with a wi-fi tablet. She seemed intent on taking a photograph of herself from various different angles.

'Grandma, could you take one of me from here? Or perhaps I could stretch out my legs?'

'Yes, I'll take one if you like,' answered Agnieska in a rather resigned tone.

'Is that going to appear on your Facebook page?' asked Izzy.

'No, I don't have a Facebook page… At least, not yet,' Ella piped up.

They settled down at the table. Isabel found herself sitting next to Ella.

'Remember,' said Ella abruptly, 'It's Halloween in three weeks' time, and of course, I shall be having my annual Halloween party – I want the theme to be ghosts, spooks, skeletons, that sort of thing… And of course, you, grandpa, you can do the sound effects.'

'I'd be only too pleased to,' was grandpa's response.

'And you, grandma, get me some Halloween decorations! And make them good ones!'

Izzy was shocked at Ella's peremptory and demanding tone. She noticed there was no sign of, 'Please could I have,' or 'Could you get me, please?'

'Yes, dear,' answered the crushed Agnieska.

'Well, before I go to bed tonight, I shall start to write a list of the friends I'm asking to come to my party,' commented the strange Ella, and then she presently added as an afterthought, 'And of course, nobody can resist my parties, EVER.'

Eventually, the meal was ended. Christopher had to leave early in order to prepare something for work the morning after and he wanted Ella to get a decent night's sleep, so he departed early in order to return to the house he was currently in the process of renovating, taking the bizarre Ella with him. Isabel helped her father to clear the table and stack up the dishwasher, and then they retreated to the front room to watch a series on television which Agnieska said she was keen to see.

'And you, young lady?' aked Izzy's father, 'Shall we go to Leeds tomorrow?'

'Yes, I would really love to.'

'Yes, provided you're happy to, my dear.'

'Yes, I certainly am.'

They proceeded to watch the television program, and Agnieska made three mugs of tea. As Izzy decided to prepare for bed and obtain a reasonable night's sleep, her father said to her, 'Well, so far, it's going really well!'

Izzy smiled and gave her father a hug. 'It is, isn't it?' Perhaps it was not turning out half as bad in reality as she had initially envisaged.

'And I'll see you in the morning, dear.'

Hence, the penultimate morning dawned. After a light breakfast of toast and coffee, Isabel and her father set off for Leeds. Leeds. Large, vital, northern city, with interesting, rather solid looking and at times bizarre architecture… Rather reminiscent of a Yorkshire version of Liverchester. 'Of course, I did two years lecturing in land law at the university,' Izzy's father told her rather proudly, 'And I also wrote some legal texts, but for the texts to be accepted by them, I would had to have paid royalties to the university… So I decided not to bother.'

They had a wander round the streets, visited a museum and the large city art gallery, then stopped for lunch in an unusual looking, interesting public house down a side street.

Kenneth bought the drinks.

'Well,' said Izzy, by way of conversation, 'Thank you for bringing me here.'

'Nonsense!' answered Kenneth pompously, sounding at this point, strangely reminiscent of James Brodie! 'The pleasure was well and truly all my own.'

'I do really like Leeds, it seems to be very similar to Liverchester.'

'Yes, it is a good town,' answered Kenneth, 'Gwyn[6] also loves it… You know, she did two years at Warwick University, and then couldn't finish off her degree course… ' at which her father looked sadly and absently towards the general direction of the public house window.

'I rather get the impression that Gwyneth doesn't like me,' said Isabel blandly, basing her conclusion for this assumption on the fact that Gwyneth Jackson had lately unfriended her on Facebook.

'Oh, I'm sure that's not the case,' answered Kenneth hurriedly. 'Gwyneth does live just round the corner, but sometimes we don't see her for weeks.'

Why had Gwyneth not completed her degree course? Why did she dislike Izzy? Why had she not been to visit her and at least say 'hello?' No, there was certainly no love lost between either of them.

They returned to Huddersfield.

---

[6] Gwyn – Short for Gwyneth, Isabel's half-sister.

'Now, would you two like something to drink after your travels?' asked Agnieska, when they returned to 35, Portland Road.

'I'll have my usual, statutory cup of tea,' answered Kenneth.

'I'll have a glass of red wine, please, Agnieska, said Izzy, 'And incidentally, Leeds was marvellous. I thoroughly enjoyed it.'

'Oh, I'm pleased you enjoyed it,' answered her stepmother.

The doorbell sounded.

'That will probably be Christopher and Ella,' commented Izzy's papa. At that moment, Izzy's mobile 'phone started to ring. James, without doubt!

'Once again, I'll take this call upstairs,' muttered Isabel. She passed through the dingy, gloomy, hallway and up to the small sanctuary of her own room.

'Oh, hello, dear,' said James, once again, clearly the worse for intoxication, 'I just wanted to... To ascertain... That all, all... Was O.K. at your end... Of the 'phone.'

'Well, it is. James, you've been drinking again!' And at this point, Isabel couldn't help smiling to herself. There was something almost quite endearing about James Brodie – he just didn't care what others thought about him, or the effect he had, or the impression he created on other people. He simply did his own thing.

'Allright...' James muttered, 'Admittedly, I have... But... A man's got to have a good time some of the time, especially when he works... He works... So hard the rest of the time.'

James, thought Isabel to herself, you really are a total crackpot! And if truth be known, she herself was also a slight crackpot! One thing Isabel was unable to tolerate was boringness.

Did that mean two crackpots together were acceptable? Possibly... And furthermore, James had taken the time, trouble and expense to 'phone her that evening... At that point, Isabel remembered a person she once worked with saying in laughing tones, 'Oh, Izzy!.......You're a barmpot!' And Isabel had been so secretly proud.

'So true, James.'

There was silence for a few seconds while James seemed to be debating and selecting what he could manage to articulate, given his severe intoxication, '...You've... You've nearly done it now... Which day... Which day... Do you depart from your... From your... From your papa's?'

'Saturday morning.'

'...Well, 'twill...' and at this point, James once again let out an almighty hiccup, then he added, '...Excuse me... I'm sorry... I'm a little the worse for wear... Drunk again is what I am... But... I do apologise for it.'

'Look, James, you don't need to be sorry. After all, I'm only your trainee.'

'Oh, but I do need to be.'

Isabel began to scratch round in the depths and recesses of her brain to try to find something else to tell James.

'Do you know, James, and this is strictly between us, I get the impression that my half-sister, Gwyneth doesn't like me, she only lives two roads away from my father, but she's not come round to see me, at least, not yet at any rate, plus the fact that she's just unfriended me on Facebook.'

'Well, dear,' answered James, his natural inclination to pomposity beginning to break through his intoxication, '...I... Really wouldn't worry if I were yourself... She's... She's just jealous of you.'

'I think she left university without obtaining her degree, also.'

'Well, that's it! As I said... I... May be drunk as... A lord... But... I can tell she's obviously jealous of you... In the words of the old... Old... Immortal phrase... In wine truth.'

'Well, maybe you're right.'

'I'm certain I… Am.' James just about managed to articulate.

'I shall need to go in a minute, why, I think the evening meal is almost prepared. I don't think it will be long now.'

'…My dear…' began James in response, 'I…I could talk…I could talk for hours… But… But there will be plenty, oh yes, plenty of time for us to… To… Talk and converse when… When… You're back in Liverchester.'

What did that mean, thought Izzy to herself, although her sojourn in Huddersfield had begun to make her see James in an altogether more favourable light, she was still not entirely convinced of his eligibility for her as a would-be life partner. Nevertheless, he was a good, decent, hard-working man, if a little unconventional, with few inhibitions, which Isabel found altogether endearing, and somewhere in the depths of her head, Izzy could almost hear her grandmother speaking to her once again.

'…Can't understand you, Izzy Jackson… Go for him! For goodness' sake, go for him… My grandson-in-law, a partner solicitor and commissioner for oaths, no less… For goodness' sake, go for him!' Should she?

Instead, Isabel calmly managed to say in response, 'Yes, there'll be plenty of chances for us to talk when I get back to Liverchester.'

'…In fact,' answered James tentatively, as though, with the passage of time he was beginning to become a little more sober, … Ben and I… Ben and I are arranging a little welcome back event for you… When you get back… Nothing… Nothing exotic… Just a little after works bonding session…'

'Well, thank you,' answered Isabel, 'That's really nice of you.'

'It will just be… At… You know, Rigby's again. And… And… By the way, young… Young leddy…' Isabel was certain at this point that James fully intended to say, 'young lady,' but bearing in mind the state and degree of his inebriation he articulated the word as 'leddy.' What a character he was!

'…There was no need… No need whatsoever… Whatsoever to thank me… We… We depend on you quite heavily for the… The day to day running of the chambers.'

'Is that so?' asked Izzy, this time rather sceptically.

'…Of course it is! Of course it is!' answered James emphatically, 'As Ben… As Ben said… We… We couldn't effectively run these… Run these… Chambers without you.'

'Well, how nice of you to say so,' answered Isabel blandly, 'And I think I really will have to go for my evening meal now, everyone will wonder what's happened to me!'

'Yes. Of course I'll let you go now,' said James a little pompously again, thought Izzy to herself, 'And I think mother wants me to lay the table… So… So that it's ready… Ready for our evening meal.'

'Goodbye, James!'

'…Good… Goodbye, dear!'

And with that, Isabel terminated the call.

Once again, Christopher and Ella had arrived for supper, and the general conversation flowed quite freely between the five of them. Isabel talked briefly about how much she had enjoyed the Victorian architecture in Leeds, and a little later helped her father to stack up the dishwasher. Christopher left early again since he was due to go to work the morning after, and Ella was due to have an early night and sleep in the other spare room across the landing from Izzy, which apparently, she frequently did.

Once again, Izzy, her father and Agnieska migrated to the front room to watch a travel program. 'Oh, incidentally, Izzy,' said her father later on that evening, 'Your mother 'phoned earlier when you were talking on your mobile. She asked how you were going on, and I told her you seemed to be having a good time and altogether enjoying things, and I told her, 'I think this young lady, my eldest daughter is absolutely super!'

'Oh, thank you father!' And Izzy gave her father another hug as she went upstairs to bed.

She would 'phone her mother when she reached the privacy and solitude of her own room.

Izzy's last full day in Huddersfield dawned. Demarcation points in human life once again, suddenly flashed through her head, quite at random, and one early one in particular. One autumn Sunday afternoon when she was nine years old, and the walk she had been on with her grandparents in Settle. They had never repeated their visit to Settle, which was a real pity since it was quite a pretty town, and Isabel happily remembered herself as the sensitive, imaginative nine-year-old who had been absolutely captivated by the sight of the rocky limestone outcrops and bastions, just slightly eastwards out of the town and which her grandmother had later on dubbed as the 'Fairytale Caverns.' On the visit to her father Izzy had visited two cities, not that she had been particularly able to reap any direct benefits from either of them, for example like doing any special shopping, since her father seemed rather loathe to visit the shops, but she was heading back to Liverchester next week so she would easily remedy the defect and be able to satisfy her predilection for Pandora jewellery and end of line cut price summer clothes at M & S on Church Street… But yes, she certainly fancied another very much overdue visit to Settle and the 'caverns.'

'Father,' asked Izzy at breakfast, 'When I was about nine, my grandparents took me for the day from Clitheroe[7], where we lived, up to Settle for a Sunday afternoon walk. We walked through the marketplace and out of the town to some rocky outcrops which formed part of the hillsides up there. I was absolutely captivated by it.'

'Well yes, dear,' answered Kenny, smiling indulgently at her.

---

[7] Clitheroe, a small market town, in East Lancashire.

'We only went there that one time,' answered Izzy, 'which is a pity because it's really beautiful, and it seems somehow appropriate for my last day.'

Kenny checked the distance on the computer. Forty-eight miles. Yes, just about a manageable distance, bearing in mind that there and back would amount to just under a hundred miles. 'Well, if we're to go and get back for a reasonable hour, we'd best set off early.' Izzy's father seemed eager for them to go.

'Yes… We'd better go soon.'

Isabel enjoyed the drive up to Settle, which seemed to rapidly alternate between vast, beautiful, wild expanses of moorland and crystal clear, tumbling, rocky waterfalls to outskirts of densely populated towns, busy motorways and urban areas. Yes, it was rather nice to be able to relax in her father's ancient car and sit and make casual conversation with him. If the absolute truth were known, she was now beginning to feel comfortable and at home with her papa, and strangely enough, although he had been absent for almost all her life, she felt as though now, even though she had only spent a few days in his company, felt as though she now almost knew him quite well.

They reached Settle at a few minutes after noon. A small market town, basking in the late summer sunshine, this, after all had formed the venue and backdrop for the nine-year old's very first momentous demarcation point. They walked through the marketplace.

'Now, we do sometimes come out here at the weekends, in fact, Ella loves the walks,' said Kenny, 'And now of course, I'm back with my dear, long-lost daughter, Katie!'

Sometimes Isabel had strong reason to believe that her father was just about as unusual as James Brodie!

'But my name's Isabel.'

'Well, it is,' answered her father, 'but so many of the Isabel's that I've known have been so... Now how do I describe it? So docile and placid… Somehow, Katie seems far more appropriate to you.' Isabel felt unable to comment, and they continued with their walk, reaching the grassy plateau in good time before the hills began to close in. The terrain was as beautiful as Isabel remembered it. A slight turn to the left, and at that point the expanse of the rocky limestone structures suddenly and abruptly burst upon the eye, conical peaks and undulations of creamy white stone, not unlike the fanciful turrets and towers of a fairytale or medieval castle, rearing up against a deep blue sky of late summer. How often Isabel had thought about and remembered them. For this moment, she had waited almost thirty years.

'Beautiful, aren't they?' Kenny commented.

'They certainly are.' And then the memories came crowding in on Isabel. The memories that the nine-year-old had liked to believe in. '…And in the caverns were fabulous, sumptuous riches. Almost all the wealth and riches known to and needed by man…'

And then another phrase from Isabel's adult years abruptly flitted through her consciousness, '…Wealth beyond the dreams of avarice.' Not that these hillsides contained such riches in reality. Without doubt, the contents of the caverns would merely comprise a few underground streams and old mine workings, but what a place! Suddenly Huddersfield and her father's house in Huddersfield, James Brodie and Ben Watson seemed like many worlds away! On this beautiful, clear, sunny day, the world up here with its fresh, clear air seemed only to consist of Isabel, her father and the caverns themselves.

Isabel noticed a small, narrow fissure or opening in the side of the nearest cavern as it merged into the rest of the hillside and the limestone of the rock gradually and eventually gave way to grass. She gingerly slid a hand into the opening, and then to her absolute and total surprise, the rock face seemed to ever so slightly give way beneath her grasp… As if almost welcoming her in. Surely not… Right now, Isabel needed to know that she could safely return to the outside… Yes, the opening would just about allow her through, or so she thought.

Isabel found herself in what looked like a dark, gloomy, sombre antechamber and somewhere she could hear the sound of fast flowing water. As she had suspected, an underground stream and the dim, gently muted light of daylight filtering through from the fissure in the rock prevented the chamber from being engulfed in total darkness. Intrigued, Isabel walked on. Into a smaller chamber about half the size of its predecessor, and then… Then in the next chamber, the cavern revealed itself to her in all its' glory, in a manner which the nine-year-old had always believed to be in reality totally untrue and way beyond the bounds of possibility… Wealth beyond the dreams of avarice indeed. Isabel was confronted by ledges piled high with every conceivable type of jewellery… Gold and silver to excess… Rings in every imaginable shape, design, style, pattern and width… Both delicate and chunky chains and bracelets were safely stored on smooth ledges and blocks of limestone and against the walls of the cavern and solid blocks of gold were arranged at reasonably regular intervals on the floor. Was Izzy dreaming or was this just a prize hoax?

Isabel was both flabbergasted and fascinated, but she decided right now that she needed to get back to her father and tell him of the singularly unusual items contained in this particular cavern. Could she manage to negotiate the opening? Suddenly Izzy found herself beginning to panic, and she tripped and fell a couple of times in both antechambers… Back through the opening, which luckily almost appeared to be welcoming her through once again… Out once again, back into the daylight… and… And reality.

'Oh, so there you are, dear,' said her father welcomingly.

Isabel looked white and her response to her father was rather reminiscent and not unlike that of Mr Carter's[8] words on the

---

[8] Mr Carter – Howard Carter, a famous archaeologist, on the discovery of Tutankhamen's tomb in ancient Egypt.

discovery of Tutankhamen's tomb in ancient Egypt, and she managed to articulate, 'I've just seen... Absolutely marvellous things.'

Chapter 5.

'What do you mean?' asked Kenny in extremely bewildered and nonplussed tones, 'What marvellous things? Where?'

'In… In the caverns!' Isabel at last managed to utter. '…Fabulous, marvellous riches! Beautiful jewellery, and solid blocks of gold! Fabulous the riches are! Absolutely marvellous!'

Kenny looked at her sceptically. 'Are you sure?'

'Well, yes. Just about as certain as I know that I'm standing here.'

There was silence between Isabel and her father for a few minutes.

'Now let me see,' he said at last, still in rather sceptical tones. 'There's only one thing for it, shall we go and look together? If there really are fabulous riches contained within, and we both witness them, then of course that's the solid, objective proof of their existence… We're both highly unlikely to be dreaming about the same subject in any case.'

Tentatively, they both approached the fissure in the rock. Once again, the rock kindly accommodated them both, and they slowly began to pick their way through the rubble of the nearest antechamber.

Suppose Izzy's imagination had simply run riot, and in reality there was nothing? Had her imagination simply worked overtime for ten to twenty minutes? Then she would look an idiot in front of her father and there was nothing to be done about that whatsoever. They approached the large cavern.

And please, thought Izzy to herself… Don't let me down! And she began to dig her nails into her palms with anxiety.

At the entrance to the cavern a deep rose pink light appeared to be casting a beautiful, gentle hue which illuminated the chamber, and somehow Izzy began to feel infused with an innately deep, positive sense of well-being, safety and general optimism. A closer inspection and examination of the contents showed that nothing had changed from the lapse of ten to twenty minutes. Solid blocks of gold and silver festooning the limestone walls... Gold rings of every width physically wearable; plain, patterned, carved, textured, hammered and engraved... An extensive collection of silver rings, necklaces and earrings... Titanium and coloured plated titanium... All was there in abundance. It really was a veritable Alladin's cave.

'You see, father... You see... It's true.' Izzy at last managed to say.

'Somehow, Izzy, dear, I didn't think for one moment that you would be likely to lie.'

Izzy stared round her entranced. She picked up a chunky gold ring from a nearby easily accessible ledge and closely examined it. At that point, Izzy vividly recalled a quote from the nineteenth century poetry she had studied for the third year as part of her English degree.

'On earth the broken arc,

In heaven the perfect round.'[9]

What a beautiful ring! And yes, it was or, at any rate appeared to be a perfect spherical shape, to Isabel's untrained eye, at least. She tried the ring on. Yes, it fitted her hand comfortably, and felt smooth against her other fingers. Not a scratch marred its' lustrous surface. She slipped it off her finger again and closely examined the ring's interior, which appeared to be adorned with a small series of hallmarks, doubtless indicating the purity content of the metal. If she came here again, she would need to reappear armed with a magnifying glass in order to be able to fully understand the hallmarking system employed. 'Always beware of jewellery

---

[9] Robert Browning, a nineteenth century poet.

displaying no hallmarks…' Isabel remembered reading somewhere from ten or so years ago… Well, true… Then Izzy thought it wise to return the beautiful item to the ledge, which she duly did, after all, it did not belong to her.

'You rather like it in here, don't you, Izzy dear?' said her father, abruptly cutting through her thoughts.

'Well, yes, I do.'

It seemed entirely wrong to both of them to start filling their pockets, after all who did all these riches belong to, and did it count as Crown property?

'I think I feel like a bit of air, dear,' said Kenny.

'Let's get back to reality then, papa.' With that, they began to pick their way back though the previous chambers, and back towards the fissure in the rock face.

Isabel's mind was in turmoil… The riches she had witnessed this lunchtime! And then her mind flicked back down the years to the twenty-two-year-old Izzy, a recent graduate of the University of Liverchester, with needless to say, little or no money, imagining all the items she would like to acquire, if only given the chance… Cherry red Montego car complete with the latest registration marks, cases full of quality jewellery, posh clothes, sexy underwear, expensive make-up and bottles of exotically fragranced, designer perfume, among other things.

'You need a rich husband!' commented her uncle Dick.

No… What ultimately mattered was to be happy… And also, probably the most vital aspect of all was to be a good person. And no… Being fabulously rich was unimportant… But conversely, of course, everyone needed to have enough money to be comfortable… That obviously raised in turn the question of how much money was needed and required in order to attain the standard of living classified as 'comfortable?' What exactly comprised 'comfortable?' To Isabel, this indicated the ability to afford such things as one decent holiday per year, purchase a luxury item of jewellery three or four times a year, be able to buy a small selection of pretty clothes three or four times per year, one for each season of the year, afford expensive make-up and the odd bottle of perfume… No, she didn't need any more make-up and had all the perfume she required for the time being at least… Smart clothing? Seriously, in reality, Isabel reminded herself, she really did have all she both really wanted and needed to make her happy.

Isabel and her father looked at each other uncertainly. Eventually, Kenny broke the silence by saying, 'Do you think we ought to tell someone what we've seen?'

'Probably, yes.'

It was a Friday lunchtime in late summer and the tourist and holiday season was well and truly over. Most individuals of employment age would be at work. Presently, a farm-hand appeared from a nearby field, equipped with a medium-sized sheep dog, obviously about to round up the sheep from the surrounding fields. Izzy's father called to him, and they hastened across to the man to ask him if he knew anything about the caverns.

'We were walking up here this morning and we, we found marvellous, fabulous riches. Hidden in this limestone outcrop!' her father told the farm-hand, '…And this, this is my daughter, and she was absolutely captivated by what she witnessed, completely captivated!' Isabel noticed that throughout her stay in Yorkshire with her father, he had rather proudly introduced her at least three or four times as, 'my daughter.' Perhaps he really was proud and pleased with her!

The farm-hand looked back at Kenny sceptically. He was silent for a few minutes, and then he eventually answered, '…The riches? In them there caverns? You don't want anything to do with 'em!'

'Are you sure?' asked Isabel.

'Oh, I'm quite sure… When those there riches were first discovered, Settle became quite a hot-spot. But you need to keep away… Stay away, that's my advice… Local people say there's a curse hanging over them… They don't do nobody no good!'

'How do you mean?' asked Isabel, and then added, 'Could you explain in a bit more detail?'

'Well, individuals came from miles, trying to fill their boots. Thought they were well on their ways to becoming multi-millionaires, pocketed many of the riches… Hoped to sell them… And in the early days some men from Leeds who raided 'em did manage to raise some cash. One Leeds businessman… He managed to raise one million from what he'd snatched. Thought he was made for life… Bought a yacht with the proceeds… Bought shares in certain companies… Bought a luxury penthouse flat in London.'

'And what happened?' By now, Isabel felt intrigued, this felt rather like opening an old perfume bottle, neglected for some time, and then suddenly becoming once again entranced and captivated by the subtle aroma. She had to know more about it.

'The yacht sank, and the buyer narrowly escaped with his life on a transatlantic tour… The company shares took an almost immediate nosedive and the companies shortly after went into… Now what do they call it? Liquidation, I think the term is. The pent-house flat was still in the process of being constructed when the other disasters occurred. The builders went bankrupt and couldn't complete the job. And due to all the stress of these things happening, left, right and centre, the poor man, he couldn't cope and he had a massive heart-attack and died… Oh, and there was a woman… She loved jewellery, it was quite her passion, and so she snatched a ring… Took it to a jeweller in Bradford where she came from. The jeweller told her it was completely worthless. Worth less than a jeweller's sample ring! She got a bit worked up about that. And guess what? Guess what? She had a series of those minor strokes, I think they call them… Ended up in hospital, she did… Then a massive one in hospital… Finished her off, finished her off, it did.'

'Oh, my goodness!' Isabel was horrified.

'…And there were other people who've tried to 'get rich quick!' and it's done 'em no good, no good whatsoever! Steer clear, that's what I say. Steer clear. The best advice I can give you two is tell no-one, keep it a secret. That way, no more harm can be done.'

'How did they get here? And who did they belong to?' asked Izzy. The mystery really was well and truly deepening by the moment.

The farm-hand was again silent for a few minutes, and then at last he answered. 'Lady Gertrude… Those riches that you've seen in them there caverns once formed part of Lady Gertrude's jewellery collection.'

'Whose Lady Gertrude?' answered Isabel, absolutely captivated.

'Well… I don't er, rightly know exactly… She was, er, Lord Roger's daughter… And from what's been said about her… Eh, she was a right good egg… A right good person… Always doing good works, she was… Loved and admired by all who saw and knew her.'

'And then what happened? What happened to her?' Isabel continued trying to probe.

'As legend has it… As the story goes, Lady Gertrude died of consumption very young. Only in her late twenties, she was. Her husband, and she'd only been married to him for about three weeks, sold some of her jewellery to raise money for the poor and destitute of Leeds, whom Lady Gertrude herself had tried to help. The problem was he was so crazed with grief and shock he hid the remainder of her collection, believing they would be safe for all time in these here caverns. Everybody wondered whether his last act was to place a curse on them, so that no mortal was ever able to profit from ill-gotten gains.'

'What happened to Lady Gertrude's husband?'

'You mean Ernest?'

'Oh, was that his name?' answered Izzy.

'Yes, Ernest… His business which had previously flourished and prospered crashed dramatically… And he too died of consumption in total penury, somewhere over near Whitby, I think… Not a happy man was Ernest.'

'No, he doesn't sound to be.'

'No, my advice to you two is simply to say nothing. That way no more harm can be done and no-one else can be hurt… Or… Or corrupted… Lie low and say nothing.'

'It's alright,' answered Kenny calmly, 'Your secret's safe with us.'

'Yes, it is,' Isabel replied.

'What was Lady Gertrue's surname?' asked her father.

'Her unmarried name? That's all I know,' answered the farmhand, 'but I think it was Rivers. Lady Gertrude Rivers. She certainly came from the Rivers family. They say her father, Lord Roger was a good, decent man too… Very good to his estate employees, he was…'

'You're fascinated, aren't you, young lady?' said Kenny.

'Yes, I certainly am.'

'That's just about all I know,' said the farm-hand, 'But I'm sure you'll be able to discover further information about Lady Gertrude from the internet… In the 1890's she was very well known round these parts.'

'Thank you for all you've told us,' said Kenny.

'Just tell no-one… And you'd be best advised not to try to remove any of the riches, always replace them when you leave. That way no harm will come to anyone. I think local people say that the riches can be safely admired in the caverns and even worn and enjoyed up to a three hundred yards radius outside the caverns…'

'And then what? What happens beyond that?' enquired Izzy.

'Eh… The goings on that have taken place up here,' muttered the farm-hand, 'Who would ever have thought that pieces of metal could cause so much trouble! It's now well and truly impossible to remove them. Beyond the three hundred yards point, I mean. Why, there's like an invisible electric fence. Some locals say it's the spirit of Lady Gertrude and her husband Ernest at work. Hey, but don't get scared. A lot of local people who love walking up round these here hills and caverns, they enjoy the walk up to here. They marvel at and admire the Lady's jewels. Wear them for an afternoon and safely return them to the caverns. These people… They've enjoyed long and happy lives. And lived to ripe old ages. Well into their eighties and nineties, in fact.'

'Is that so?' asked Kenny, equally captivated by now at the farm-hand's narrative.

'Oh, yes… Most certainly. It's often been said round these parts, Lady Gertrude looks after her own. And it's a fact.'

It suddenly came to Izzy in a blinding flash and she fully understood and caught the farm-hand's drift. Treat the caverns with respect, and they will respect and look after you, but try to exploit the caverns for your own selfish ends, and no good will come of it, no good whatsoever.

'Thank you for your advice, and yes, we will take that on board,' answered Isabel.

By now, it was almost lunchtime. Izzy and her father walked on for a further half hour, both well and truly shell-shocked and their minds reeling, from what they had witnessed and heard. They then spent a further pleasant couple of hours at a country public house in Settle, and then drove a little further towards walking distance of the three peaks. What a day it had been! Certainly momentous to say the least! They had both enjoyed such intrinsic naturally occurring beauty, the riches and obvious opulence of the items contained in the caverns apart, and slightly beyond Settle, they took a left turn up a winding road that led up towards Ingleborough, a long-backed, flat-topped peak, its' uppermost reaches scored with dark grey, slightly mysterious looking screes beginning to bask in the gentle, orange glow of early sunset.

'Probably best be turning round and heading homewards,' said Kenny, smiling across at his new-found daughter, 'After all, we've got quite a long way to go, and it's been quite an eventful day.'

'And father,' replied Izzy, 'Let's do as the farm-hand advised and keep this strictly a secret between us. Why, it can't do any harm.'

'Too right, dear. Let's keep it a secret. That can remain our little secret.'

'Did you two have a nice day?' asked Agnieska when they returned to the house.

'Oh it was marvellous. I thoroughly enjoyed it.'

'Oh, good, I am pleased.' Agnieska passed a glass of wine to Izzy, after which she poured one out for herself.

Somehow, Isabel had a sinking feeling somewhere in the pit of her stomach that conversation that evening might prove difficult. After all, most of the conversation which had passed between the three of them had already been exchanged. What could she find to talk about?

'I think we drove quite near Bronte land, didn't we father? And those long, low-lying open moorlands were absolutely marvellous and timeless.' The reference to 'Bronte land,' suddenly reminded Isabel of the Bronte sisters' novels, which, of course was an obvious talking point.

'Agnieska, have you read any of the Bronte novels?' asked Isabel.

'Oh yes, I've read quite a few. Do you know? I loved that book, 'Jane Eyre',' answered her stepmother.

'Yes, I did too. I loved the original early 1970's dramatisation on television.'

'Yes, it was excellent.'

'And there was a particular point at which Jane tells Mr Rochester that she does not find him handsome, why, my grandmother and I laughed our heads off when we watched it the first time.'

'Yes, that really is funny.'

Suddenly, Isabel's 'phone began, once again, to make its' presence felt in the pocket of her jeans.

James. No doubt about it, whatsoever.

'I'll just take this call upstairs… If you'll excuse me, just a minute.'

Izzy rushed upstairs.

'Oh, hello, dear.'

James! Surprise, surprise! This time he did not sound totally intoxicated.

'Hello, James. Oh, you are a good lad. Thank you for 'phoning.'

'Well, it's quite some time since I've been called a lad – It must be, well, forty years, at least.'

'Oh, you are funny, James.'

'Just think, dear, you'll be on your way home tomorrow morning, and I shall be so pleased to have you back at work.'

Yes, I'm sure you will, Isabel thought to herself. Instead, she managed to say, 'We've seen some absolutely marvellous things, especially today.'

'Have you had your evening meal yet?' James enquired.

'No, but we are about to.' And what, thought Izzy to herself are we going to talk about? Why, almost all possible sources of conversation now seemed to be well nigh exhausted. Somewhere down in the depths of the house, Isabel heard the doorbell ring once again. Christopher and Ella, no doubt.

'Well, remember dear, we've got our special 'welcome back do' specially arranged for you for when you get back.'

'Yes, I believe so…' answered Izzy uneasily, and then she added in an attempt to be good mannered, but shortly afterwards felt extremely guilty since the comment was, in reality nothing more than a bare-faced lie, '…And I'm looking forward to it!'

'Yes, I thought you might be,' answered James, once again, Isabel noticed, rather pompously. 'Incidentally, Ben and I are going out for early evening drinks, so I can't stay on the 'phone too long this evening!'

Well, thought Izzy, she could cope with that only too easily… Certainly not a problem from her point of view, but instead she managed to calmly and casually articulate, 'Oh, are you going somewhere nice?'

'Hannah's.'

'Well, you two enjoy it.'

'I'm sure we shall, but you know, Izzy, I would enjoy it still more with your good self.'

Yes, I'm sure you would, thought Isabel to herself, and the sinking feeling in the pit of her stomach seemed to be almost, she felt trying to warn her that further sexual harassment might be the, 'order of the day,' once she returned to work… A trainee solicitor's lot was, after all, not a happy one.

Suddenly James interrupted her thought processes by saying,

'What time are you leaving in the morning?'

Isabel was unsure of the exact time, but she had imagined it would probably be about mid-morning.

'I'm not exactly sure, but I was thinking the middle of the morning.'

'Yes, that sounds sensible, dear,' answered James in his characteristically heavy-handed tones, 'Then I could possibly 'phone you tomorrow morning about the time you wake up, just to wish you 'bon Voyage,' and all that sort of thing.'

'Well, thank you, but you really don't need to.'

'Nonsense! The pleasure, and it will be a pleasure will be all my own, and I shall be absolutely delighted to do so.'

'Well, thank you James,' answered Isabel.

'And Izzy, you know when you return, why, I have good things planned. Very good things.' Isabel's heart quietly sank. At this point, all she could imagine was herself, the luckless trainee having to fend off her employer's unwanted sexual advances. In fact, the very thought revolted her!

'What do you mean, good things?'

'Oh, but that's for me to say, and you to find out,' answered James non-comitally. Somewhere in the distance at James's end of the 'phone, a doorbell seemed to sound.

'I think that's Ben now.'

Thank goodness! This, thought Izzy to herself, was her cue to end the 'phone call, and James would not want to hold up and delay Ben while he idly chattered on the 'phone to his hopefully, would be 'lady love.'

'I'll leave you two gentlemen to it then. Goodbye, James!'

'Goodbye, dear.'

Izzy terminated the call. She retraced her steps downstairs. Luckily, Christopher and Ella were sitting at the tea table, and Christopher appeared to be animatedly in conversation with Agnieska about something. Gratefully, Isabel resumed her place at the table, and attempted to focus on the drift of Christopher's conversation.

'…Well, I don't feel as though I was at fault if this woman injured herself,' he said in slightly irritated, aggrieved tones.

'What happened, Christopher?' asked Izzy.

'Outside the house that I'm busy renovating, a woman fell down a shallow manhole and injured her left leg, and I'm just sincerely hoping that I'm not in any way responsible.'

Isabel's legal brain clicked into activity.

'Well, that really depends on who the roads are owned by. I'm quite happy to investigate the matter for you, if I can.'

'Oh, thank you.'

Isabel had also been debating over the prospect of purchasing a new camera for a few weeks now, and since Christopher worked in a photographic shop, he seemed the best person to ask and provide advice. Additionally, Isabel felt secretly very relieved that Christopher was present tonight, since he did most of the talking and appeared to be quite skilled in the art of casual conversation.

Christopher left early in the evening as he was due to meet a friend at the local public house, and Ella got herself prepared to go to bed in the spare room. The rest of the evening passed quite easily, and later, Isabel, her father and stepmother migrated to the front room.

'Well, it's gone so well,' said Kenny before Isabel eventually went to bed.

Strangely enough, it had somehow. Yes, there had been some difficult, awkward silences at times, in particular early this evening until Christopher had arrived, but on the whole it had passed as well as was to be expected, given the circumstances. Next time, of course would be considerably easier, although Isabel was uncertain as to exactly when the second visit would occur, if it occurred at all.

As Izzy got herself into bed, her mind was in turmoil concerning the events she had witnessed during the day... The caverns, their secret and treasures would need to remain a secret, and she felt confident that her father could also be trusted to allow the subject of the caverns to remain a strictly well-guarded secret. And James? Well, James had been his usual slightly irritating, yet strangely endearing self... And then suddenly Isabel's grandmother seemed to be speaking to her once again, and so clearly too!

'Well, Izzy! You were right and I was wrong…' Concerning her choice of legal career, and then on a more personal note, '…James Brodie! Partner and Commissioner for Oaths! For goodness' sake, Izzy! Just take him… And he sounds a nice, decent man! For goodness' sake, don't look the proverbial gift horse in the mouth!' This in turn, reminded Izzy of someone else she had known from the past, and her grandmother's recollections of this individual, 'Now, that German man, I really do like the sound of him!'

The specific man in question, was not, in reality a German man at all. In actuality, he was an Englishman who taught GCSE and 'A' level German, and Izzy had met him through a singles' group whilst she had been employed in Preston a few years ago. Strangely enough, Isabel's mum, Edith had briefly encountered him only a few weeks ago whilst on a shopping trip to Preston, whereupon Carl appeared to have made quite a deep impression, although not by any means a favourable one.

'Personally, the mystique of the German man completely passes me by. I, for one, will never speak to you again if you marry Carl Dawson!' Not that Izzy particularly wanted or intended to do so.

And then there had been the haunting story of Lady Gertrude… Lady Gertrude, admired and loved by all who saw and knew her, renowned for her philanthropic works and a consumptive. Strangely enough, the scenario appeared quite similar to that of James and Alison. Yes, she had to know more about the enigmatic Lady Gertrude.

Izzy collapsed into bed with a view to sleeping both soundly and thoroughly. Either James with his morning call or her father would wake her in the morning.

True to form, Izzy's 'phone rang out at precisely eight p.m. James, doubtless. By now, Isabel had ascertained which train she would travel on, Agnieska having very kindly checked out her route and availability for Saturday morning.

'Hello,' answered Isabel uncertainly. If truth be known, she wished James had left the telephoning until a little bit later in the morning, in which case she would have slept a little longer.

'Hello, dear! It's only James… You know, just your old supervisor.'

'Oh, thank you for 'phoning James.'

'So, when are you leaving, dear?'

'Here? Oh, at quarter to eleven.'

'And are you going straight back to Liverchester, or going back to Cumbria?'

'Well, both really. I'm getting the train back to Liverchester, picking up two changes of clothing and then heading back to Cumbria.'

'Well, you know,' answered James in a strangely simpering tone, infused with false jollity which sounded strangely out of character for him, 'When you get back to Liverchester I shall want to know all about it… Yes, all about it! And I mean all.'

Well yes, thought Izzy to herself, she could tell James almost everything, with one major exception… No, she was not, repeat not going to let slip anything about the late Lady Gertrude and her jewellery, after all, she had no idea how James would interpret the concept of a stash of jewellery hidden in a Yorkshire hillside, and good, decent, caring, sensitive man though he was, there was still the very real prospect that he might wrongly believe that the riches could be raided and plundered to increase his own personal wealth.

No, best to say absolutely nothing, when the subject of the last day fell under discussion.

Instead, she would merely speak of the beauty of the walk and the memorable views across to the three peaks in the early evening sunset. 'And I will tell you everything,' answered Izzy calmly. Then she suddenly thought of a topic of conversation which she could ask James about, his visit of the night before to Hannah's Bar.

'How did you go on at Hannah's last night?'

'Ah, it was most, most agreeable!' answered James in a typically pompous and heavy-handed manner, 'In fact, we both became, er… rather blotto, and Ben had to go and recover his car this morning by means of a taxi, so I believe a generally good time was had by all.'

'Oh, I'm pleased to hear it,' replied Izzy.

'But of course,' James continued, 'it would have been nicer, much nicer still with my dear Izzy.'

Oh horrors, thought Izzy to herself, and she had managed very easily without James, thank you, for many years. As of next week, she would be back with a vengeance to reality, yes, back to reality, the world of work, James and whatever he decided to throw in her path.

'Well, James, I'm going to be back very soon, just give me forty-eight hours to rest and recoup at home.' Izzy managed to articulate in response.

'Of course, dear, of course,' wittered James, 'and now, if you'll excuse me, I'm going to get a little more sleep.'

So why had he 'phoned at this unearthly time of the morning? Oh well, he was only trying to be kind.

'Yes, and I shall sleep a bit longer. After all, I've a long way to travel on the train this morning. Goodbye, James! We'll speak again soon.'

'Goodbye, dear!'

Isabel thankfully terminated the call and managed to sleep for a further hour and a half.

She was next woken by Kenny, asking her whether she would like a cup of morning tea. Izzy had packed most of her clothes and belongings the night before, so there remained little more now than to pack her overnight essentials. She consumed her tea, had a ten-minute shower courtesy of the ensuite facility in her bedroom, donned a clean set of clothes and went down to breakfast. Ella sat at the table, grumbling about something.

'Once and for all, I don't like salmon, either ordinary or smoked.'

'It's alright, dear, I haven't made you any,' said Agnieska, placatingly.

'Well, all the more for us!' laughed Kenny.

'And I'm thirsty,' continued Ella in lofty, superior tones, 'Grandma, get me something to drink!'

Isabel had noticed for a few days now how unpleasant Ella was to Agnieska, and there was still no sign of the use of the word, 'please,' or 'could I have?' Furthermore, she couldn't help but notice how her stepmother without question or grumbling simply carried out Ella's wishes. Isabel quickly reminded herself that her grandmother would never have stood for such talk.

Large helpings of scrambled egg on toast complete with substantial slices of smoked salmon began to appear at the table.

'Oh, thank you, Agnieska – this looks really good.' Isabel told her stepmother as her helping appeared at the breakfast table.

Her stepmother smiled. She was a plump, straightforward, straight-talking woman with absolutely no hidden agenda, and whom Isabel instinctively liked.

'You're extremely welcome.'

The rest of breakfast passed happily enough and Izzy helped her father to clear the table and load up the dishwasher.

'And now, of course, you young lady need to catch your train,' said her father.

As Izzy retraced her steps upstairs to collect her case, and perform one last examination of the bedroom just to check that nothing had been left, she reflected on her brief sojourn in Huddersfield. It had gone surprisingly well with few embarrassed silences, she and her father had got on so well, they had so very much in common and she felt that Christopher and Agnieska both liked her too… Not too sure about Gwyneth or Ella but, oh well, thought Izzy to herself, 'Impossible to please all of the people all of the time.'

Once downstairs, Izzy gave her stepmother a hug and thanked her for all the good food and hospitality she had received over the last few days and ended by saying in laughing tones, 'And please don't let Ella boss you about.' At which her stepmother laughed.

'Don't worry, I shan't!'

At Huddersfield station, Izzy and her father stood on the station, awaiting the next train to Leeds.

'Well, thank you, it's been so good, father, why I'm sure I shall be back in the not too distant future.'

'We've been only too happy to have you, my dear.'

'This of course, is only the start of us really getting to know each other.'

'Well, yes.'

At that moment the train arrived, and eventually ground to a halt. Izzy gave her father one last hug.

'Let me help you with your case.'

Kenny gallantly lifted Izzy's case, and placed it in the train vestibule.

'Oh, thank you, father,' replied Isabel, and as her father disembarked from the train they both began to wave frenziedly to each other through the train window.

Izzy found a vacant seat on the train and settled herself comfortably into it. Gradually, the industrial Yorkshire landscape began to give way to the more salubrious open moorland, fields and fresh, clear waterfalls, but not for long, for only too rapidly the fast mid-morning train began to enter the outer reaches of suburban Leeds.

'You'll need the 1.30 p.m. train to Liverchester, love,' Isabel was confronted with as she got her ticket checked at the ticket barrier at the station in Leeds.

'And where does that depart from when it leaves?' enquired Izzy.

'Platform 6. You can reach it by means of the lift.'

'Thank you.'

At approximately 1.20 p.m. the Liverchester train pulled in, and Izzy duly boarded it. Once Izzy had had time to unpack her laptop and browse briefly through its' contents, she had work to do. The magnet of Lady Gertrude was once again calling Isabel. Once the train had departed from the station, Izzy connected her laptop. Much to her surprise, the device connected at the first attempt.

Now to check out Lady Gertrude's details, Izzy thought to herself. Using Google as a search tool, she duly typed in, 'Lady Gertrude Rivers.' Strangely enough, the search yielded thousands of possible Lady Gertrude Rivers results, far too many than she was able to cope with, among which was listed a Gertrude Rivers of California. Certainly not what she required. Izzy proceeded to scroll down what she believed to be the feasible and plausible entries which she believed to be relevant and useful to her search. Eventually, something possible appeared.

Page 3. Gertrude Rivers, Lady. North Yorkshire. Victorian philanthropist – woman of letters – nurse - renowned diary writer/keeper and consumptive. (Dates were provided of 28th February 1867 to 3rd November 1894.)

That sounded exactly what she needed! Isabel clicked on the entry. An entire web page seemed to be devoted to the benevolent acts of the idealistic, philanthropic Lady Gertrude and further sections and sub-divisions appeared to be added along the top of the home page, namely, birth and origins, work and activities, diary, personal life and death.

Izzy felt immediately intrigued by Lady Gertrude's writings. Much of the rest of the web page was equally interesting, but she longed to discover further information concerning Lady Gertrude's daily life, and for the time being at least, she only had a strictly limited amount of time to spare.

She clicked on the diary section. The moment the page had fully loaded, a series of subdivisions materialised which appeared to comprise early life, the events of October 1886 to November 1894, romantic liaisons, marriage and death. Yes, the entire website looked fascinating. Bearing in mind that time was limited, almost at random Izzy clicked on 'Events of October 1886,' whereupon a section of Lady Gertrude's diary promptly began to unfold.

Wednesday, 15th October, 1886: I'm so very, very happy! So happy in fact, that I could shout from the rooftops of Riversdale Hall! Oh my goodness! My visit to Leeds at the end of last week resulted in success. The director at the School of Nursing has accepted me for the first year of the Lady Probationer Nursing Scheme… Above all, I'm so thankful to my marvellous father for allowing me to do this… He is just quite simply the best papa that ever was! At last, I can make something of my life! I turn twenty years old on 28th February, 1887. On 5th April (of the same year), I begin the nurse training…. And yes, I received official written confirmation in this morning's post.

I initially believed that my papa would be opposed to all my nursing plans, but now that I have officially been offered a place, he appears to be delighted… This is all so exciting… I need to pick up my probationer uniforms next week, which of course will mean a further visit to Leeds.

Leeds. I do so love that city. The shops are quite marvellous… The town is so vital…

At this point, Isabel's 'phone began to make its' presence felt. Probably James.

'Hello, dear!' It was indeed James.

'Oh, hello, and thank you for 'phoning.'

'Nonsense! As I said previously, the pleasure is all my own. Just think, you're heading home!'

'Well, I shall be back at work on Monday morning.'

'Yes, both Ben and myself will be extremely pleased to have you back.'

'Actually, James, it wasn't half as direful or as difficult as I had imagined... When, and if I go again it will be much easier.'

'Yes, I'm sure it will be... Well, I've just finished mother's shopping, so that's out of the way for another week, I think I've just about got everything we need.'

'Well, that's very nice of you.'

'Oh, it's the least I can do for my mother at her time of life and I certainly don't want her to go in a care home – I want her to retain her independence and dignity, well, hopefully for the rest of her life, and she has a home carer in five mornings per week, just to get her washed and dressed. Of course, I can manage her at the weekends, why, she does so well for her age. Fingers crossed, of course.'

James was so caring and sensitive, Izzy thought to herself, such a good and decent man, and these were traits which she found endearing. Admittedly, he could be irritating and pernickety, but everyone could fall into the trap of being irritating, that was just an inherent characteristic of human nature. Oh, and the pernickety trait? Why, that was simply an integral element of being a member of the legal profession, and of course, James had that down to a 't.'

'Well, James, I'll speak to you soon. I'm just checking something out on my laptop.'

'Oh, really?' enquired James, 'then I'll leave you to it.'

'I'll speak soon, James, goodbye!'

'Goodbye, dear!'

Relieved, Isabel returned to Lady Gertrude's diary. Which point had she reached when James interrupted her? Oh, yes.

The shops are quite marvellous... The town is so vital... I've always been interested in architecture, and I find the style of architecture employed in the centre of Leeds fascinating. So obviously built to last and endure, with a quiet dignity too... But best of all, and absolutely the best of all, this unusual and in places extremely beautiful city, is to be my home for the next two years, at least. I simply feel so lucky. This is my first step on the ladder towards making something of my life.

Captivated, Isabel read further. She suddenly found another entry worth noting and worthy of her attention. This happened to be Gertrude's second visit to Leeds, exactly a week later.

Wednesday, 22nd October, 1886. Papa and I paid a second visit to Leeds, since papa had business to attend to at the Wool Exchange in the centre of town. I collected my uniforms from the School of Nursing in the grounds of the hospital. The uniforms are just so pretty, a beautiful dusky pink. I shall really look like a professional in these!

For lunch, we visited the Central Dining Rooms, relatively close to the Wool Exchange. Incidentally, lunch was excellent! We both thoroughly enjoyed the roast topside of beef, rinsed down with claret, followed by raspberry trifle and then ended our meals with strong coffees. It was quite delightful.

Papa told me that he was so pleased with my decision and my recent success at the School of Nursing that he would buy me another piece of jewellery to add to my already extensive collection, as a treat. He is such a good papa, one of the best papas who ever walked the face of the earth, in fact. The item of jewellery, style of the design and metal were to be entirely my own choice. I had a brief wander around the city centre and dipped in and out of some large jewellers on main thoroughfares, but saw nothing I felt overly tempted to buy. Quite by chance, towards the end of the afternoon,

I noticed a small rather 'down-market' looking shop down a side street, over the top of the window, a decrepit and shabby looking sign proclaimed, 'A. Summers,' and Mr Summers styles and describes himself as a, 'Manufacturing Jeweller.' I then took a casual inspection of the items on display in the window, and there it was! A ring to rival all the others in my collection. Plain gold borders with a patterned inlay, 'inlay', I think, is the correct word. Yes, I'm sure that inlay is the correct word to use. Such a pretty inlay has been used to create the ring, why, you could say the design of the inlay is almost like a reversed comma and I think there is a name for it, now it comes to me, Paisley Pattern. Yes, that's it, Paisley Pattern. That will sit beautifully in my jewellery casket. Not only that, I shall enjoy wearing it. Papa and I entered the shop and asked the assistant if I could take a closer look at the ring in question. I tried it on, but it was a little tight on my hand. The excellent Mr Summers himself sized my fingers and told me it was possible to make the ring in exactly the same style and design but to a larger size, and my papa ordered and paid for it. Seventy pounds, it cost, which makes it rather on the pricey side, but as my grandmother would have so correctly said, 'You get what you pay for!' Mr Summers has told us he will notify us by telegram when the ring is ready for collection, which of course, means a further visit to Leeds, but that is no penance since I already love this town, and so it will be additional practice into acclimatising myself into spending prolonged time spans in this city, which is, of course, what I shall be doing when I'm nursing full time in this metropolis.

When we left the shop, I thanked papa profusely for his generous gift, and also told him what a marvellous and profitable day I had had. He told me he had thoroughly enjoyed the day too, and asked me if there was anything in particular that I wanted or needed for Christmas, to which my response was to tell him that there was absolutely no contest, I would probably like either another ring, a chain or necklace, purchased from the excellent Mr Summers' shop.

At that moment, Isabel's reading was interrupted by the arrival of a text message, bleeping and generally making its' presence felt in the pocket of her jeans. She clicked on it to open it. James again. It read:

'I'm not in the general habit of texting, and on the whole, do not like it in the least as a means of communication, but I couldn't help noticing as I checked the holiday rota, that you still have unused, paid holidays for this year, my dear Izzy. I wondered whether you might like to spend a couple more days at your mother's house resting and relaxing, and hence, not start work this coming week until Wednesday morning. It's a pity to lose your paid holiday, at any rate. Best Wishes, J.'

Well, that was very nice of James! Immediately, Izzy 'phoned him on her mobile.

'Yes, James! I would love those two days off. Mother will be pleased to see me for a few days more, anyway.'

'Good!' answered James in his usual lugubrious style, 'So I shall await your arrival back at chambers on Wednesday morning.'

'You certainly shall.'

'And then, of course, we shall have our welcome back session. Ben and I are making all kinds of plans for you.'

What was that intended to mean? Instead, Izzy managed to answer, a little uneasily, 'Oh, I shall look forward to those, I really shall.'

'Yes, I thought somehow you might.'

'Well, I'll speak to you soon, James. Goodbye!'

'Goodbye, dear!'

Quickly, Izzy terminated the call. She wanted to return to the writings of Lady Gertrude. After telephoning her mum to explain about her impending prolonged stay in Cumbria, and the time of train she would be arriving on, she once again began to carefully scrutinise the entries comprising Lady Gertrude's diary. Lady

Gertrude never seemed to miss a single day with her thoughts, views and recollections, even if it was to merely express her dissatisfaction, irritation or frustration.

Wednesday, 24th October, 1886. Went walking this afternoon with my stepmother. Not a pleasant day, not pleasant at all. All too surprisingly, it was extremely cold, not a hint of the usual mellow, golden October days we have formerly been accustomed to. To be honest, the walk was a boring waste of time, but a little later on when we returned to the hall, I managed to complete a prodigious amount of writing. I love writing, and I feel as though I am quite good at it.

Thursday, 25thOctober, 1886. My maid, Emma, came to attend to me this morning in order to provide general assistance with helping me to dress and carefully arrange and style my hair. 'My goodness, ma'am… You know, if you don't mind my saying it, but you're growing up to become a real beauty… And you going to Leeds in April next year, I'm sure you'll find yourself a rich husband there!' Was what she told me.

'Oh, I'm not so sure about that,' was my singularly cynical response, 'but I really do want to make something of my life.'

'Well said, young lady… And, of course, you're not simply going to be based in Leeds town, but in the hospital, and I'm sure there'll be a few young members of the medical profession who'll have their heads turned by the likes of a beauty like yourself.'

'Oh, Emma!' said I, gently and light heartedly chastising her, 'I want to make a contribution… But I have to admit, I am quite excited about going, and besides, I love Leeds, but as I have private study time at weekends I shall still be travelling back to Riversdale by means of the post chaise on Friday evenings.

'I'm so pleased for you, ma'am… I'm sure you'll do well,' and with that, Emma gave me a hug. I value Emma in so many ways, and not simply in the capacity of an employee to assist me with my morning dressing routine, but she is, in fact, more like a close friend, confidante and advisor, whom I can tell all my closest secrets to, is always there for me in my hour of need, is there with the advice concerning my clothes, hair and make-up, in addition to being, as they

say, 'As honest as the day is long.' Why, she is a veritable maid servant in a million!

Isabel was by now, almost back in Liverchester. She caught a taxi back to her flat and sorted out some clothes requiring a wash and added some clean changes of clothing to her suitcase. What time was it? Three thirty, and it was Saturday afternoon. She still had time to go to Hannah's Bar for a glass of red wine and possibly a sandwich, since no food had crossed her lips since the scrambled egg, smoked salmon, toast and coffee of this morning. She could easily walk to Hannah's Bar in ten to fifteen minutes. Once in Hannah's Bar, Izzy 'phoned her mum to inform her of the time she would be reaching home and also to enquire whether or not she was required to buy any food shopping in   the city centre before she departed for Cumbria.

Approximately two and a half hours later, Izzy safely reached home, slightly weighed down by the food shopping she had purchased and already burdened with the weight of her luggage.

'Oh, Izzy, love! I'm so pleased to see you, and I really have missed you!'

It felt really good to be back for a few days.

'I'm pleased to see you too, mother,' answered Izzy, 'and what's more, I've got plenty to tell you.'

Chapter 6.

Izzy and her mother enjoyed a couple of days of wining, dining and a few small self indulgences, nevertheless, when Tuesday afternoon arrived, Izzy was feeling rather ready once again for both her independence and the bright lights of the great metropolis of Liverchester.

She continued to dip in and out of Lady Gertrude's diary. Once she had changed trains, she reconnected her laptop. Yet again, she was feeling the innate pull of the need to discover further information concerning Lady Gertrude's activities.

Saturday, 9th November, 1886. A telegram arrived at Riversdale Hall this morning by today's post. The wait is over! The glorious Mr Summers has completed my new ring, so that I may now take possession of it! I feel so excited and delighted with my purchase, or more correctly, I should say, the ring which papa bought for me. When I am released onto the wards of the hospital in Leeds – I think it is known in common parlance, as St. James's, I had best become acclimatised to referring to this most noble institution by this name, I will be unable to wear my jewellery, which is a pity, since I feel partly undressed without it. Incidentally, I believe the best course of action is for me to leave all my jewellery safely behind stored in their caskets and boxes at Riversdale Hall, so that I can wear my precious, treasured items only at weekends. As I said before, that's a pity, but there it is.

Tuesday, 12th November, 1886. Once again, papa travelled to Leeds today, since he had further outstanding business matters which needed to be attended to at the Wool Exchange. As I said previously, he is simply the absolute best papa that ever was, and I am so lucky to have him as my father. Guess what? Yes! Papa brought me back the ring from the exemplary Mr Summers. It is so beautiful, in fact so beautiful, I shall guard it with my life!

Isabel was almost back in Liverchester. She collected her belongings together and descended from the train. Somehow, she felt infused with an innate sense of satisfaction and completion; she had met up with her father and spent a few days staying at his house. It had gone extremely well, and she had fulfilled her obligation towards him.

'But do you like your father, Izzy?' her mum had asked her at least twice during this last visit to Cumbria. Izzy's answer, on both occasions, had been exactly the same.

'Yes, I certainly do.'

'Well, that's all that matters.'

Izzy caught a taxi back to her flat on Percy Street. Better prepare her work clothes for the morning. Up the rickety staircase to the first floor flat she inhabited. Yes, it was just exactly as she had left it. Izzy began to sort out her washing and place it in the machine. She retraced her steps to her lounge-cum-dining room and then she suddenly noticed and became fully aware of her answer 'phone bleeping persistently. Izzy played it back. 'You have one message. The call was left for you at ten thirty-five p.m., Thursday, 28th September. 'Izzy,' said the disembodied voice at the other end of the 'phone, and by the sound of the voice, it sounded to be becoming rapidly more intoxicated by the moment, 'Izzy… It's Ben… We just hoped you were… Or are… Going on O.K. at your father's. All's well at… At our end of the 'phone… We're both… We're both in Hannah's Bar, at the moment… Having a good time…' And at this point, he too, let out an almighty hiccup. 'Oh, er… And James… James has something to tell you… Go on, young James… Tell her… And do it NOW!' Silence prevailed for a least a couple of minutes. Then it was abruptly back to Ben who then started trying to explain the reason for James's failure to materialise at the other end of the 'phone, who airily continued to stoically say through his drunken stupor, '…No, he's not coming to the 'phone… Too embarrassed, he is… What he really wanted to say was… He… He really likes you!' Well, that was nothing of a surprise, it was simply what Izzy had begun to suspect for the last few months now. How was she going to face work in the morning? '…That's all we wanted to tell you… Speak soon. Goodbye!' And here, the call abruptly terminated.

Well, both as drunk as lords in Hannah's Bar on Friday night? What should she do? Izzy debated the possible options for a few minutes, and then came to the conclusion that the best course of action open to her was simply to appear at work as though nothing had transpired whatsoever. She could, after all, always let slip a caustic comment later on in the day about them both being as drunk and incapable as lords, and were they restored to their normal selves? Yes, that's what she needed to do.

After an early evening meal, Izzy nipped quickly out for a couple of glasses of red wine at Hannah's herself… Yes, an hour and a half's general relaxation and reading her book in the depths of Hannah's wine bar, seemed both a feasible and attractive proposition this Tuesday evening before she returned to work tomorrow morning. It was just so good to be back in her home from home of Liverchester, to watch the cars and taxis sliding past the windows of the wine bar, to imagine the city's chaotic and hectic nightlife just a matter of a few streets away, and doubtless wild parties at this very minute in progress. Somehow, inevitably, Isabel found her thoughts returning to Lady Gertrude… Her visits to Leeds… Proposed nursing career… Her writing… The remainder of the Rivers family… The relationship Gertrude had with her father, Lord Roger, who she seemed to be particularly close to… What she had already read of Lady Gertrude's life seemed to already comprise enough useful information to write a book about, in fact, the subject was rapidly becoming compulsive!

Izzy returned to the bar for a second glass of red wine. After this glass she would begin to wend her way back home to the flat.

Once back home, Izzy duly connected her laptop. Needless to say, the inevitable pull of Lady Gertrude was once again exerting her magnetic effect on Isabel.

Friday evening, 15th November, 1886. Here at Riversdale, we are quite in the festive spirit already! I somehow have a feeling, a deep-seated feeling that a change is in the air, although I feel uncertain of the exact nature of the change. Maybe it is the prospect of the change which is making me feel excited!

Papa entertained a new business colleague at supper this evening. His name is Ernest Watkins, and I believe he is a lord. Papa speaks so highly of Ernest. To my mind, and of course, beauty is essentially subjective, he is extremely handsome, witty, suave and charming. Why, I should consider the world well lost for Ernest! But enough, absolutely enough of my witterings, Lord Watkins is twenty-five to my nineteen years old, and I have nurse training to undertake in the great metropolis of Leeds… Besides, as far as men are concerned, I am painfully shy, and could think of very little to converse about to Lord Ernest, with the exception of my impending move to Leeds in order to begin probationer nurse training, which he himself thought to be an excellent idea. After Lord Ernest had departed from Riversdale, I accidentally let slip to my stepmother that I thought Lord Ernest handsome, and she replied by saying that possibly papa should invite his new colleague for supper a little more often, in order that we may get to know each other better. Oh, my goodness! I quite literally turned crimson! I felt as though I could die of embarrassment. The entire estate might begin to talk!

Ernest, thought Isabel to herself. So, this was the man that Lady Gertrude eventually married… And he was one of her father's business colleagues. When Gertrude had met Ernest, she had been nineteen, almost twenty years old, and Ernest had been six years her senior at twenty-five. Hardly like the age gap between James and Isabel. It was now eleven thirty p.m. She had better get herself off to bed. She could return to Lady Gertrude's writings when she returned from work.

Isabel got herself off to work, as normal. At ten past nine, Ben came to her room with two sets of requisitions to be completed. He was looking slightly embarrassed, and apparently decided to come straight to the point immediately.

'Oh, Izzy, I'm so sorry about all that silly business on the answer 'phone that transpired on Friday night! We were both of us singularly the worse for wear!'

Isabel laughed light-heartedly. 'You two, my goodness, you were both as drunk as lords Friday night! Do you make a regular feature of that?'

'No, of course not. In fact, I was just having, as they call it, a 'bit of a laugh!' You know, 'seeing how far I could go,' as they say... It all seems a little bit infantile now!'

'Well, it was rather... Don't worry. I'm quite prepared to forget it ever happened!'

'At any rate, if you could sort out these two pages of requisitions, dear, we would greatly appreciate it.'

'Oh, I can easily do that for you.'

'And remember,' added Ben, 'We have our works bonding session this evening... Don't forget, we'll both be waiting for you.'

I'm sure James will, thought Izzy to herself, but instead, she managed to say quietly and calmly, 'I shall greatly look forward to it.'

James appeared that afternoon, since he again needed to visit a hospitalised client that morning and Isabel also suspected he had been feeling a little mortified over the episode that occurred on Friday night. At any rate, he was more than a little relieved when Izzy behaved as though nothing had happened.

'Dear, I am so sorry about the events of Friday night,' he muttered, 'why, we were both well and truly intoxicated!' And then he abruptly changed the subject, 'Did you get on O.K. at your father's?'

'Yes... Well, it went as well as was to be expected. No, seriously, it went very well.'

'And we've got our bonding session tonight. 'Twill be starting about eight-thirty.'

'Yes, I believe so.' Isabel made a few rough, mental calculations, if she left work at exactly five o' clock, that would provide her with enough time to walk home, buy some food, prepare it, consume her meal, change her clothes, conduct a little more of her research concerning Lady Gertrude and then get back into town for the start of the works event? Surely that would be sufficient time? At present, Lady Gertrude almost appeared to be taking over her entire life.

Isabel was fully occupied for the rest of the afternoon with the rules relating to new properties and application of the relevant legal rules to the prospective buyer, so she temporarily forgot all about the mysterious and enigmatic Lady Gertrude, in fact, she had also, for the time being at least, also even forgotten about the impending bonding session, until Ben casually sauntered into the room, saying,

'So, I'll see you in Rigby's this evening at eight-thirty!'

'Oh, yes, of course. Do you know, I was so wrapped up in the rules relating to new properties, I absolutely clean forgot about the bonding session!'

'Just get yourself there, it's eight-thirty for nine o'clock, and you don't need to buy any food, Izzy, there's going to be food provided.'

'Oh, thank you… In fact, you're too good to me.'

'Nonsense! We really value and appreciate you. Quite frankly, you're considerably better than the average trainee, and I've thirty years of experience in this profession.'

Izzy wondered how many years of experience James had, but decided it prudent to refrain from asking, so instead, she simply said casually, 'Anyway, I shall get myself to Rigby's for eight-thirty this evening. I'm quite looking forward to it.' Izzy glanced at her watch. Quarter to four. Still an hour and a half to go. Presently, James brought some official copies of the register[10] through for Isabel, in her role as a trainee, to comb through.

---

[10] Official copies of the register = official copies obtained from the Central Land Registry, and often obtained by the buyer's legal representative.

'Now, young lady, I'm delighted to tell you that once these are completed, you're free to leave for the afternoon... And don't, don't under any circumstances, forget our staff bonding session!'

'Oh, don't worry, I shan't,' answered Isabel confidently, and then continued, 'how could I ever say no to two such delightful gentlemen?'

'Well, that's part of our irresistible mystique!' Ben laughed, 'At any rate, shall we leave this young lady to it? I still have a bit of correspondence to complete, and I'm anxious to finish it by five.'

James and Ben departed for their back offices, and Izzy resumed the work allocated to her. Carefully, she began to note down any matters which appeared to indicate that further clarification would be required. By ten to five, it was concluded. Either James or Ben was now needed for the purpose of a careful examination, then provided all was well, she could leave.

Isabel was just about to stand up when who should appear but James, and strangely enough, his face looked to be unusually flushed, as though he had just enjoyed an extremely rapid but heavy drinking session... My goodness! James was such a strange man!

He sat down in the vacant client chair, and began to closely examine Izzy's writing in his own inimitable and slightly myopic style. Silence prevailed for a few minutes, then at last, he uttered in a tone which certainly did indicate that he had imbibed quite heavily in the past hour, 'Excellent! Excellent, young, young, young leddy! Found... I found just one error... Which I... Shall point out to you now.' Slurred speech already.

'James, are you O.K.? You sound as though you've been drinking!' Isabel looked horrified.

'Well, and if... And if, I have... This, after all, is my chambers!'

'Well, of course,' answered Isabel, 'Now, I think it's almost time for me to go...Can we sort out the error in the morning? And

I need to prepare for this evening... And you, why you need to sober up if you're to grace us with your presence this evening!'

'Yes, of course, young leddy, of course,' James answered meekly, making what appeared to be an enormous effort to sound relatively sober. He then abruptly stood up and muttered, 'Sorry about this... I'll see you later.' And with that, he staggered precariously back to his room.

Isabel swept up her things, vacated her room and stepped out into the busy, noisy depths of Dale Street. No, she didn't need to buy anything with the exception of a box of tea bags, jar of coffee and a carton of milk. Once again, Lady Gertrude was calling her.

Friday evening, 21st November, 1886. We have been graced by a visit from my dear, older brother Harry. Or possibly I should give him his full name, Henry Edward Bernard Rivers, who has been so busy beavering away at university, especially since he began his third year, and so is consequently under quite a lot of pressure.

I told him with great pleasure this afternoon, that I would very soon be joining him in the great metropolis of Leeds, not of course at the university, why, I believe to be in Leeds in that capacity would probably be a little beyond me, but that said, nevertheless, I shall be resident in the great metropolis in both a useful and worthwhile capacity, since I shall be caring for the sick and poverty stricken!

And now, of course, for the subject which is a sheer pleasure for me to both write and think of! My beloved, beautiful Lord Ernest. But I shall not raise my hopes too much regarding this paragon of a young man... He is, after all, six years my senior, so he may well regard me as a little too young for him, and additionally, I do have my nursing career to consider... A career, or possibly a vocation which I am entirely committed to. Furthermore, I consider myself so very fortunate to be training in a city which I know and love, and the director of nursing, understanding and realising how much I wish to retain my family ties and how much they mean to me, has very kindly allowed me to return to Riversdale Hall every Friday evening, where I shall complete all my written and theoretical work for my studies. I somehow, have a feeling that things are going to progress very well, once I have settled in, of course.

Isabel glanced at her watch. She could lose herself for hours in Lady Gertrude's diary and the details of her life and times, but it was by now, almost time for her to leave for her evening out. She switched off and disconnected her laptop, began to sort out her evening clothes, hopefully the new embroidered jeans would at last 'come into their own,' those coupled with a pretty evening blouse. Izzy then made her face up with a minimal amount of make-up, ran a brush through her hair, a few rapid blasts of perfume behind each ear and on both wrists and she was once again, ready to go.

Ten minutes later, Izzy was wending her way down Bold Street. To be absolutely honest, she really would have preferred not to attend, and simply enjoyed a quiet evening in the flat, and nipped out about an hour later to read her book for an hour or so in Hannah's Bar, but no, Ben and James had gone to enough trouble to arrange the event, hence, for that very reason, Isabel felt under a very real obligation to attend. Onto Church Street, and past the familiar shops, M and S, Clarks the Shoe Shop, the small branch of Boots, numerous clothing shops and boutiques. How relieved Izzy would feel when she was wending her way home once again, and the bonding session was successfully completed and behind her! She crossed onto Lord Street… Getting closer with every step… This just simply had to be done… Izzy turned onto North John Street, past Boodle's the Jewellers, numerous offices and a newsagent's shop, past Steven Jones, also a jewellers' shop and a shop she found extremely tempting. At about this point, the shops stopped, the shopping quarter ended and the business, finance and commercial quarter began to start. I'll be glad when this is over, thought Izzy to herself, and then mentally reprimanded herself… Stop it! They've been really good to you! She spied a solitary figure standing outside Rigby's… James, in all probability, although she was only guessing, since Isabel's eyes were not too good in the distance. Much to her surprise it was not James, but Ben and he had already noticed her.

'Welcome, Izzy! Come in! Come in!' he shouted to her. Ben seemed genuinely pleased to see her, and he directed her inside.

'Oh, hello, Ben!'

'You see, we're all in that back room, the function room, I suppose you could call it.'

Isabel allowed herself to be led by Ben to the back room. Once again, Izzy noticed that James and Tanya both looked extremely relieved at her arrival.

'Hello, James! Hello, Tanya!' Isabel greeted them warmly.

'The lady herself!' said James, with his usual and characteristic pomposity, nevertheless, he was beaming affably from ear to ear, 'What will you have to drink?'

'Oh, I'll just have my usual glass of red wine, please.'

Rigby's was it's usual, busy, crowded self that Wednesday evening, and James had to almost fight and pick his way to the bar. In his absence, Ben once again raised the subject of the visit to Huddersfield.

'So last week in Huddersfield went reasonably well?'

'Yes, we saw some marvellous things… We went to York and spent a good two hours looking at the minster, spent a day in Leeds which I thoroughly enjoyed, oh, and went to that place you love so much, Ben, Settle. Why, we had an absolutely marvellous walk up there, so dramatic.' At this point, Isabel remembered the farm-hand's words, no, not under any circumstances whatsoever, was she going to let slip the secrets of the wonders and marvels of the caves.

'Did you enjoy the shops in York and Leeds?' asked Tanya, 'I've heard they're very good.'

'Well, they are, but father didn't want to look at any, he's not exactly into shopping. Typical male, you could say!' laughed Izzy.

'Now women always say that! Always! Lilian always seems to be able to spend money faster than I can earn it!' Ben grumbled in a half self-pitying sort of way, Oh, and of course, it's Lilian and I's twenty-seventh wedding anniversary on Friday, so I shall have to take my good lady out for a meal.... More like a flippin' life sentence!'

At this point, James returned from the bar, and hearing the reference to the life sentence, he asked suspiciously, 'Ben, what flipping life sentence? Were you talking about life sentences?'

'No. Only that Lilian and myself are just approaching our twenty-seventh wedding anniversary, in other words, more like a life sentence for me!'

'Well, I wouldn't know,' answered James rather stiffly. At that moment, he cast Isabel a rather strange look, which she felt unable to interpret, so she quickly looked downwards. Attempting to quickly change the subject, Isabel said blandly to no-one in particular,

'You know, someone said to my cousin, Lawrence, when he was a trainee in the litigation department, 'Oh, we'll let the dog pick those papers up,' and he proceeded to empty the entire contents of a client file out onto the floor, according to what Lawrence told me!'

'Did he really?' asked Ben, scarcely able to believe what he was hearing, and then he added as an afterthought, 'And did he?'

'Those were his exact words according to what Lawrence said, and I don't see why he should invent things, and as far as I'm aware, he did pick them up. Incidentally, the associate solicitor who shared an office with Lawrence told the supervisor off rather sharply, saying, 'You've no call to speak to him like that!'

'And quite right too,' answered Ben emphatically, 'that the associate told him off, I mean!'

'Well, we're not like that, I'm extremely pleased to say,' answered James, 'We're a little more, how do I express it? Trainee friendly, so to speak.'

'I'm relieved to hear it!' Izzy laughed. And of course, this was true, she was so lucky in many respects to have found a sympathetic and trainee friendly chambers.

'I think you tend to find the larger companies are rather more that way oriented,' said James and then he said rather abruptly, 'And now, I would like to propose a toast to my most valued and extremely talented trainee, without whose exceptional endeavours and invaluable, dedicated hard work, we would be quite simply unable to effectively operate these chambers. To Izzy!'

Izzy turned crimson, as everyone else clinked their glasses around her. She glanced casually across to a seat beneath a window, where she had sat on a few occasions with an ex-boyfriend quite a few years ago, and then strangely enough, she thought she heard her grandmother once again speaking to her... Yes, speaking to her quite clearly through the noise and general hullabaloo of the back bar ... '...Honestly, Izzy! He seems like quite a nice young man, and he keeps 'phoning up! He's obviously very serious!' And Thomas had been, the only problem was that Isabel had not felt the same towards him... A bit of a pity, but there it was. And then Isabel's grandmother seemed to be once again speaking to her, 'Isabel, for goodness' sake! Do I have to spell it out to you? Now this nice James, why, I think you could be really happy with him! Take him! A partner, no less! Now, what more could you want?!'

Just at that moment, Ben interrupted her thought processes by saying, 'Isabel, you've gone very quiet suddenly. Are things all O.K.?'

'Yes. I was just taking the proverbial mental 'trip down memory lane,' I used to sit at the table across the way with an ex-boyfriend, more years ago than I care to remember... One thing's for certain though, I'm so glad that he's well and truly in the past!'

'Well, we've all got those skeletons in the cupboard, and usually best left there!' said Tanya in response.

'Yes, best left there,' echoed Ben.

By this time, the drinks were beginning to run a little low, and Ben got to his feet in order to buy the next round.

'Well, this is all very nice, and thank you to all three of you for going to all this trouble to arrange it,' said Izzy.

'You are extremely welcome, dear,' answered James, 'And after all, we're Brodie and Watson, and we like to look after our trainees, we're not like those devils who run the partnership your hapless cousin Lawrence works for!'

'You mean Mason-Jenkins?'

'Oh, does he work for them?' Isabel saw recognition in James's eyes.

'And he sometimes has to work until three in the morning, and then as if to add insult to injury, come back in at nine o'clock of the same morning. Horrendous it is!'

'It sounds as though it is,' answered James and Tanya simultaneously.

'No, we look after our trainees,' James repeated, and Isabel wondered for a moment whether his intoxication of a few hours ago, were once again beginning to manifest itself, '...All our employees are treated fairly and equally!'

'I'm relieved to hear it,' answered Izzy blandly.

'I don't know about you two, but I'm feeling in the mood for something to eat,' said Tanya, 'Is there a menu anywhere about, seeing as I'd like to look at it?'

'Certainly, young lady.' James looked about him suspiciously, and a man from the table next door, passed one across.

'Choose whatever... Whatever... Whatever you like,' answered James. By now, his intoxication was quite clearly beginning to show in his slightly slurred speech, which seemed to be resulting in him having extreme difficulty in articulating the simplest words. 'And... And don't... Don't worry about the cost, it's... It's... It's all on the house... Courtesy of... Courtesy of... Brodie and Watson!'

By now, Tanya was intently studying the menu.

'I'll have the steak, please, James.' She passed the menu over to Izzy, who also decided on a steak. Just then, Ben returned from the bar with the next round. He then had to nip back to the bar since there were more drinks bought than he was able to carry.

'We're just debating over the menu,' explained James, when Ben returned to the table for the second time, after having quickly scanned the menu himself and chosen the roasted belly pork. Ben, in turn, examined the menu and came to the conclusion that he would like to order the venison casserole.

The rest of the evening passed easily enough. Tanya was first to leave saying that she would need to leave at ten thirty at the latest, since her father became worried if she regularly got home late, and after all, she needed to go to work in the morning. James even very kindly gave her a ten-pound note to pay for a taxi back to her home in Litherland. Quarter of an hour later, Ben decided to leave, thinking he also needed a good night's sleep before facing a day's work tomorrow. That just left James and Isabel.

At being left alone with Izzy, James initially looked a little embarrassed. After a silence of a few minutes, he at last said, 'I'm afraid I've drunk a little too much, dear... I... I don't want to lose my licence. I shall 'phone for us a taxi.'

'Yes, that sounds sensible.'

James promptly proceeded to telephone for the taxi. In due course, the taxi arrived. They reached Isabel's flat on Percy Street. Did she invite James in for a little night cap? The evening had passed far better than she had imagined, and it would appear rude if she did not at least make the offer. And after all, James was an absolute gentleman of the first order, she was absolutely certain that he would not try to have 'his evil way.' Outside the Percy Street flat, Izzy tentatively asked, 'James, would you like to come in for ten minutes or so, just for a little night cap?'

'I'd be delighted, young leddy!' was James's rather surprising response.

'Please come in then, and make yourself comfortable.'

Once again up the staircase to her first floor flat, door unlocked and Izzy was home again. The elegant, full-length sash window of her small dining cum living room looked out onto the now blackened street, across which Izzy pulled the rather tasteful, dark purple curtains. A medium-sized television stood in the nearest corner of the room, its blank screen staring vacantly into the rest of room, a neat, grey three piece suit comprising two armchairs and a small two-seater settee were centrally located in the middle of the room and three of the room's cream walls were adorned with pictures of rather average quality. Isabel indicated a chair for James to sit down in.

'Oh, and the bathroom's through my bedroom, should you need it! That's one of the plus factors with this flat, the convenient en-suite facility! And incidentally, the bathroom's nothing to be ashamed of, rather state-of-the-art in fact, I think the landlord told me it had only been installed about eighteen months ago.'

'Oh, so you rent this place?' asked James, rather diffidently.

'I do indeed. Now, James, what would you like to drink as your night cap? Now I have…' And at this point, Izzy nipped next door to scan her kitchen work top. '…I've got brandy, sherry, either dry or sweet, gin or pink gin, red wine, or there is a small bottle of whisky… Oh, and yes, I've just noticed it, two bottles of strong Belgian beer.'

James debated for a minute, then at last he said, 'A strong Belgian beer, please.'

Izzy vanished, and presently reappeared with a tumbler glass, a bottle of strong Belgian beer and a bottle opener.

'Now if you'll just excuse me for one minute.' Isabel again departed to the kitchen and again reappeared a couple of minutes later, a pink gin in hand.

'What a pretty colour!' James commented.

'Yes, it is rather.' Just like the beautiful, benign, rosy pink and intrinsically welcoming light which illuminated the fairy-tale caverns, as noticed by Isabel on her sojourn in Yorkshire, but no, she was not going to make any reference to the contents of the caverns to James. That must remain a closely guarded secret.

'So, how long have you lived here, dear?'

'What? In this flat? Oh, about five months so far. Before that I was living in temporary accommodation up at the Embassy in Faulkner Square. I do feel really lucky to have got a flat like this, I mean as beautiful and elegant as this. I'd had my eye on accommodation in the Georgian Quarter for some time, and O.K. this isn't the complete lap of luxury, but it's perfectly adequate for my needs, and so convenient for town.'

'And the visit to your father's went reasonably well, as I understand it?' James enquired.

'Yes, in fact it went remarkably well, much better than I had initially envisaged. We had a visit to York and spent a couple of hours in the minster, there was so much to look at in there and I was quite intrigued by those 'choir transepts,' even though I've seen them many, many times before. We then went to Leeds the day after, and then for the last day we went walking in Settle, yes, all in all, I've seen some marvellous things!'

'And are matters O.K. between your father and yourself?'

'Oh, why they couldn't be better!' answered Izzy airily, 'But I have to admit I'm pleased to be back to my own things and, of course, my spiritual home of Liverchester!'

'Well, of course, that's entirely understandable,' answered James, as he sipped his strong Belgian lager.

Yes, thought Izzy to herself, James was a bizarre and definitely off-beat man, but he had a strange, endearing quality about him, there was no guile or devious, hidden agenda to him whatsoever. What you saw was certainly what you got… Utterly straightforward… No pretence or attempts to impress anyone,

James was simply his own man, and a man of absolute integrity and principle at that. Isabel shifted slightly and made herself comfortable on the two-seater settee, and she remembered something she had read in a magazine from years ago, '…For me to like a man, he has to be a bit of an oddball, in fact, I remember so vividly I was completely captivated by the psychiatrist who had more problems than his patients!' Needless to say, the story had comprised a singularly unusually paired-off couple… A bit of an oddball… Yes, Isabel herself had rather a penchant for oddballs, and James was certainly that!'

'For goodness sake, Isabel! As I said before, don't look the proverbial gift horse in the mouth! What more could you want?' Once again, Izzy could almost hear her grandmother speaking to her. Could she possibly be right? No, thought Isabel to herself firmly; after all, she might like James as an employer, but she did at least certainly need to find out more about him and no, he was certainly not going to be permitted to share her double bed tonight! She would ask him to leave after a couple of drinks! No ifs or buts.

At that moment, James abruptly cut through her views and recollections by suddenly saying, 'Do you know, dear? That was the best night out I've had for, well, years! I really thoroughly enjoyed it!'

'Good! I'm so pleased.'

'In fact, we could do it again in a few months, but may be possibly this time we could arrange it for Friday night, then of course, no-one has to get up for work the morning after… Why, after our meal we could even go clubbing!'

Somehow, never, ever in Isabel's wildest dreams could she ever envisage James in a booming, strobe-lit cell, frenziedly shaking his hips… No, the prospect was rather abhorrent, equalled only by the very real memory of Carl Dawson awkwardly shaking his hips at a Christmas party in 2001.

The only real difference was that Carl was rather younger than James.

'Well, er, I'm not sure about the clubbing aspect,' answered Isabel, 'but I think possibly the wining and dining aspect, say once a month could be highly beneficial.'

'I shall put it to Ben tomorrow morning.'

'Yes, that sounds good.' At this point, Izzy noticed that James's glass was almost empty. She would offer him the other bottle of Belgian beer, and then she wanted him gone, gone back to the depths of sunny Woolton! She glanced at her wristwatch. Eleven thirty… James needed to be gone by midnight, and of course, she needed her sleep.

'James, your glass looks almost empty. Would you like another bottle?'

'Don't mind if I do!'

Isabel got up and departed for a few moments into the depths of the kitchen, which was incidentally right next door. She also poured herself a glass of fruit juice from the carton in the fridge and returned to the dining room.

'Yes, that was a most agreeable evening! And, why, I hope we have many more!'

'Yes, I hope so too!' answered Izzy blandly.

'And tell me,' James began to probe, 'You said you lived in Falkener Square before moving here?'

'That's right. I love Georgian architecture, well, probably because I grew up in a Georgian house, the proportions and the symmetry are just so beautiful. So yes, it's what I'm used to. In fact, I've always been interested in architecture, it's so much better than the rubbish that they throw up now, why it looks as though it will all collapse in ten years!'

'Too true! My feelings entirely… Er, Izzy?'

'Yes?'

'That's something else we have in common… I'm also interested in architecture, do you know? It all started when I was about eight years old, and my mother used to take me round cathedrals. Well, you see my late father was himself an architect. At any rate, we loved looking at cathedrals, all three of us and my mother told me about things to look out for and look at, for example, the style of the arches, the design of the chapter house, the size and exact layout of the transepts, all that sort of thing.'

That struck a cord in Isabel. 'Yes, my grandmother did that with me.'

James was then silent for a few minutes, then at last he said, 'You see, Izzy, dear, I strongly suspect we have many more things in common.'

Once again, Isabel began to feel acutely embarrassed. What exactly was James building up to? She longed to say to him, 'Like what?' but refrained, and instead managed to answer in an essentially non-committal tone, 'Well, very possibly.'

James took another sip of the Belgian lager, he then leaned across, and placed his left hand on Isabel's right knee, the signet ring on his little finger twinkling faintly in the electric light of the dining room, at which point, Izzy felt definitely uneasy, embarrassed and uncertain of what James might next decide to utter, and then a faint smile played round the edges of his lips, and at last he broke the silence by saying in quite a matter-of-fact tone,

'You know, Izzy… Both Ben and myself were both saying during the time you were staying in Huddersfield that you really are a pleasure to work with! Young Ben… Well, I suppose not so young now, said you're just about the best trainee he's ever had!'

'Well, that's very nice of you both to say that, and thank you.' So James was not trying to make a pass at her, at least not yet, or so she hoped… And it was almost midnight by now and Izzy was beginning to think it was time they both repaired to their beds… Separate ones, of course… And then somewhere

Isabel heard her grandmother speaking to her once again, '…Take him, Izzy, take him! What more could you possibly want!'

'Er, James, I have, well, I have work in the morning. So, er, I'm rather eager to get to my bed. Can I 'phone for you a taxi?'

James glanced at his watch. Eleven fifty. He drained the last few inches of his Belgian lager and said, 'Well, dear, it's been an absolute pleasure, er, especially the last part, but I don't want to outstay my welcome, and yes, I need to get back to my bed… I need my sleep, and if I'm much later, mother will start to worry and wonder what's happened to me!' Yes, James Brodie was indeed the perfect gentleman. Together, they descended the staircase and James managed to almost immediately flag down a taxi, before wishing Isabel a 'goodnight, and sweet dreams, dear.' With that, Izzy went to bed, and no, James and Isabel had not shared her double bed… Her grandmother would have been so pleased about that.

Chapter 7.

Izzy arrived at work slightly late the next morning, late, yes, but only by a mere three or four minutes. When she arrived, she noticed there was no Tanya to operate the reception desk, unless she had been held up in traffic somewhere between the city centre and Litherland. Another five minutes elapsed, and then the front office 'phone began to ring insistently. Isabel, who had just been in the process of making herself comfortable at her desk went to answer it.

'Hello, Brodie and Watson, can I help you?'

'Well, yes, er, it's Tanya… I'm feeling so grotty I just don't feel fit to come in.' Isabel could tell that the reason for her absence was genuine, since she could hear rather graphic sound effects at the other end of the 'phone of frenzied coughing, snorting and intermittent sneezing.

'You give yourself a few days off and spoil yourself, and I hope you're feeling better soon,' replied Izzy.

'Oh, thank you, Izzy,' said Tanya gratefully, and then she added casually as an afterthought, '…It was rather good last night, I right enjoyed it!'

'Good, I'm pleased to hear it. Did you get home safely?'

'I did, thanks to brilliant Mr Brodie, in fact, he gave me more money than I needed. I shall bring the change in to him when I'm feeling better.'

'You just focus on getting better, Tanya, and give yourself tomorrow off if you need to, I can happily answer the 'phone for a few days, and I'll tell James and Ben you're not coming in today.'
'Oh, thank you, Izzy… Goodbye!'

'Goodbye!'

At this point, James, looking rather sheepish appeared in the front office.

'Good morning, James! Did you get home allright?'

'Yes, dear, I was back at just after twelve… As I said last night, that was the best evening out I've had for years!'

'Oh, James, incidentally, Tanya's not coming in today, she's come down with 'flu and feels really grotty!'

'Izzy, could you do me a big favour?'

'Yes, if I can.'

'Could you stand in for Tanya, for say a couple of days if need be, and act as our receptionist? Of course, I'll still pay you at trainee and paralegal level. If you can move your possessions into the front office for the time being, I would greatly appreciate it.'

'Yes, of course, that's no trouble at all,' replied Izzy. Somehow, she was quite looking forward to temporarily sitting at the reception desk in the front office and it would be a change of immediate environment from sitting in the middle office, effectively sandwiched between Tanya and the partners. Fingers crossed, hopefully it would be a nice easy morning. For the first ten minutes, Isabel found she actually quite enjoyed it, since being the temporary receptionist was obviously less stressful than her regular job, but then she found herself consciously waiting for the 'phone to ring, in fact, she was willing it to ring, which then, of course, it so awkwardly and perversely refused to do so. Out of sheer boredom, she slid open the top compartment of Tanya's desk. It contained two bottles of nail varnish; one a dark cherry red by Rimmel, and the other, Cutex, 'Pink Shimmer.' So this was how Tanya spent the bulk of her working day! Izzy opened the drawer below it. That contained another bottle of nail varnish, and, from the look of the bottle the contents looked to be becoming impossibly thick and congealed, entitled, 'Apple Green,' a half-used blue Bic biro and a hairbrush thick with hairs. The drawer below that was empty apart from an emery board, a nail file and a small, half-full box of tissues.

Presently, much to Izzy's intense relief, the 'phone began to ring. It was a simple transfer to Ben, and Isabel duly completed it.

Lunchtime came and went. James, being the probate partner went to see an old established client regarding the re-writing of his will, at a care home in Croxteth and Ben needed some routine correspondence attending to, which Izzy was only too easily able to complete. My goodness! What a boring job this was! Oh, well, thought Izzy to herself, one day less. But was that the right attitude?

Suddenly, her desk in the middle office seemed infinitely preferable, yes, the comforting, familiar, old leather-topped desk! Thank goodness she was only on the front desk temporarily! She stood up to take the completed correspondence through to Ben for signature, grateful for the leg stretch and on the way back to the desk, Izzy glanced casually at her watch. Four o'clock.

Presently, ten minutes later, the 'phone began to ring once again. Relief!

'Hello, Brodie and Watson, can I help you?'

'Oh, hello,' answered a voice at the other end of the telephone, 'It's Martina Brodie. Is that, er… Er, James's young lady? Oh, I'm sorry, my mouth gets me into all kinds of trouble!'

Isabel felt as though she had been hit hard between the eyes. What had James said to his mother last night when he got home? For a moment, Izzy felt embarrassed and uncertain of how to quite answer… Think… Think… Then she managed to answer blandly, 'I'm James and Ben's trainee, Mrs Brodie, can I get James to call you back?'

'I've already tried him on his mobile but couldn't get through, but yes, I would be grateful, dear.'

'I think he had a client with him whom he went out to see, so he's not in the office at present but he should be back any minute now if you want to try again in ten minutes or so, or I can tell him the minute he arrives back, whatever.'

'I'll try him again on his mobile,' answered Mrs Brodie.

'Allright then. Goodbye!'

'Goodbye, dear!'

Izzy replaced the receiver on the 'phone. Well, that was a little premature at this stage, his young lady indeed! Shell-shocked, Izzy glanced at her watch. Quarter past four, and she was now beginning to feel the pull of Lady Gertrude in Riversdale Hall and her writings – what pearls of wisdom and beautifully polished prose were going to flow from Lady Gertrude's pen this evening? Izzy was just debating this question when presently James appeared, armed with a mass of paperwork.

'Successful day, James?' Isabel asked.

'Oh, hello, dear. Has my mother just been on the 'phone?'

'Yes. She certainly has.'

'Oh, she is a character! She gets things so confused. I've just talked to her myself outside chambers on the street.'

'Oh, well she 'phoned here just ten minutes ago.'

'Oh, she gets things all wrong… I'm sorry to say that my mother's just heading in one direction at the moment… Well, sad, but there it is!'

Was James trying to imply his mother was losing her faculties and was facing the rapid onset of Alzheimers'? Doubtless, he was simply trying to explain away Martina's rather indiscreet comment concerning his 'young lady!'

At that moment, they were interrupted by Ben returning the typed up correspondence, duly signed and ready to be sent.

'Izzy, do you know of any nice restaurants in the centre of town? You know, the sort that do a decent three course meal for two people?'

'Yes, there's a good one opposite Lees' department store, mother and I sometimes dine out down there, and that usually works out as two courses with a bottle of wine for fifty-one or fifty-two pounds, the main courses are usually really good, they do steaks and roast belly pork, plus the puddings are also good, they serve cheesecake and apple pie, that sort of thing!'

'Excellent! The reason why I'm asking is because of my wedding anniversary tomorrow night, you know my twenty-seven years of total serfdom, submission and servitude! There'll be a ton of bother if I forget it!'

'Oh, we know!' laughed James.

'I'll go there on my way back from work and reserve the table.'

'There's a few clustered together on that corner… It's not Brown's, not the Jamie Oliver either, that's just a burger house, it's the next one after the Jamie Oliver restaurant, you'll easily find it,' Isabel explained, 'and it really is good there, a real pleasure to dine in,' she added.

'Yes, I can imagine. Well, I'm collecting my things up, and then I shall be off home… Oh! And… My goodness! I nearly forgot! I need to buy the old trout a card and present! Thank goodness, I remembered! Just in time!' Ben exclaimed.

Of course, nobody took Ben's rantings seriously, and everyone knew full well he was secretly very happy with Lilian, and would probably easily reach his fiftieth wedding anniversary or maybe even a few years beyond. This was all little more than a front that Ben regularly put up, i.e. that of being the 'hen-pecked,' long suffering husband with the difficult and lonely furrow to plough, but it was more often than not a source for amusement and general entertainment purposes.

'Try Lees' toiletry and cosmetics department,' Isabel suggested, trying to be helpful, 'I personally, love their boxes of expensive soap.'

'I may just do that,' Ben muttered.

'Oh, and Clintons sell beautiful cards,' Isabel answered, 'and the nearest Clintons is in Liverchester One.'

'Well, Izzy! You have saved my life!'

'Well, I do like to be of assistance.' Izzy answered ingratiatingly.

'Right, I'm off! I'll see both of you in the morning.' And with that, Ben vanished to his room, leaving James and Isabel facing each other.

Isabel folded up the letter and placed it in the envelope. This, of course, would need to be posted on her way home.

'Well, tomorrow's the anniversary of my big day, and quite frankly, I'll be glad when it's over, at any rate, I'll see you both in the morning!' said Ben airily as he retraced his steps back through the front office and exited by means of the front door to the chambers.

Isabel and James faced each other. It was ten to five in the afternoon. Silence prevailed for at least the space of a minute or so, which incidentally, seemed more like an absolute lifetime. Eventually, James broke the silence by asking, rather gingerly,

'Izzy, could you do me a favour?'

'Well, yes, if I can.'

'Well, you see… It's, er, two favours really. One is, if Tanya is absent tomorrow could you sit here and answer the calls? I know it's boring, but it just has to be done.'

'Yes, with pleasure.'

'And the second one is… Er, this one's a little more difficult, and, er, delicate… I decided I would like to sample the Brazilian restaurant halfway along Hanover Street next Wednesday evening for supper, er, would you be interested in joining me?' There, for better or worse, he had said it.

Isabel debated for a moment, and just then one of her grandmother's well-worn clichés hammered somewhere in the depths of her brain, 'Honestly Izzy! Why, you could go a lot further and fare far worse than James Brodie! Don't be so choosy! For goodness' sake, take him!'

Isabel smiled and answered with, 'I'd be absolutely delighted, James. At what time on Wednesday, approximately?'

'Shall we say eight thirty for nine, like our last bonding session which went so well?' James beamed with gratitude and relief, then quickly added as a sudden afterthought, 'I really don't want to tread on any other man's toes... Do you have a man in your life?'

That was rather a leading question!

'I don't have a young man.'

'Well, now you have one... Or, possibly, I could say, a middle-aged man!' replied James, again in his characteristically heavy-handed manner. Later on in the flat, Isabel could not help but quietly laugh to herself, not at James, but at the way in which he had made his request.

'Well, then I shall call for you at eight-thirty on Wednesday evening.'

'Sounds good to me,' answered Izzy. 'And now, James, it's time I was leaving so I will see you in the morning. Goodnight!'

And at that point, James snatched hold of Izzy's right hand and once again kissed it, and again, Izzy felt herself uncontrollably blushing a shade of deep crimson. What a day it had been! Now she really was James's young lady!

'James, I really do need to go now,' said Izzy, 'It's time I was attending to my evening meal.'

'Yes, of course, dear,' with which he released his grasp, 'And goodnight, dear!' he called out after her departing figure as Izzy vanished into the depths of Dale Street.

Yes, Izzy wanted to get home, and Lady Gertrude's diary was once again calling. Isabel called at Sainsbury's at the top of Bold Street. So, James had now made a pass at her and she had accepted it. And the hand kissing episode? Izzy remembered reading something on the subject of hand kissing years ago. '…When a man kisses your hand, it means he likes you, but is keeping you at arm's length.' Best if it was kept that way Izzy thought to herself. Isabel suspected that James felt a little too embarrassed to go any further, at least for the time being.

Isabel bought a couple of ready-made meals. She also bought a small carton of milk, teabags, coffee, bacon, eggs, bread rolls, fruit juice, two bottles of Belgian lager to replace the bottles which James had consumed, an average-sized slab of French cheese and two small puddings. The provisions should keep her going well into next week.

Once back at the Percy Street flat, Izzy unpacked and stored her purchases. And now, Lady G was most certainly calling.

Saturday, 22nd November, 1886. My dear, older brother, Harry is still gracing us with his presence. From what I have heard, he lives what can only be described as a, 'wild life,' in Leeds, which appears to largely comprise the imbibing of vast quantities of alcoholic liquor. To be honest, Harry greatly displeased me when he told me that from what he had heard of Lord Ernest he sounded like a 'pathetic little gold digger,' who was, 'too old for me at any rate,' and whom he would prefer kept well away from me, at all costs. What a character he is! Henceforth, I shall make absolutely no references to Lord Ernest whatsoever whilst Harry Rivers is at home; since if I do, general trouble inevitably results.

Sunday, 23rd November, 1886. We visited church this a.m. My half-brother, Edward, who is aged ten and his younger sister, Rachel, who is eight, are becoming really over-excited already at the prospect of Christmas, but before we had our lunch, father reminded us all of how lucky and fortunate we are to be of considerably rich, comfortable and substantial means and we needed to complete our estate visiting before Christmas, which means we need to distribute the families of the estate cottages, who of course are our employees, with some additional basic provisions and also some food producing animals, for example, pigs and chickens for rearing on their small holdings.

Additionally, Harry completed an essay which he was extremely pleased and relieved to finish, which is due for submission on Monday morning. He leaves by means of the post chaise service at quarter past five which should see him back in Leeds by half-past seven approximately.

And of course, I shall be joining my dear brother in the great city of Leeds in early April, which I really do feel so excited about!

Not a day seemed to pass which escaped Lady Gertrude's observations, views and perceptions, thought Isabel to herself. She did seem to be a woman of many parts. Intrigued, she read on.

Monday, 24th November, 1886. Once again, Papa had business to attend to in Leeds, so he took me with him. I found a fascinating little shop, a little less expensive than the splendid Mr Summers' shop, but nevertheless charming, named the Silver Box, where I bought a pair of beautiful, very elegant, dropper earrings complete with purple balls at the end of each. To be honest, I'm quite unsure what the name of the stone is. The price was twenty pounds. Later on, my stepmother told me off for making this purchase, as a result of which I did not feel particularly kindly disposed to her for a while after that… At any rate, she should not examine and scrutinise my property which should obviously remain out of bounds to her! After all, I had used entirely my own money to finance the purchase, so I believe chastisement to be a little unfair! Anyhow, enough of my stepmother's peculiarities!

At lunchtime, we once again dined at the Central Dining Rooms in the city centre, near to the Wool Exchange. The meal was absolutely excellent! Both of us dined on venison casserole, rinsed down with a bottle of claret and for our pudding, we enjoyed lemon sponge, in addition to strong coffees to end our meal.

Before we left Leeds, we paid a rapid visit to Mr Summers's shop, where once again, I browsed through his tempting wares… And guess what? Then I presently spied, and I can only describe it as the ring of my dreams, a thin, gleaming, delicate band of eighteen carat yellow gold, rather reminiscent of a curtain ring, although considerably more valuable! The ring felt so comfortable and looked so pretty on my hand… Yes, the hands that will soon be roughened with hard, manual nursing work! My papa placed what Mr Summers calls a 'Special Order,' and furthermore, Mr Summers allowed papa a small discount off the total price, in view of the fact that we are now quite good and valued customers of this jewellers' business. The ring is to be ready for collection the week before Christmas. I shall be such a happy woman when I open papa's very special Christmas present on Christmas Eve, which of course is when our family open our gifts, and begin to celebrate the festive season. This is a family tradition which we have observed for many years.

Isabel glanced at her watch. Almost seven fifteen and time she was making a meal of some sort for herself. She rummaged among the ready-made meals bought earlier in Sainsbury's… Steak and kidney with two dumplings… To be boiled up in the bag in water, and Isabel remembered she had consumed that meal once or twice previously, and quite enjoyed it. She began to set to work to prepare it. Inevitably, she found her thoughts returning to James. How would he be spending the evening? Perhaps about to enjoy a pre-supper dry sherry, whilst his mother lovingly prepared a meal for them both. Possibly he was thinking of his beloved trainee… His Izzy, and the good time he was going to give her when they visited the Bem Brasilia restaurant.

After Isabel had consumed her meal, washed and cleared away after it, her thoughts returned once again to Lady G.

Tuesday, 25th November, 1886. Exactly a month to Christmas! But I am not wanting Christmas to arrive just yet. In fact, no-one should wish their life away, that is quite the wrong attitude! After all, experiences in human life are to be savoured and enjoyed, if at all possible, as they present themselves. To be absolutely honest, I am and I think always have been, and particularly over the last two years or so, been a person who notices and appreciates things. So, at this time of year, I always notice the black, empty, gnarled branches of the winter trees, looking like black skeletons against the cold, clear, winter sky, or in early spring, the delicate exquisiteness of the pale yellow primroses on the estate fields and at the edges to the woods. Of course, this coming year, I will largely miss the burgeoning of spring at Riversdale since I will be deep amid the sick and afflicted of the great metropolis of Leeds, but hopefully enjoying many new experiences, and God willing, making some new friends.

There was something rather endearing about this woman's diary entries, thought Isabel to herself, as she disconnected her laptop this evening, with a view to spending an hour in Hannah's Bar. That was it! Gertrude was always so positive, and was clearly a sensitive, perceptive woman and there was something else which appeared to suggest itself from her writings, and at this point, Isabel remembered some of the sayings of her grandma, '…Our Izzy! I take her for a day out and a glass of orange juice or lemonade, and she always enjoys it!' Yes, thought Isabel, Lady Gertrude and herself both had certain things in common, in addition to the fact that Gertrude, like herself, noticed, enjoyed and appreciated extremely diverse aspects of human life from the beauties of early spring in North Yorkshire, to the glories, temptations and vitality of urban Leeds.

Once in Hannah's Bar, Isabel consumed two small glasses of red wine whilst reading a novel, after which she began to make her way home, and back to the flat.

It was just after eleven when she reached home. No, she was not going to have one further visit to Lady Gertrude's diary, thought Izzy to herself, fighting the temptation, after all, she needed to be at work tomorrow in good time, and furthermore, she needed her sleep.

That next morning, Izzy stepped in at eight fifty-five exactly. She had been sitting at the front office desk a mere eight or nine minutes when the 'phone began to ring out.

'Hello! Brodie and Watson, can I help you?' Isabel answered, as she picked up the 'phone. '…Oh, er, Izzy? Izzy, the trainee? Is it Izzy that I'm speaking to? You see… It's Tanya… Well, I am better, but… Well, still not right. Not… Not right by a long chalk!' And in the background Tanya let out an almighty sneeze, then she resumed the conversation by saying, 'I shall have to take today off… No, definitely not coming in… I just can't, why, I'm so full of cold!'

'Look, Tanya, it's alright, I will happily fill in for you, you just focus on improving!'

'Oh, thank you, Isabel.'

'And don't worry, I'll tell both James and Ben that you're not coming in.'

'Oh, thank you. 'Bye then.'

'Well, I hope you're feeling better soon, Tanya. Goodbye!'

Isabel replaced the 'phone. Now she had to sit here until lunchtime. Presently, the 'phone rang out again. It was Mr Melville, one of the partners at a partnership on an adjacent street, wishing to speak to James, so all that was required was a simple transfer. Half an hour later, Ben brought some filing in for storage in the front office.

Well, thought Isabel to herself, she really was a Jack of all trades, both trainee solicitor and receptionist cum-typist-cum switchboard operator! Furthermore, her cosy office sandwiched between the front office and the partners' rooms afforded her rather more privacy than this one which simply looked straight out onto Dale Street and was rather more akin to sitting in a goldfish bowl, being on full view to most of the street! Oh, for her back room!

At that moment, the 'phone began to ring one again. Much to Isabel's surprise, it was Steven, her next door neighbour wondering what progress was being made concerning his dispute with Bertram. 'Would you be able to come in some time, so I can explain the terms, Steven? In actual fact, I think you may, I repeat, MAY, have a good case here.'

'I'll have to check my work schedule, Isabel,' answered Steven.

'Well, it does look as though Bertram has broken some of the terms relating to the tenancy, but I'm unable to advise you right now as I'm acting in the capacity of Brodie and Watson's temporary receptionist-cum-typist... If you can come in next week some time, fingers crossed, Tanya the receptionist will be back, and I'll be in a better position to advise you.'

At that moment, James appeared in the front office with yet further filing for storage, which he duly deposited on Isabel's desk, or more to the point, Tanya's desk.

'For filing!' He whispered and then vanished back to his room.

'Now, I think you may have a decent case – and I'm stressing 'may', since I don't want to falsely raise your hopes at this point. But you check your work schedule and get back to me with a time that's convenient for some time next week.'

'Yes, I'll do that. 'Bye!'

'Goodbye.'

Lunchtime came and went. In the early afternoon, Ben brought in yet further filing, until there was a small mountain piled up on Isabel's desk. In fact, that would keep Isabel gainfully occupied for the bulk of the afternoon. Izzy set to work to sort it out.

Presently, she was once again joined by a visit from James. Whatever masculine charms or male winning ways James might have acquired under the tutelage of Alison, his erstwhile lover, they had comprised neither subtlety or finesse. As Isabel bent over the filing cabinet he strategically placed both his hands on her behind, not surprisingly, Izzy flushed a deep shade of crimson and stared for a moment at her employer in absolute horror.

'Now, how does that feel, dear?'

'Well, er, that's not exactly what I'm used to.'

James's response provoked still further revulsion in Izzy, and as she was mentally recoiling, he answered breezily, 'Well, there's always a first time to learn, and after all, you won't learn younger!' At that point, much to Isabel's relief, Ben appeared with a letter and attendance note for typing up, and thankfully, James rapidly removed his hands, just, but only just in time before Ben had had time to notice. The mystery of James was rapidly becoming stranger with every passing day. At the sight of Ben, James casually turned and retreated quickly back to his room, Izzy noticed.

Luckily there were no further embarrassing episodes that afternoon and once again, James needed to leave the office in order to interview a client charged with assault and currently held at Bootle Police Station. There was one matter about which Isabel had absolutely no doubt whatsoever. James would fight his or her corner to the bitter end. Isabel would ask him how the afternoon had progressed when she next saw him, which would be Monday morning. Izzy sat at the desk until five o'clock that afternoon, by which time she was more than ready to leave. As she left and walked back through the town, Izzy sincerely hoped that today was her last day in the role of temporary receptionist.

Her weekend passed singularly uneventfully and Izzy once again frequented Hannah's Bar for two glasses of red wine on Sunday evening. The week ahead was certainly going to be eventful, especially Wednesday, since that heralded her romantic rendezvous with James… A rendezvous which, for the time being at any rate, she was trying hard not to think about too closely.

But before Izzy went to bed, she still had at least a good half hour for another read of Lady G's diary. Yes, the mysterious and enigmatic Lady Gertrude who now appeared to be occupying much of Izzy's free time.

Wednesday, 26th November, 1886. Father did some more entertaining of some of his business colleagues this evening. I am extremely sorry to say that my beautiful Lord Ernest was not among the party of revellers, which is a pity, but I am sure there will be other occasions for me to meet up with him.

I have to admit that I consumed a little too much claret myself and became more than a little merry, laughing and joking sometimes a little out of turn, but after all, I am nineteen, almost twenty years old, so I am in actual fact, quite at liberty to do so!

I do so love this ancient, ancestral and beautiful country seat! With the coming of spring, in three to four months, it will be still more special… Of course, by then, I hope to have seen my marvellous and beautiful Lord Ernest a good few more times! Yes, as I said just two lines ago, this is such a lovely, stately old pile to have as my home, and always so very secure, so I count myself as extremely fortunate to have Riversdale as my home, roots and heritage. Nevertheless, I am almost twenty years old, and I am starting to feel a strong desire to, 'spread my wings,' so to speak. I know and am fully aware that there is a wider reality beyond Riversdale Hall, so yes, I certainly need to leave it for a few years in order to experience a wider society, and of course, I really wish to at least try to, 'make something of my life.' I have to admit, I feel as though I have an innate talent for nursing, so I am sure I would be capable of making a very special contribution, and absolutely best of all, I shall be training in the great urban environment of Leeds! Yes, Leeds, where I somehow, strangely enough have this gut feeling that I am going to be really happy in, at least, I really do hope so.

By now, Izzy needed her sleep. She closed down and disconnected the laptop, sorted out some paperwork required for the morning and snuggled into bed with her hot water bottle.

Chapter 8.

O n her arrival at chambers the next morning, Isabel was highly relieved to see Tanya, once again, at the front reception desk.

'Are you feeling better, Tanya?' Isabel asked her.

'Oh, yes I am, thank you… I'm glad the bug or whatever I had has passed, why, I had my head in a bucket most of Saturday!'

When Isabel deposited her possessions at her desk in the middle office, there was a note from James on it. It read:

I'm going to be tied up most of the day at Bootle Police Station, representing this man, Barry. I somehow have the feeling that the coppers are extremely predjudiced against him, which is an absolute disgrace!

I have left you some work to be getting on with on your desk, which Ben can probably check through once completed. Any problems, of course, and give Ben a shout.

I'm really looking forward to our date on Wednesday evening, in fact, I'm counting the hours! J X.

Well, no unwanted sexual advances for most of today at least, thought Izzy to herself. She could easily cope with that. Isabel happily settled down to complete the work which James had allocated to her. Isabel satisfactorily completed the task, which Ben later carefully examined and this time, confidently awarded a hundred percent to. Lunchtime came and went, and in no time, five o'clock had arrived.

Still feeling pleased at Ben's award of full marks, Isabel began to wend her way home. No food shopping was required, due to her recent food stock up on Thursday of last week, and besides she wanted to read up about the latest activities of Lady Gertrude.

Thursday, 27th November, 1886. I did not exactly feel my absolute best this morning, and of course, I have no-one to blame apart from myself! This was entirely self-inflicted! I feel terrible, and I am only too fully aware of the cause. I consumed too much red wine last night! All I was able to manage at breakfast time were two extremely strong cups of coffee, and three pieces of thickly buttered toast. This is not remotely like me, since under normal circumstances, why, I eat almost anything and everything, in fact, I eat like a cormorant!

I am starting to feel a little better now, and enjoy watching the birds fly past my window in the winter morning sunlight. I need to place some scraps of food out for them to feast on, possibly some scraps of bacon, bread, some fat from the remains of our roast meals, nuts and obviously some fresh water.

I also need to take my pet dog, Scamp, for a mid-morning run. Scamp is a three-year-old Springer Spaniel, and such a lively dog! I am certain he has far more energy than I have, and if left to himself, why, he will eat all day! The typical dog you might say. In fact, I love all dogs, all animals really… And Scamp is such a character! He has belonged to me since I was sixteen, and one of the estate employees brought him to us, since he had more puppies than he was able to cope with. I was extremely pleased to hear that all the puppies from that litter went to good homes, since I hate and despise any type of cruelty to animals. In fact, even as I write this diary entry, he is sitting with his head comfortably resting on my right knee. To be absolutely honest, he is quite the best dog that ever was.

Just at that instant, Izzy's landline 'phone began to ring. Isabel answered it at the second ring. 'Hello, Liverchester 707 4396!'

'Izzy? It's James!'

'Oh hello, James. Er, do you have something to tell me?'

'Well, not really, dear. I was simply 'phoning to say that I may not be back in the office tomorrow, as I'm probably going to still be tied up with this Barry business. Seriously, North Merseyside Police are behaving abysmally towards him, I've tried to tell them three or four times they're flouting vital sections of the Codes of Practice, but they won't have it! My goodness, sometimes I really do have a furrow to plough!'

'Oh, I'm sorry to hear it. What are you doing now, James? Are you back at home?'

'Yes, but I've only just got home, I've been back, what? Ten minutes, absolute maximum, do you know? I am so stressed out that I'm going to give myself a small treat! I think possibly a large, strong G and T is most certainly in order, I'll also offer mother one as a little aperitif before our evening meal.'

'Oh, you poor soul... Well, you both enjoy your G and T's, and try to switch off.'

'So the chances are, I shan't be in chambers tomorrow... Needless to say, I'm sure a capable, competent girl like yourself can manage perfectly well in my absence, meanwhile, my blood will almost reach boiling point, tried and tested by those beggars who run Bootle Police Station!'

'James, try not to get so het up. I know you're doing what you can for this man, Barry.'

'Yes, you're quite right, dear, and I know... I know you'll miss me tomorrow.'

Well, not particularly, thought Izzy to herself. Instead, she answered by saying, 'Look, don't let the beggars grind you down... Just go in and earn the money.' At the other end of the 'phone she thought she could hear somewhere in the background, the sound of someone shouting, '...James! I'm putting the evening meal in now! It will take about an hour to thoroughly cook.'

Mrs Brodie, no doubt.

'Yes, I'm coming mother. Come and get your G and T.' Izzy heard James say.

'Mother's calling, so I'd better go!' James answered, by way of explanation.

'Alright, James.'

'I'll see you on Wednesday, when I should hopefully be finished once and for all with this wretched Barry business. I know you'll miss me, and I'll certainly miss my darling Izzy, goodbye!' 'Goodbye, James!' Izzy replaced the receiver on the 'phone feeling shell-shocked. James had actually called her 'darling,' and also, whatever in God's name was currently in progress at Bootle Police Station? Oh, well, that would be a talking point between herself and James when they went for their Wednesday evening rendezvous.

She resumed her scrutiny of Lady Gertrude's diary. Which point had she reached when James had disturbed her? Oh, yes… Something relating to Lady Gertrude's dog, and Scamp being quite the best dog that ever was.

According to certain members of the Rivers' family, during Scamp's first year, when he was just short of a year old, he possessed a rather cheeky and naughty habit, which I was not always privy to, that of snatching or stealing food from the table; a joint of roast turkey which my older brother, Harry and my father were going to eat, some freshly cooked sausage, three or four meat pies, newly baked in the kitchens, cheese, bread rolls and biscuits, he will eat quite literally anything! I find it quite hard to become seriously angry with him, since his eager little face is always so appealing! It's a pity that I am unable to take him with me to Leeds when I go in April.

Time for Izzy's evening meal. She rummaged in the freezer in the kitchen and found a Sainsbury's ready-made meal. Yes, that would satisfy her for this evening.

Once Isabel had consumed her supper, she returned once again to the inevitable Lady Gertrude's diary. Simultaneously, her thoughts were also partly with James… He missed his darling Izzy and furthermore, believed North Merseyside Police were not playing fair with his client, Barry.

Friday, 28th November, 1886. My dear, delightful brother Harry has again returned to Riversdale for the weekend from the urban delights of Leeds! Both father and I are so pleased to see him, although once again he will need to spend the bulk of his time in studying and writing an essay.

Of course, as we wined and dined this evening, my darling Scamp, almost, I might as well say, ALMOST joined us at the table! My goodness! This dog, if left to himself, will eat all day, and yes, he will quite literally, eat anything and everything!

Isabel nipped out to Hannah's for a quick two glasses of wine, after which she retraced her steps back to the flat and once again snuggled up in bed with her hot water bottle.

The next day passed singularly uneventfully, and once again Izzy was quite happy to leave chambers when her work had been completed and approved, at ten past five that afternoon. Needless to say, the enigmatic Lady Gertrude was again calling.

Izzy reached her upstairs flat. She had no sooner set foot in her dining room when she became almost instantly aware of her answer 'phone persistently bleeping.

'…Izzy, it's James Brodie again. I'm sorry to keep phoning like this, but North Merseyside coppers are really getting my goat, big style! Poor old Barry, that's what I say! I'll tell you all about it when we meet up on Wednesday evening… Just wanted to say that I've really missed you all day, in fact! I just want to get this Barry episode sorted out in as fair and as equitable a manner as possible, and I'll be really pleased and relieved when it's over. Anyway, I'll pick you up at eight-thirty tomorrow evening, and that, young lady, will be a treat in store for me. Goodbye, dear.'

Well, that was nothing that she did not already know thought Isabel to herself, as she relaxed with a glass of wine. No communication from her father, she suddenly realised… Had she said something wrong when they last communicated? Oh, well, she had written to him only five or six days ago, it really was now down to him to respond, and no, Izzy was not going to lose sleep over her papa. Once again, she resorted to Lady Gertrude's diary.

Saturday, 29th November, 1886. I ordered some new dress material this morning, since my stepmother advised me that I may need some new clothing, especially leisure time clothing for when I transfer to Leeds next year… Leeds!

I am feeling so excited in many ways, yet not in others! Will I fit in and make any friends? Will I adapt and become acclimatised to living away from Riversdale Hall? Harry told me that I had no reason to worry at all, since he suspected I would be exactly like him, and settle in within a matter of a mere three weeks! I really do hope so.

Isabel continued to scrutinise the diary entries. At present, when she returned from work feeling drained and exhausted, there appeared to be no better way to chill out and destress than a delve into Lady Gertrude's diary. A little later, after having briefly prepared for the next morning, Izzy decided to call it a day, or more appropriately, to call it a night, after all, her bed seemed a rather inviting place in which to spend some free time, and at eleven fifteen she curled up gratefully into the depths of the flat's double bed complete with her hot water bottle.

The bulk of the next day passed uneventfully, and Isabel was in the process of collecting her possessions together with a view to leaving, when her 'phone started to ring. Once again, she picked it up to answer it.

'Hello!'

'Izzy, it's Tanya! I've got James on the 'phone. I'm assuming you can speak to him?'

'Yes, of course. Transfer him, please.'

Tanya duly transferred the call.

'Oh, hello, dear!'

'Hello, James.'

'Izzy, I think I've managed to secure a fair, reasonable outcome for Barry. Thank heavens! Oh, I am looking forward to our meeting tonight, and I'm not returning to chambers today, no, young lady, no! But I shall pick you up at the Percy Street flat this evening at eight-thirty! Incidentally, I have loads to tell you!'

'Oh, really? So, you're going to keep me guessing until this evening?'

'Well,' answered James in his customary rather pompous manner, 'All I will currently say is that's for me to say, and you to find out.'

'Well, I'm looking forward to it,' answered Isabel, a little uncertainly.

'Yes, and so am I!' answered James emphatically, and then he proceeded to add, 'Now I shall call for you at Percy Street at eight-thirty prompt, and you know me, I'm always on time!'

'Yes, I know!'

'Alright then, goodbye, dear!'

'Goodbye, James! I'll see you very soon.'

Izzy replaced the receiver. What, in God's name, did James have to tell her with the exception of the entire sorry, unfortunate business concerning Barry? He was madly in love with her? Isabel thought he had already made that abundantly clear. Was he preparing to unburden his soul regarding the unfortunate demise of his ex-lover, barrister-at-law, Allison Maitland? Well, that was nothing new since Ben had enlightened her on that subject a while ago. No, she was unable to guess, so she would be forced to wait until her rendezvous with James later this evening, thought Isabel to herself, as she began to wend her solitary way back to the flat.

At eight o'clock, Izzy selected her clothing. Once again, she decided on the partially embroidered, relaxed-fit jeans and the new green blouse, with white floral motif, courtesy of M and S for their meeting, a minimal application of make-up, thorough brush of her hair and rapid blast of perfume behind each ear and at both wrists and she was ready to leave. Twenty past eight… She felt as anxious as an eighteen- or nineteen-year-old on a first date… No, she had nothing to fear, surely… Twenty-five past eight. Now the minutes appeared to be passing like years, and hopefully, James would do most of the talking, oh, surely he would, especially since he had told Isabel that he had plenty to tell her… And the nature of all he had to tell? '…That's for you to find out!' resounded somewhere in the depths of Izzy's brain.

Izzy was shaken out of her speculations by the abrupt sound of the flat doorbell. James, without a doubt. She descended to answer the front door. Sure enough, James stood on the doorstep, once again beaming from ear to ear.

'Your carriage awaits you, young lady!' James greeted her with, indicating a large, two-year-old, evergreen BMW car.

'Hello, James,' answered Izzy, and feeling as though she needed to make a favourable comment concerning the car, she added, a touch uneasily, 'Oh, what a marvellous car, and I do so like the colour!'

'Oh, it's only a piece of metal to me! All I really need from a car is that it gets me from A to B with the minimum amount of fuss and that it's comfortable. Well, for the past three days, this motor has rarely been out of Bootle Police Station!'

'Oh, that business! Are you going to explain to me?'

'I will when we reach the restaurant, yes.'

A few minutes later they reached the restaurant and were shown to a table.

'Now, young lady,' enquired James, 'would you like anything special to drink? Just think, this is the first of many, many dates we are going to enjoy!'

'Er, a glass of house red wine, please,' asked Izzy tentatively.

'No, no, I insist on something a little stronger, to start off with at least. Why, I feel as though both of us have earned a glass of reasonable quality Champagne. After all, it's not every day that I get the chance to entertain a young lady as nice as yourself.'

Isabel flushed puce with embarrassment, and then she managed to respond by saying, 'Well, that's so nice of you, James, and thank you. What exactly occurred in the Barry business?'

'Oh, why I think that is eventually grinding towards what I sincerely hope is a satisfactory outcome.' James pushed his glasses further up his nose and looked fleetingly exasperated for a moment. 'Poor soul,' he continued, 'well, in a nutshell he's being discriminated against due to his, er, sexual proclivities. A lover's tiff erupted between Barry and his partner, Martin. According to Barry, the relationship between himself and Martin, for the last few months has been anything but happy at any rate, and Barry strongly suspects that Martin's now cheating on him with a prospective new lover, Robert. Apparently, only last week Martin taunted Barry with the fact that,

'You're not as good as the new man in my life! You have no education, at least none to speak of!

My new man, he has four 'A' levels, two of which are grade A's, first class honours and a P.hD!'

Of course, as is the usual custom, I checked the custody record on arrival at Bootle police station and Barry is a peaceable, quiet, hard-working man who runs a successful building business with only one previous criminal offence, which occurred five, almost six years ago, but the beggars! They're prejudiced against Barry due to his homosexuality!

'And what was the offence?' asked Isabel.

'The theft of six rashers of bacon, a packet of four bread rolls and a small carton of milk from Sainsburys'… Goods totalling six pounds, forty pence. My goodness, it was so minor, and as a result of the theft he appeared before Crosby Magistrates' Court and paid a small fine of five hundred pounds.

'And this taunting by the partner, why, that sounds as though he may be eligible for the defence of provocation.'

'Too true. My feelings entirely.'

At this point, they were interrupted by the waiter, enquiring as to their need for drinks.

'As this is such a special occasion, I would like to order a bottle of champagne,' said James boldly. Once the waiter had departed, James resumed the topic of conversation by adding, 'And as if to add insult to injury, I think Martin's beating up and abusing poor old Barry. He looks to have some quite visible injuries to his head and upper arms, so I've requested for them to be seen by the police surgeon.'

'And has he got back to you with the results?'

'Yes, but they're not conclusive, at least not at the moment, and Barry doesn't like to say anything since he's terrified of reprisals from Martin. The good news is I've applied for a restraining order[11] on Barry's behalf.'

'So, what was suspected?'

'The injuries were said to be consistent with the application of a blunt-ended object, applied with considerable force, something like, for example, a baseball bat. I think one was actually recovered at the crime scene.'

Isabel made a mental note that she needed to refresh her memory concerning the subject of domestic violence and abuse.

'North Merseyside coppers questioned the poor soul for six solid hours with no break in questioning whatsoever and no offer of refreshments, not a cup of tea, a sandwich or cake! Nothing!'

At this point, the waiter returned to the table, complete with the champagne. James allowed him to fill their glasses.

'Well, it's not every day I have this pleasure,' he said, once again beaming from ear to ear.

'This is all marvellous,' answered Isabel, 'And thank you for bringing me here.'

---

[11] Restraining Order – The offender, or suspected offender must refrain from all contact within a certain specified radius of the victim and his or her home.

'Seriously, the pleasure is all my own. Do you know, Izzy? You remind me so much of someone I knew from the past.

Was James referring to Alison? Isabel took a rather anxious, hurried sip of the champagne, the bubbles of which began to shoot up her nasal passages.

'Yes, you remind me so much of a girl who was once very dear to me,' James continued, at this point looking rather sad and wistful.

'Was her name, Alison Maitland? James, I am so very sorry about, er her passing,' answered Izzy.

James gave her left hand which was resting on the table a small squeeze.

'Izzy,' James persisted, 'You are so like Alison, although in many ways entirely different, and no, I don't wish to speak ill of the dead, I somehow have this intrinsic gut feeling that you are a rather better balanced and less volatile character.'

'How do you mean, exactly?' asked Izzy. She was absolutely intrigued and fascinated about James opening up so bluntly, but as she had discovered the week before there was no pretence whatsoever with James, and what you saw was exactly what you got. Was that what he originally intended telling her?

James took another sip. 'Poor Alison,' he said quietly, 'she always had to be succeeding. She once told me that the day she received her 'O' level results, her father, Eric, roundly told her off, due to the fact that she had only obtained three grade 'B's' and three grade 'C's'. According to Alison, she was similarly told off in the aftermath of her 'A' level results three years later, since she had only managed to score two grade 'B's' and a grade 'C.' She didn't manage to get any grade 'A's.'

Isabel laughed uneasily.

'Yes,' answered James, 'It's absolutely laughable, 'aint it? In fact, Alison once told me she never really wanted to be a barrister. I think she would have been far more comfortable and at home with being a staff nurse or a bank cashier.'

Isabel was rapidly obtaining the picture. Pushy, go-getting parents and a seemingly dysfunctional family, with love being conditional, subject to and highly dependent on academic prowess and ability. Isabel again sipped at her champagne.

'You know Alison lost the court case she was defending and various members of the court staff later told me that Miss Maitland was devastated.'

'Actually, Ben did tell me something like that.'

'Yes, the first few years in the aftermath of Alison's… Er, how shall I put it? Passing away, were quite hard, but as someone said, 'the hole eventually fills up.' And yes, I've always been quite a religious person and I believe in life after death.'

'Yes, I likewise.'

'But do you know, Izzy, I've so enjoyed the last few weeks, in particular the welcome back party which we arranged for you; in fact, as I said before, I'd not enjoyed a night on the town for years quite as much as that one.'

'Oh, really?' asked Izzy, and with that she took another mouthful of her champagne. Once again, the bubbles seemed to shoot to the top of her nose and produced a temporary strange feeling. 'Oh, most certainly. I don't say things I don't mean. Yes, Alison…' said James returning to the subject that at one stage had dominated his life, 'Alison once told me that she was sick to death of being a consistently grade 'B' achiever, when she should have been a consistently grade 'A' attainer.'

At this point, they were once again interrupted by the waiter enquiring whether James and Isabel were ready to order their meal. James managed to stall him by quarter of an hour. 'Er, no, not yet, we're still enjoying the champagne.' At the waiter's departing form, James muttered, 'I absolutely hate doing that!'

'Sorry, what exactly were you referring to?' asked Izzy, once again taking a mouthful of her champagne.

'Going out for a meal to wine and dine and ordering instantly!'

'Oh, my feelings entirely!' answered Isabel emphatically, which of course, inevitably reminded her of certain members of her family who quite repeatedly employed this technique, much to Isabel's irritation and frustration. Certain matters seemed to be being hammered home to Isabel, and although herself and James did need to get to know each other better, they appeared to have plenty in common.

Isabel finished her glass, at which James promptly refilled it. James's previous conversation relating to Alison and being a consistently grade 'B' attainer, reminded her of her second-year study of Philosophy and the writings of a rather erudite German philosopher. The vast majority of the issues he raised had been long since forgotten, but one point stuck indelibly in her brain. '…Man needs to ultimately realise that his situation in the world is essentially limited and restricted, in particular with regard to and concerning such aspects as material wealth, physical health and academic ability.' So true.

'Just returning to Alison,' Izzy said gingerly, 'that reminds me of something I studied in the second year of my degree course. A German philosopher raised a point about every individual being limited and restricted in the world in terms of such things as material wealth, intellectual and academic ability, bodily health, you know what I mean, that sort of thing.'

'Well, yes. It's just part of human life, 'aint it?' answered James wisely.

That, in turn, reminded Isabel of someone else. Her cousin, Oscar. If Alison had at one stage grumbled about only being consistently able to attain grade 'B's', Oscar was consistently a grade 'C' attainer, yet he continued to entertain fanciful ideas that had he received the education received by their cousin Lawrence, the two would have been easily on a par, 'at least,' according to Oscar. Nonsense, of course. Oscar, having left school with a mere handful of GCSE's had at one stage been briefly employed as a police constable, promptly proceeded to have an altercation with the supervising sergeant, whereupon, he instantly resigned.

Isabel took another mouthful. 'Oh, my cousin Oscar's like that. Well, not exactly, no… I'm sure Alison was far cleverer than Oscar,' she added quickly, for a moment feeling as though she had insulted the memory of Alison. No, nothing wrong with being a grade 'B' attainer, but why, Oscar is consistently a grade 'C.' Bone idle, I think he was, at school.'

James smiled indulgently. 'And what category is my Izzy?'

Izzy blushed and then said, 'Well, you know I think I'm firmly in the Alison category.'

By now, Isabel had finished her glass. Yet again, James refilled it. If Izzy were absolutely and entirely honest, the rendezvous was turning out to be not half so bad as she had initially anticipated. The more she came into contact with James, the more Isabel was rapidly discovering that she intrinsically liked him as a person, they had quite a few things in common and she regarded him as a decent and principled man. The memory of her grandmother's words from years ago, suddenly resounded for the umpteenth time in her head:

'…Honestly, Izzy! Don't be so choosy… For goodness' sake, take him and have done with it! I don't think you'll find better than James Brodie! You don't want to end up sixty-five and stuck on your own!' …Stuck on her own… No, Izzy certainly did not want that.

'…Just think, with this middle-aged man… You could have a nice house in Woolton…' This last sentence, was of course, all Isabel's own invention regarding what her grandma might all too easily have said.

Presently, it occurred to Izzy that by now she was feeling well and truly in the mood for something to eat, and she picked up the menu and began to scan it thoroughly. Eventually, she decided on a Bem Brasilia steak. James chose the beef casserole.

'Right, we will order next time he appears,' he said, 'And we'll also order a bottle of red wine.'

'Sounds good to me,' answered Izzy, although to be honest she was feeling a little uncertain regarding how much more she could consume in the alcoholic department.

James, as if sensing her worries said blandly, 'Don't worry at all, dear. If we've consumed a little too much, we can get a taxi back and I shall foot the bill.'

'Oh, thank you, James.'

Once again, he squeezed her hand, and Izzy beamed back at him. The waiter took their orders and then left. Once they were alone again, James broke the brief silence by abruptly saying, 'Izzy, I've got a small present for you.'

'Well, I wasn't expecting anything, but thank you.'

He rummaged in his left-hand jacket pocket and passed a neat, compact, leather-covered box across the table. It was the type of box that jewellers stored engagement and wedding rings in before purchase. At this point, James began to hastily and anxiously explain, 'I want to give you this as, well, like a commitment ring… It was originally, er, originally, going to be Alison's wedding ring, until she was of course, so abruptly snatched from me… It's been languishing in my boxer shorts and sock drawer at home for years… And to be honest, you may find the style and design a little old-fashioned, but back then, back then in the early eighties, why, this was considered state-of-the-art wedding ring technology.'

Isabel opened the box. Comfortably nestling on a black velvet cushion was a flat, yellow-gold ring. To be brutal, it was not the piece of jewellery of Izzy's dreams, although Izzy could tell it was obviously a quality ring, with its' flat, even surface and neatly bevelled off edges, the lid of the box carefully lined with a white silk-like material, proudly proclaimed in gilt letters, 'Stephen Jones, Manufacturing Jeweller, 30, North John Street, Liverchester, L1 3BJ.' No, it was not or by any means the ring of Izzy's dreams, and what she had seen of Lady Gertrude's jewellery collection comprised some far more impressive pieces, but obviously to express her dislike of it to James would simply have been plain rude and ill-mannered, so instead she managed to say, 'James, it's absolutely beautiful… In fact, I'll try it on now.'

'Now, dear, if it doesn't fit, and is either too large or too small, I can return it to Stephen Jones for re-sizing and adjustment. I just wanted you to have it.'

'Well, it's beautiful, James, and thank you. You know I love jewellery.'

'Yes, I did know.'

Izzy tried it on the third finger of her right hand. Like the rings in Lady G's collection, it was absolutely flawless and fitted her finger comfortably.

A few minutes later their meals and wine arrived. The waiter filled their glasses with wine and once again left the table.

'Well,' said James at last, 'I'd like to propose a toast to us, I think, and also to happiness!'

'To us, and also to happiness!' repeated Isabel, as she clinked her glass against James's, and then proceeded to take a sip.

'And furthermore,' continued James, 'I'm full of plans, in fact, absolutely bursting with them!'

'Oh, really?' asked Izzy, 'Could you explain a bit more?'

'Well, do you know, I've been thinking of possibly in the not too distant future, of taking on another partner.'

Talking of partners, Isabel was just reminded that her cousin Lawrence had just obtained a partnership at Mason Jenkins, and as a result, friction had inevitably arisen between Lawrence and Oscar, who now, of course was insanely jealous of Lawrence. Oh well, thought Izzy to herself, that was so often the case in families, friction and rivalry inevitably resulting.

'Oh, do you know? My cousin Lawrence has just got a partnership with the dreaded Mason-Jenkins.'

'Well, you know us, we're not like them!' James laughed, 'No, not at all! Now, obviously I was not thinking of recruiting the partner immediately, no, certainly not yet, no, more like in about two years.'

Isabel took another sip of her wine. Somewhere in her memory she remembered her mum saying to her, 'Now, how about that nice German man…? But of course, she rapidly changed her tune on actually seeing him in person, but how different was James from Carl Dawson, yes, Carl who was detached, cold, distant and impenetrable and frequently present at social gatherings, but largely there in the capacity of a strange, brooding and uncomfortable presence. Conversely, James was warm, welcoming, entertaining and good-natured. Yes, of the two, James was far preferable. No, she could have no future whatsoever with Carl Dawson!

'…Just think…' James continued, 'Brodie, Watson and Partners, now that sounds better than mere Brodie and Watson… And now, wait for it… I'm actually hoping to change the name of the chambers… And now young lady, I'm going to make you an offer you are in no position to refuse, yes, if I have my way, in a few years, the chambers will be re-named as… Brodie, Watson and Jackson-Talbot… The partner I ultimately had in mind was yourself.'

Isabel felt as though she had been hit hard between the eyes… So James considered her partner material? She managed to reply with, 'James, well thank you! But, you're just too good to me! Too good by a long chalk. To be completely honest, I'd never, ever envisaged myself as a partner, never in my wildest dreams!'

'Nonsense! The pleasure is entirely my own! And you'd never imagined yourself as a partner? Izzy, if you have the innate ability which I believe you intrinsically do, then you might as well try for it, at least. When I initially interviewed you back in the spring, I had this feeling that this young lady will go far.'

'Oh, really, did you now?' enquired Izzy. Then something else clicked in deep in the recesses of her brain… Not one, but soon two partners in their family, and that would really make her cousin Oscar who was a basic level paralegal, absolutely hopping mad and furious… Stop it! Izzy, she thought to herself, that's not particularly nice!

'Yes, I certainly did… You've done an awful lot for me, and why, I used to think that Alison was good for me, but you are better still, I think somehow that you are a bit better balanced and less serious minded… Oh, excuse me, I didn't mean you were not serious minded, but I find you far more relaxed and less intense than Alison… In fact, you relate very well to others, or at least you appear to. So, you see, the offer of the partnership, should you require it, is my way of thanking you.'

'Well, James, what can I say? This is so very nice of you.'

'You see,' James persisted, 'I would absolutely hate to lose you. I simply can't imagine the chambers being able to effectively function without you now. After all, some trainees just complete their articles contracts and that's it, you never see them again, they prefer these cut throat companies where the prospects are better, you know, the likes of Mason Jenkins!'

'Oh, don't worry, as far as I'm concerned Mason Jenkins, you can keep 'em!' answered Izzy emphatically, 'When I initially considered a legal career, I imagined a small high street company, that's all I've ever wanted, no, Mason-Jenkins 'aint exactly my bag.'

'I'm highly relieved to hear it.' Once again, James leaned forward and gave Isabel's hand a light squeeze. Then he suddenly added as an afterthought, 'Just back-tracking on an earlier conversation, Izzy dear, should you not particularly like the design of Alison's ring, we can easily return it to Stephen Jones for melting down and reshaping.'

'Well, that's very nice of you, James, but I'm actually quite happy with it as it is in its' present form.'

144

'Well, the offer still stands, dear... Both offers still stand, I mean, the offer of the eventual partnership and the offer of the ring restructure.'

Izzy took James's free hand as he sipped a little more of his wine, and said, 'James, dear, as I've already said, you're too good to me. I already love the ring as it is.' Isabel felt an abrupt rush of love for James. Yes, she could easily face the world with James beside her, to help, support and guide her once she had completed her articles contract, be it in the capacity of associate solicitor or even partner.

'Twill' be so nice, so very nice, darling, when you have a set of rings of your own choice, of course, to fit on the other hand.'

'Well, yes.'

They completed their meals and progressed to desserts and to conclude their meals ended with strong coffees. Isabel came to the conclusion that the evening rendezvous with James had passed considerably better than she had originally envisaged. Yes, she was now well and truly involved in a work-based relationship, something she had hitherto neither wished for nor needed, yet there was something rather endearing about her supervisor, James Brodie, the absolute man of principle. True to form and true to his word, James called a taxi which he paid for at his own expense, and being the true gentleman that he was, dropped Isabel off at her flat before travelling back to his Woolton home.

Chapter 9.

James was once again absent from chambers the next day, since he was still busy fighting Barry's corner at Bootle police station.

'Ooh, get you, young lady!' said Ben laughingly, as he checked through Izzy's completed, allocated work load for the day, 'You're rapidly becoming more competent by the day... I don't know, it must be all those late nights with James!'

Isabel laughed.

'Yes, I know you two are now an item. I know everything that goes on in these chambers. There's nothing happens in here that escapes my notice.'

'No, somehow I didn't think anything escaped you, Ben,' Isabel answered laughingly.

'Partner in two years, you are on the up and up.'

'Well, put it like this. I'm still undecided about that. I'm currently debating both possibilities.'

'Izzy, dear, I don't want to deter you, but it's both lonely and stressful... being a partner, I mean. Always being responsible. No, had I known then what I now know I would simply have stayed as an assistant or associate, it's far easier.'

Just at that moment, Izzy's 'phone sounded and a cold sounding woman's voice asked at the other end of the 'phone;

'Is that Miss Jackson-Talbot?'

'Speaking.'

'You've got a flipping nerve!'

'I don't know what you're talking about,' Isabel answered calmly. Sensing that the nature of the call was personal, Ben discreetly left Izzy to it and returned to his own room.

'No?.......You don't know?' answered the angry voice, 'It's Gwyneth Jackson, well, all I can say is you damned well should! I was quite happy with my father for thirty-odd years, and then you come oiling in, wanting to be all touchy-feely, the long-lost, once prodigal daughter, but now prodigal no longer, Super Izzy! Well, I for one, am thoroughly sick of Super Izzy!'

James's words resounded in Izzy's brain. 'Dear, she's just jealous of you!' Izzy hated any unpleasantness like this, but thank goodness she did not have to face the furious Gwyneth face to face.

'Look, I do understand how you feel, Gwyneth. But I'm not asking for anything from father. I just wanted him to be aware of my existence, so to speak.'

'Oh, you've done that alright!' Gwyneth was still clearly furious with her and was obviously in no mood to try to humour, or even attempt to laugh off any of her rantings and caustic comments. And what's more you come to our house for a few days eating our food and drink and costing my parents money! Yes, costing money that father would have loaned me to start my own business! It's just complete sod's law!'

'…She's just jealous of you…' It was beginning to sound as though James might be right. Conversely, Izzy had successfully completed her degree and was still working at self-improvement, that was doubtless another determining factor in Gwyneth's dislike of her, but that was no comfort to Isabel, who right now was simply feeling shell-shocked. At last, she eventually managed to say in response, 'I really don't know what you mean.'

'I would have thought it was absolutely obvious to the meanest intelligence, father spent money on your entertainment and wining and dining for your general benefit, which I could easily have made use of! But, oh well, I shall just have to let it pass!'

'Well, he happens to be my father too, or had that matter escaped you?' Isabel answered.

'Oh, he's my father too!' Gwyneth mimicked Izzy's voice in a sneering way, 'Furthermore, young lady, I would advise you, for your own good, not to darken the doors of this house, and I mean it… You prize B I T C H… Ever again.'

Somewhere in the background, Izzy could not fail to hear an angry, raised voice; it was the voice of her father,

'…Gwyneth! That's enough! Now will you please leave?'

'I'll be only too pleased to!' shouted Gwyneth in response, and a loud slam was promptly heard.

Doubtless, the front door.

'Izzy, love?…….Izzy, I'm so very sorry. Gwyneth's been having a go at me all day!'

'Oh, is that what happened?'

'Yes. Seriously, she can be a right grumpy devil! All this arose because I wouldn't give her any further money to try to start her own business.'

'Oh, I'm sorry, father.'

'Not at all, dear. You are not at fault, at all.'

'I'm relieved to hear it.'

Izzy glanced at her watch. Five to five. Almost time to go.

'Look, I was just going to say, if you would like to pay us another visit in about a month's time, you would be extremely welcome,' her father asked rather tentatively.

'…I would advise you not to darken the doors of our house…' hammered in Isabel's memory; obviously with Gwyneth in this frame of mind, just about the last thing Isabel felt tempted to do was pay her father another visit.

'I'm not so sure about the welcome part, father.'

'Look, Gwyn was feeling in a bad temper, which does sometimes happen, but I'm sure it will soon all blow over. Can I call you later on this evening?' her father asked placatingly.

'Yes, if you wish. It's almost time for me to leave, so you can catch me on either my mobile or landline, goodbye, papa!'

'Goodbye, dear, and lorry loads of love.'

Feeling highly relieved, Isabel replaced the 'phone receiver. Her father was obviously now feeling highly embarrassed at Gwyneth's behaviour and general attitude towards Isabel, and possibly his evening call was going to represent an attempt to smooth over matters and repair any damage which had arisen in relations between Gwyneth and Isabel.

Izzy began to slowly wend her way home. Once again, it was Thursday and she needed to do her shopping. Once in Sainsbury's she bought her essentials, a small carton of milk, four bread rolls, cheese, unsmoked bacon, yoghurts and three ready-made meals. Lady Gertrude was calling, yet again. Ten to six in the evening. Once back at the flat, Isabel checked her watch. Storage of her purchases was now required, and furthermore, the answer 'phone was bleeping. Izzy played the machine back.

'Hello, Izzy! Izzy, it's James again. Almost concluded the Barry business, apart from the fact that I'm going to have to represent him in court. I'll be really pleased when it's firmly in the past; just 'phoning today to see all's O.K., and I'm really missing you… I've been back at home for approximately quarter of an hour, and I'm about to have my G and T… Love you, bye!'

After the torrent of verbal abuse which Izzy had been subjected to that afternoon, James's words sounded like music to her ears. Oh for James to stroke her hair and tell her there was nothing to worry about, which in actuality there was not really, and he loved her, so what did Izzy need to fear?

Izzy cast her mind back to something someone had told her years ago, which of course, was so true…' When someone's nasty to you, it's not you who has the problem… It's them!' Izzy then remembered casual conversations with her cousin Oscar from years ago, '…I don't like Izzy! Shall we throw Izzy in the water?' This last comment was always guaranteed to drive their grandma wild, since her response was always the same, and furthermore, it never varied, '…No, or I'll throw you in the water! Stop being so nasty about Izzy!' Well, he was obviously jealous of you, so many others had told Isabel. Yes, the same principle probably applied to Gwyneth, James had said as much himself.

Izzy stored her food, and once again, took refuge in Lady Gertrude's diary.

Sunday, 30th November, 1886. We visited church this morning and dined this lunchtime quite royally on venison freshly culled from the estate. It was marvellous!

Harry successfully completed all his written work, which is now ready for submission on Monday morning and left by means of the post chaise service this afternoon, at just after five. To be entirely honest, I would also have been happy to be departing to the urban temptations of Leeds, since I feel well and truly ready to savour and experience a wider reality, a small taster of which I have already sampled, and so far thoroughly enjoyed when I have accompanied papa on his business visits to Leeds.

Early this evening, I sorted through my jewellery collection. Yes, my jewellery collection which now easily fills three jewellery caskets and I will very soon be requiring a fourth box! Who would ever have envisaged when I was twelve years old that I would develop a total fixation and compulsion for all types of jewellery. In actual fact, I believe this predilection began when my grandmother bought me a small silver bracelet complete with my name engraved on it for Christmas, when I was twelve years old. I still have it in my possession. To be honest, my jewellery constitutes my most prized and valued possessions, and as the brilliant man at the Silver Box so correctly said, '…Provided you safeguard, care for and don't lose jewellery, you should possess it for the rest of your life, which obviously isn't so with clothes or shoes, why, they inevitably wear out eventually.' So true. Yes, I have clothes and footwear aplenty, but I am always happy to add to my jewellery collection. Furthermore, I see my jewellery purchases along the lines of an investment, so hence, for this very reason, I always like to purchase good quality items, often found in small family businesses downside streets and alleyways, and as papa so rightly told me that is where one is most likely to pick up some really tempting bargains! Additionally, I do so love to support the exemplary Mr Summers, since he really is a master craftsman and a goldsmith of the highest order.

Monday, 31st November, 1886. Once again, papa had business in Leeds which needed to be attended to, so he took me with him.

Over the last few months, I have been saving up and holding back small amounts of money, for example, quite a substantial amount of my birthday money, which I have clung onto and added to, so that I was yet again able to visit Mr Summer's shop. Guess what? Surprise, surprise! I was totally unable to resist the charms of the shop, and I bought a small silver charm bracelet; well, for the time being at any rate, the bracelet only, but the jeweller told me that he produces a vast array of complimentary charms which can be manufactured to order, to mark almost any special event, for example, a twenty-first birthday, a wedding and success in an examination, to name a few. In fact, he has even told me that he produces a special Christmas bracelet, complete with special 'Christmas theme' charms, comprising such motifs as Father Christmas, wrapped up presents and loveable little reindeers! I think I shall refrain from purchase of his Christmas theme, since the charms may only be worn for a maximum of a single week in an entire year, and of course, Christmas comes but once a year! But acquisition of the all year round collection of charms to add to my growing stash of jewellery should happily keep me going for years.

Isabel made herself a meal, and then returned to her study of Lady Gertrude's diary. No 'phone call was forthcoming from her father, but as her stepmother, Agnieska had said, he was becoming increasingly forgetful, so maybe that was only to be expected. Besides, thought Izzy to herself, she did not feel as though there was anything more which could be said, especially in view of the drubbing she had received earlier on at the hands of Gwyneth.

We again dined at the Central Dining Rooms, near the Wool Exchange, this time on roast pork with plenty of roast potatoes and green vegetables, rinsed down with the quality red claret which papa loves so much and chocolate sponge to conclude our meal. It was all absolutely excellent, and I so enjoyed it. I think papa enjoyed it too.

Later that evening, papa told me something that he said he had suspected for years, and something about which I was only very dimly aware of. I found this so disturbing and shocking, that in retrospect, it quite tarnished and detracted from my enjoyment of my visit to Leeds. The great and noble city of Leeds, like any other city in the United Kingdom has terrible problems with poverty and deprivation. Papa, in fact, felt so unhappy about the plight of the woollen weavers, some of whom were facing possible starvation and destitution in view of the fact that production of wool was greatly reduced this year, that he very kindly donated several thousand pounds to a charity specifically established to deal with these types of problems. Yes, without doubt, my papa is the best papa that ever was, and I do so love him for it. Yes, I really am quite the, 'daddy's girl.'

Sadly, there is not a great deal that I can do for the poor and destitute of Leeds, which makes me unhappy, apart from when I go there to learn my nursing skills, which will of course, entail attending to the sick, poverty-stricken and bedridden of the city. I am sure that this will present a bit of a challenge, but this is a challenge I am only too happy to meet.

Izzy was brought abruptly back to twenty-first century living by the sound of her 'phone. James was calling.

'Hello, Liverchester, 707 4396!'

'Oh, hello dear!'

'Oh, hello, James!'

'How did today go? Did it go well?'

'Well, yes, until right towards the end of the afternoon. I was just about to leave chambers, when I received an incoming call from my half-sister, Gwyneth. Well, in short she subjected me to some extremely unpleasant verbal abuse, and the long and the short of it is, she advised me never to darken the doors of the Jackson household ever again, and my father had spent money entertaining me which she could have made use of to fund establishing her own business. I heard her say it! My father, who was himself clearly quite exasperated with her, then asked her to leave. She then stormed out of the house, and slammed the front door without even bothering to replace the receiver. Father was then quite apologetic, told me how sorry he was and invited me to stay again, would you believe it?

'Oh, I am sorry, Izzy. But it sounds as though this is what I originally suspected. Izzy, she's simply jealous of you!'

'I thought after the altercation Gwyneth and I had, which I might add, I did not start, another stay at my papa's was just about the last thing I would want!'

'Well, precisely,' answered James.

'Father said he would call me back either on this number or my mobile, but so far he hasn't… I know he's prone to being rather forgetful. He may 'phone tomorrow, but I'm certainly not intending losing any sleep over the fact that he's forgotten to call.'

'No, and quite right too. Also, seriously, Izzy, if you don't want to visit your father's house again, you really don't need to, remember, you're not under any obligation.'

'Somehow, at present, I don't fancy sitting down to eat my evening meal with Gwyneth glowering across the table at me!'

'Well, no, I shouldn't think you would!' James responded.

At this point, at the other end of the 'phone, Izzy heard the frenzied bark of a dog, and strange, rapid, steam locomotive-like breathing somewhere in the background. Then she heard James say in a slightly irritable tone, '…Manc, that's my shoe! Without my shoe I can't take you for a run in the park!'

James then quickly added, 'Izzy, I'm sorry, that's my new dog! He has a strange fetish for my shoes, God knows why!'

Izzy never knew James possessed a dog, she would question him a little more closely about the dog when next she saw him. Presently, in the background, she heard James say, this time quite irately, 'Manc, will you please give me back my shoe!'

Izzy was rapidly beginning to feel better and she asked, 'So, James, how are you going to spend the rest of the evening?'

'Well,' answered James, 'The moment I've recovered my shoe from this here hound, I shall take him for a run in Woolton Park, if and only if, he'll give me back this shoe! Then it's back here for G and T's with mother, and then we'll have our evening meal… Oh, this hound… You go and retrieve the shoe, and if you're not wearing the other, he runs back and snatches that one! He's such a character, but I wouldn't be without him, not for anything!!! Now Manc, you just drop this here shoe… I also need it for wearing to go to work tomorrow morning to earn some more money to keep you in dog food! Please will you drop the said shoe?'

Izzy started laughing, 'Remember, James, he doesn't understand English!'

'No, but he can tell when I'm displeased with him, don't you, young sir?'

Somewhere in the background, a few snatching, lunging and barking noises were heard, and Mrs Brodie was heard to say, 'Here we are James. I've got your shoe back.'

'Right, I'm going for a rapid, and it will be a rapid tour of the park.'

'Well, I hope you enjoy it,' answered Izzy, 'And thank you for making me feel better!'

'Not at all, dear… Oh, and er, I probably won't be in chambers tomorrow, but I will be next week. This is the last day of the Barry episode, and it will probably comprise writing up all the paperwork, then of course there will be his hearing but that will not be for seven or eight weeks, at least. Yes, I shall be in chambers as of next week onwards.'

'So I'll see you next week then, you enjoy the park!'

'Oh, we shall, we shall, goodnight dear! And forget all that silly business with Gwyneth, why it's quite blatantly obvious she's jealous of you… Oh, and er, Izzy, darling, would you be interested in meeting me, say, next Tuesday night at Hannah's Bar with a view to progressing onto the East Garden, Chinese restaurant? Mother and I have wined and dined there before, and we've found it really good.

'Yes, I'd be only too pleased.'

'Well, until next week then, dear, goodnight!'

'Goodnight, James!'

Izzy replaced the 'phone receiver.

Where had she reached in Lady G's diary when James disrupted her? Oh, yes…

'…But this is a challenge I am only too happy to meet.'

There are so many people around who say that education is wasted on a woman… What absolute, complete and total nonsense! In fact, I am nineteen years old and wish to further improve my knowledge and education. In my book, it is impossible to be too well-educated. I would love to be given the chance to obtain a university degree, and stretch and stimulate my mind in an intellectual capacity… And after my degree? Yes, I have to admit that my aspirations are possibly on a grandiose scale, why, I would have loved to have become a Member of Parliament, or even possibly a lawyer or novelist… Pity I am the wrong sex to do either of these jobs. But I have so very much to be grateful and thankful for, and I am quite certain that I shall enjoy my new nursing role.

Izzy glanced at her watch. Eight thirty. After the earlier emotional abuse at the hands of her half- sister, she felt well and truly ready for two glasses of red wine at Hannah's Bar… Of course, Izzy reminded herself that next week she would be visiting Hannah's with James. In fact, she was just walking along Rodney Street to the bar, when once again, Izzy felt certain that her grandma was again speaking to her.

'…Well, this middle-aged man's obviously extremely keen on you, Izzy… To my mind, you won't do better than James Brodie, for goodness' sake, take him and have done with it!'

Izzy sipped her wine. So James owned a dog? Somehow, she had never imagined him as a man who was into pets. No, Izzy had imagined him as more of an animal disliker, rather than an animal lover. But no, James, like herself, loved animals. That was something else they had in common… And Lady Gertrude, who would loved to have become a Member of Parliament, a lawyer or a novelist, but believed herself to be the wrong sex to fulfil any of these roles? Yes, Isabel had to admit she had enormous difficulty prizing herself away from Lady G's writings, which seemed to Izzy to be fast becoming a source of inspiration, wisdom and pleasure to her. All simultaneously. She finished her glass of wine, left the bar and returned to the Percy Street flat.

Yet further requisitions occupied the bulk of Izzy's time the next day, and she was only too happy to complete them.

Her weekend had passed all too quickly, and once again it was Monday morning. Once again, there was no sign of James, since he was still embroiled in the Barry business, but was hoping to conclude the process over the next two days. When Isabel received this information by means of Ben, she was a little surprised at her own feelings and response, no, she was not missing him, not by any means, and James's non-appearance at the chambers ironically proved to be a source of relief rather than displeasure. Now she was feeling an overwhelming sense of relief at the fact that there would be no James in chambers today… Thank goodness! But then, if she was feeling this way, could she possibly have a future with James? Yes, James, the man of principle and perfect gentleman, and again, Izzy could almost hear her grandma speaking to her, 'Izzy, love! Don't be so choosy! Just take him! After all, you might not get another chance! Just imagine, Isabel, you can have a nice, comfortable house in Woolton… What more could you possibly want or need?'

'…Well, grandma, he does just happen to be twenty-four years my senior… Old enough to be my father, at least!' Obviously, that reminded Izzy of someone else entirely. No, he had still not called Izzy, but he was possibly feeling a little embarrassed, especially in the aftermath of the singularly unpleasant showdown with Gwyneth.

Once again, five o'clock eventually came round, and Isabel was quite ready to leave chambers, her week's shopping needed to be completed, and Lady G was again exerting her strange, magnetic charms. The moment Izzy had stored her food purchases, she went straight to Lady Gertrude's diary.

Tuesday, 1st December, 1886. Just under a month to go until Christmas, so we will soon begin our Christmas visiting. This entails providing our estate employees with additional foodstuffs, for example, joints of beef, bacon, turkey, venison, gammon and mutton, all freshly culled here on the estate, and of course, papa will, as always, do his employees proud and give his entire workforce extremely generous Christmas bonuses, he really is quite the papa in a million, and I love him for it!

Incidentally, my mind has wandered over to and worked its' way around to the inevitable subject of my marvellous, handsome and extremely dashing Lord Ernest. Why, I have not seen him for almost two months now… And as far as I am concerned, this is two months far too long! Perhaps he no longer visits our house due to the fact that he already has another woman in his life! If he has, I consider that woman to be the luckiest and most fortunate in the world, after all, in view of the fact that he is so suave and handsome, this is only to be expected. Possibly, I need to steel myself for the absolute worst, that he has another woman in Leeds whom he is happy with, and regards 'little old me,' as a mere sideline, a much younger woman, who still has plenty of growing up and maturing still to do… Oh, well, if that is the case, it is a great pity, but there it is.

The build-up to Christmas is quite magical and precious, and this year seems to almost entirely comprise beautiful cold, clear days with the black, skeletal branches of bare trees rearing up against a brilliant blue winter sky, contrasting exquisitely with the bleached, pale green fields drained of their natural colour and hillsides heavy with old and decaying brown masses of bracken… All so subtly beautiful and an absolute refuge from the hurly burly of city life, and marvellous though the estate is, I am nevertheless beginning to find my day to day life at the hall a little narrow, constricting and restricted…

Yes, I have to admit that I really do hope that when I transfer to Leeds to learn and practise my nursing skills, my life will widen out a little.

Izzy glanced at her watch, seven-fifteen, and then almost on cue, the 'phone rang out. Probably either James or her father.

'Hello, Liverchester 707 4396!'

'…Is that a certain person?' Isabel knew of only one person who addressed her in this manner, in an attempt to be funny. Her father.

'Oh, hello father.'

'Hello, Izzy, dear.'

'Do you have something to tell me?' Izzy asked gingerly, not even sure why she was asking that question.

'No, not really dear, but I can only say that should you wish to visit us in a few months' time, you would be extremely welcome.'

No, thought Izzy to herself, after the savage verbal attack which she had been subjected to at the hands of Gwyneth, that was just about the last thing on her mind, but instead, she managed to calmly answer, 'I don't think Gwyneth likes me! Why, I think for the time being, it's probably best if I lie low here and say nothing!'

'Oh, come now. Of course not! And if there is a problem with Gwyneth, I'm absolutely certain it will blow over soon, why to be honest, she'd been having a go at me for most of the day yesterday.'

'Well, possibly,' answered Izzy in a singularly non-committed tone. When, and if she did decide to pay her father another visit, it would need to be quite some time in the future, certainly not for a good few months, at least and furthermore, she had her work and her relationship with James to occupy her time.

'Well, you know I do hope you'll be able to pay us a visit at a not too distant date, but at any rate I fully intend to come over to visit your good self in Liverchester some time, maybe in the next few weeks, just the minute my left foot feels a little better. We can even wine and dine.'

'You've hurt your left foot, papa? Oh, I'm sorry to hear that,' answered Izzy, taking a leaf out of Lady Gertrude's book when addressing her father.

'Oh, it's nothing to worry about. It's nothing that the G.P.'s tablets won't cure, why, it simply makes walking and standing for any length of time quite painful.'

'Well, you be careful,' Izzy replied. Slowly but surely, Isabel was once again warming to her father, despite the temporary hiccup caused by the angry exchange which erupted between herself and her half-sister. Then she added quickly as an afterthought, 'And I shall look forward to our meeting up to wine and dine in Liverchester. I know a lovely Brazilian restaurant which serves excellent food and is good value for money.'

'I shall too, my dear. Now, I think I'd better go as I think I'm being summoned by your stepmother, anyway, lorry loads of love, dear, and we'll speak again soon.'

'Goodbye, papa!'

'Goodbye, dear!'

Izzy replaced the 'phone. Well, relations were restored with her father, at any rate. Thank goodness. Not sure about Gwyneth, but that did not really matter and besides, on the occasion when Izzy had paid her visit to her father's house, Gwyneth appeared to have gone to almost excessive lengths to avoid Isabel's company. Oh well, as Izzy's grandma had once passed comment, 'It was quite impossible to please all of the people, all of the time!' Hence, there was no point in trying.

Izzy next set to work to prepare her evening meal. The ready-made meal she had placed in the electric oven appeared to be progressing nicely, when she was once again interrupted by the 'phone.

This could possibly be James.

'Liverchester 707 4396!'

'Oh, hello dear, I'm sorry to disturb you early this evening,' James asked a little uncertainly.

'No, you've not disturbed me,' Izzy answered.

'Well, if the truth be known, I just wanted to hear your voice,' James replied, a little sadly, 'Those beggars at Bootle Police Station are still playing fast and loose with poor old Barry, and at times I've come quite close to losing my temper with them. At any rate, I believe Barry has a perfectly valid and credible defence, and what's more, I intend to fight his corner to the bitter end.'

'Oh, I'm certain you'll do that,' answered Izzy. This was the side of James that she did so admire and love.

'I was just going to say dear, that when I represent Barry in court, you may want to come with me to watch the entire process, only for one day of course, but just to see the court process. You know, the 'Bow to the judge' and 'The Court Will Rise' and all that business, why, it will be good experience for a trainee like yourself.'

'Yes, I would love to.'

'Excellent… Oh, er, and incidentally, how are relations with your father? Still a bit strained?'

'Not really, I'm pleased to say. I think my father was a bit embarrassed over Gwyneth's behaviour and her general attitude towards me, rather than anything else, so he was trying to smooth matters over and minimise the damage caused by our altercation.'

'Oh, that silly business. As I've said before, it all boils down to Gwyneth being jealous. I really wouldn't give it another thought. Anyhow, I've really missed you these last few days, and shall be only too pleased to see you when we meet up tomorrow evening. Will it be O.K. for me to pick you up at, say eight forty-five?'

Unable to say no, and desperate to avoid any further unnecessary unpleasantries, Isabel answered, 'Yes, with pleasure.'

'No,' answered James emphatically, 'As I've previously said, the pleasure is quite unreservedly, all my own... Oh, and I shall now have to go, Manc's getting restless, he needs his supper and his evening run in the park! Manc, your lord and master is on his way!'

Izzy laughed at the other end of the 'phone, 'Well, you be careful, and don't go losing your temper at Bootle Police Station – Don't let your blood pressure rise too much, oh, and I shall want to know all about Manc when I meet you tomorrow!'

'You shall hear all, darling! 'Till tomorrow evening then! Goodbye, dear!'

'Goodbye, James!'

Izzy replaced the 'phone receiver and rapidly retrieved her evening meal, now thoroughly cooked from the oven, saved, just in time from being burned and reduced to a cinder.

Izzy decided to spend a quiet, uneventful evening at the Percy Street flat. It was Monday night, after all, and not by tradition, an evening for wild nights on the town. Instead, Izzy watched a thriller on television, and then crawled exhausted, into her bed complete with hot water bottle. To be able to collapse into bed and fully relax in the aftermath of very recent traumas seemed like absolute bliss,

'...To sleep, perchance to dream,' and the very precious, 'Sleep which knits up the ravelled sleeve of care...' to summarise the situation in purely Shakespearian terms. There was one certain, undoubted factor that evening, Izzy needed it.

A personal injury matter occupied the bulk of Isabel's working day on Tuesday, together with a lengthy 'phone call from Stephen attempting to ascertain when would be the most mutually convenient rendezvous for Isabel to provide him with the advice and information which Stephen required relating to his tenancy. After much haggling and negotiation, the two eventually settled on Monday afternoon of the week after, at four o'clock.

Today, of course, was the fateful day of her meeting with James, and, true to form, it had come round far too fast. Once back at the flat, Izzy selected her clothes and make up, frenziedly combing through her wardrobe to find something smart, suave and appropriate. Eventually, Izzy decided to wear the exact same clothes combination she had worn the previous week, of green and white floral blouse and embroidered relaxed fit jeans, a minimal application of make-up and a quick drag through her fair tresses with a hairbrush, a few brief squirts of perfume behind the ears and on each wrist and she was once again, ready for James.

Sure enough, at quarter to nine exactly on cue, Izzy's front doorbell push sounded. Mr Brodie, without a doubt… And it was.

'Oh, Izzy!' James greeted her with, 'Why, you look beautiful!'

'Oh, thank you, James, how nice of you to say so!' was Izzy's reply, as she climbed casually into the passenger seat of James's two-year-old, dark green BMW.

'So now we're on our way to Hannah's,' said James airily, as they crossed Upper Parliament Street heading for the wine bar. I think I might well choose something to drink from their extensive cocktail list… Can't say that I've ever tried it before,' he added as an afterthought.

'No, I haven't either, but you know what they say about there being a first time for everything, and all that business?'

'Too true,' James answered.

Once in Hannah's, they found seats and a table beneath one of the many television video screens that graced the wine bar. Rum Fuego cocktails were ordered, although conversation turned out to be a little difficult due to the noise generated from the juke box. After an hour in Hannah's and four cocktails later, they decided to call it a night, and began to wend their way down past the bombed-out church and down towards China town and the East Garden restaurant.

Once in the East Garden restaurant, James ordered a bottle of red wine.

'To us, eh?' asked James, raising his glass rather diffidently.

'Yes, to us!' Izzy raised her glass in assent, then added, 'You know that Monday was rather fraught with the irate 'phone call I received from my half-sister, not good at all!'

'No, I can fully understand that.'

'And now I want to know all about your new dog.'

'Oh, Manc, you mean? Oh, he's a character alright!'

'And that's his name? Manc?'

'Yes. It was me who dubbed him Manc. The reason for this was, when I got him, he looked so scruffy and, well, er, quite frankly, Manky and down-at-heel, so to speak. Hence, Mancky. Manc for short.

Izzy took another sip of her wine and attempted to probe a bit more. 'What type of dog is he?'

'One of those that's used for hunting, now, what do they call them? A lurcher, I think.'

'And where did you get him from?'

'Oh, Liverchester Animal Rescue Centre, what, six or seven weeks ago, in fact. Do you know? When I was younger, my mother used to get a dog from the Animal Rescue Centre every few years. She liked to provide them with a decent home, if she could. Manc's original owner was a hopeless character. According to the rescue centre, he was a crack cocaine addict who lived on the streets and this poor hound slept on a regular basis in the old tobacco warehouse, you know where I mean, down on the docks.

Izzy was learning more about James with almost every passing day, quite literally. He really was such a good person.

'Well, that's very nice of you,' she answered.

'Poor hound,' James continued, 'Yes, you're getting the picture, his owner spent much of his time begging from Mr Joe Public on Church Street, now, I've no objection to beggars, in fact, I occasionally give to them myself, but they should under absolutely no circumstances whatsoever possess dogs. That is a practice I absolutely deplore. There are not many beggars dogs in Liverchester I'm pleased to say, but obviously, there should not be any, at least, not if I had my way.

Yes, as you can imagine, Manc's owner eventually could no longer cope and handed him in to Liverchester Animal Rescue Centre.'

'Yes, you're quite right,' replied Izzy emphatically.

Presently, the waiter appeared attempting to take their order, but luckily James managed to stall him by quarter of an hour to twenty minutes.

'At any rate, I gave the Rescue Centre a donation for a hundred pounds which made them quite happy, and I left with my new dog, which made me equally happy and do you know? I quite regularly talk to him as though he's a human being, why, I was already speaking to him as we left the dog's home, '…No more sleeping in the Tobacco Warehouse for you, young sir, you will now be sleeping in one of our many dog baskets, protected and enveloped in tartan rugs, I wouldn't be without him not for anything now, in fact, it's quite a wonder that I managed without him for as long as I did.'

Izzy started laughing. 'You are funny, James, I mean about talking to the dog.'

'Well, he has to learn sometime and somewhere,' laughed James, 'but seriously the practice of beggars with dogs, if they are genuinely homeless and of course, they not all are, really does make my blood boil in my arteries.'

'Yes, I do know what you mean.'

'Now, you know, young lady, I really am feeling quite excited about yourself and this partnership business, and I mean that. Yes, in fact the more I think about it, Brodie, Watson and Jackson-Talbot has rather a good ring to it.'

Izzy was again at a loss for exactly what to say in response. Silence descended for two minutes. Then eventually Isabel managed to say in response, 'Well, I never really gave it any serious thought until you referred to it last time we met up, but Ben said that at times he found it both stressful and lonely.'

'Not at all!' James said dismissively. 'Why, when I obtained my partnership, I saw it more as a bit of a challenge, the 'Can I Really Do It?' approach, that was my attitude, whereas Ben's just thinking, 'All for a quiet life,' and since he's about to turn fifty-nine, he's into, how can I put it? Er, 'winding down' mode. No, dear, I believe you are fully up to the challenge.'

'Well, I do hope so,' answered Izzy, a little uncertainly, taking another sip of her red wine. Once again, it occurred to her that her date with James was progressing far more easily and smoothly than she had initially envisaged, and, like herself, he had an easy, relaxed manner and was quite a good conversationalist. No, this would never be exactly the romance of the century, but, thought Izzy to herself, James and herself were two lonely souls together, who furthermore, happened to have quite a lot in common.

'I don't think so, I know so,' answered James, abruptly cutting through her reflections.

'And how's the Barry business progressing?' enquired Izzy, by this time quite keen to change the topic of conversation. Isabel finished her glass, at which James promptly refilled it. She also took a quick scan of the menu. Like James, Izzy had dined at the East Garden many times before, so she thought she would probably choose the meal she invariably ate there; duck Cantonese served hot, with egg fried rice.

'Oh, the Barry business!' James threw back his head and laughed, 'Sorry, I shouldn't be laughing, but that's becoming almost farcical!'

'How do you mean, farcical?'

'Well, North Merseyside Police, they're just prejudiced against the poor beggar due to his homosexuality. They keep saying to him, no, trying to coerce him, I think is the correct expression, saying such things as, '…Come on, Barry, we know you're guilty of attacking Martin, just own up and admit you're guilty as sin and we'll release you on bail… All that sort of silly business.'

'Sounds like sections 76 and 78 Criminal Justice Act, 1994 apply,' said Izzy in response, taking another sip of her wine.

'Precisely. Evidence obtained by unfair means and oppression,' answered James, pushing his glasses further up his nose and picking up the menu. With his characteristic slightly short-sighted scrutiny he began to scan the list of dishes, once again, choosing the crispy belly pork. 'At any rate,' James added, 'in the interests of justice, I insisted that Barry's interview was tape recorded, of course, the beggars were trying to get away with not taping it, and I'm pleased to say that I already have a copy of the said interview in my possession.'

'Thank goodness for that.' Izzy took another sip.

'Once that's replayed in court, I strongly suspect that Bootle coppers won't have the proverbial leg to stand on.'

'Good. I'm relieved to hear it.'

The waiter appeared, and this time, successfully took their orders.

'Do you know? At the end of Barry's interrogation this afternoon, he actually personally thanked me.'

'Oh, really?'

'Yes, and, well, that's a reward in itself. When a client thanks you it's one of the perks of the job.'

'Well, yes, it must be.'

'But the rest of the time, why, it's a completely thankless task!' James answered laughingly. 'Do you know, just before Barry and I parted company this afternoon, Barry asked me rather a personal question, and this is what it was: 'Mr Brodie, do you have a very special person in your life, someone that you're really close to, who to you is, 'the reason for everything?' You know, the reason you get up in the morning, the reason you sit at the table and eat a meal, go to sleep at night, that sort of thing, I'm sure you know what I mean, Mr Brodie, yes, I'm absolutely certain those were Barry's exact words.'

Isabel took another mouthful from her glass, and then she responded by saying, 'And what was your reply?'

'I did at one stage have a lady friend in my life, who was extremely dear to me, but she was snatched from me quite abruptly, when she was only twenty-four years old. I then spent years unattached and alone, but now I have a new woman in my life, who is actually very similar to the first, yet somehow better; I suspect the new woman I share my life with is rather better balanced, takes herself less seriously, knows how to relax and party. Without in any way wanting to insult the memory of Miss Maitland, I feel the new young lady is more liveable with. In short, I believe I ultimately got the better deal.'

Izzy blushed crimson. 'Well, that's really nice of you to say that, and thank you.'

'Not at all, dear, you don't need to thank me for anything, but I really do mean that.'

'Oh, but you haven't seen me in the mornings,' laughed Izzy, taking another mouthful from her wine glass. 'Why, my grandmother said that in the mornings I was like Dr Jekyll and Mr Hyde, and Mr Hyde was certainly riding high in the mornings!'

James laughed uproariously, and answered by saying, 'Oh, but I have seen you in the mornings, what about in chambers in the mornings?'

'No, the very early mornings, I mean.'

'Oh, well, I shall have to be very careful what I say to Izzy Jackson-Talbot Hyde in the mornings in future!'

At that moment, the waiter returned with their meals, and James ordered another bottle of wine. Once again, they clinked glasses. The rest of the evening passed very easily and painlessly, and a good time appeared to have been enjoyed by both parties. Izzy and James concluded their meals with strong coffee and James called a taxi.

In the taxi, James sat close to Izzy. She strongly suspected he was really keen to be invited in for night-caps. Well, it was late in the evening, although not that late, only twenty-five to eleven and both had work in the morning. One night-cap and then James could be sent on his way back to Woolton.

'Would you like a little night-cap, James, dear?'

'I would love one.'

They disembarked at the Percy Street flat. Up the rickety staircase to the first-floor.

'That was an absolutely excellent meal, and a marvellous night out. Thank you, James.'

'Absolute pleasure.'

'Now, what would you like? I've got the usual, you know, whisky, which I scarcely ever drink, brandy, gin – either white or pink, red wine or strong beer.'

'Now this, young leddy, is an offer I find extremely hard to refuse. I'll have a bottle of strong beer, please.'

Once again, James sat down in the same armchair he had last occupied. Izzy vanished into the kitchen to obtain the drinks. She returned with two glasses, one three quarters full of pink liquid and tonic water, the other empty, a bottle and a bottle opener. 'Well, this is all very nice, Izzy, dear, and I do so love your flat.'

'I've always wanted to live round here, and of course, eventually I got my wish!' This, in turn reminded her of her grandma's antiquated, old fashioned pre-war attitude to living away from home, which, if truth be known, really irritated Isabel, since Izzy herself had managed to live quite easily and happily away from home for years, but nevertheless, stray thoughts of past contretemps flitted through her brain, 'I had a flat in Manchester before the war, and I hated it!' That, I might add, reflected Izzy, was all her grandmother's own fault, since from further conversations which came to light, Izzy's grandma had taken the, 'nose in the air,' superior approach towards her housemates, believed her fellow housemates were inferior to herself and generally not to be trusted. In addition, she had more than once commented, 'I don't want you living in grotty digs!' which was inevitably a source of friction between them and frequently led to angry exchanges, with Isabel responding, 'I'm a free spirit, grandma! You will never tame me!'

At this point, James suddenly cut through her recollections, and quietly asked, 'You're very quiet, Izzy, and that's not like you.'

'Oh, I was just thinking when you made the reference to the flat being nice about what my grandma used to say about living in a flat, away from home.'

'And what did she say, dear?'

'So often, times without number, in fact, she used to say, 'I had a flat in Manchester before the war, and I hated it!' Although that was all her own fault, she wasn't prepared to make the remotest effort to be friendly with her housemates, far too busy being Miss Superior was my grandma! Another of her much bandied sayings was, 'I don't want you living in grotty digs!' That was totally guaranteed to completely get my goat!'

'Well, of course, she was a few generations removed from yourself, I expect,' answered James, taking a sip of the strong beer.

'Well, yes. It still completely got my goat though!'

Once again, James leaned forward and placed one hand on Izzy's knee, and yet again, his signet ring gleamed in the muted electric light.

'This has been a brilliant ending to a magical night on the town,' said James.

'Yes, it has been marvellous, and thank you again, James!'

'Not at all, t'was nothing… Er, Izzy, darling, next week, I should be once and for all free of the Barry business, er, well, for the time being at least. Would you like to meet mother and come and have a meal at our house? Why, I'm certain mother would really like to meet you?'

'Yes, I would love to,' answered Izzy and anxiously took a sip of the pink gin.

'Is that liquid good?' James asked, suddenly and abruptly changing the subject, 'I remember I tried a few glasses of it when I was in my late twenties, but I decided I preferred the ordinary variant.'

'Well, I do quite like the fruity flavour, you know, the essence of raspberries, strawberries and red- currants.' Izzy took another mouthful. Time she was going to bed, and pronto and yes, it was high time James was making his way back to Woolton, after all, his mother might be starting to worry. Izzy glanced at her watch, eleven o'clock… Still quite early.

James noticed. He took another sip of the strong Belgian lager, and said, a touch pompously, 'It's alright, darling, my intentions are honourable, I shall only take a further ten minutes to drink my lager. After all, mother will start to worry and Manc needs his evening walk to allow him to do what he needs to.'

Izzy took another mouthful from her glass and answered in response, 'You don't want your mother believing you've been captured by the new femme fatale trainee of your chambers?'

James started laughing, 'You do make me laugh sometimes, Izzy Jackson-Talbot, and that's why you're so good for me.'

'I'm pleased to hear it.'

'Oh, incidentally, I'm probably not going to be in chambers tomorrow. In fact, I don't think I shall. The Barry business is well nigh concluded, but I shall need to sift through all the available evidence and relevant information that we have to hand, which I shall do from home before depositing a copy at H.M. Courts in town, and the other copy stays with myself for general reference, for the time being, at any rate.'

'Do you like working from home?'

'Well, yes, put it like this, it has its' compensations. Mother loves it, and she waits on me hand and foot, bringing up mugs of coffee to my bedroom, every hour on the hour. Manc curls up at my feet, he doesn't seem too perturbed by the stink of them and its' good.'

Izzy dissolved into fits of laughter.

'Now you're making me laugh!'

James drained his glass, and with that he stood up. 'Right, it's ten past eleven, it's time I made myself scarce.'

'Let me wait with you.'

James made his way down the rickety staircase and out onto Percy Street, closely followed by Izzy. Presently, a taxi stopped on the opposite side of the street, from which exited three individuals, which James hailed. As the taxi pulled up, James held Izzy close to him and whispered, 'Thank you, darling, for the best night on the town ever, our meetings seem to get progressively better, and I'll see you very soon.'

'Goodnight, James, darling, and happy working from home tomorrow!'

With that, James vanished into the black depths of the taxi, and back to his Woolton home, Mrs Brodie and his unusual dog. Izzy returned to her first floor flat, and curled up in the luxurious double bed, complete with her hot water bottle.

Chapter 10.

*W*ednesday, 2nd December, 1886. Once again, I'm feeling happy and so very excited. Through today's post I received a recommended reading list from the School of Nursing in Leeds. The explanatory information which the list arrived with and provided to all probationary trainees, gave us specific instructions to provide tangible evidence in our written work of wide background reading, the inclusion of which should lead to the award of high marks! I shall ideally aim for an average of at least 70% for all my written work. Always aim as high as possible, to quote my marvellous papa.

In fact, papa has business in Leeds to attend to tomorrow, once again at the wool exchange, so I circled and wrote down a few of the titles, together with the names of the authors, so that he will be able to order them for me at a Leeds bookshop. Obviously, when these arrive, I can then start my reading. Furthermore, I suspect papa will secretly feel rather proud when he tells the bookseller the reason for his wish to order these books, i.e., his eldest daughter is about to study nursing at Leeds School of Nursing. Yes, he will inform the bookseller with pride!

Unfortunately, I have not seen my marvellous Lord Ernest lately, and papa has not seen anything of him either, but suspects that he may be spending time with his parents over in Bolton, in Lancashire, which is where he comes from… Come back soon, Ernest, since I really miss you…

And right now, I have my cheeky little canine friend to attend to and also to take on his morning walk. He really is a sheer delight. In fact, when I release him from his lead he charges on ahead of me totally unfettered, but at regular intervals, he turns round back to me, I bend down to welcome him and he charges back into my open, outstretched arms. What a dog he is. If I sit in one of our comfortable armchairs in the evening, he likes nothing better than to rest his head on my knee so that I can stroke his head. He really is such a character, and I have to admit, I do not like to envisage a time when he is no longer with us, but I shall not think of that since he is with us now, and has a good, decent and comfortable home. As I think I have previously said, he is an absolute dog in a million, and I love him for it!

I have been extremely busy lately and very gainfully employed in reading some of the writings of the good and noble Bronte sisters, in particular, Jane Eyre, and in fact, this book is so well written, I am almost unable to lay it aside and can so clearly picture in my mind's eye, the sequence of events occurring, '...There was no question of taking a walk this afternoon...' Absolutely excellent! I must read for pleasure while I still can, since when I start at the School Nursing, much of my time will be fully occupied with all the prescribed background reading which has been set.

I'm just thinking, there were so very few openings and chances for women to make anything of their lives in the times of the Bronte sisters, still very few fifty years later, even in the mid- eighteen eighties, but that said, I am extremely lucky, I have a stable, secure and rich home and family, and furthermore I now have my nursing career, so on the whole, matters are not altogether too bad. Hence, for this very reason, I should under no circumstances, grumble or feel sorry for myself.

True to my word, I took my marvellous little Scamp for his mid-morning exercise, and I am ashamed to say that on this occasion, he rather disgraced himself and greatly embarrassed myself by incurring the wrath of a farm-hand in chasing sheep! But I have to admit, I was unable to chastise him for long with his little eager face. I now maintain that Scamp needs to remain at all times on the leash when sheep are present, and I will only take him for his good long run-in sheep-free territory. He really does never cease to entertain me, although sometimes for the wrong reasons!

Thursday, 3rd December, 1886. When we sat down for our supper this evening, father told me that he had placed an order for the books I requested, he really is so very good, and additionally, there was another piece of jewellery ordered for me at the marvellous Mr Summers's shop. Oh, father, you really are so very good. The new mystery jewellery item will obviously need to go away for Christmas, but this ultimately means yet another item to be added to my jewellery collection which is steadily, slowly and surely growing. I have no idea whatsoever the item comprises or consists of, but I do not find this a problem, since I am more than happy to wait until the festive season arrives. Yes, I am *perfectly happy to wait for my surprise item, and papa is perfectly confident that I will love it, since I believe that if papa has chosen it, I am absolutely certain that I too shall love it, in view of the fact that papa's personal taste is so very similar to that of my own. According to papa, he again ate his lunch at the Central Dining Rooms, feasting on roast turkey this time, rinsed down with two large glasses of claret and a generous helping of apple pie, both courses of which were excellent and of the highest quality. I might also add at this point, that according to papa, he felt a little guilty with his recent gastronomic overindulgences, together with the presents he so kindly purchased for the members of his family that he made yet another donation to the poor and destitute of Leeds fund. I believe it was as much as a hundred pounds!*

It had been a singularly uneventful day in chambers for Izzy. She had had a few client proofs of evidence to record, and then yet further requisitions, which Izzy was almost an old hand at, by now having had so much practice.

As Izzy began to prepare her evening meal, her mind wandered to the subject of the caverns. She remembered the conversation which had passed between herself, her father and the farm-hand… 'Best tell no-one,' the farm-hand had advised, 'That way no-one can get hurt!' Yes, thought Izzy to herself, probably best to maintain silence, 'the less said the better,' discretion being the better part of valour and all that business. It would not be particularly hard for her father either, Izzy reflected to herself, after all, his only concession to jewellery being a wristwatch. Suddenly, the flat felt extremely quiet and Izzy was acutely aware of her solitude, or was she? Presently, she remembered the funeral service words… 'Like a flower, man or woman springs up, and then the wind changes direction, and he is blown away…' And then, the immortal phrase, '…Life is changed at death, not ended.' So true. At that moment, Izzy began to sense she was not entirely alone in the flat, she felt almost certain that her grandparents were standing on either side of her, and now her grandma was speaking to her directly and clearly, in a manner which could simply not be ignored.

'Well, Izzy, love, you were right, and I was wrong!'

'What about, grandma?'

'About the library work versus the law… Ignore me, I say a load of things I shouldn't.'

Oh that silly business her grandmother had at one stage indulged in… 'I wish to God our Izzy would realise that she's ideally cut out for library work, why, she could have done that library course blind- folded!' The library course had been a one year postgraduate course that Izzy's grandmother had, to all intents and purposes, forced Izzy to attend on completion of her undergraduate English and Philosophy course. Almost effectively from day one, Izzy had hated it and found the course to be deadly boring and dull as ditch water, as a result of which, she began to find excuses not to attend timetabled classes, and left the course permanently at the end of the second term.

But no, this time her grandparents were not there in a censorious, condemnatory or judgmental capacity, Izzy sensed. No, Mr and Mrs Talbot seemed to be present in an essentially supportive role, 'Izzy, love, you're doing the absolute best you can… We've gone on ahead of you, and you're on your way,' and then a little later on, '…I'm really sorry I lied to you about your father… You were absolutely right to contact him! Yet again, you were right, and I was wrong!'

'Yes, hopefully I am on my way, grandma!' Izzy actually verbally uttered, 'And yes, grandma, I do try to always do my absolute best… And yes, I do try to be a good person…' Somehow, Isabel had for years possessed the innate feeling that with her grandma on the chase, almost anything was easily possible.

At that point, Izzy's reveries were abruptly shattered by the 'phone ringing out. James, no doubt about it.

'Hello, Liverchester 707 4396!'

'Oh, hello, dear! I'm sorry to disturb you after a hard day at work, I, er, well, just wanted to confirm that I shall come to pick you up at, say, eight-thirty, next Wednesday evening at the Percy Street flat.'

'Well, yes.'

'You know,' James added with a slightly conspiratorial air, 'Mother's really keen to meet you!'

'Oh, really?'

But, thought Izzy to herself, was she extremely keen to meet Mrs Brodie? Wasn't this all a little rushed? Of course, James would then in all probability introduce Izzy to his mother as, 'his young lady,' and then Izzy remembered something she had read years ago, which had quite literally been, 'romantic rubbish,' '…When a man introduces you to his mother, it means he's really keen and serious about you.'

'She certainly is!' James interrupted her thought processes, and he then went on to further explain, 'Well, I've been working from home today, and I've really missed you, as always, I'm sorry darling, but I think I shall have to also do the same tomorrow, but don't worry Izzy, love, I shall be back in chambers Wednesday morning, and for the time being at least, I've completed this Barry business.'

'Thank goodness for that!' Izzy answered emphatically, but if she really came clean and admitted to herself, it was a secret relief to her that James was not going to make his presence felt in chambers tomorrow, so no inept, embarrassing, quasi and unwelcome passes… But if James's absence resulted in a deep-seated sense of relief for Izzy, what was the point in those two being together and a couple? Izzy was thirty-eight years old to James's sixty-two years old… Could they possibly have a future together? And inevitably, this reminded Izzy of the inescapable fact that when Izzy was forty-six years old, and still young to all intents and purposes, James would have reached his seventieth birthday. A twenty-four-year age gap. Yes, as Izzy was starting to suspect, it was too much.

'Well,' said James, 'I shall pick you up next Wednesday evening, and then we'll go to mothers.'

'Er, yes, I shall, er, I shall be looking forward to it,' answered Izzy uneasily and by no means convincingly.

'And I know almost exactly how mother will respond,' said James in reply.

'And how will she respond?'

'She'll say, Oh, you two! You're a perfectly matched couple! Izzy, oh she was well worth waiting all these years for!' Yes, she will love you, you mark my words.'

'Oh, how nice,' answered Izzy half-heartedly.

'At any rate, I will now probably see you in chambers on Wednesday morning, and until then, goodbye, dear!'

'Goodbye, James!' With that Izzy replaced the receiver. Today had been an uneventful day in chambers, with client proofs of evidence to be recorded and checked through and a few 'phone calls to be made and answered. Now, with a sense of innate relief, Izzy returned to Lady Gertrude's diary to read and enjoy her words of wisdom.

Friday, 4th December, 1886. To return to the point I made two days ago, I do so enjoy the writings of the Bronte sisters, especially Charlotte Bronte and Jane Eyre… What an original story, I only wish I had had the inspiration to concoct a story with that particular theme myself! Do you know? A few years ago, my governess told me that descriptive and creative writing was one of my absolute fortes, and one of my strongest academic subjects… Of course, unless one is lucky enough to possess the intrinsic and inherent talents of the Bronte sisters, there is no money or livelihood to be made in literary talents, especially if one is a woman… It is, to my mind, a real pity, but sadly it is just a fact of human life.

Oh, and quite incidentally, my beloved and naughty Scamp did so enjoy his daily exercise, yesterday, today and the day before! No chasing sheep this time, thank goodness, I am extremely pleased to say.

I am also highly pleased to record that my newly ordered dresses arrived complete from the dressmakers in Harrogate, by this morning's post. Furthermore, I have tried them on and they fit very comfortably, and in such beautiful colours too, I am quite in love with my cherry red ball dress, and my maid servant, my loyal and truly devoted Emma told me this morning that it contrasts so perfectly with my raven black hair, and she also explained that the dress and its' effect will be beautifully finished off with a necklace, choker or some other form of neck embellishment from Mr Summers's shop. Why, I shall look quite the elegant, upper crust young lady when I am out and about in Leeds in just a few months' time.

As we wined and dined this evening, I eventually managed to sum up the courage to ask papa if he had heard anything from my marvellous, delightful and gallant Lord Ernest. According to papa, he had so far heard nothing, which was quite unlike the gentleman in question, but papa quite unequivocally told me that he suspected he would probably hear any day now... Besides, I do not wish to raise my hopes too much concerning this exemplary young man, since he may regard me as far too young, immature and without doubt, probably already possesses a small coterie of admiring and devoted women, all only too pleased to lap up his attentions! But I have to admit, the image of his handsome and extremely well-proportioned face continues to materialise in my mind's eye, and I have to admit, I am quite unable to help myself, as far as he is concerned at any rate. Additionally, papa explained that he needed to make a further visit to Leeds tomorrow and would I also like to attend? Most certainly, was my clear and quite categorical response, in fact, I am looking forward to it already!

Saturday, 5th December, 1886. This is almost becoming a habit now! Once again, I am sampling the 'flesh pots' of urban Leeds to enjoy a day's shopping, wining and dining... And of course, as of early April onwards I shall be spending the vast majority of my time in this most noble city!

I did spend a rather wistful ten minutes admiring the jewellery so proudly displayed in Mr Summers's shop but did not enter the premises or bother to place an order, since I did not wish to place too much temptation in my way and decided that on this particular occasion, I would save my money! Yes, I believed that I would save my money for when I am based in Leeds rather more permanently, which, of course, I soon will be, a fact of which I am really excited about! Father is buying me further jewellery for Christmas, so I have all I need for the time being.

We again dined at the Central Dining Rooms, on roast topside of beef and Yorkshire pudding… Yes, true Yorkshire fare, all rinsed down with plenty of red Claret and slabs of chocolate sponge. 'Twas all excellent.

As we were leaving the dining rooms, a really memorable event occurred, and an event that I shall remember for the rest of my entire life! As papa and I set foot in the street, who should we encounter but Lord Ernest, oh my goodness, I am quite sorry to say that I turned crimson at the sight of him! Papa invited him to feel free to spend further time with us at any time he felt so inclined, to which my beautiful, eloquent Lord Ernest answered that he would be only too pleased to do so, but he would furnish papa with plenty of warning beforehand, being the gentleman that he so obviously is! I do hope he will spend at least some time with us, and then I shall attempt to employ all my feminine wiles and charms in order to entrance him!

Before we left Leeds, papa made yet another very generous donation to the poor and destitute benevolent fund of the city; a hundred pounds, yet again, would you believe it? If Lord Ernest is half the man that my excellent papa is, then he will do very well and very nicely, thank you.

What time was it? Izzy glanced at her wristwatch. Eight-fifty. It was almost time she got herself to Hannah's Bar for a little liquid refreshment. Once the laptop had been closed down, that was the direction in which she inclined her footsteps.

Izzy spent a further two uneventful days in chambers and returned to Cumbria for the weekend. When she reached her flat on Sunday night, she found further communication from her father, requesting that she spend a little more time with him in Huddersfield. No, Izzy's heart did not leap at the prospect, and for obvious reasons she was not overly keen to have any further contact with Gwyneth, her half-sister. She would do nothing for at least a couple of days and give herself sufficient time in order to compose an appropriate response. In the interim, however, she was going to have to meet Mrs Brodie, and currently, she felt totally unable to see beyond this particular little rendezvous.

Monday passed uneventfully, Stephen, Izzy's neighbour, visited the chambers and obtained the advice which he required. On returning to the flat, after having indulged in a small amount of retail therapy, Izzy found her answer 'phone bleeping with one new message from James. Surprise! Surprise!

'…Well, dear… I really have missed you this last week. I can't believe it… In less than twenty-four hours, you'll be meeting mother. I'm so looking forward to it.'

Well, quite frankly, and to express matters totally bluntly, Izzy was not. Most certainly not. No, thought Isabel to herself, she was not going to 'phone James back either, why, that might give James the impression that she was a little too keen. Once again, whilst preparing her evening meal, she took refuge in Lady Gertrude's diary. As Izzy switched on and connected her laptop, she reflected on the fact that just lately, Lady Gertrude's diary and Hannah's Bar were becoming her treasured and much valued havens. Don't resort to Hannah's Bar too often, Izzy reminded herself, after all, we don't want you becoming an alcoholic! My goodness, Isabel Jackson-Talbot, she thought to herself, you sound just like your grandma! And at that moment, Izzy became intensely aware of her grandmother in the upstairs flat with her, and once again the same old message seemed to be being hammered home.

'Take him, Izzy, for heaven's sake, take him… A partner solicitor and commissioner for oaths, why, you won't do better than James Brodie!'

Izzy resorted to Lady Gertrude's diary.

Tuesday, 8th December, 1886. Momentous information was brought me by my excellent papa this morning! He has received news from Lord Ernest that he would like to pay us a visit on Wednesday evening of next week! What an absolute paragon of a man! Do you know? I do not wish to in any way pre-

empt matters too fast, but I feel as though Ernest and I might have a real future together!

At this point, Izzy decided to call it an evening. She had her scaly ordeal tomorrow to face, so she needed maximum time in order to prepare for the events of the evening.

All too soon it was the next morning. During the morning, both Ben and James were present, although James vanished at lunchtime, providing Izzy with specific instructions that he would call for her at half past eight at the Percy Street flat. Once back at the flat, Izzy selected her clothing, somehow, she had an innate feeling that Mrs Brodie would approve of smart, conventional clothing in rather muted, subtle colours. Izzy scrutinised the contents of her wardrobe, eventually choosing a pair of black relaxed fitting jeans, a pink linen blouse newly purchased from M and S and black, flat, slip on shoes; two ethnic beaded bracelets, Alison's wedding ring and silver dangling M and S earrings completed the jewellery effect for the evening, next, she applied a small amount of make- up, carefully bearing in mind that James would probably prefer his women with a more natural look.

Now she was ready to meet James, but it was only seven-thirty p.m. Still an hour to go, and once again, Lady G's diary seemed to be calling Izzy, and for the umpteenth time exerting its magnetic effect on her. Almost instinctively, she connected the laptop.

Wednesday, 9th December, 1886. The deep and true meaning of reality. Is there one? I really do hope so. To be absolutely honest, I have spent years trying to work this question out, and I am still no nearer the answer, whatsoever. Lets face it, the only conclusion I have ever been able to reach concerning this subject, is that we are all mortal, and will all eventually die, but as I see it, all one can say is that a person should do, is be the absolute best person that he or she can be, and do good whenever or wherever he or she can. I really firmly believe this. Papa tries to do this, and as far as I am concerned, why, he is the best man that ever was!

As I write these diary entries, my little character of a canine friend, Scamp, nestles at my feet... You know what they say, 'Man's best friend!' or in this case, 'Woman's best friend!' Every evening he loves to lie slumped in front of the fire in the great hall and I really do so wish that I could take him with me to Leeds, but sadly, this is not a possibility, and he would greatly miss his exercise and fresh country air.

I am extremely pleased to say that some of the nursing text books papa kindly ordered for me in Leeds, arrived at Riversdale Hall this morning. I am really so enjoying the physiology, even at this very early and elementary level, and from my reading so far, I have gathered that the natural processes and functioning of the human body is designed to maintain it in as balanced and stable a condition as is physically possible for the duration of the natural lifespan of the individual, however long that might last for.

James should now be arriving at any time. True to form, precisely on cue at eight-thirty, Izzy's flat doorbell sounded. Now her ordeal would begin. Izzy quickly switched off and disconnected the computer and made her way down the stairs.

'Well, hello, hello, darling!' James greeted her with, and then added as a casual afterthought, 'And once again, you look beautiful!'

'Oh, how very nice of you to say that,' answered Izzy, 'I'll just nip back upstairs and get my jacket.'

'Er, James, would you like something to drink here, before we go to Woolton?'

'Don't mind if I do. Mother's expecting us to arrive at approximately nine.'

'What would you like? Your usual?'

'Please.'

Izzy vanished into the depths of her kitchen. A few minutes later, she reappeared with James's bottle of strong Belgian beer and a liberal gin of the pink variant.

'That's that pretty-coloured liquid,' James commented, on Izzy's reappearance in the lounge, and seeing Isabel's rather worried face, he added, 'You look really anxious, dear, don't be.'

Izzy took a large mouthful, rinsed it round her mouth and then swallowed it. What should she say to Mrs Brodie? She had absolutely no idea whatsoever. Anxiously, she took another mouthful of the gin.

'And how's the Barry business going?'

'Oh, I've managed to conclude that for the time being, at least,' James answered airily.

'Are you feeling relieved?'

'Yes, I certainly am. Anyhow, I've done all I can for the time being, and Barry's staying at his sister's for the moment, so he can't come to any harm at the hands of his now, ex-lover, Martin.'

'I'm relieved to hear it.' Izzy took another sip of her gin and revelled in the delicate, fruity taste. She really would be pleased when her evening out was over.

James leaned forward. Once again, he placed one hand on Izzy's knee. Izzy took another gulp.

There was silence for a few minutes, which James eventually broke by saying, 'Have you heard any more from your lazy cousin, Oscar?'

'Oh, him, would you believe it? He's supposed to be getting married next year, I don't like to think how he's going to be able to pay a mortgage, not with only a temporary job!'

'Oh, my goodness!'

'But he's so busy shouting his mouth off, he's probably telling his fiancée he's going to be coining in £500K a year... He's all mouth, he is.' With that Izzy took another sip to fortify herself, and then beginning to warm to the theme of her conversation she added, 'He was ghastly when he was taking his law degree, too.'

'Oh, really?' asked James, appearing genuinely interested.

'Oh, my goodness, yes. It was, '...My tutors tell me my knowledge of law is so sound and thorough, I ought to become a law lecturer, and after the second year, one told me that I was well and easily in line for first-class honours! Why, Oscar Talbot, you are always absolutely spot on!'

'Silly boy!' James answered laughingly.

Beginning to relax as the gin took effect, Izzy also added, 'And that day at the British Museum, my God, he really reached his finest hour…'

'Did he now? What happened?'

'Why, this young man, he loves intellectual matters and a bit of culture,' explained Izzy sarcastically, 'Now admittedly, not all those rooms in the British Museum are interesting, but you would think he would have found something that was worthwhile and worthy of looking at, but no, in a nutshell, he couldn't be bothered and had no interest whatsoever in looking at anything, well, to put it bluntly, I was flabbergasted!' Izzy took another mouthful of her gin.

'You mean your gast was flabbered?'

This time it was Izzy's turn to burst into fits of laughter. Whatever her intrinsic attitude to James Brodie was, at times he could be extremely entertaining, made her laugh and was the perfect gentleman.

Eventually Izzy managed to respond when her laughter had subsided, 'I mean I've always loved the Ancient Mesopotamiam Room, and the jewellery there, which is true to form and typical, absolutely typical and when I was nine, I was absolutely captivated by the Saxon warship discovered in deepest Suffolk; the workmanship on the daggers, swords and shields, oh, and the year after, I loved the Sarcophagi and the wall paintings to the various gods in the Egyptology section, but Oscar, no, he just couldn't be bothered and had no interest whatsoever between you and I, he's a prize burk… He simply saw the British Museum as a meeting or rendezvous point.'

'So, he got your goat?'

'Precisely.' Izzy laughed again.

'It's probably time we were making tracks, darling. And please don't be anxious, mother will love you.' James stood up and drained his glass, replacing it on the side table.

Izzy followed him down the staircase and out to his car, by now she was feeling quite relaxed and happy to take the meeting with Mrs Brodie in her stride.

Fourteen, Princess Crescent, Woolton. The home of James and Mrs Brodie. Now they had arrived. Izzy scrutinised the house as best she could in the rapidly developing dark. From the exterior, the house looked to be a comfortable, detached house. Somewhere from within the depths of the house, a scrabbling noise was heard, followed by an insistent bark. Manc, no doubt. James slipped his key in the lock and opened the front door. The minute James had set foot inside the hallway, from some back room, out bounded a medium-sized, rather scruffy-looking lurcher dog, which began to frenziedly bark and very rapidly wagged his tail. He then proceeded to gambol at James's feet.

From somewhere upstairs, Izzy heard a voice shout, 'Is that you, James?'

'Yes, I'm here with Izzy,' was James's response.

'Don't be intimidated by Manc, incidentally, his bark's far worse than his bite, quite literally! This is just a welcoming bark!'

Izzy squatted down and immediately began to stroke Manc, who like many dogs, revelled in and thoroughly enjoyed the fuss and attention.

Now that James had switched the hall light on, Izzy had a better chance to see the room in greater detail; mock, black-oak panelling lined its walls and the staircase leading to the upstairs looked to be rather high pitched and steep and appeared to give way to a deep, muted red landing and upstairs walls.

'James, I'm on my way down!' repeated the voice.

'Mother, let me help you!' James shouted in reply, and a minute later, an elderly, white-haired lady appeared, tastefully dressed in a dusky, pink cashmere jumper and loose-fitting, stretchy, black crimplene trousers. She looked to be approximately in her late eighties.

'Oh, hello Mrs Brodie!' Isabel greeted her warmly.

'Oh, please, call me Martina.'

James helped his mother down the stairs.

'This… This is my young lady, mother.'

'Oh, I've heard so much about you,' said Martina, 'please, come into our lounge and make yourself comfortable.'

James and his mother led the way in, with Manc capering at James's heels. Izzy carefully scrutinised the room. Strangely enough, it was very similar to the room she had imagined during her stay at her father's house, but the contrast between this and her papa's house could not have been starker. A roaring log fire burned brightly and cheerfully in the grate, and to the right of the brick fireplace, a bookcase full of volumes reached right up to the ceiling. A dark red, three piece leather-covered suite consisting of two armchairs and a three-seater settee comprised the sitting area, an elegant, deep pink and white striped wallpaper, almost exactly as Izzy had imagined it, lined the walls. A medium-sized television, currently switched off occupied the front left-hand corner and beautiful, sumptuous, blue brocade curtains, embossed with what looked to be a Paisley-like pattern blacked out the windows. Two tasteful paintings of central Liverchester graced opposite facing walls and a few family photographs completed the personal touches. The entire effect was finished off by a thick, deep blue carpet and the overall impression was one of superior taste, quality and cheer. Martina, assisted by James, parked herself in a comfortable armchair, Izzy chose an end seat of the settee.

'Izzy, would you like a gin? Do you know, I bought a bottle specially in honour of a certain very special young lady, just this Saturday at Tesco's in Woolton.'

'Oh, well yes, why, I'd not say no.'

'Consider it done,' answered James, 'And mother, what would you like to imbibe?'

'Oh, I'll just have a glass of red wine, please, Jim.'

As James vanished to the drinks cabinet which turned out to be in the room next door, Martina repeated to Izzy, 'You know, Izzy dear, I've heard so much about you, Jim's hoping to offer you a partnership, or so I believe.'

'Well, er, that may be a few years off yet,' answered Izzy modestly, 'I shall obviously have to prove myself first! Obviously, James will need to be absolutely certain that I'm real partner material.'

'Oh, I am sure you will be.'

Only too keen to change the subject, Izzy asked quickly, 'And how long has James possessed this hound?' She had only just uttered the comment, when she realised that she had asked James the very same question last week.

'About two months now. I have to admit, I was not too pleased when our Jim appeared with him that Friday evening, but since then, I've got used to him. We wouldn't be without him for anything now.' At that point, Manc charged over to Izzy and began to gambol and roll at her feet.

'I think he likes you,' Martina added.

'Well, I love all dogs, although I have to admit, I'm not much of a cat woman,' Izzy replied.

'No, I myself have always been a dog woman,' answered Martina.

Just then, James reappeared with the drinks and aperitifs.

'Here we are, mother, fresh from the local wine store in Woolton village. Pink gin for this young lady and a normal, dare I say it, white gin for myself.'

Another awkward silence descended for a minute or so, which James broke by adding, 'Well, bottoms up! Hopefully, this will be the first of many! And at this point, I would like to propose a toast… To friendship!'

Izzy walked across to Mrs Brodie and their glasses connected, James also rose and clinked his glass together with Izzy's and Mrs Brodies's. Izzy took a sip of the pastel-coloured liquid, it was a touch on the strong side, but at present, she felt too embarrassed to ask James for a top up of tonic water. When all three were resettled in their seats, Isabel uncertainly asked James,

'So, is this Barry business finally resolved?'

'Most certainly, yes,' answered James, emphatically. 'I still maintain that Bootle police are predjudiced against Barry due to his sexual tendencies, which in my book, is an absolute disgrace… Why, every person is entitled to a fair hearing regardless of their sexual inclinations.' Later on, Izzy came to realise the strange irony of that last sentence.

'Well, yes, of course,' answered Izzy and Mrs Brodie, almost in unison.

Izzy took another sip of her gin. In actual fact, the previous gin consumed in the flat, combined with consumption of the present stronger one now seemed to be taking full effect and she felt far less on edge and anxious than when she had first arrived at Princess Crescent. Nevertheless, thought Izzy to herself, that said, she had to refrain from, 'putting her foot in it.'

'Now, I've made venison casserole for the evening meal,' said Mrs Brodie, brightly, 'In fact, I spent most of the day making it, so I hope you both have good appetites.'

'And incidentally, that's one of the meals I enjoy best of all.'

'And, obviously,' continued Mrs Brodie, slightly guiltily, 'I had to give our Manc a helping also. He loves it too.'

James shot his mother a pained look.

'This dog, he now sleeps on silken cushions, doesn't he mother?' said James laughingly, '...One extreme to the other... Honestly, I don't know!'

Izzy and Mrs Brodie both began to laugh.

'But you wouldn't be without him now, and well you know that!' replied Mrs Brodie.

At this point, James got up and vanished into next door for further drinks. The next minute he reappeared with two bottles of gin which he deposited on a neat cane coffee table, complete with a glass surface top centrally based in the middle of the room. He then vanished again and re-emerged with a large bottle of tonic water and the bottle of red wine for Martina.

'Would you like a bit more wine, mother?' he asked Mrs Brodie.

'Don't mind if I do, love.' James obediently refilled his mother's glass.

He then turned to Izzy. 'Izzy, dear?'

'I could easily use a top up.' At which James slopped an extremely liberal measure back into Izzy's glass.

'James, that's enough! I'm going to be blotto!' answered Izzy, desperately reaching for the tonic bottle.

'Oh, you need to live dangerously sometimes!' said James casually.

'Well, here's to friendship, once again!' James repeated. Yet again, glasses connected.

Izzy was rapidly beginning to feel better as she took another sip of the gin, and then, beginning to lose her inhibitions, asked Mrs Brodie, quite boldly, 'So, Martina, were you employed in the legal profession originally?'

'Oh, good heavens, no,' answered Martina airily, 'No, I was a simple country girl from Ormskirk who took a Biology degree at the University of Birmingham, at the end of that, I then added on a P.G.C.E. certificate, and moved to Liverchester, but a year out of university, I met Bernard, that was Jim's father and he was earning his forty thousand per annum as a partner in the architect's practice he worked for, so when we married, I very happily dropped down to part-time work.

'And did you enjoy Birmingham?' Izzy enquired, rapidly feeling more confident by the moment.

'Well, yes, I did, but by the time I left after four happy years there, I was feeling quite ready for a change.'

'And of course, mother, once you were back in Liverchester, which was your nearest large town when you lived in Ormskirk anyway, you met my papa,' added James in his customary and characteristically heavy-handed tone.

'Now, James and Izzy, if you'll excuse me a moment, I'll just check on the casserole and see if it's anywhere near cooked.' With that, Mrs Brodie vanished briefly to the kitchen.

Silence descended between James and Izzy for a moment, which James eventually broke by saying, whilst beaming broadly, 'I've got the impression that mother really, really likes you, and after all, who could disapprove of a girl as nice as yourself?'

Izzy blushed a delicate shade of crimson, and at last she managed to respond by saying, 'Good. I'm so pleased to hear it.'

'Yes, the evening meal is served!' shouted Mrs Brodie from the depths of the kitchen, 'And we can now go through to the dining room!'

James led the way through to the back room. In contrast to the front lounge, the back room was yet again, tastefully decorated in a pale blue and white striped wallpaper, with a rectangular-shaped oak dining table standing squarely in the room's centre. Attractive paintings graced the walls and a few family photographs were carefully dotted about. Once again, a deep blue carpet covered the floor and dining chairs with blue silk seats and back rests were carefully pulled up to the table, indicating dinner for three tonight.

Again, what a stark and complete contrast to the back room at her papa's house! In both the rooms which Izzy had so far seen, the general atmosphere and aura was one of comfort, luxury, cheerfulness, affluence and innate positivity. On one side, French windows gave way to an elegant and well-proportioned conservatory, which itself in turn gave way to a small, neat and trim-looking garden.

'We call this room the blue room, for obvious reasons,' James explained, as he switched on a standard lamp in the right-hand corner of the room which proceeded to give off a gentle, soft, muted glow and then lit a few candles in the centre of the table.

'Both these rooms are so pretty,' answered Izzy, 'And I love the wallpaper, the elegant pastel-coloured regency stripes are beautiful!'

'Nice, aren't they?' answered Martina, 'We've lived here almost thirty years, but I came into some money my father gave me when he passed away, and at that stage the house needed quite a large amount of money spending on it, added to which the kitchen and bathroom required totally re- gutting and refurbishing. I saw the household renovations and improvements as adding on to and increasing the value of the property, so I was only too pleased to spend the money.'

'As I said before, mother, they were worth every penny you spent on them,' said James.

'Too true,' answered Mrs Brodie.

Martina's casserole was excellent, and Izzy even had a second helping. Needless to say, during the meal, Manc sat extremely close to James, in fact almost up at the table, and in order to satisfy him at least temporarily, James threw him a couple of thickly buttered bread rolls, which he gratefully bolted down.

'Well, that was all absolutely excellent, Mrs Brodie,' said Izzy when she had completed her second helping.

'Oh, please, call me Martina,' Mrs Brodie reminded her, and then she answered, 'Oh, thank you, dear, it's always nice to know that one's efforts are appreciated. But no need to thank me, that was an absolute pleasure.'

James took an additional few minutes to finish off his meal, and when he laid down his knife and fork on his empty plate, he uncertainly asked, 'Is there a pudding on offer, mother?'

'There certainly is. I bought lemon cheesecake at Tesco's in Woolton village yesterday. I'm not too keen on it myself, but I though you two might both enjoy a piece.'

In retrospect, reflected Izzy later on that evening, the meeting and meal with Mrs Brodie had gone extremely well and not been half as bad as she had initially envisaged. Both James and Izzy opted for the cheesecake, every mouthful of which, Izzy relished. On completion of the cheesecake slices, James announced that he would take Manc for a run in Woolton park, and Isabel offered to help with the clearing away and washing up.

'No need to help with washing up, dear, that's just not required, we've got a dishwasher, but you can help me clear the plates and cutlery away and stack the dishwasher, if you wish.'

'Yes, with pleasure,' answered Izzy.

James connected Manc to his lead, and man and hound vanished through the front door. Izzy began to clear away the plates and cutlery and took them into the kitchen. Similarly, the kitchen, like the other two ground floor rooms, looked to have had no expense spared on it whatsoever. What looked like pine wooden cupboards lined the walls, below which the effect was complemented by neat, cherry- red wall tiles. For a few moments, an awkward silence seemed to have descended between Isabel and Mrs Brodie, which Mrs Brodie eventually broke by saying, 'Do you know? I'm so very pleased James has got himself a young lady as nice as yourself, at last after all these years!'

'Well, that's really nice of you to say so, and thank you.'

'Not at all, dear… The pleasure is all my own… The pleasure is entirely my own. In actual fact, James could have done with meeting up with you at least ten years ago.'

'Oh, really?'

'Yes. Of course, so much of the time he's been so shy and so busy at work, it left no time for romance and affairs of the heart. He met Alison in his late twenties, and when she died, that really sapped his confidence, but you, Izzy, you've done him no end of good, in fact, he's almost a changed man.'

'Well, I'm really pleased to hear that,' Isabel replied.

'And you see, I'm not so young either, I'll be ninety in early November, so it's obvious I won't go on for ever,' continued Martina, 'I was getting so worried, endlessly thinking to myself, 'If only our Jim could get himself a nice, decent young or middle-aged lady,' and now he's found one!'

'Seriously, Martina, I'm only too pleased to care for James,' answered Izzy, 'he does make me happy, and I feel as though we may have a future together.' Although as Izzy later herself recalled, 'May' was indeed, very much the 'operative word,' to express it in legal terms.

'You know, I'm absolutely certain of that, dear!' answered Mrs Brodie.

Presently, James and Manc returned. At that point, Izzy remembered the present she had bought for Mrs Brodie a few days ago at Lees department store, safely stored in the glove pocket of James' car, and before Izzy left she gave Martina the box of Crabtree and Evelyn's 'Gardenia' bath soap and matching shower and bath gel, which luckily Mrs Brodie loved and appeared at any rate, to greatly appreciate.

'Now,' said James absently when he had safely returned Manc to the house and released that hound from his lead, 'We need to get you home safely, and I think I've consumed far too much booze to drive safely tonight and I want to see you safely back home to the flat.'

'I should think you have,' Mrs Brodie tut tutted.

'I know, I'll order us a taxi, then once you're safely home, I'll flag another taxi down on Upper Parliament Street, or thereabouts and come back here.'

James promptly 'phoned for a taxi on his mobile. Ten minutes later, a radio cab arrived into which both Izzy and James piled.

Relief began to rapidly envelop Izzy, as she sat close to James in the taxi and he gently held her hand. She had successfully got through her mighty ordeal.

'Would you like to come in for a small nightcap?' Izzy ventured to ask James as they approached her flat.

'I would love one.'

Once again, up the rickety, creaky staircase and back into the Percy Street flat.

'That was an absolutely marvellous evening, and you did so well, Izzy. I'm so proud and pleased with you.'

'And I'm so pleased I didn't disgrace myself or put my foot in it!' answered Izzy emphatically, and then she added, 'And your mother's really nice, she obviously went to so much trouble to make us a really excellent meal tonight, I just really do hope she enjoys her present.'

'Oh, she will, without doubt. It's alright, I'll not stay long, and you know me, my intentions are strictly honourable.'

'Yes, I'm certain they are.'

Izzy glanced at her watch. Ten past eleven. It was still reasonably early.

'Would you still like your night cap, or would a strong coffee be more in order?'

After a few minutes careful consideration, James chose the coffee option. Izzy decided to do the same. There was now another vague worry steadily coursing its' way through Izzy's brain… Was James secretly expecting to be asked to stay tonight in the flat? And if so, could he sleep on the settee? There was only one way to express this, and the gin and wine had singularly loosened Izzy's tongue, furthermore, to cap it all, at that moment it all suddenly came abruptly spilling out. 'James, darling, it's getting late. Would you like to stay here tonight?' There, she had now said it, for better or worse. They were two lonely people together.

James was silent for a minute and then he answered, 'Yes, I would love to. I'll sleep on the settee, oh, or in the spare room if you've got one.' Izzy thought of the spare room, it was clean and the bed made up, but it was full of her mum's clutter.

'Well, I have got a spare room, but it's full of my mother's things. Can you face the settee?'

'Of course I can. I'll just 'phone mother to tell her I'm not coming back tonight, but don't worry, Izzy, love, I shall be gone at eight a.m. tomorrow morning,' answered James, producing his mobile from his jacket pocket. He began to 'phone, and the next thing Izzy heard was, 'Mother, thank you for an absolutely marvellous evening, I've decided after careful thought to stay at Izzy's flat tonight, so I'll see you in the morning.' A slight commotion seemed to arise at the other end of the 'phone, to which James's reply was, 'Now don't start expostulating, mother! I'm going on Izzy's settee in the front room!' Izzy was unable to help secretly laughing to herself, and James's next response was true to form, when Izzy heard him reply, 'You know me, I'm always the perfect gentleman, and you know full well, my intentions are honourable.'

Izzy found the bedding from her airing cupboard and still smiling to herself, made up James's bed on the settee. They were just about to retire to their separate bedrooms when Izzy, her inhibitions by now well and truly rinsed away, decided that she ought to ask James into her bed. 'This is just silly. You might as well share my double bed.'

How many unmarried women down the years had been intimate with their partners in those rooms before? Well, that night Izzy Jackson-Talbot was the latest one to be added to the list.

Chapter 11.

Izzy was gathering her things together at approximately quarter to five the next day. She had seen neither hide nor hair of James that day and he had vanished by the time she had surfaced from her sleep at eight o'clock that morning. In fact, as Izzy scanned and scrutinised the lounge that morning, the only item to indicate that a visitor might have been present the night before was James's used coffee mug from last night, sitting on a side table. Izzy would wash the mugs up, once she arrived home. According to Ben, he was spending one last day working from home, and just as Izzy was debating the prospect of leaving chambers, she began to get the impression and sense the feeling that her grandmother was once again speaking to her, or, what was rather more to the point, chastising her. And nor was it good.

'…You ought to be ashamed of yourself! Is it really asking too much to observe the, 'no sex outside marriage rule?' I really am extremely disappointed in you, young lady… And to think of how I brought you up… A decent, respectable, middle-class Catholic girl!'

Oh, don't be so straight-laced, grandma, thought Izzy to herself. 'Besides, I thought you altogether approved of James, yes, James Brodie, partner solicitor and commissioner for oaths!'

'Yes, I did, but I think it may now be time to revise my views on that particular young sir, besides, I'm thinking he may be a bit on the old side for you, young lady… Fancy a sugar daddy, do you?'

If truth were known, something along those lines had been haunting Izzy for the best part of the day. She had to admit, she was feeling slightly unclean, and now guilt was also added to her array and jumble of emotions. Just as Izzy was actually in the process of leaving chambers, who should appear at chambers' front door, but James, armed with files.

'Oh, hello, dear!' said James pompously. 'That was an extremely agreeable evening!' he added, sounding very like one of Izzy's uncles.

'Yes, it was!' answered Izzy, for a moment at a total loss for words and almost struck dumb. Then something flashed through Izzy's brain which she thought she might dare to ask James.

'Was your mother alright with you, when you got back this morning?'

'Oh, yes. She was a bit frosty for the first ten minutes, but she came to. Incidentally, mother believes I used the settee all night, so I didn't like to correct the impression, I simply thought it might lead to yet further trouble… She's absolutely riddled with Catholic guilt.'

'I didn't know you were R.C… Incidentally, so am I.'

'Yes. Didn't you see the silver/gilt crucifix we have in our lounge?'

In retrospect, Izzy did recollect that she had noticed a rather pretty, delicate looking crucifix on the wall above the fireplace at Princess Crescent, but on her initial arrival at the house she felt too stressed and under pressure to fully realise and appreciate the implications of what that might mean. Well, that was something else they had in common.

'Do you practise?' James asked.

'Yes, I certainly do. Do you?'

At this point, Ben appeared at the opened door of his inner office.

'Oh, I'm sorry, am I interrupting something?'

'No, not really,' answered James, 'Er, young lady, could I buy you a drink and we'll continue this conversation in Rigby's?' Then, being the gentleman that he intrinsically was, he added, 'You're very welcome to join us, in say, twenty-five minutes to half an hour?'

'That's an offer I can't refuse, and thank you,' was Ben's response.

'Oh, and you, Tanya, come over the road in half an hour, over to Rigby's?' James added as an afterthought.

'No, thank you, Mr Brodie, but thank you for the invitation, I'm actually going out clubbing with my cousin.'

'The answer to that, young lady, is yes I do practise. I'm an every Sunday morninger, eleven o'clock in the cathedral.' James led the way to the left hand bar, and added, 'You make yourself comfortable and I'll get you a gin.'

When James returned, he was proudly bearing two glasses of gin, neither of which were pink, but one James proudly told her was s special 'Liverchester Gin', brewed at and on the Rigby's premises in central Liverchester.

'No, seriously,' said James when they were comfortably settled in Rigby's back room, 'mother really likes you.'

'Does she regard me as the femme fatale of your chambers?'

'No, of course not!' answered James airily.

'Thank goodness for that!'

'No, mother when she came round from her initial frostiness said eventually, 'Look, Jim, love, I'm only being like this because I don't want you to get badly hurt. My response to that was, 'Somehow, I don't think this young lady will hurt me. Oh, and incidentally, due to the religious nature of mother she originally wanted to name me Dominic, but Bernard, my father, being an agnostic, greatly objected to the choice of name, I believe he thought it a little too redolent of the Church of Rome, but quite acceptable as a second name… So hence, those initials on the partnership letter headings, James Dominic Martin Brodie.'

'Oh, I wondered what the D.M. Brodie stood for,' answered Izzy.

'Oh, and Benjamin S.T. Watson; Benjamin Samuel Thomas Watson, oh and er, Izzy?'

'Yes?'

'Look, I'm not your average man, not by a long way, and last night, contrary to what you may believe I was not simply attempting to have my evil way, I regard our relationship as a serious and lasting one, and if you are really not comfortable about it and, well, er, would like to… discontinue the physical side for now, I will respect that decision, and furthermore, I'm quite happy, no, not quite happy, I'm more than happy to do so.'

Izzy was a little unsure of how to respond, so she quickly came to the conclusion that possibly the best way to answer was to simply, 'hedge her bets,' so after a silence of a couple of minutes, she answered, and this time, with a strangely new-found confidence, 'Shall we see the way in which matters develop?'

'I'm only too happy to,' James responded, and then he suddenly noticed Ben's approaching form beginning to materialise in the back bar. 'Oh, and here comes the man himself, our Benjamin,' he casually commented.

Benjamin purposely made his way across. 'Can I get you two anything?'

'Oh, just a glass of house red wine, please, Ben.'

'And yourself, young Jim?'

'I'll have the same please, Ben, just a house red wine, please.'

Ben vanished to obtain the order at the bar.

'And seriously, everything I've just said, I really did mean,' said James boldly, and at the same time he gave Izzy's left hand a small squeeze. Once again, cosy, happy coupledom was restored.

'I really do like your house, James,' Izzy ventured to say, 'And your mother's redecorated it very tastefully.'

'Yes, I think so too, I think, between you and I, mother had a strange fixation or fetish about striped wallpaper about twenty years ago… You know, she thought it looked neat and clean and the upstairs is on similar lines; my room is yellow and white striped and mother's is pink and white striped, of course, that blends well with the pink of the bathroom…' Izzy recalled the neat, compact, pastel pink, Twyfords bathroom suite, complete with back-to-wall, hidden toilet cistern, neat shower combined with bath and washbasin units, the effect of which was complimented by cream tiles, as she had had reason to use it on one occasion yesterday evening. Yes, it was a pleasant, presentable, highly acceptable bathroom by the strictest of critics' standards.

'Oh, and the two spare rooms are similarly clad in purple and white stripes and again, pink and white stripes, so… We've plenty of rooms for guests,' James added as an afterthought. 'It really is a nice, comfortable house.'

At this point, Ben reappeared from the bar, equipped with liquid refreshment.

'Well, and here's to friendship… Bottoms up, eh?' Ben announced.

Izzy began to snigger to herself, since the use of this phrase recalled the occasion last night when James had employed it, when dining with Izzy at Princess Crescent.

'What are you laughing at?' Ben laughingly asked immediately.

'Oh, nothing really. James here, also passed the exact same comment when we dined at his house yesterday evening.'

'Well, you see, great minds always think alike,' replied Ben.

'Oh, yes I did,' James answered rather vaguely, and then abruptly changing the subject, he said, 'And I'm hoping that possibly, in a few years, this young lady will be joining us as a partner.'

Izzy felt a little embarrassed, and she managed to say in answer, 'Oh, are you sure? Do you really think so?'

'I don't think so, I know so,' was James's confidant response, 'And just think, we will then be a three man and woman partnership,' he took a mouthful of the wine and then added, fast warming to the theme, 'Brodie, Watson and Jackson-Talbot, it has a nice ring to it – James Dominic Martin Brodie, Benjamin Samuel Thomas Watson and Isabel Jane Jackson-Talbot, as the said partners. No, we couldn't run this here partnership without our Izzy, so this is to be her reward. And mightily well- earned, I might add.'

'Oh, thank you, James,' Izzy managed to reply.

'Just as you wish,' was Ben's rather subdued response, as he took a mouthful of his pint of beer.

'Yes, that sounds good,' James repeated, 'Brodie, Watson and Jackson-Talbot in embossed gold lettering… Personally, I never was too keen on the name of Brodie myself, far too similar to Brady, as in Ian Brady and also infamous, due to Deacon Brodie, the body-snatcher in Edinburgh, but coupled with Watson and Jackson-Talbot it has a strange, acquired, 'je ne sais quoi' about it…' He took another sip of the house-red and then added as a casual afterthought, 'Perhaps we could even market ourselves under the caption, 'Whatever your legal query, Brodie, Watson and Jackson-Talbot can be guaranteed to fight your corner, be it divorce settlements, personal injury matters, clinical negligence, conditional fee agreements, land and property disputes, conveyance matters, business advice and criminal issues… No job is considered too small or trivial and we assure you of a quality and professional service at all times.'

Ben turned to Izzy and said light-heartedly, 'Do you see, Izzy? He's at his best when he's had a skinful!'

'Yes, I was actually only too aware of that fact!' Izzy laughed.

In response to this comment, James laughed uproariously, and not in the least offended, he answered good naturedly, 'Precisely. It's when I lose all my inhibitions.'

He took another liberal mouthful of the house-red and then commented, '…And of course, there's one individual we won't be employing in a hurry…'

'And that is?' Ben asked, trying to probe for further information.'

'What's his name, Izzy? That rather obnoxious individual who's always boasting and gets everyone's goat?'

'Oscar Talbot.'

'The man himself,' answered James in his customary heavy-handed manner, 'No, we won't be employing him!' At this point, he took another mouthful of the house-red, this time draining and emptying his glass, and then adding for further emphasis, 'And I'm head of chambers, so I know best.'

'Furthermore, I think he intensely dislikes Northerners… Although God knows why!' Izzy commented.

'Well then, there is absolutely no way on this earth that we will ever employ him!' answered James resolutely. 'Incidentally, would anyone like a top-up?'

'I'll not say no, James, love. Another house red, please.'

'Pleasure,' answered James in his characteristic style, 'Consider it done. Now, my good Benjamin, what would you like to consume?'

'Oh, just a pint of Rigby's best, please.'

James lurched to the bar, threading his way through the assembled crowds.

'Well,' said Ben, when James was out of earshot, 'All seems to be hunky dory between you two… Good, I'm so very pleased.'

'Well,' said Izzy casually, deciding now was about an appropriate time to change the subject, 'I need to write to my father tonight, I think he's expecting me to pay him another visit in the not too distant future, which I don't really feel in the mood to, at least, not yet.'

'You've got the perfect excuse,' answered Ben, 'Say the chambers can't manage without you, and furthermore, that's at least partially true.'

'Plus, my half-sister, Gwyneth, absolutely hates my guts and had an enormous row with me down the 'phone, a verbal altercation, which I might as well tell you, she initiated, so for obvious reasons I'm not exactly desperate to go.'

Ben laughed contemptuously. 'She'll just be jealous of you, there's no mystique about that. Incidentally, what's your half-sister's job?'

'Oh, she's currently out of work, and was trying to start her own knitwear business. I might also add, she didn't finish off her degree course at the University of Warwick.'

'Well, there you are,' answered the savvy Ben, 'I'll just drink this second pint and then I'm off home; I don't want to incur Lilian's wrath by arriving home late for my evening meal.'

'Oh really?' asked Izzy.

'Most certainly yes… Rules me with a rod of iron, she does.'

Izzy suspected that this in reality, was not the case at all. After all, Ben had previously told Izzy that they had completed twenty-seven extremely happy years. It was nothing more than a front he presented to the outside world. Izzy began to mentally envisage what she needed and wanted to do with the rest of her evening. Surprise, surprise, Lady Gertrude's diary entries were once again calling. Ben took another mouthful of his beer.

'So is your daughter settling in well in Glasgow?' Izzy asked.

'Yes, I think so. She found the first three weeks a little difficult and could only manage by coming back to Liverchester Friday nights, but she now seems to have taken to university life like the 'proverbial duck to water.'

'I'm pleased to hear it.'

'…And her work seems to be going well, she seems to be getting decent grades for her essays, and needless to say, she loves the strobe-lit cells that seem to form Glasgow night life.'

'Well, being a student wouldn't be being a student without some clubbing,' answered Izzy, draining her wine glass.

'Too true… Takes me back to when I arrived at the University of Newcastle, I think the first two terms largely passed in oblivion, then I came to the conclusion that I might be asked to leave if I didn't do a modicum of work.'

'You didn't did you, get asked to leave, I mean? Surely not?'

'Oh no, I'm highly relieved to say. No, luckily it was a case of, 'All's well that ends well,' a safe two/one; an average percentage of sixty-three, I think I managed… That obviously, was more years ago than I care to remember.' There was something quite endearing about Ben, Isabel thought to herself; he was an extremely capable, competent partner, yet so modest and self-effacing.

At this juncture, James returned with the latest round of drinks.

'What, er, what was more years ago than you care to remember?' James asked.

'Oh, nothing really. When I was a student at the University of Newcastle.'

'Right, bottoms up? Yet again, dare I say it?' answered James in reply.

'Yes, this does seem to be getting a bit of a habit, doesn't it?' Izzy laughed as she raised her glass in response.

'Oh, that's the name of the game at Brodie and Watson's,' said Ben, 'so you might as well learn that as soon as possible.'

'Yes, I'm quite sure of that.'

Presently, Ben stood up, muttering something about needing to attend to the calls of nature. When Ben had vanished, James lowered his voice and moved slightly closer to Izzy and said, 'What

I intended to say before Ben arrived was, I'm only too happy to wait until this relationship is on a, how can I say it? A regular footing. In other words, for the time being, I'm more than happy to go with the wishes of my lady fair.'

'Well, that's very nice of you, James. I always knew you were a gentleman.'

Once again, James reached slightly across and took Izzy's free hand.

'And you see, you have mother's seal of approval… Why, what more could you need?'

Izzy laughed, slightly anxiously. She was still feeling the pull of wanting to return to Lady Gertrude's diary, yet she managed to say quite boldly, 'I think I'll just finish this glass and then it's probably time I was making tracks, I've a few things to do this evening.'

'Just as you wish, dear. I suspect that I may now be over the limit, but Ben's not, I'm sure he'll quite happily take me home. Well, it's either that or a taxi.'

Presently Ben returned from the gents.

'Izzy's going to leave us after this glass,' James explained, 'She has a few things to do at home.'

'Yes, like write to her father, for example?' asked Ben.

'Oh, don't remind me!' muttered Izzy, 'I haven't got the slightest idea what I'm going to write yet.'

'No, I did get that general impression.'

'Just say to him that you're being corrupted and most certainly being led astray by those couple of horrendously debauched partners that you work for,' said James.

'Well, you never know,' answered Izzy non-commitally, 'I may just do that.' She casually glanced at her watch. Quarter past six. Had they already spent an hour in Rigby's back bar? The time had absolutely flown past. She took another mouthful. A quick dander through the shops, a rapid tour of Sainsbury's for the week's essentials and then, at last, the pearls of wisdom which flowed so freely from Lady Gertrude's pen, and Izzy had been unable to fully enjoy the writings yesterday evening, since she was feeling entirely pre-occupied with her impending rendezvous with Mrs Brodie. Izzy took one last mouthful and drained her wineglass.

'Right, gentlemen,' she said reaching for her handbag, 'I must love you and leave you now. I don't, after all, want to outstay my welcome!'

'You, darling? Outstay your welcome? Never!' James answered emphatically.

Izzy blushed. 'Goodbye, James! Goodbye, Ben!' With that, she began to pick her way through the still present crowd. After a brief visit to the ladies' toilet, she then left the bar for the evening.

Half an hour later, after a brief and unproductive visit to the shops, Izzy returned to her flat. In the depths of her flat freezer, she found a ready-made meal and set to work to heat it up. Yet again Lady Gertrude was exerting her extremely magnetic effect. Strangely enough, very little was recorded for Thursday, 10th October, 1886, with the exception of the following terse entry:

Thursday, 10th October, 1886. An exceptionally uneventful day, with cold, foggy weather, and today, strangely enough, I find myself with almost next to nothing to write down. 'Tis a time to really batten down the hatches. I feel as though I need to focus on attempting to be a better person. Possibly, I may be able to try to put this into effect when father and I do our Christmas visiting and distribute our Christmas presents and pre-Christmas bonuses to our estate employees.

Oh, and my marvellous brother, Harry, will be returning from Leeds next week for his Christmas holidays, so I shall have the perfect excuse to ask him about, 'life and times' amid the urban temptations of Leeds… What an exciting town!

Contrary to what Izzy had earlier believed, there were no entries whatsoever for Friday, Saturday or Sunday, the 11th, 12th or 13th December. Izzy returned to the top of the page to ascertain the other contents of the website. She clicked on 'gallery.' Sure enough, the portraits of Lady Gertrude were exactly as Izzy had begun to imagine her nineteenth century role model. A girl with delicate, well- proportioned features and a cascade of long black, gently undulating hair materialised on the laptop screen, piercing blue eyes and a smiling mouth, wearing what looked to be a dark green velvet dress. Below the photograph of the full-length portrait, an explanatory note clearly specified that the lady in question was, 'Lady Gertrude Rivers, on her 21st birthday.' The painting below that portrayed Lady Gertrude in an equally sumptuous red, silk ball dress, doubtless one of the series of dresses which Gertrude had lately referred to in her diary entries and formed part of the collection newly arrived from Harrogate. This time, Lady Gertrude lovingly cradled a rather cheeky looking black and white Springer Spaniel on her knee, without doubt her beloved Scamp, and according to the explanatory notes the portrait was, 'Lady Gertrude Rivers, at the age of twenty-two.'

Izzy then returned to the diary entries.

Monday, 14th December, 1886. What a day this has been! Father and I, assisted by my stepmother began our Christmas visiting, and I will quite freely say that I really enjoyed it. I do so like to help those less fortunate than myself. Yes, we just about managed to get round the entire estate to give out the Christmas fare: This comprises turkeys, joints of bacon, beef, gammon and mutton and extra fuel bundles for their fires… There is one thing for certain, our employees will go neither cold nor hungry at Christmas (in fact, they rarely do the rest of the time!) And additionally, we also took along some of the marvellous pies and puddings which our resident cook works almost night and day to produce and is famous for. My papa is very highly thought of amongst his estate employees, in fact, at the last cottage we visited, we were told by the man of the house that he was, 'A master in a million!' I know he is certainly a papa in a million!

Just in time, Izzy remembered her evening meal and retrieved it from the electric oven. She had only just placed it on a plate and was locating a knife and fork to eat it with when the 'phone started to ring out. Izzy went next door to answer it.

'Hello, Liverchester, 707 4396!'

'Oh, hello, dear.'

'Oh, hello, James, love. Did you manage to get home safely? I'm sorry I rushed off, but I had a few things to do at home.'

'Oh, yes, I got home O.K. Ben very kindly took me.'

'So, are you at home now?'

'Yes, and you can be certain of one thing, at any rate, no booze is crossing my lips, for the time being at any rate.'

Izzy laughed, 'Well, thank goodness!'

'Oh, er, Izzy?'

'Yes?'

'Er, I was thinking of our next romantic rendezvous. Now, when I got home I scrutinised the holiday entitlement allocation list. But you've still got three weeks and two days so far untaken holiday – I'm assuming you'll want to take some over Christmas, and I've got some time as I've so far taken nothing this year yet. So, I was wondering whether I could meet you next week during the daytime, I know a marvellous little restaurant on the Wirral, which I'm sure you would enjoy!'

'James, you know I would love to.'

'Excellent! So incidentally, which days would you like to take as paid holiday?'

Izzy had a rapid mental debate with herself, then she thought to herself that it would be quite nice to take Wednesday off along with Monday of the week after, which meant if she went back to Cumbria Friday night, she would only need to leave Monday lunchtime and could consequently spend Monday evening resting, relaxing and preparing for Tuesday back in the Liverchester flat.

Suddenly, this all seemed quite exciting and furthermore, she scarcely knew the Wirral!

'Well, James, can I take Wednesday of next week off and Monday off the week after?'

'Yes, with pleasure. You know, dear, I do so miss you when I don't see you; so, I shall also take Wednesday off this week, it'll be a blessed release from all this preparation for the flippin' Barry business.'

'Yes, I can imagine.'

'Oh, and have you managed to do it?' James suddenly enquired.

'What, exactly were you referring to?' Izzy queried.

'Written to your father.'

'Oh, don't remind me! I only wish that I had.'

'Incidentally, mother sends her love.'

'Oh, how nice.'

'So shall I call at the Percy Street flat, say, Wednesday morning at a mutually convenient time?'

'In which case, it won't be too early, not from my point of view. As you may well know by now, I'm never at my best in the early morning.'

'No, I do understand. I likewise. Although I now have to get up early every morning, seven days per week since Manc needs his morning run.' This comment was met with further laughter from Izzy. 'Anyhow, you will be sure to love this lovely little Italian restaurant in Oxton village, and we could also go to the sculpture park overlooking the River Dee estuary before we dine.'

'James, that sounds marvellous.'

'Say, eleven-thirty?'

'Yes, that sounds good.'

'Yes, we'll speak soon, dear. I shall have to leave you now, mother's calling me and Manc needs his dog food! Goodbye, dear!'

'Goodbye, James.' Izzy replaced the receiver. She took her plate and cutlery over to the laptop and continued to scrutinise Lady Gertrude's writings.

Tuesday, 15th December, 1886. A singularly unremarkable day which was extremely cold and swept by searingly bitter, chilling, biting winds. Another day to, 'batten down the hatches' and stay warm.

Wednesday, 16th December, 1886. I can scarcely believe it, it is just eight days to pass until Christmas Eve, and I have to admit that already I feel so excited! But Gertrude, stop it! Stop it here and now! That is no way to live, you should enjoy everything as it comes along, and remember, do not wish your life away!

Once again, I went with papa to Leeds, where I am extremely pleased to say that I completed all my Christmas shopping, we wined and dined again at our usual venue quite royally, papa donated very generously yet again to the Poor and Destitute of Leeds Benevolent Fund, true to form is was a liberal amount too and dare I say it, he collected the special, pre-ordered items from Mr Summers's shop. Papa has given me very specific instructions that they are not to fall into my possession until 24th December, in other words, Christmas Eve! That is no problem for me, since I am more than happy to wait. I somehow suspect that this will be our last visit to Leeds, this year.

During the early evening on our return from Leeds, I further entertained myself with the writings of Charlotte Bronte, and according to various individuals in our family the writings of her younger sister, Emily Bronte are also quality works and equally well-written.

I was then called away from my reading by my stepmother, Alice, and our entire family was entertained for at least the next two hours by the Mummers' play. Of course, refreshments were provided for the performers afterwards in the Great Hall, and overall, an excellent performance was staged.

Thursday, 17th December, 1886. Another bitterly cold day and another uneventful one at that, with the exception of one occurrence. A mystery parcel arrived for me by the special delivery post which papa informed me needed to be placed safely and securely away out of harm's reach and also needed 'to go away for Christmas.' I had just a brief glimpse of the packaging this morning, and the writing I simply did not recognise and was totally unfamiliar with, although whoever has addressed the parcel, at any rate, knows me well enough to be aware of where I live, and furthermore, I rather think the little packet bore a Leeds postmark. Oh, my goodness! A thought has just this instant occurred to me! I do not like to think too much about this, since it may be tempting fate, and obviously I shall be held in suspense until Christmas Eve, but do you think it could be from my marvellous, dashing Lord Ernest?

The remaining two days of the week passed uneventfully and on Friday, Izzy returned to Cumbria to spend the weekend with her mum. Izzy was half-way home, when in fact the thought was suddenly driven home to her that if she was to enjoy a lasting, serious and enduring relationship with James, then she would have no alternative than to tell her mum, Edith about the presence of James in her life. She was also going to need to tell her father about her relationship with James. After all, Izzy reasoned to herself, it would be a little unkind to simply abruptly announce her engagement out of the blue to a man neither of her parents had either met or knew anything about. Perhaps she could gradually introduce the subject of James that evening. That evening, supper-time came and went uneventfully and still Izzy had said nothing. In fact, Izzy was just again debating with herself how to explain the presence of James in her life, when the matter was entirely removed from her hands by the 'phone quite abruptly deciding to alert it's owner to the fact that it was still fully functioning.

Edith went to answer it.

'Oh, Izzy, there's someone for you on the 'phone... Sounds really nice.'

James without doubt. Izzy went to take the call.

'Oh, hello, dear. I just wanted to know you'd got home safely and in one piece.'

'Well, I have and thank you for 'phoning.'

'Not at all! Incidentally, I'm really looking forward to our sortie onto the Wirral on Wednesday.'

'Yes, so am I.'

'And the restaurant, you know you will really love it. It's named, would you believe it, 'Fresh!' It really does live up to its' name. Just think, we've been a couple for almost a month now, young lady.'

'Yes, that thought had actually just also occurred to me.'

'And the sculpture park,' James added, quickly warming to the theme, 'I'm not really into sculpture, well actually, not at all, but I do love the views across to the hills of North Wales, it's very atmospheric. Mother and I sometimes go for our Sunday lunch to the restaurant, it's so good and then we often take Manc for a run in the park afterwards, he loves it! Oh, and this is by the by, we'll take Manc with us on our travels on Wednesday, after all, I don't want to leave him out now that I've got a young lady.'

'Oh, no,' answered Izzy emphatically, 'We certainly don't want that.'

'Er, Izzy?'

'Yes?'

'Was that your mother?'

'Yes, you mean Edith.'

'She sounds very nice and I'm hoping I'll be speaking a lot more to her in the not too distant future!'

'Well, er, yes,' replied Izzy, a little uncertainly.

'Well, I'll leave you now, and leave you two to enjoy some quality time together. Oh, and by the way, mother sends her love, she really approves of yourself.'

'Good, I'm so very pleased to hear it.'

'Yes, very much so. She said she thought you were a very special young lady.'

'Oh, how very nice.'

'Do you know? Mother actually told me she was actually becoming really worried about me, wondering what was going to happen to me when she passed away; she really wanted me to find a nice, decent, appropriate young or middle-aged lady, after all, mother's not as young as she once was!'

Izzy suddenly remembered the conversation she had had with Mrs Brodie when she had helped to stack up the dishwasher.

'Yes, your mother did actually tell me something about that this week when you were taking Manc round the park.'

'At any rate, you enjoy the rest of your evening, and we'll speak again very soon. Goodbye!'

'Goodbye!'

Izzy turned round to walk back to the fireside.

'You don't mind me asking, but who was that? He sounded very nice,' asked Edith, rather tentatively.

'That was Mr Brodie. My employer.'

'Izzy, your eyes are shining. Is there, er, something you haven't told me about?'

'Were they? I wasn't particularly aware that they were.'

'Izzy, will you just answer my question.'

'Oh, alright. If you really want to know, I've been seeing James, Mr Brodie,' Isabel quickly answered, 'for almost a month now. He's one of the partners at Brodie and Watson.' There, she had said it.

'Well, he sounded really nice,' replied Edith, 'And how old is this James?'

'Well, he's rather a lot older than me,' by now, Izzy was beginning to feel acutely embarrassed. She desperately wished that she had kept quiet.

'Come on, how old?' Edith continued to probe.

'…Twenty-four years my senior.'

'Oh, Izzy! Well this time, you really have got yourself a sugar daddy!'

Izzy laughed uneasily and she presently became acutely aware of the stark realisation that James was closer in age to Edith, than he was to herself.

'Mother, he's really nice, a real gentleman and it's not remotely serious. At any rate, not at the moment.'

'Are you sure?'

'Most certainly. And now, I would like to leave the subject of James Brodie and focus on my free time. Oh, and incidentally, I don't need to go back this week until Monday afternoon.'

'Oh, marvellous!' Edith responded.

Later that evening, the subject of James did reappear, and Izzy explained to Edith about James's previous one and only lover, Alison, her untimely death and the fact that he lived out in Woolton with his mother and a stray dog he had picked up from Liverchester Animal Rescue Centre. Izzy then spent an uneventful two days resting and relaxing at home, during which time she actually managed to write a brief letter to her father, remaining at home until Monday afternoon when she then began to wend her way back to Liverchester.

Once again, the moment Izzy set foot in the flat, true to form, Lady Gertrude's diary was again calling. Surprise! Surprise!

Friday, 18th December, 1886. Another rather boring day, and an intensely cold one. I am persevering with my reading for my probationer nursing.

Saturday, 19th December, 1886. We dined royally on venison casserole, I believe it is one of our cook's specialities, freshly culled from the estate, for our evening meal. I might also add that my dear brother, Harry, entertained us with his tales of life and times amid the urban fleshpots of the great city of Leeds. I get the general impression that some of his behaviour whilst in town is certainly a little suspect and questionable, and without doubt, drinking until the early hours of the next morning appears to play a large part. What a character he is!

Sunday, 20th December, 1886. Again, an uneventful day, apart from the fact that we attended church in the morning. I laid aside Jane Eyre since I had finished reading it, and turned my attentions to Emily Bronte's 'magnum opus,' Wuthering Heights. I have to admit, I find it's beginning a little slow-moving, but nevertheless, I shall continue to persist with my reading of it, since it appears to be extremely well-written.

Monday, 21st December, 1886. We began to make our final preparations for the festive season, which I feel really quite excited about. Furthermore, Harry again entertained us all with tales of his exploits and escapades in Leeds. At one point, he was mildly chastised by papa, who was obviously reflecting on the financial consequences from his own viewpoint, but this failed to deter 'Our Harry' from further boasting.

At this point, Isabel's reading was abruptly shattered by the 'phone ringing out. Probably James or her papa, no doubt.

'Oh, hello, Izzy dear.' It was James.

'Oh, hello, James.'

'Hello, darling. I just wondered what sort of a day you'd had. In fact, it was quite boring and routine in chambers today, just not the same without you, Tanya had to go home early at four-thirty with a stomach bug and vomiting, and that's just about all that transpired today.'

'Oh, really?'

'Yes, just about. Oh, er, Izzy?'

'Yes?'

'Would you mind excessively standing in for Tanya tomorrow in chambers; you know, 'twill be full trainee and paralegal pay, but general secretarial and receptionist duties.'

'Yes, with pleasure.'

'Good. I know I can always count on you. My goodness, where would I be without yourself?'

Izzy laughed.

'No, I mean it,' James persisted, 'And what's more, I'm really looking forward to our day out on the Wirral.'

'Yes, so am I.'

'So, dear,' asked James in reply, 'What are you doing at present, I'm sorry, please forgive me, I very possibly shouldn't be asking a question like that?'

'Oh, not at all,' answered Izzy breezily, 'I'm just messing around on the internet and then I shall prepare my clothing for the morrow and the day's work ahead of me, then eventually I shall nip out to Hannah's Bar for a couple of glasses of red wine, or even, dare I say it, I might really push the boat out and have a couple of cocktails.'

'That sounds like an excellent idea. Do you know? You seem to be like my mother, she's a devotee of red wine.'

'Well, you know what they say? Great minds think alike.'

'Too true.'

'And James,' asked Izzy, 'Are you doing anything special right now?'

'Well, not really, apart from the fact that it's almost G and T time, or will be in about ten minutes – normal, white, transparent gin, of course. And then, mother and I will have our evening meal.'

'Well, you enjoy it, and I'll see you tomorrow morning in chambers.' Goodbye, James!'

'Goodbye, dear!'

So, Izzy was facing a boring day ahead of her in the morning. But right now, it was Hannah's Bar time, so she disconnected the laptop and made her solitary way down to Hannah's on Leece Street.

Sure enough, the next day passed uneventfully and unremarkably enough with filing of old correspondence, coffee-making and answering the 'phone making up the bulk of Izzy's day, so that by five in the afternoon she felt well and truly ready to leave. Before Izzy left chambers, she thought it wise to inform James of her impending departure.

'Right, James, I must now love you and leave you and I'll meet you at eleven thirty tomorrow morning!'

'You will indeed!' answered James, 'Well, at any rate, I shall look forward to our meeting up tomorrow morning, goodbye, darling!'

'Goodbye, James!'

And with that, Izzy closed the door to James's inner office and went out into the noisy hustle and bustle of Dale Street.

After a brief wander through Liverchester One, Izzy began to make her way back to the Percy Street flat, where she treated herself to a lengthy hot bath. A rapid rummage through the freezer for a meal to prepare this evening and then it would back to Lady Gertrude's diary.

Tuesday, 22nd December, 1886. Yet again, an uneventful day for the most part, except for the fact that we distributed Christmas presents to our estate employees, and then the latter part of the day, we were fully occupied in making the final preparations for our own festive season! The Christmas season is so almost upon us, I can scarcely believe it!

Izzy had just retrieved her own meal from the microwave, when the telephone abruptly rang out, shattering the peace and calm of the first floor flat. Either James or her papa, doubtless.

'Hello, Liverchester 707 9643!'

'Oh, is that a person?' asked a heavy-handed voice at the other end of the 'phone, 'At least I hope it's a person!' It was her papa.

'Oh, hello, papa!' Isabel answered uneasily, not quite knowing exactly what to anticipate.

'Well, I just want to thank you for your previous epistle, which I read with great pleasure.'

'No, the pleasure was all my own, father.'

'Now, I was simply going to say that should you want to spend some time with us over the next few weeks, you would be extremely welcome to do so.'

At this point, Izzy felt acutely embarrassed and at a complete loss for words. After a brief and rather tense silence, Izzy finally managed to utter, 'Well, I shall need to see how my work progresses.'

'You see, you're always welcome at our house.'

'Good. And father, have you been up to Settle, lately?'

'No. But, dear, if you decide to grace us with your presence over the next few weeks… Er, well, I shall arrange for us to have a special outing up there.'

'That sounds good.'

'Obviously, I shall need to check my diary, since I have visits to both Norwich and Manchester to make in the immediate interim time.'

'Yes, I fully understand, papa.'

'And, I would also like to come up and see you some time… Well, er, maybe in Liverchester or even up to Cumbria.'

'Well, Liverchester is obviously going to be easier for me.'

'Oh, I don't really like Liverchester,' answered her father, a touch dismissively. To a person like Izzy who loved Liverchester, her papa could not have made a worse, more unfortunate comment.

'Well, that's rather a sweeping statement,' Izzy replied, feeling slightly shocked and aghast.

'But that road to the airport, dear, it's so grotty!'

'Well,' Izzy answered calmly, 'That's true, but that's not to say that the whole of the town is like that, no, most certainly not. Not by a long way.'

'You know, I think we're going to have some really good times when we next meet up,' answered Izzy's father, purposely Izzy suspected, attempting to change the subject.

'Yes, I think so too.'

'At any rate, I will need to check my diary. Oh, er… I think I'm being called… So I shall have to love and leave you.'

'Goodbye, papa.'

'Goodbye, dear.'

With a deep-seated sense of relief, Izzy replaced the receiver. Why did her father dislike Liverchester? Was this simply all due to the fact that the road leading to the airport was grotty? Well, that was so absurd! The immediate environment around many airports were often quite unpleasant, but that was not to say that the entire town was equally unpleasant and nasty!

That evening, after her evening meal, Izzy met her friend, Francoise at Hannah's Bar for early evening drinks and they made loose plans for meeting up the week after to go out clubbing for the evening, after which, Izzy wandered homewards and back to her flat on Percy Street. When she returned to the flat, her 'phone was persistently bleeping with an answer 'phone message. '… Er, Izzy, dear, pity I couldn't catch you tonight, I'm just looking forward to meeting up with you tomorrow morning… Goodnight!' Needless to say, it was James.

On receipt of that, Izzy crawled into bed with the company of her hot water bottle, and within a few minutes, she was soundly asleep.

The next morning at ten thirty, Izzy was sorting through her wardrobe, attempting to find something she considered, 'appropriate,' for her date with James. Fortunately, it did not take her too long at all, and she selected the new, jade green M and S linen blouse and the black, relaxed fitted jeans. Somehow, Izzy had the feeling that 'smart/casual,' was the order of the day. She then proceeded to make up her face with a minimum amount of make-up, a brush of her hair, rapid blasts of perfume from the reduced counter at Boots, the Chemist behind each ear and on each wrist and she was now ready to go. At precisely eleven-thirty sharp, James presented himself. Sure enough, his strange- looking dog, Manc was curled up on the back seat and greeted Izzy with a raucous bark.

'Now, don't be scared, dear,' James advised her, 'That's a welcoming bark, as I've said before. And I might also add, you look beautiful.'

'Oh, thank you. How nice of you to say that.'

'Not at all. It's yourself who is doing me the honour.'

'Well, hopefully we'll have a nice day,' answered Izzy, feeling it was time for a change of subject.

'Of course we will, we always have good times together,' replied James, emphatically.

Once they had arrived at the park, James released Manc from his lead, who proceeded to promptly charge off into the middle distance, looking neither to right nor left.

'Oh, James! This is a really beautiful little spot, I never realised either quite how impressive the views are!' The park faced towards the Irish sea, and was backed by blue, low-lying hills in the distance.

Yes, and very atmospheric it is,' answered James, 'mother and I love spending Sunday afternoons here.'

'Do you know?' said Izzy in response, 'this has renewed my interest in the Wirral peninsula as a whole. I rather think it was created during the last ice age by glacial activity, when a tongue or fragment of the ice pushed out into the Irish sea.'

'Yes, it was something like that.'

'I've always enjoyed local history, and I do find discovering the origins of places interesting.'

'Yes, I enjoy local history too,' was James's response.

Izzy was beginning to notice that James and herself kept discovering hobbies and interests they shared in common; and as Izzy reminded herself, this could only be good.

'Have you heard from your strange cousin, you know, Oscar, who gets everyone's goat?' James enquired presently.

'Well no, and I'm not sure I particularly want to, either!'

'Not wanting to be nasty, but he really does sound like a prize burk.'

'Yes, that's right; he is,' answered Izzy, at which point, she found herself starting to laugh.

'Well,' said James resolutely, 'you can be sure of one thing, there's no job for him at Brodie and Watson's!'

'And I have to admit, I'm relieved to hear it. Just imagine, him employed at Brodie and Watson!' Izzy looked across to the hills of North Wales. For many years now, she had always loved the area round Conway with its' ancient castle and quaint, medieval gatehouse. Then, rather uncertainly, she asked James, 'Just think, James, we could have a short break over in Conway, I remember going there a few years ago and I was absolutely captivated by it. We could find a nice hotel and spend a bit of time there.'

'I hadn't thought of that. But yes, I would love that, yes, let's do that. I'll check the holiday entitlement folder when I get home. Honestly Izzy, you really are so good for me.' Somehow, Izzy had the feeling that this could certainly be the case.

At that point, Manc abruptly bounded back to James, his pointed ears flying wildly.

'My goodness, Manc! I almost thought I'd lost you for a moment!' said James, as he bent down to stroke the errant hound who was by now bouncing and frolicking at James's feet. 'And it's nearly time for lunch, shall we make our way to the restaurant?'

Izzy beamed in assent, 'Yes, what an excellent idea.'

James had ordered a table a few days previously, and Izzy found herself running an approving eye over the restaurant premises, décor and furnishings. Cream walls arrayed with tasteful paintings led the eye to neat yellow tablecloths and the dining area was lit by a gentle, muted lighting.

'Mr Brodie?' asked the waiter.

'Er, yes, I ordered a table for two a few days ago.'

The waiter proceeded to lead the way to the reserved table.

'Well,' said James when the waiter had departed, 'this is turning out to be one of the best days out I've had for quite some time.'

'Good. That's so nice to hear.'

'And how are matters progressing with your father?' James asked.

'Well, to be absolutely honest, not too good at present.'

'How so?'

'Well, we talked on the 'phone, now when was it? Oh, just last night. Would you believe it? He launched into a tirade about not wanting to come to Liverchester because he hated it, especially and in particular, the road that leads to the airport. Well, admittedly, the road leading to the airport is not too pretty, but that's not to say that the entire town is ghastly, I mean think of the Georgian quarter where I live and the streets leading down to the Pier Head! It's absolute nonsense!'

'Well, he's wrong!' answered James vehemently, pushing his glasses further up his nose, with his left middle finger, and then proceeded to add, 'I've never heard such rubbish in my life.'

'Too true. My feelings entirely.'

'So for that sole reason, he's fallen out with you?'

'Well, I'm not entirely certain, but I'm beginning to suspect that he might also have taken great exception to some of the things I've written in my latest communication to him, and yes, I did say I thought he was wrong about a couple of things. But after all, we live in a democratic society, and in any event, I'm entitled to my own views.'

James laughed. 'He who has to be obeyed and never contradicted, eh?'

'Precisely.' At this point, the waiter appeared and asked James if they required drinks. James ordered a bottle of Beaujolais.

'Oh, and he wants me to spend further time staying at his house, which I've probably already told you; so maybe he's not fallen out with me. But to be honest, I would rather have our short break to North Wales.'

'Now that, young lady, sounds rather good.'

The waiter returned with the ordered bottle of Beaujolais. James carefully swirled it round his glass, and then sampled a sip of it.

'Excellent! And if you could please fill the young lady's glass.' The waiter obediently filled up Izzy's glass and then left them to debate over the menu.

'I'm already looking forward to our North Wales holiday,' said James confidently.

'Yes, so am I.'

'Well, here's to our North Wales holiday, darling!' And with that, James tapped his glass against Izzy's.

'To our North Wales holiday,' Izzy replied, 'And just think, we could drive down to Barmouth one day and go for fish and chips, I think the fish is specially line caught and freshly hauled from the Irish sea.'

'Oh, really?' asked James, as he took another mouthful, 'Oh, er, and Izzy?'

'Yes?'

'Be it separate rooms or sharing a room, I really don't mind at all, I'll leave that to yourself to decide, I'm entirely easy,' said James, dropping his voice a tone.

Izzy took another sip from her glass. 'Oh, James, you really are so good,' Izzy managed to utter in response. She had to admit, she was still a little undecided on this particular topic, so she would leave its' cogitation until a little nearer the time.

'No, not at all. It's you who are doing me the favour and honour of being my young lady.'

'Well, I'm delighted to be so,' Izzy replied. She carefully began to scrutinise the menu.

James reached out and gave Izzy's free hand a little squeeze. Izzy decided on the sirloin steak. 'A wise choice, dear. I had the sirloin last time mother and I dined here, and it really was extremely good. Mother had the sausage casserole and she found that excellent too.'

'So, James, have you decided?'

'I think I'll also have the sirloin.'

'So do you dine here regularly?' Izzy asked, taking another mouthful from her glass.

'About twice a month. Incidentally, the puddings are also rather good, the apple pie is absolutely first-rate, and so are the strawberry meringues.'

'MMMMMmm, that sounds good.'

'Oh, and as I said before, we will under no circumstances whatsoever be employing a certain young gentleman named Oscar Talbot.'

Izzy laughed and conceded, 'I know it's wrong, but thank goodness! Quite frankly, I don't like to think what he'd get up to if he worked for Brodie and Watson; make a few catastrophic errors I should imagine, like undertaking to clear a client's mortgage for them with insufficient funds present in the client account… Well, he has been known to.' At this point, the waiter appeared with pen and paper poised, ready to take the order, but James managed to stall him by a further ten minutes.

'Really?' James persisted, his eyes widening in sheer horror as he took another mouthful from his wine glass.

'Oh, yes. Boast, boast, boast. That's Oscar Talbot for you. Sorry, I know this doesn't sound too nice, but the problem is, he's such an irritating person. Apparently, he's also had a fall-out with two of his other cousins.'

'And who are they?'

Izzy drained her glass, at which James promptly refilled it.

'Their names are Simon and Angharad, and they both live in South Wales. Simon's a G.P., and Angharad, his older sister, did Biochemistry at Cambridge University and now has a job in publishing.'

'Well, those two must be clever.'

'Yes, they are.' Izzy took another mouthful from her glass.

'I would have loved to have been a G.P.,' said James rather wistfully, 'and talk about a worthwhile job; but sadly I'm no use at Maths or scientific subjects. At any rate, I like to think I'm the next best thing.'

'You're not good at scientific subjects?' queried Izzy.

'No, not at all. I had a real struggle to pass Biology 'O' level with a grade 'C' pass. I might also add, my mother was a Biology teacher as you may well already know, but she was unable to help me a great deal.'

'I'm exactly the same. I never enjoyed scientific subjects myself.'

'That's something else we have in common,' laughed James.

'Yes, it is.'

'And did you say something else about Oscar now trying to obtain a mortgage?' asked James, in complete disbelief.

'Yes, I may have already said, but I can't for the life of me imagine how he will get one, especially at present, since he only has a temporary job.'

'Nah, that'll be the day!' laughed James.

'And I'll bet you he's getting heavily into debt. You know, buying expensive furniture, designer clothes, an expensive, posh car, you know, all that sort of thing.'

'Is all he cares about his image?'

'Yes, it seems so at present, anyhow.'

'Silly, shallow boy!' answered James.

At that point, the waiter reappeared, attempting to once again take their order.

'Are you ready to order, sir?'

'Yes, we'll have two sirloin steaks.' After further questioning concerning James and Izzy's preferred degrees of cooking, the waiter vanished to the kitchens with the order. After a silence of a couple of minutes or so, James broke the silence by quite unexpectedly saying; 'Somehow, I never, ever for a moment thought that I would ever have a work-based relationship. Never in a million years, in fact! Well, I mean at one stage I was seeing Alison, but we were not employed by the same chambers.'

'No, to be absolutely honest, nor me.'

'And of course, why, I always thought that going round eyeing up colleagues, was, er, well, strictly unprofessional.'

'So true,' answered Izzy, 'my feelings entirely.'

The comments James had just made about unprofessionalism summarised her own feelings in a nutshell. Quite possibly she and James had far more in common than Izzy had initially envisaged.

'But, of course,' James continued breezily, 'you're a bit different yourself.'

Izzy smiled and after she had taken a mouthful from her glass, she responded by saying, 'Well, I like to think that I am. According to Edith, that's my mum, I get all my unusual qualities, of which there are many, from my papa.'

'Oh, really?' asked James, and then he added quickly almost as an afterthought and abruptly changing the subject of conversation, 'Please, dear, if you really don't want to go to your papa's again, just make the excuse of work, and it is at any rate, at least partially true; the chambers can scarcely manage effectively without you. Besides, I don't want it to interfere with our short break to North Wales.'

'No, I don't either.'

'So, Izzy,' James enquired, 'Did you say your cousin, Oscar Talbot is always boasting?'

'Oh, yes, boasting with a capital 'B.''

'Don't worry, we are not in the habit of employing individuals like the likes of him, and furthermore, we never will be.'

'Good.'

'And I can't imagine him going down very well with our Benjamin, either,' said James, matter-of-factly, and then added, 'Ben hates people like that, about as much as I do.'

'I do so like Ben,' Izzy answered, 'there's no pretence about him, he's just a case of, 'What you see is what you get!''

'Yes, excellent man, and I'm so lucky to have him as a partner!' commented James, and at this point, he took a bread roll from the basket sitting on the table, buttered it quite liberally and threw it to Manc who was neatly and compactly curled up beneath the table, and who instantly and gratefully bolted it down. 'Oh, no! I've really done it now!' James grumbled, 'He'll now never stop trying to snatch food!'

Presently, the waiter returned with the ordered food.

'Now, young lady, and future partner, I do so hope the steak meets with your approval.'

Izzy cut into the meat, and gingerly took a mouthful. Needless to say, it tasted excellent.

'Future partner, eh? I would never have imagined that a few years ago,' said Izzy casually, and then added as an afterthought, 'Please don't go telling Oscar 'Boasting' Talbot, otherwise he will want one too.'

'Do you know? I think I am quite rapidly becoming allergic to that young gentleman.'

Izzy thought it now might possibly be prudent to change the topic of conversation, and steer it as fast as possible away from Oscar Talbot.

'So, James, have you lived in Liverchester all your life?' Izzy probed.

'No, I'm from Stockport, near Manchester originally. I moved over here when I was, what? Fourteen. My father, you see, got the chance of a partnership at an architect's practice over in Liverchester. It took a while for us to settle in, but then we found we far preferred Liverchester to Stockport, and with my mother having worked for a few years in Liverchester and coming from Ormskirk, it really was like going 'back to her roots.'

'So, a popular move then?'

'Most certainly. You know me – I've always been a bit of a solitary, shy, lonely character.'

Izzy took another mouthful from her glass; she somehow had the feeling James was building up to telling her something. Eventually, Izzy could cope with the suspense no longer, and she managed to say, 'James, do you have something to tell me?'

'Yes. When I finished my legal training, I had, er, well, other aspirations.'

'Which were?'

'I studied for eighteen months in Durham... Yes, you've guessed it... I was busy with my priestly studies.'

Izzy took a sharp, abrupt, intake of breath, and at that juncture, she once again could almost hear her grandmother speaking to her, 'Well, how appropriate!!! A decent, respectable, middle-class Catholic girl... This becomes better by the moment... Take him, Izzy, you won't do better than James Brodie!! Oh, and incidentally, don't feel guilty about the fact that James left the seminary, why, it all occurred years before you met him!' Quite true, Izzy reminded herself.

After silence of a couple of minutes, Izzy managed to say in response, 'James, it's quite alright with me... So, how were your parents about it?'

'Not good. Father ranted and raved. 'You can't do that! You'll end up stuck on your own and growing old. My response to that was, 'No. It means I'll just grow old with the Almighty. I'm perfectly happy to dedicate myself to Him. As far as I'm concerned, those men who run our parish have chosen the better part, like Mary in Martha and Mary.'

Izzy laughed uneasily.

'Anyway,' James added casually, 'this all transpired years ago, why, it was before I met Alison, and that was quite some time ago, too.'

'Yes, I believe so,' Izzy answered.

They spent an extremely agreeable further three-quarters of an hour finishing off their meals, whereupon James asked to see the desert menu. Similarly, Izzy ran her eyes down the mouth-watering list of puddings. Izzy chose a raspberry meringue and James opted for a piece of apple pie.

'No, if you really don't feel in the mood to visit your papa, I would just say, as I've said before and furthermore, it's partially true; the chambers is unable to manage without you. Oh, and er, Izzy, if you do decide to spend a few more days with your papa, will I be able to 'phone you each night like I did last time?'

'Yes. You're extremely welcome to do so.'

'Good. Well, in the event that you do go, I'll speak to you every night.'

Presently, the waiter returned to take the orders.

'This has been such a marvellous meeting up, James, I really have enjoyed it.'

'Not at all, it's me who should be thanking yourself.'

'And we seem to be getting to know each other better every time we meet up, James,' Izzy added.

'Too true. I'll need to check the holiday entitlement folder when I get home. Then, of course, we can start to plan our holiday to North Wales.'

'Yes, that sounds good. I feel quite excited about it already.'

James asked for the bill as they finished their puddings which the waiter then duly brought.

'Well, how much was it?' asked Izzy a little uncertainly. James inspected the bill, with his characteristic, myopic and pernickety scrutiny.

At last he said, 'Fifty-six pounds, eighty pence – worth every penny!'

Izzy attempted to do some rather feeble mathematics, and came to the conclusion that she probably owed James twenty-eight pounds, forty pence, approximately.

'How much do I owe you, James? Twenty-eight pounds, forty pence, or thereabouts.'

'No, I will pay the whole bill, I don't want anything, and I mean it. I absolutely insist. After all, it's not every day I get into the company of a young lady as nice as yourself.'

Izzy instantly coloured and managed to respond by way of answer, 'Oh, thank you, James.'

They took one last drive past the sculpture park in order to take one last look at the hills of North Wales.

'…Just think, we'll be spending some time over there in the next few weeks,' James casually commented.

'Yes, and I really am looking forward to it.'

Chapter 12.

*T*uesday, 22nd December, 1886. *A particularly uneventful day. We finally completed our preparations for Christmas. To be absolutely honest, there is one small matter which is giving me a great deal of worry. Papa has not heard from Lord Ernest. At times, I really do feel as though the worry is driving me mad.*

Somehow, I have this sinking feeling in the pit of my stomach that Lord Ernest and I are simply not intended to be romantically linked at all.

Wednesday, 23rd December, 1886. Yet again, a boring day, but nicer and more liveable with in terms of the weather; bright, cold and clear. And furthermore, still no word from Lord Ernest. Perhaps we would have spent more time together already, had we intended to be together. Yes, I am almost ninety to a hundred percent certain that Lord Ernest regards me as a silly, immature little girl far too young for him.

Scamp and I went for a good, long, winter walk through the woods, and my dear brother, Harry told me that Scamp required further training, especially and in particular in the walking-to-heel department. My marvellous little Scamp charged on ahead until he reached a bridge crossing a fast-flowing stream in a small clearing, in the middle of some woods on the estate. Scamp really was doing so well, in fact, until he had progressed half-way across the bridge, whereupon he quite abruptly stopped dead, right in the middle, turned round and trotted back to myself.

'Oh no!' I shouted.

'He really is the most useless dog!' muttered Harry, quite venomously this time and proceeded to inform me that a certain particular hound was fit for nothing better than being tied up in a sack and drowned! Of course, according to papa he did not really mean this, in fact, papa believed this to all be part of a 'front' which Harry presents to the outside world, i.e. that of being a, 'hard man of the world.' Well, as far as I am concerned, a certain dog can sleep on silken cushions and eat the finest food on our estate, well, not quite. I will not offer him caviar or smoked salmon.

Thursday, 24th December, 1886. Christmas Eve. The most magical, special, best and precious day of the year. Again, the weather was bright, cold, crisp and clear. Typical Christmas weather, you could almost say!

This lunchtime, we dined rather frugally and sparsely on a selection of cold meats, largely saving ourselves for the banquet in the great hall tonight… What an event that will be! My younger half siblings, Edward and Rachel, are already becoming so very excited! In fact, I remember both vividly and very clearly throwing myself at the grand staircase in Riversdale Hall, almost falling over and losing my balance, the Christmas Eve when I was ten, on being informed that there were surprise presents hidden and secreted all over the house! My goodness, I was a character! That was nine years ago, and I am now almost twenty.

So far, this is turning out to be the best Christmas I have ever had. This evening, after a selection of aperitifs, we progressed to wine, obviously, it is our own estate bottled; the Christmas Eve meal cook prepared for us was excellent and we all seemed to enjoy every mouthful, whereupon my excellent papa and Harry retired to the smoking room in order to sup on the port. In fact, my half-brother, Edward, says that he is very much looking forward to being a little older so that he can similarly consume port after dinner. Quite the young gentleman he is!

We then, of course, progressed onto, and I really mean this, the absolute best and most marvellous time of the entire Christmas celebrations after the first-rate, Christmas Eve banquet… Yes, giving out and receiving of presents and gifts!

Just before we began our formal gift and present-giving session, my papa, Lord Roger handed me the mystery parcel which arrived at Riversdale a few days ago. For the life of me, I was quite unable to even begin to imagine who should have sent me this little packet… At any rate, I opened the packaging, and what should it contain but a small, extremely delicate, simple gold crucifix, and it was accompanied by a note, penned in exquisite writing. This is what it read:

45, Queen's Square,

LEEDS,

West Yorkshire

My darling Gertrude,

I'm not quite sure you will welcome any further communication or contact with myself, but I wish to apologise for not visiting yourself or your papa before Christmas; I have been so extremely busy with business matters. At any rate, hopefully we can meet up some time during the new year. Again, I am sorry to have been so very remiss, and I also wish to tell you how much I have missed your smiling, benign, kindly and cheerful presence.

I now need to make it my new year's resolution to see you on a more regular basis, if, and only if, it is agreeable to yourself.

Your loving and ever devoted servant,
Ernest.

P.S. I hope the small crucifix meets with your approval. I purchased it from a rather 'down market' looking jewellers hidden down a dubious looking alleyway in Leeds City Centre.

Why, this is absolute music to my ears! This really has been so far the best, most perfect Christmas I have ever celebrated! Furthermore, hopefully, I would love to take our relationship to a higher level, and of course, hopefully there will be every chance of this when I move to Leeds in the early spring!

I now feel both excited and really happy simultaneously, if this is possible, which I think somehow it must.

All in all, this evening I received some marvellous and quite beautiful presents, the crucifix from my glorious Lord Ernest aside. I received a pretty, thinly-wrought gold ring from my papa, which really is a ring for all seasons and so very comfortable on my hand and an additional ring, slightly wider in gauge, but nevertheless a truly quality piece of jewellery… Of course, no prizes for guessing who the manufacturer is! The splendid Mr Summers, without doubt! What a man he is! Also equally precious were the books I received from Harry, I will get round to finding the time to read them at some stage. Yes, I most certainly shall, even though I do need to bear in mind that as from April onwards my time will be singularly more limited and restricted. My step-mother, Alice, gave me a bottle of perfume, the fragrance of which is quite enchanting and a bag of toiletries which comprises two tablets of expensive, highly fragranced soap, bath additives and lavender water, which she believed might come in useful when I am based in Leeds next spring. Needless to say, I was highly delighted with the gift – I really am a lucky person! As for my half-siblings, Edward and Rachel, I received from my half-brother two large notebooks, I suspect for me to write my diary in and from my half-sibling, Rachel, I obtained a year's supply of pens and general writing equipment… I will always find use for them, and I have to admit that I find the useful and practical presents almost as delightful as the decorative ones!

After our present session, Harry and papa retreated to the smoking room in order to consume the port, which they apparently did with considerable gusto! Of course, needless to say, they were both most certainly, 'the worse for wear,' in the morning! Oh, my goodness!

As far as my dashing Lord Ernest is concerned, why, I suddenly feel like the happiest young lady in the whole of Yorkshire, if not the entire United Kingdom. My cup feels almost well nigh full to overflowing. I certainly do need to write and thank him for his extremely generous Christmas present, wish him well for the new year and invite him to my twentieth birthday celebrations at the end of February. That, without doubt, certainly will be quite a 'party and a half.'

Friday, 25th December, 1886. Christmas Day. We attended church again this morning, and I think, to be completely and entirely honest, all of us adults were guilty of the excesses in which we over- indulged the night before, so none of us were exactly feeling at our best!

Since, like yesterday, it is another very special, precious day, I wore my new cherry red velvet ball dress and slipped Lord Ernest's crucifix around my neck, coupled with the thin gold ring which papa so very kindly gave me last night, along with the delicate silver bracelet which I purchased in Leeds for myself.

After the church service, I took my beloved Scamp for a brief walk and exercise along some of the estate roads and paths, especially those which are closest to the hall, since we did not envisage spending much time outside the house today. I do so hope that he has worked up an appetite for his Christmas Day lunch, for that is what he is going to get this lunchtime!

Once again, we dined quite royally in the Great Hall and I thoroughly enjoyed every minute of our family celebrations. Incidentally, papa promised to take me some time in the new year to York for the day, and having not spent any time in York whatsoever for at least the past ten years, I will be only too pleased to pass a day there. Hence, that will be a treat in store to look forward to.

The afternoon was again bright, cold and clear and until our dinner that evening, I once again entertained myself with the writings of the marvellous Emily Bronte. What a woman she was!

Saturday, 26th December, 1886. Boxing Day. What a Christmas it has been, so far! As far as I am concerned it has been the best one as far as my memory serves me! Yet another day of princely dining and consuming some exquisite wines.

I'd love to know about Lady Gertrude's experiences in Leeds! Izzy actually muttered to herself that evening. She, of course, had also spent an enjoyable day with James and now they were planning their first short break away together.

Presently, Izzy was sharply brought back to reality by the persistent ringing of the telephone. She reached over to answer it.

'Hello, Liverchester 707 4396!'

'Oh, hello. Er, is that… A certain person?'

None other than her own papa, Mr Kenneth Jackson.

'Oh, hello, father. Why, er, I thought you'd fallen out with me!'

'Now, why should I do that?'

'Well, I hadn't heard from you for a few days, so I was beginning to think I'd either written or said something out of turn.'

'If you had dear, I would have told you straightaway. I don't like to keep my nearest and dearest in the dark, so to speak.'

'Good.'

'All I telephoned to say was, in a month's time it will be my seventieth birthday... So of course, you're extremely welcome to join us for the general celebrations.'

At that moment, Izzy felt a sharp, abrupt, inexplicable sense of panic sweep across and envelop her... Her father's birthday celebrations! Why hadn't he told her earlier! The fact that she was now sworn enemies with her half-sister, Gwyneth and was this going to mean she was going to be unable to enjoy her short break in North Wales with James? Manners, thought Izzy to herself. Remember your manners. Given the nature of the new-found relationship between Izzy and her papa, Izzy felt somehow as though she were obliged to attend; after all, her father was a good age and nothing in this world could ever be said to be entirely certain. After all, how much longer he had left to live on this earth was a matter of pure speculation and anyone's guess.

'Yes, papa,' answered Izzy eventually, although admittedly, not entirely truthfully, and then added, 'I would love to come.'

'Excellent! And of course, you and I can have a day up in Settle. I know how much you love it up there.'

'So true.'

'Oh, er, and Izzy?'

'Yes, papa?'

'Could you do me a favour?'

'If I can, yes. What is it?'

'To be absolutely honest, I don't like all this formal 'papa' business, why it sounds like a Victorian novelist. No, I really, really want you to call me, 'dad.'

For at least thirty years, the name of 'dad,' for Izzy had been reserved for her grandfather, a quiet, sensitive, good-mannered, unassuming, hard-working Lancashire man; Edith's father, who had spent the bulk of his working life employed as a chartered surveyor. In fact, he had been quite the 'man of many parts,' and had himself been an extremely talented pianist and organist and a veritable maestro at the keyboard. Not surprisingly, due to the fact that Eric Talbot was known to all the other members of the Talbot family as, 'dad', Izzy herself, also used the very same title. My goodness, thought Izzy to herself, this really was going to prove difficult! Eventually, after a moment's silence, Izzy managed to respond by saying, 'Yes, with pleasure.'

'And at this point, my dear, I shall be forced to leave you, since I think Agnieska's shouting for me.'

'Well then, we'll speak soon, dad.' Izzy had to force herself to articulate the last word, and if truth be known, the very use of the word wrankled with Izzy and made her generally squirm.

The next couple of days passed quite uneventfully and Izzy was more than ready to return to Cumbria on Friday for two days' recuperation. In fact, when Izzy returned to the Percy Street flat on Sunday evening, her answer 'phone was bleeping with a new message. Her papa. Furthermore, he appeared to be quite excited about his forthcoming birthday. Yes, thought Izzy to herself, she would attend, but it was not going to be by any means with, 'a song in her heart.' It really would be a relief when her second sojourn in Huddersfield was behind her and safely relegated to the past. Izzy paid a brief visit to Hannah's Bar for a little liquid refreshment and then returned to Percy Street. Again, the call of Lady Gertrude's diary had to be answered.

Monday, 4th January, 1887. We spent a comfortable but uneventful New Year's Eve and day. Guess what? I actually managed to sum up the courage and will power to write and thank my exemplary Lord Ernest for his extremely beautiful gift… I am so happy with it! In fact, it is one of the most beautiful pieces of jewellery that I have ever owned in my brief, short span! I dropped the brief note in today's post, and hope that it reaches his charming presence soon. What a man! That said, I certainly do not intend to hang around desperately waiting, maybe fruitlessly, for a response! I still have a substantial amount of background reading to undertake and complete for my probationer nursing course and to which I am entirely committed; in addition to having much of my life still to savour, experience and hopefully to enjoy!

As I said before, we are now into a new year, 1887, which is a special year for me as I am due to turn twenty years old, in about eight weeks' time. Why, I think in the next few days, I will spend some time in planning my birthday celebrations.

Tuesday, 5th January, 1887. A savagely cold day with a biting, bitter cold wind chill and essentially and predominantly a day to stay safely indoors and keep warm. I took Scamp for his morning run and then a brief trot in the afternoon, after which I gratefully retreated back into our ancestral home, feeling greatly relieved that the stately, noble, four-hundred year old of pile of limestone is there to protect me. I am so lucky to have a beautiful, comfortable and secure base which I am able to call home. It is a fact which I should never forget.

Wednesday, 6th January, 1887. Yes, I've done it! What, you may ask is 'it'? I've started the plans for my twentieth birthday celebrations! Papa says that it will be quite a grandiose event. Already, I feel excited!

Thursday, 7th January, 1887. Guess what? Papa and I spent an absolutely enchanting day out in York, and due to the fact that I had not visited York for at least the past ten years, why, it was largely all new to me! We wandered down the charming ancient streets and walked round the Minster, imbibing and savouring the prevailing atmosphere of calm and serenity. I was intrigued by the late medieval architecture of the choir, and I believe there are guided walks available where the visitor is actually able to climb the tower; well, I have to admit that here my nerve fails me! Quite frankly, I am simply not able to climb the tower, much as I would love to.

True to form, we dined excellently at a local restaurant, both of us enjoying the beef and Yorkshire pudding… 'Twas good Yorkshire fare in every sense of the word!

Friday, 8th January, 1887. Another uneventful day, apart from the fact that I continued to make my plans for my forthcoming birthday and completed some further background reading.

Saturday, 9th January, 1887. Guess what occurred today? A most momentous occurrence! I received a reply, oh my goodness, I treasure it, and have already read and re-read it three or four times at least! It was a reply from my dear, gallant Lord Ernest thanking me for my communication which according to my exemplary fellow he himself thoroughly enjoyed reading. He hopes to visit us at Riversdale Hall very soon and has decided as his new year's resolution, to see me on a rather more regular basis! As far as I am concerned, he is just the best young man that ever was! Furthermore, he accepted my invitation to my twentieth birthday celebrations. Again, I feel so happy and so very excited!

Sunday, 10th January, 1887. Another quiet, unremarkable day; I completed a small amount of tapestry work which I rapidly tired of, and then resorted to Wuthering Heights, which I greatly enjoyed reading. I also managed to respond to Lord Ernest's missive which will need to be placed in tomorrow's post.

Monday, 11th January, 1887. Yet another singularly uneventful day.

At that particular point, Izzy's reading was again interrupted by the 'phone. She leaned over to answer it.

'Hello, Liverchester, 707 4396!'

'Oh hello, dear!' It was James.

'Oh, hello, James!'

'Oh, incidentally dear, I've just checked the holiday entitlement folder. You're still owed some holiday time, and that gives you time to visit your papa's, should you so wish; and we can also have our short break to North Wales.'

'Marvellous,' answered Izzy, envisaging Conway Castle with its' backdrop of romantic looking, mysterious blue hills; the expanse of Conway Bay in the foreground.

'Are you doing anything special right now?' James casually enquired.

'No, not really. Just flicking about on the internet.' Just then, James let out an almighty sneeze. 'Oh, excuse me!' he said, by way of explanation, and then added, 'You know, I don't think I shall be in tomorrow, I've got the beginnings of an almighty head cold, so it's probably going to be best if I simply work from home. You know me, I scarcely ever have time off and what's more, I rarely do anything by halves, but when I get a cold, my goodness, I'm good for nothing for days. Yes, I'm going to give myself at least two days off; if not a few more.'

'Yes, and quite right too,' replied Izzy, 'and I'm sure your mother will wait on you hand and foot.'

'Most certainly. Mother's very good that way.'

Once again, Izzy felt a strange, deep sense of relief.

'Oh, and if Tanya's not back, you may have to cover her job again. That said, pay will obviously remain at the normal rate.'

'Gladly.'

'Well, dear, I must leave you now. If, for any reason you wish to talk further, just give me a call on my mobile. Goodbye, darling!'

Izzy replaced the receiver.

Tuesday, 12th January, 1887. I am absolutely sick to death of my stepmother. Lady Alice Rivers! She really is one of the most vacuous individuals I have ever had the misfortune to meet! Yes, we have had a row, dare I say it? Or, a 'family disagreement,' so to speak. What was the disagreement about? My 'dear, so revered and respected' step-mother, and that I mean sarcastically, believes that I spend too much money and I will need to pull in and trim 'my horns,' when I am based in Leeds in three months' time! According to her, I spend too much money on luxuries! What a woman! She has no thoughts whatsoever in her head beyond scandal and the exploits of our neighbours. Why, the last original idea in Alice Rivers's head probably died of loneliness quite some time ago! At one stage, I will admit, I actually did like her, but certainly not at present, and I am so pleased to be leaving her company on a fairly permanent basis, which I shall be as of April onwards. In fact, I felt so provoked and irritated by her, that I told Alice with great glee that I would be only too pleased to fairly permanently remove my offensive presence from her sight and take refuge in what I have the feeling will become my spiritual home, i.e. the urban delights, pleasures and fleshpots of Leeds! At present, I really shall be only too pleased to leave Riversdale. In any event, in my absence, Alice Rivers may even begin to miss me.

Thursday, 14th January, 1887. Relations between my step-mother and myself have largely improved, although a slight, small rift still lingers and, for the most part, I have occupied myself with making grand plans for my birthday. Best of all, I received further communication from Lord Ernest, which of course, made today a very special, magical day! Without doubt, I shall treasure it along with his two previous epistles and I shall take it with me when I move to Leeds. They will be lovingly tucked into my suitcase before I even begin to pack my clothes!

Tuesday, 19th January, 1887. I chose some new dress material; a pretty, deep, powder-blue from the dressmakers in Harrogate. Apparently, the dress in question will be complete, made up and ready for my birthday celebrations in February. How exciting!

At that moment, Izzy decided to stop for a few minutes to read and re-read the latest missive from her papa, which she had received in today's post. He seemed desperate to meet up again with her in Huddersfield. There would be no escape from his seventieth birthday celebrations, it seemed. And the relations with Gwyneth, now that they were scarcely even on speaking terms? No, it was highly unlikely to be a particularly festive event! Izzy then paid a solitary visit to Hannah's Bar for a little liquid refreshment after which she made her solitary way back to the Percy Street flat and was easily back for midnight.

No James the morning after in chambers and strangely enough, how quiet it was without him and once again, Izzy was forced to acknowledge and face up to the fact she was able to complete her allocated tasks with a bizarre sense of relief! What a good team Ben, Tanya the typist and herself made!

After a brief sortie round Liverchester One and the shops on Church Street, Izzy was just a few paces from her Percy Street flat, when her 'phone bleeped with a text message. Text from James. It read:

Missed you all day, darling. I hope your day was better than my own... Why, I shall be counting the hours until I see you again. Love J XX.

Izzy had just set foot in the flat when the 'phone proceeded to ring out. Doubtless James, or alternatively it could be her papa.

'Hello, Liverchester 707 4396!'

'Oh, hello, my absolute darling!' It was indeed James. 'What a day it's been! I've been finding it extremely difficult to focus today due to my streaming cold, and I've missed your smiling, cheerful face... Oh, by the way, dear, have you decided to pay your father a visit?'

'Yes, I have. Although I shall come clean – it's not something I'm desperately looking forward to.'

'Well, don't worry, dear, it will soon pass. I shall 'phone you every night, most certainly!'

'James, you really don't need to.'

'Nonsense! I absolutely insist!'

'Well, thank you.'

'Not at all. Oh, er, and Izzy?'

'When you return from your papa's, well, er, I have something to ask you.'

Whatever did James want to ask her? Izzy scoured her brain for possibilities... The partnership was hers should she want and require it? No, surely not. James had already told her as much in previous conversations. James thought that it was now time that he moved into her flat? No, he was far too straight-laced and conventional for that, and besides, Mrs Brodie would never approve. No, never in a million years. Last of all, Izzy's mind eventually resorted to the inevitable. Did James have a marriage proposal in mind?

'James, what's all the suspense about? Could you give me some sort of clue what it might be about?'

'No… All I will say is, that's for me to ask and you to find out, and I might as well add, not until the time is right… Or approximately right.'

'Oh, Mr Brodie!' laughed Izzy, 'You really are a one!'

''Aint I?' laughed James himself this time. 'No, as I said before, this is for me to ask, but only when the time is right, which, I suspect it will be when you return from your papa's.'

'Don't worry. I'll not probe any further.'

'And very relieved I am to hear it,' answered James.

'How are you spending the rest of the evening?' asked Izzy.

'Well, the mighty Manc needs to go out for his evening run, and it won't be for very long with me feeling as grotty as I do at present. Then it will be back here for G and T's with mother and then time for our evening meal.

'Oh, that sounds nice and civilised.'

'Well, dear, I shall need to say goodbye soon, as I think mother's calling me.'

'Yes, we'll speak soon.'

'Oh, and I feel so grotty at present, I'm certainly not coming in tomorrow. Another day safely in doors, for me, I suspect is in order.'

'Yes, you spoil yourself.'

'I shall do that with pleasure, dear. Goodbye!'

'Goodbye, James.'

Izzy replaced the receiver. 'I have something to ask you, but only when the time is right,' resounded in Izzy's brain. It was fruitless to speculate, so Izzy dismissed the possibilities. Instead, she took refuge in Lady Gertrude's diary.

Friday, 22nd January, 1887. Another bitterly cold day and extremely foggy too. Nevertheless, it was especially memorable and special since I received another missive from my glorious Lord Ernest. Of his own admission, he freely states that he finds me an extremely delightful and charming young lady whom he would like to get to know better! All this unanticipated praise of me is quite music to my ears! That said, I firmly believe that possibly the best course of action is to, 'wait and see,' bearing in mind that a man as attractive and accomplished as Lord Ernest may have many women far suaver than me, only too eager to pursue him, and as far as Lord Ernest is concerned, 'little, humble old me,' is not really a serious proposition! I obviously do not wish to get hurt in any way by this man, so I had probably best retain a strictly 'open' mind. I had best reply to Lord Ernest at my earliest convenience.

Furthermore, I completed the final preparations for my birthday which is still just over a month distant! I ended the day by snuggling into bed and entertained myself with the writings of Emily Bronte. What enormous strength of character was shown by the Bronte sisters, living as they did such lonely, isolated and restricted lives incarcerated at Haworth parsonage. I am forced to admit, I find my own life a little solitary and limited at Riversdale, but I hope that that will all change when I arrive in Leeds.

The diary contained a few irrelevant and inconsequential entries which comprised Lady G's growing frustration and irritation with her step-mother's behaviour and the limitations and loneliness of Gertrude's life at Riversdale Hall, which Izzy proceeded to rapidly skim through. In fact, the next major entry of any note was 28th February, 1887.

Friday, 28th February, 1887. My twentieth birthday. What a party it is going to be tonight! I have already received some delightful presents! (Yes, even from Lady Alice, my step-mother!) Come on now, Gertrude, do try to be fair and give your step-mother the benefit of the doubt! Try not to be too judgmental. But I have to admit that it is so difficult sometimes.

When we were fully dressed for the evening, (of course, needless to say, I was wearing the new powder-blue ball dress, newly arrived from the Harrogate dressmakers,) we proceeded down to the Great Hall to begin the evening's festivities. Papa was already welcoming the guests as the Master of Ceremonies began to announce their names. It obviously goes without saying that best of all was my glorious and gallant Lord Ernest, what a man; so opulently dressed in his smart, black knee breeches, matching jacket, white cotton lawn shirt and elegant waistcoat of dusky pink watered silk. The sherry and wine flowed so freely, as did the music from the minstrel's gallery. My papa has quite clearly expended so much time, trouble, money and effort into attempting to make my twentieth birthday a memorable one… And go on, Gertrude, be fair, so has my step-mother!

The food was also excellent and yes, the cook did us proud. After our meal, Ernest and I enjoyed many a dance and I believe tongues began to wag freely amongst our guests; but I did not regard this as a problem, since I have already made my feelings for Lord Ernest perfectly clear and unequivocal; I greatly admire and respect him. Eventually, our evening, magical as it was, began to draw to a close, well, so must all good things; and eventually our guests began to depart.

As our guests started to leave and dwindle in number, my Lord Ernest told me that he must speak to me over an important matter. Furthermore, the matter in question required privacy. When we were alone together on the side terrace overlooking Hurrock Woods, Lord Ernest told me what I regarded as his sad and highly disappointing news!

'Gertrude, dear, this morning I received a telegram from my long-lost Aunt Ethel. She freely states that she has far more money than she will ever need, hence, for this very reason, she will pay for me to go on the 'Grand Tour of Europe' for eighteen months! This is such a generous offer, I fear I simply cannot refuse it!'

I have to admit, I felt singularly less than happy at the prospect, no, that is to express it mildly, in fact to summarise the current state of my mind at that specific moment, I felt absolutely devastated and shaken to my core. Quite suddenly and abruptly, my life is meaningless, or to put it in Shakespearian terms, 'full of sound and fury, signifying nothing.'

For a few moments, I felt numbed into silence and shock. This was just not the future I had envisaged for either of us.

'Oh, Gertrude! I'm so sorry!' Lord Ernest eventually managed to articulate.

At that moment, I could begin to feel my eyes rapidly welling up with tears. What should I do? Allow him to go, in which case, I might never see him again, or dissolve into floods of tears, presenting myself as dependent, needy and clingy. After a couple of minutes debating with myself I chose the former course of action. After all, I had to be strong, since I am ultimately a strong woman. 'If your aunt so wishes, you must go,' was my reply, 'and I hope you'll remember a girl who really loves you.'

'Oh, Gertrude! We can still stay in contact. We can write, at least once a month. This is such a chance for me! Once in a lifetime, in fact!'

'Yes, and I'm so happy for you!' I replied, although as concerns the latter part of the sentence, I was blatantly lying though my teeth.

Lord Ernest looked saddened himself, and as his tears began to flow freely, he gasped and stammered,

'This… This… Is just… Just so difficult!'

'Ernest, darling,' I managed to respond, 'provided we can stay in contact, I'm sure we can cope. I might as well go to Leeds, after all, there is little to keep me here now and I wanted to go to Leeds at any rate – why, those were my original, initial plans in the first instance!'

'Yes, you have to, dear, and besides, when I met you the first time you told me that you wanted to nurse in Leeds, which I thought was an excellent idea.' I cast my mind back to my first meeting with Ernest in the autumn of last year, and at that moment it seemed like almost a lifetime away.

'Ernest, darling, I shall be strong. You know me well enough by now; you know what a strong woman I am. When are you due to leave for the continent?'

'The end of next week.'

Just then, Lord Ernest found himself being called by a friend due to the fact that the carriage had just arrived at the front entrance to convey them back to Leeds. Wiping his tear-stained face, he sadly stumbled after the friend towards the carriage.

Once back in Riversdale Hall, I thanked papa for all the trouble he had expended and threw my arms round his neck. He really is the best papa any girl could ever wish for! The perfect birthday which has ended on a sad and poignant note! 'Tis a pity. I feel in a strange and peculiar way as though today I have grown up. I am now a grown woman, who has her share of both good and bad luck. Additionally, perhaps I was right in my original supposition that Ernest and I were simply not intended to be together.

Saturday, 1st March, 1887. When one feels in this frame of mind, it becomes extremely difficult to see the point or purpose of anything. Almost everything becomes an exercise in futility. I feel so furious and not exactly kindly disposed towards Ernest's Aunt Ethel. In many ways, I feel furious with Lord Ernest himself. He quite obviously does not intrinsically overly care much for me, otherwise he would never have agreed to go... Go to Leeds, Gertrude, and forget all about him!

The next morning I confided in my maid servant, Emma about the singularly unfortunate occurrence of last night, and furthermore, about my resolve which has now been forged more clearly than ever; to go to Leeds and forget Ernest, which incidentally, she believed to be an excellent idea. Here, I will quote her exact words:

'Ma'am, you do know what they say? They say that everything that happens to a person occurs for a reason, so therefore, it cannot be altogether bad!'

'So very true!' was my response.

'Go and get yourself to Leeds, ma'am... As I said before, what you need to do is to latch onto a rich patient or a member of the medical staff... I'm absolutely certain that Lord Ernest won't be the only man in your life very soon, you mark my words.'

I laughed mirthlessly, and wondered to myself whether I was ever likely to meet a man who measured up to the high, exacting standards set by Lord Ernest.

Sunday, 2nd March, 1887. I feel extremely vulnerable. I suppose every mortal is. Human beings are, by their very nature, vulnerable and subject to basic accidents of existence, bad luck and fate. Yes, the human being, with the innate capacity for acts of extreme self-sacrifice, and at the opposite end of the spectrum, the depths of selfishness and depravity. In fact, to quote Mr Shakespeare:

'Oh, what a piece of work is man!

How noble in reason, how infinite in faculty!'

The very real sense of rejection is biting into and crippling me. The feeling is extremely unpleasant.

And once again, Mr Shakespeare sums up the situation in a nutshell:

'Oh, that this too, too solid flesh

Would melt, thaw and resolve itself into a dew,

Or that the Almighty had not fixed his Canon

'Gainst self-slaughter.'

Yes, I shall be only too pleased to move to Leeds. I am certain that I would feel so much better if I could forget Lord Ernest Watkins.

Monday, 3rd March, 1887. Another bitterly harsh, cold and windswept day. I occupied myself with quietly completing yet further background reading for my probationer nursing and took refuge in the writings of Emily Bronte. I am grateful for both these worthwhile pastimes in my life, since in the absence of them, I might simply sit and brood about the planned departure of Lord Ernest!

Tuesday, 4th March, 1887. Now this really is the proverbial, 'turn up for the book!' Through today's post I received a lengthy epistle from the wayward Lord Ernest. This is how it read:

'My dear Gertrude,

I'm a little unsure how you will receive new communication from me, since I know how extremely upset and traumatised you were to hear my news that I shall soon be departing to travel to foreign parts.

At this point, let me stress that you have every right to feel angry and betrayed by my decision to travel and I only accepted the offer because

I believed it to be quite simply, 'A once in a lifetime's chance,' which would be highly unlikely to materialise and present itself again!

It is only a tour which lasts a mere year and a half, hence, I shall be back in no time at all!

In the interim time, what I would really like you to do for me is to apply yourself to the absolute best of your ability to your nursing studies, and also please enjoy the city of Leeds, with its' shops and many attractions, and if you meet another man, please do not carry a torch for me alone. I somehow have an innate and intrinsic feeling that you are worthy of a man considerably better than myself.

I am only too keen to write to yourself, but this can only occur when I am comfortably and securely settled in my first port of call. At this particular moment, I expect this will be the Alps.

I remain your devoted servant and send you all my love,

Ernest.

But was I ever likely to meet the likes of a man anywhere approaching Lord Ernest? Somehow, I suspected not. With a black, hopeless despair and deeply-rooted sadness, I crawled into bed and eventually I was unconscious.

Chapter 13.

Izzy spent an average sort of day in chambers and completed a holiday request form to cover the three or four days she intended to spend at her papa's home in Huddersfield. She then spent a further unsuccessful and fruitless three-quarters of an hour scouring Lees' department store looking for a birthday present. She eventually decided to buy an expensive pen, but refrained from purchasing it. No, she would buy it closer to the time that she was due to go. On her way home, she bought a small amount of basic food shopping at Sainsbury's and stopped off at Hannah's Bar for a glass of wine or cocktail. After a 'Tierra del Fuego' cocktail she returned to the Percy Street flat. If Izzy admitted it to herself, she was feeling anxious. For what reason?

If truth were known, two factors were fuelling Izzy's anxiety. The first cause for her worry was due to the impending visit to her papa's in Huddersfield, and her fairly recent verbal altercation with Gwyneth; the second source of anxiety was the result of the question which James was still to put to her. Eventually, after a few moments of mental turmoil, Izzy came to the conclusion that it was useless to speculate on either; she would simply take the visit to Huddersfield in her stride, come what may, and James's question? Well… That too, could be faced and coped with in good time, when as James himself had expressed it, 'the time was right.'

Later that evening, Izzy and her friend, Francoise spent a couple of hours in the Cavern Club which they both enjoyed, and Izzy was once again more than ready to return to Cumbria to spend the weekend in recuperation. But before her evening, once again, the pull of Lady Gertrude's diary began to exert itself on Izzy.

Wednesday, 5th March, 1887. I exercised Scamp along some of the estate roads, but it was another fiercely cold day, and I spent the bulk of the day mentally debating with myself what I should write in response to Lord Ernest's latest letter.

Thank goodness for my marvellous little Scamp! He really is such a joy to me. Of course, he is his usual, unchanged self, unaware and totally unperturbed by the ways of human beings, entirely uncomplicated and best of all, totally devoted to me! He certainly is, 'my canine friend,' in every sense of the word, curling up at my feet as he did later in the evening as we, the adults, sat in the Great Hall before the roaring log fire drinking our sherry and wine, and even at times, placing one paw or sometimes even resting his head on my knee. Yes, he even has the temerity to do that! He is just so very loveable.

Thursday, 6th March, 1887. After considerable self-conference and mental debate, I eventually managed to pen a reply to my Lord Ernest… Although I really feel as though he is no longer 'my' Lord Ernest. This is what I wrote:

Dear Lord Ernest,

Thank you for your previous letter which arrived safely at Riversdale a few days ago. Yes, I fully and freely admit I was saddened by your recent decision, but I firmly believe you need to do as your conscience sees fit – it is indeed a, 'once in a lifetime,' chance.

I am now more certain than ever that I also need to 'go with my instincts,' as I said to you on my twentieth birthday celebrations, there is nothing now to keep me at lonely, isolated Riversdale Hall any longer, and I will need to, 'spread my wings' sooner or later, in any event! Yes, I believe you are absolutely right, I shall go to Leeds and I remain entirely committed to my nursing studies, which I am prepared to complete to the absolute best of my ability. I shall be back at Riversdale Hall from Friday to early Sunday evening, so you can safely address any correspondence to me here and it will easily reach me. I shall look forward to your missives when they arrive.

Lastly, it simply remains for me to say that I hope your travels are safe, enjoyable and extremely profitable.

I remain your ever-loving and extremely devoted servant,

Gertrude Rivers.

Friday, 7th March, 1887. I received further paperwork from the School of Nursing in Leeds, which I duly signed, dated, returned and posted at one and the same time as my Lord Ernest's note.

As I posted the nursing correspondence, I felt a strange, abrupt sense of excitement rinse over me at the prospect of spending lengthy time spans away from Riversdale Hall, where I have spent the entire brief span of my twenty years to date. But what will happen if I do not settle in Leeds? Or do not make any friends? To be honest, I do not like to contemplate either of these possibilities in too much detail. All I can say at this point is that I am about to be given the chance to do a job I really believe will be quite my 'life's work.' Quite frankly, I am prepared to 'give it all I've got,' after all, I ultimately like to regard myself as a strong woman, easily able to cope with the vicissitudes that human life can throw at me, whilst still retaining my sanity and equilibrium. Now… now I need to cease my incessant wittering and go and take Scamp for his morning run.

Saturday, 8th March, 1887. I devoted much of the day to a substantial amount of background reading and then spent a cosy, domestic evening with my papa, stepmother and my older brother, Harry. Of course, my beloved Scamp was there to entertain me; he really is such a comfort to me!

Sunday, 9th March, 1887. We attended church this a.m. and dined on beef and Yorkshire pudding, the beef being as always freshly culled from the Riversdale estate. Harry departed early at just after five, since he had work to submit at the university in the morning.

At this point, Izzy decided it was probably time to call it an evening with her reading. As Edith and Izzy sat on the garden drinks terrace enjoying the view across the blue expanse of Morecambe Bay, Edith asked her, 'So Izzy, how's James been this past week?'

'Well, largely his usual self. We enjoyed a nice meal at a real quality restaurant on the Wirral on Wednesday… We, er, we both had a day off work, you see.' At this juncture, Izzy thought it prudent to refrain from any references to what James might have to ask her when she returned from her sojourn in Yorkshire, after all, it was a matter of pure speculation and she did not wish to pre-empt matters.

'He sounds really nice, even though he is, er, well, a little older than yourself, dear,' answered Edith.

'Yes, he is nice, mother.'

Just then, once again Izzy could almost hear her grandmother speaking to her, clearly and unequivocally. 'Take him, Izzy, for goodness sake, take him! You could go a lot further and fare a lot worse than James Brodie!'

Izzy then remembered the telephone conversations that had passed between herself and her father this past week.

'Oh, er… And mother, apparently it's coming up to papa's seventieth birthday and he's extremely keen for me to pay him another visit. You know, over to Huddersfield.'

'Do you really have to?'

'Well, no, but it's not every day that a father turns seventy. It's alright, it won't be for at least another three weeks.'

'Can you get the time off work?'

'It can form part of some so far untaken time off, according to James.'

'Well, provided you're happy with that, dear.'

Izzy reflected on the last few months. She had grown up in what she believed to be a single parent household. Now, quite contrary to what her grandmother would have led her to believe, she had two parents, admittedly, that particular couple had split up some time ago, but Izzy felt obviously permanently and irrevocably linked to both her parents by a strong bond of love. Her father could inevitably irritate her at times, but she still loved and cared about him.

'And how's the rift with Gwyneth?'

Izzy groaned. 'Oh, that! I'm trying not to think too much about that!'

'I'm sure she's just jealous of you!'

'You may just be right!'

The rest of the weekend passed without event, and Izzy returned to Liverchester Sunday evening. Before preparing for the week ahead, Izzy paid a brief visit to Hannah's wine Bar for a couple of glasses of red wine, before getting out her Monday morning work clothing which she hung in its usual position outside the wardrobe before settling into her double bed for a reasonably early night.

The next afternoon she was in the process of checking and scrutinising a client proof of evidence, when she was approached by Ben Watson in a strangely light-hearted and jovial frame of mind.

'Hello, Ben!' said Izzy casually as he approached.

'Suddenly, I'm feeling really happy!'

'For what reason?' answered Izzy.

'Lilian's aunt, the Lord rest her soul left her a nifty little seventy-five thousand pounds!!! Call it serendipity! Well, I'm not really pleased that she's passed away; incidentally, she was a bit of a crabby old bat… The upshot is, James and I are going out for a few drinks in three-quarters of an hour, oh, only over to Rigby's for a few after work drinks, which will be strictly on me of course!

'Tanya!' he shouted through to the front office, 'Brodie and Watson are out on the booze again in three-quarters of an hour and you're extremely welcome to join us!'

'Well, that's very kind of you, and thank you, Mr Watson. I've got a few things to do tonight, but I'll come for a couple of cocktails.'

Ben then turned to Izzy.

'Izzy, how about yourself?'

'Yes, I would love to.'

'Of course, all liquid refreshment will be strictly on the house, house of Ben Watson, I mean.'

'A treat in store. Yes, I shall look forward to that at quarter past five.'

'Excellent!' answered Ben, 'Oh, and incidentally, young lady, James and I are planning a small send-off for you when you next go on your travels over to Yorkshire to visit your long-lost papa.'

'Oh, that's very kind of you.'

'Not at all. Why, we could scarcely run these chambers without you; as I've already said a few times.'

'Good. I'm so pleased to hear it.'

Izzy was more than ready to leave chambers at quarter past five. Izzy sat with James and Tanya as Ben fought his way to the bar to buy the round.

'All well today in the front office?' James asked Tanya.

'Yes, Mr Brodie, but I have to admit, I do sometimes really struggle with your writing.'

'Oh, do you now? I'm sorry, I'll try to write more legibly in future. The same goes for my dictaphones, I will try to speak in a more articulate manner next time!'

'I'm not really grumbling. You're one of the best employers I've ever worked for.'

'Thank heavens for small mercies!' James laughed.

Presently, Tanya looked a little embarrassed to be in the company of James and Izzy, and suspecting Izzy might like to be left alone with James, she hastily muttered something about needing to use the toilet.

In Tanya's absence, James turned his face to Izzy, as if now fully able to give her his full attention, and he said casually, 'That was a really nice day last Wednesday, the day we spent on the Wirral.'

'Yes, it certainly was.'

'And the moment you return from your papa's, why, we can start to plan our North Wales holiday … Why, I'm really looking forward to it, already.'

'Yes, so am I.'

'And we'll find a good hotel in Conway, wine and dine every night, go walking during the day and well, all I really want is for you to safely return from your papa's in one piece.'

'I'm sure I can manage to do that.'

'Yes, and I'm sure too,' answered James.

Somewhere in the depths of Izzy's brain, her grandmother began speaking to her again. Albeit, rather briefly. 'For goodness' sake, Izzy! This man can't get enough of you! Take him, and once and for all have done with it! Why, after all, I think you two could be happy together!'

'Dare I ask, what are you sure of? Am I interrupting something?' asked Ben, who at this precise moment, returned from the bar with the round of drinks balanced on a tray.

'All I said was, I'll be pleased when this young lady gets safely back to Liverchester from Huddersfield.'

'Oh, most certainly,' Ben responded.

Presently, Tanya reappeared from the toilets. When they were all four comfortably settled at the table in the back bar, Ben proceeded to raise his glass in order to propose a toast to Lilian's aunt Brenda.

'Well, here's to Lil's aunt Brenda; she was often a crabby old bat, but she did have a nice side to her. In any event, we're in the happy position of now being seventy-five thousand pounds richer! 'Bottoms up, ladies and gentlemen!' Ben proceeded to declare.

Everyone raised their glasses and drank freely. James began to laugh.

'There's always plenty of drinking goes on in these chambers!'

'Well,' answered Ben casually, 'any excuse for a little liquid refreshment.'

'So true,' answered Izzy, and then she thought to enquire, 'and have you any plans concerning what you're going to spend the money on, Ben?'

'Well, we thought we might possibly have a nice autumn, winter or spring break, you know, possibly spend ten days in Sicilly and Sardinia or Malta, somewhere like that; and as regards possessions, we've both of us got most of the things we really need and want, so I think we'll probably just save the rest. Of course, a small amount might just go to help finance our Helen through her university studies.'

'Last of the big spenders!' laughed James, after he swallowed a mouthful of his pint of bitter. At this juncture, Ben shot James a suspicious look, and then said, 'I, er, thought the title of 'Last of the Big Spenders,' went to my business partner across the table?'

James threw back his head and laughed.

'Ah, but things are different now! Now that I have my Izzy!'

Ben then cast Izzy a knowing look.

'Just you insist that our James spoils you, young lady!'

'Oh, don't worry. I shall,' Izzy answered. His Izzy? James's Izzy? It was still with a little difficulty that Izzy struggled to mentally get her head round the concept of being James's Izzy. After all, was this really what she wanted?

'Well,' answered James defiantly, 'I might add that Izzy and I are planning a short break to North Wales. We'll do plenty of wining, dining and general self-indulgence then.'

'I'm pleased to hear it,' answered Ben; Izzy suspected only half-jokingly.

'Oh, and Tanya, will you be coming to Izzy's send off in a few weeks' time; we're planning an early afternoon late lunch to give our Izzy a decent send-off before she revisits her papa in Huddersfield. Will you be joining us for the event?'

'Well, I shall need to check my diary,' replied Tanya, in a slightly evasive tone, 'but I shall probably grace you with my presence for an hour or so, at least, Mr Watson.'

'Good! Oh, and please call me Ben!'

Izzy took another sip of her red wine. For obvious reasons, she did not like to reflect too closely on her impending visit to her father's home. Attempting to change the subject of conversation, she asked casually, 'James, I find it difficult to imagine you as the 'Last of the Big Spenders?' In fact, you always seem only too keen to, 'splash the cash?''

James took another sip of his beer and laughed indulgently. Eventually, he said in response, 'Well, there was a time when I was a bit loathe to spend money; that was when I first became a partner, now, when was it? Twenty-two years ago; I could scarcely believe it, all that extra cash – and furthermore, I was desperate to manage my money wisely and sensibly. It was just caution really, and in addition, I didn't want to be dependent on and beholden to either of my parents to sort me out.'

'So true,' Izzy added in response. What a sensible, middle-aged man James was, thought Izzy to herself. James's former parsimony could be a possible talking point between them on their next date, she reminded herself. Although he was scarcely the man of her dreams, no, he was certainly not, not by a long chalk; Izzy was increasingly finding herself liking and intrinsically admiring his sensible, down-to-earth habits. Was it possible they might have a future together? Izzy remained silent and quietly drank her wine.

Quite surprisingly, the next person to break the silence was Tanya. 'Oh, Mr Brodie, as I said before,' she then suddenly began to simper, 'I couldn't wish for a better employer... Oh, and you're rather special too, Ben!'

James took another sip of his beer, and responded in his usual characteristic manner, 'You know, young lady, we pride ourselves on being both a fair and equal opportunities employer.'

'...And we're approaching a very special time,' Tanya continued, undeterred, 'why, I've worked for you for almost two years! I bet a girl like me would struggle to find employment anywhere else... You two, you're too good to me!'

'Not at all, Tanya...' James and Ben uttered, almost in unison.

At this, James drained the last few inches of beer from his pint glass. He glanced across at Ben who was also just about to drain his glass, and asked, 'Would anyone require a refill?'

'Yes, please; another medium-sized house red, James, if I may.'

'Of course you may. Ben? Tanya?'

'Another Rigby's best.'

'A pint, young sir?' James queried.

'Yes. But I insist on paying for the round; after all, I'm a rich man now.'

'Oh, are you now?'

Ben passed James a fifty-pound note across the table. It looked like a new one; all clean, crisp and freshly extracted from the cash dispenser.

'Oh, and James?' Ben added, 'get a few bags of crisps, please.'

'I shall do that small thing,' James answered.

'Now then, young Tanya? What would you like?'

'Oh, er, I'll have a Liverchester Gin with tonic water, please, Mr Brodie.'

'Oh, please, call me James!' With that, James departed and began to pick his way through the crowded back bar.

'Yes, I'm now a rich man,' said Ben in James's absence, 'and it would be nice to stay that way too!'

'But if you don't intend to spend any of it, what's the point in having it?' asked Tanya, quite abruptly.

'Security, dear. It's rather good to have security,' Ben replied.

'So true,' answered Izzy.

Ben then turned his attention to Izzy.

'James told me that you two were planning a short break in North Wales sometime.'

'Yes. Possibly planned for some time when I return from my papa's.'

'Well, if you go somewhere nice, perhaps you could note down the name for me; I might like to take Lilian there at some stage.'

'Yes, most certainly,' Izzy answered, and then quickly added as an afterthought, 'We're not even going to start planning our holiday until I return from my papa's in Huddersfield.'

'Now, come on young lady. Once you get there, you never know, you might even enjoy it!'

'Well, I'm not so sure about that,' Izzy answered in a resigned sort of tone. At times, she wished she had never bothered to establish contact with her papa. Wouldn't it have been far simpler and far less complicated to simply have done nothing?

'Oh, don't be so modest! I'm sure you will love it once you get there!'

Izzy didn't say anything, but quietly smiled to herself. Her next visit to her papa's was currently scheduled for approximately three weeks away, so she would try to switch off from that for now. 'How are you two gentlemen getting home?' Izzy enquired.

'Well, we'll both of us probably be over the limit, but we'll get a taxi. Incidentally, being a man of considerable financial means, I shall pay the taxi fare,' Ben answered, in a tone more reminiscent of James.

Izzy laughed. 'I always knew you were a gentleman!'

'That's right, I am!' Ben laughed.

Presently, James returned from the bar with the order and a fistful of change and notes which he passed over to Ben. Ben opened a bag of crisps and proceeded to offer them to the other three. Izzy, James and Ben took a few. Strangely enough, Tanya declined, which was a little surprising since she was rather a plump girl who appeared to enjoy her food.

'Oh, no thank you, Ben! I'm trying to lose weight for my holiday in November. I'm going with my cousin to Grand Canaria, and I want to look good in a bikini!'

Izzy didn't like to picture the thought of Tanya spilling out of a bikini on the beaches of Grand Canaria. She imagined Tanya might be quite likely to clear the beach. James smiled uneasily and looked acutely embarrassed.

'And we're hoping to pick up some nice, decent men at Manchester airport!' Tanya added as a casual afterthought.

'Are you able to get home, safely?' James asked, desperate to change the subject.

'Yes, I'll just have this G and T and then I'll get the bus back to Litherland. So, I must love and leave you soon. But, oh, James and Ben, I've had such a nice day; really marvellous it's been, I've so enjoyed it! In fact, I'll go so far as to say that Brodie and Watson are the best employers I've ever worked for… The past two years have sped past!'

James beamed and then answered, 'Well, of course, we're a small partnership and we aim to please, at all times.'

Tanya sipped at her gin. 'I've so enjoyed it,' she murmured, 'I've sometimes had a bad time with previous employers, but that day in April two years ago when I came for my interview I had good vibes at 79 Dale Street, why, I thought to myself, 'Tanya, young lady, you're going to be O.K. with Jim and Ben!' And I have been!'

'Yes, you have!' answered Ben.

'And I love these bonding sessions!' she added, quickly warming to her theme, 'Why, why even though I am a little challenged in the intellectual department!'

Izzy smiled secretly to herself. At least Tanya was honest.

'Oh, not at all,' muttered James.

'What's more, I hope to work for you for many years to come,' Tanya continued unabashed.

'I'm sure you will do, dear,' answered James.

Tanya took another sip of her gin and continued, this time, again in the same simpering tone, 'It would be my greatest pleasure, James.'

'Have you any further plans for the rest of the evening, Tanya?' asked Izzy.

'Not really. I might watch a film and have a couple of strong beers with me da. Apart from that, nothing special.'

'Have you any plans, Izzy?' James enquired

'Not really.' Although, of course, this was only partially true. Once again, Izzy was feeling the magnetic effects of Lady G's diary.

'Anyhow, I've really enjoyed our works bonding session tonight,' Tanya piped up again, 'and I'm really looking forward to the next one.'

'Good. I'm so pleased you've enjoyed it, dear,' answered James, a little stiffly.

At this point, Tanya drained her glass and announced, 'Well, ladies and gentlemen, now we shall be forced to go our separate ways; I shall be forced to leave you, sad though that makes me feel.' With that, she placed her empty glass on the table and began to fight her way through the crowd.

'Did you two gentlemen say you were taking a taxi?' Izzy asked.

'Well, it just depends,' Ben said vaguely, 'you see, I shall also need to leave pretty soon, since Lil's making a special meal in honour of Aunt Brenda and she'll give me hell if I'm late, so I'll be leaving in a few minutes, but you two...' and at this point, he dropped his voice a tone and added, '...Of course, you two lovebirds can stay as long as you wish!'

James laughed nervously and Izzy blushed crimson, and in fact turned puce at Ben's next comment, 'And you, young leddy, of course, don't do anything I wouldn't do, this James Brodie, you need to watch his sort!'

James laughed uproariously this time and answered in response, 'Oh, Ben, you really are a one!'

'You mean I'm funny when I become intoxicated?'

'In a nutshell, yes.'

'Right, I'll see you two in chambers tomorrow a.m.'

'You certainly shall.' James responded.

In the aftermath of Ben's departure, James and Izzy were plunged into silence for a couple of minutes, until James abruptly broke the silence by boldly saying, 'Now, young lady, I need to take you home. We'll get a taxi. Oh, incidentally, don't take Ben's comments too much to heart. He doesn't mean half of what he says.'

'Yes, you two really are the proverbial chalk and cheese.'

'Yes, but we get on so well, like the proverbial, 'house on fire,' so to speak! He's the mouthy one and I'm the quiet one.'

In the taxi, James held Izzy close to him and firmly held her right hand. Possibly she had better invite James into the Percy Street flat, after all, it was only basic manners and they had enjoyed a few extremely enjoyable dates together so far.

'James, would you like to come back, only for a couple of drinks, of course; you know, just early ones?'

'Don't mind if I do!'

James paid the taxi fare and they retraced their steps up the rickety staircase.

'I do so like this flat!' said James as they arrived in the first floor lounge.

'Yes, so do I. Eventually, I got my wish; my wish of living in the Georgian quarter, I mean. James, please sit down and make yourself comfortable.'

James settled into his usual armchair.

'Now, what would you like to drink? I've got gin, both normal and pink, whisky, red wine, sweet sherry, brandy, oh, and of course, the inevitable, the strong Belgian lager.'

'Sounds like a fairly extensive drinks cabinet. I'll have a strong Belgian lager, please.'

Izzy vanished to the kitchen to get it. A few minutes later, she reappeared with the bottle of lager, a whisky glass and a bottle opener. Then she vanished again; returning with a three-quarters full bottle of pink gin and a full bottle of tonic water. Izzy sat down on the settee and began to pour herself a measure of gin. Topped it up with tonic water.

'Well, my dear,' James announced '...And I would like to propose a toast... To us!' At which point, he leaned forward and James and Izzy's glasses connected.

'To us!' Izzy repeated.

'Just think we've been, er, an 'item,' dare I say it? Although I personally dislike the phrase; for two months now.'

Come to think of it they had. An unlikely couple to say the least, but it had not been an unpleasant two months, by anyone's standards. Izzy looked across at James, and answered, at this stage, truthfully,

'You know, James, I really have enjoyed it and I do hope we have many more to enjoy.'

'Well, I really don't see why we should split up… And you and I, we're both of an age to know our own minds and know what we want from this life.'

'So true.'

Izzy smiled to herself remembering the previous occasion on which James had visited the flat. 'If you don't mind my asking, what are you thinking about, young lady? Something has obviously entertained you? Oh, I'm sorry; I shouldn't be asking.'

'No, it's quite O.K., James, if you really want to know, I was just thinking that last time you came here, we shared my bed.'

'Yes, we did… It's alright, I don't expect that tonight, it's too early in the evening right now and mother will have a fit if I'm not back tonight, and besides, if a girl tells me or I sense she's not comfortable with, er, the physical side of our relationship which is still, of course, in its' infancy, then I'm not the type of man to force himself upon her.'

'Good. I'm pleased to hear it. In fact, James, I always knew you were a gentleman.'

'Oh, did you now? Well, I try to be, at least.'

Izzy attempting to change the subject, casually enquired, 'So did you enjoy the latest works bonding session?'

'Oh, very much so. Ben's a character, isn't he?'

'Yes, he is, and you two, you couldn't be more different, but you work so well as a partnership and, er, well, you know the old phrase, 'opposites attract!''

'Too true,' answered James, and he took a sip of his Belgian beer, and then he added, 'And Tanya's a bit of a strange girl, I only employed her initially on the strength of the fact that she typed up a faultless piece of correspondence in the typing test we set for all our interviewees. I have to admit I was baulking at the thought of her in a bikini on Grand Canaria Beach.'

Izzy laughed. 'Yes, and she was hoping to pick up a man at Manchester Airport, I can't imagine for the life of me who would be the man of Tanya's dreams.'

'No, nor I.'

Once again, James leaned forward and placed his left hand on Izzy's knee, Izzy placed her right hand on top of his and gave it a small squeeze. With her free hand, she took another sip of the gin. True to form, it tasted excellent.

'No, I can't imagine Tanya in a bikini either… Incidentally, darling, I can imagine you in a bikini, only too easily!'

'Well, that's very nice of you, James, and thank you for saying so.'

Just at that moment, they were disrupted by the 'phone. Izzy went to answer it.

'Hello, Liverchester 707 4396!'

'Oh, er, is that a certain person?' It was her papa.

'Well, yes. At least, I hope so.'

'I'm just making a few plans for my birthday and wanted to check you were O.K., hence the reason for my call.'

'And did you succeed in your plans?'

'I think they were largely successful,' answered her papa, in a manner extremely reminiscent of James.

'I'm pleased to hear it.'

'And how are you entertaining yourself this evening?'

'I'm just spending some time with James, I, er, work with him.' By now, Izzy felt as though she were fast running out of possible sources of conversation.

'James,' Izzy said, 'could you come and speak to my papa, just for a few minutes?'

'Yes, with pleasure.'

Greatly relieved, Izzy passed the 'phone over to James.

'Hello, Mr Jackson!' said James, and then Izzy was a little surprised at the next comment which James uttered, which came abruptly, and quite out of the blue, '…And I think you're very lucky to have a daughter as nice as Izzy!' Izzy was unable to hear what was said at the other end of the 'phone in response, but James's next comment consisted of, 'Well, of course, we're three legal professionals together!' Silence for a couple of minutes at the James end of the 'phone, doubtless whilst James waited for her papa to finish his sentence, and then James answered, 'Well, I would have loved to have attended, but sadly, I'm not able to, since that week I'm required in chambers!' Without a doubt, that was James declining an invitation to Izzy's papa's seventieth birthday celebrations, 'Which is a real pity, because I would have done the driving over to Huddersfield!'

Come on, James, you know you don't really mean that, thought Izzy to herself; after all, you don't want to walk into a room full of strangers and be forced to make stiff, polite, formal conversation with them; never in a million years!

Silence again, for a minute or so, doubtless whilst papa made a comment or statement, and then James answered, 'Yes, Izzy is my young lady! And your Izzy is perfectly safe with me, why, unlike a lot of the male sex, my intentions are strictly honourable!'

In an uncertain world, thought Izzy to herself, that was one certain factor.

'Well, I had best leave you now, Mr Jackson,' said James, 'Izzy, are you going to speak?'

'Yes, just pass the 'phone over, please, James.' Izzy took the receiver.

'Goodbye, papa! We'll speak very soon, oh, er, and James sends his love.'

'Lorry loads of love, dear. Goodbye!'

Izzy replaced the receiver on the 'phone; at which James smiled indulgently, and then at last said, 'He sounds like a nice, decent man!'

'Oh, he is!'

'Now, when are we going to plan our North Wales escape?'

'How about when I arrive home from my papa's?'

'Well, we can do. I could always be 'phoning round some hotels to try to find the best value for money.'

'Yes, you do that, for now. So, obviously papa is now aware that we're an item?'

'Well, yes, but I'm pleased about that – I mean he was going to find out sooner or later, wasn't he?'

'So true. I'm also pleased it's now out in the open… And mother loves you.'

'Oh, really?' asked James, a little stiffly.

'Oh, yes. Most certainly.'

James resumed his hand on the knee stance. Once again, his signet ring glinted in the electric ceiling light. He was silent for another minute and then said, in a singularly uncertain manner, 'Do you know? I'm quite feeling in the mood for another Chinese meal; how about us paying the East Garden another visit on Wednesday evening?'

'Yes, any time, James. In fact, you know I would love to.'

Once again, James smiled with gratitude and relief. At this point, he casually muttered something about needing to get back to his mother and Manc, since it would soon be time for the Brodie household evening meal; at which he drained the last few inches of the Belgian lager and declared that he would stand outside on the street to wait for a passing taxi.

Outside on Percy Street, James held Izzy close to him, but he did not have to wait very long, only a matter of minutes, since a taxi soon pulled up and conveyed him safely back to Woolton, Mrs Brodie and their strange, unkempt hound.

Saturday, 8th March, 1887 and Sunday 9th March, 1887. Two very unremarkable days. I continued with my preparations for my sojourn in Leeds; which I am really looking forward to. I certainly do not intend to back out now, since my trunk is already packed.

Intrigued, Izzy read on.

Monday, 10th March, 1887. Spring seems to be arriving! All at once. Banks of primroses are springing up en masse into a veritable lemon carpet on the estate woodlands, and we seem to be beginning to enjoy the occasional warm and balmy day. I still feel vulnerable and my confidence has taken a savage blow, but as a result of this hardship, I now quite abruptly and unexpectedly begin to find myself feeling considerably stronger. After all, you are a strong woman, Gertrude, and are fully able to put this episode behind you; yes, where it belongs, in the past. Perhaps I interpreted too much in Lord Ernest's friendship, and maybe the best course of action is simply to stay friends with him.

He will have far 'better fish to fry' on the continent than too young, 'little me,' still with much of my growing up still to do. Don't expect much, Gertrude, since if you do, you may well end up becoming hurt, disappointed and generally let down. No, simply don't raise your hopes unduly.

Tuesday, 11th March, 1887. The weather now appears to have taken a severely retrograde step, and once again, the Riversdale Estate has been besieged by bitingly cold winds and by mid-afternoon, we suffered an almost torrential downpour. Scamp and I took refuge indoors, needless to say; and then I proceeded to entertain myself with the writings of the famous Bronte sisters, in particular, Charlotte Bronte; which I thoroughly enjoyed.

That Wednesday evening, Izzy met James at her flat and they spent an agreeable two and a half hours at the East Garden Chinese restaurant, then finished off with cocktails at Hannah's wine bar; where Izzy further queried James a little bit more about the sarcastic title with which he'd been dubbed, i.e. that of, 'The Last of The Big Spenders.'

'So for what reason were you referred to as, 'Last of The Big Spenders,' James?'

'Oh, that was just in the aftermath of Alison's passing away. I decided there was nothing I either wanted or needed. At any rate, however much money I earned, it would still not bring Alison back.'

'No, I fully understand. I'm really sorry, and I won't raise that subject ever again.'

'No, not at all, dear. Remember, it all occurred years before I met you. At any rate, I have my Izzy now to make me happy, so I can spend my cash on her.'

'Thank you, James. You really don't need to feel under too much obligation. You know me, I'm used to paying my own way and being generally independent.'

Once again, they said goodnight at the door of 8, Percy Street and James caught another taxi home to Woolton.

Well, in two weeks' time, Izzy had her second visit to Huddersfield to complete. All too soon, the day arrived. After the royal send-off given by the Brodie and Watson Partnership, Izzy was once again on her way to Huddersfield. During the interim time, Izzy had still been religiously and assiduously studying, reading and scrutinising Lady Gertrude's diary entries, which she read almost every night. What a wise, well-balanced, well-adjusted woman she was!

Monday, 8th April, 1887. I left the noble Riversdale Hall on the ten-thirty post-chaise service, which arrives in Leeds, West Riding of Yorkshire at precisely twelve-thirty. Last night, I was plagued by last minute nerves and doubts. After the sumptuous riches of Riversdale Hall, will I ever fully adjust and adapt to squalor, urban poverty, disease and deprivation? At times, I firmly believe no, is the answer to that question. I have been so keen to leave my narrow, at times rather lonely and circumscribed existence at Riversdale for quite some time; I believe the precise timespan is probably two years, but now that the actual date and time of departure has finally arrived, I feel nothing but dread, negativity and gloom.

'Come now, Gertrude, Leeds will soon be your home from home in just a few weeks' time!' My excellent papa told me. Quite frankly, I did not feel so certain.

Alienation… Unfamiliarity… An entirely new, different, strange town and streets which are entirely unknown to me, is all that I see around myself in the sprawling, enormous urban jungle which comprises Leeds city centre. But I have set my hand to the plough, and am a woman of my word. I will see it through.

On arrival in Leeds, we went straight and immediately to the hospital, where I was shown to my nursing accommodation. Henceforth, this is to be my base in Leeds; Sunday through until Friday evening, for the next two years. It is a first-floor room, with pale lemon-coloured walls; bright and cheerful and by no means unattractive. The building itself is probably about a century old, and my room has an elegant, long, Georgian window, which reaches to floor level and is hung with sumptuous purple curtains and the window itself provides good overall views of the city. It also has a modest, single bed pushed against the furthest wall, a small storage cabinet, complete with a china basin and ewer for washing purposes against the opposite wall, a small writing desk, basic wardrobe, a hard, upright chair and a single, rather more comfortable armchair to relax in… But it is a mere convenience cubicle compared to my bedchamber back at Riversdale! A mere place in which to eat, sleep and complete my theoretical work!

My trunk was left in my room and my excellent papa announced that he was taking me to our beloved old haunt of the Central Dining Rooms for what he termed, 'a good send off.' What a marvellous man he is! I have no wish whatsoever to betray or let him down in any way, hence, for that very reason I really wish to see this Leeds business through.

True to form, we dined excellently on roast of turkey with accompanying vegetables and lemon sponge, all rinsed down with a bottle of finest quality claret; I shall not dine like this again until I reach Riversdale on Friday evening! I have to admit, I did not enjoy the food quite as much as I would have done under normal circumstances, since I knew full well later in the afternoon, my dear papa and I would be parting company!

Papa also checked the post-chaise times from the city centre, which was so very good of him. The service is indeed excellent and is available at half-hourly intervals. As I waited for papa as he went to enquire at the information office, with the urban chaos sprawling about and enveloping me, I suddenly, abruptly and quite without warning began to feel a fleeting and transient sense of being at the hub of an intensely exciting and vital entity and I began to suspect that ultimately, all would be well and intrinsically positive.

I wonder how long it took Lady Gertrude to settle in Leeds? Izzy thought to herself. Meanwhile, she had her visit to Huddersfield to complete. Izzy's papa and her stepmother once again met her at the station, and she spent a reasonably pleasant few days with them, during the middle of which, Izzy's father celebrated his seventieth birthday. No, all appeared to be well, to all outward intents and purposes at least, and even the soured relations between Izzy and Gwyneth appeared to be thankfully relegated well and truly to the past. Also, needless to say and true to form, James continued to call every evening. James!!! If Izzy began to admit it herself, she was finding that possibly her attitude towards James was starting to change. He was no longer simply the avuncular figure, who she could frequently and all too easily and painlessly manage without! Yes, he was rapidly becoming her security in a fast-changing world, her rock, who would always be there for her!

On the last day of Izzy's stay, they paid a second visit to Settle, and inevitably inclined their steps once again, up to the caverns. Of course, the caverns remained just as Izzy and her papa had left them. Entirely unchanged. Still the caverns possessed their sumptuous array of treasures – rings, chains, bracelets and earrings of every width, design, style, pattern, texture and finish conceivable to man. Izzy tried on some rings and in almost no time at all, fast-filled all the fingers of both her hands. She was unable to prevent frequently looking down to admire the lustrous metal, gleaming in the late October sunlight as she sat outside the caverns with her father; the neighbouring caverns with their white, bright limestone, catching the early autumn sunlight and rather reminiscent of enormous slabs of crumbling white cheese. Of course, almost all of Lady Gertrude's jewellery was a perfect, comfortable and exquisite fit. But far more important than the attraction and lure of the jewellery, was the fact that Izzy had discovered and eventually made contact with her father, and, irritate her though he might at times, they were connected inexorably and irrevocably by a strong and enduring bond of love. Furthermore, the internet had brought them together.

Thank heavens for the internet!

Before Izzy left Settle early that evening, she took especial care to replace all the items of jewellery which she had worn that afternoon. She also purchased some small 'thank you' presents for her step-mother and her papa – a box of cherry-filled liquor chocolates for her step-mother and a bottle of quality claret for her papa.

Her sojourn in Huddersfield had once again been quite profitable and surprisingly not unpleasant in the least, especially bearing in mind her earlier altercation on the 'phone with Gwyneth.

Nevertheless, by now Izzy was quite ready to return to her spiritual home of Liverchester.

Additionally, if truth be known, she was finding the inexorable pull of Lady Gertrude's diary once again calling her. Oh, how she hoped that Gertrude had settled in in Leeds!

Izzy departed the next morning after breakfast. Once she had changed trains at Leeds and had had sufficient time to settle into a comfortable seat on the Liverchester train, Izzy immediately duly connected her laptop.

Monday, 8th April, 1887. New people, like myself, appear to have been arriving all afternoon. But I was hopelessly unprepared when at about four o'clock, my marvellous papa uttered the ominous words, 'Well, Gertrude, your step-mother and I will have to be leaving you!'

Almost instantly, I felt tears spring to my eyes, I could scarcely bear the impending prospect of being deprived of my papa; and even my step-mother, despite our earlier altercations and contretemps, I would happily have allowed her to stay with me a few weeks until I had fully acclimatised to my new environment!

'Do you have to?'

'Yes, dear, we have to. We have to be back in Ripon before nightfall. Just think, you will be back at Riversdale on Friday evening, for which we will hold a special celebratory banquet!'

'Very well, then, papa and step-mother, I'll not keep you.'

I gave papa a deep and long-lasting hug and my step-mother a rather more muted one and then bade my goodbyes.

With a deep-seated sadness and feeling extremely vulnerable, I sat down on the bed and folded my arms, not quite knowing what to do next. Presently, about ten minutes later, a plump, cheery woman in her early sixties knocked on my door and announced, 'Could all lady probationers meet in the hallway downstairs on the ground floor at half-past four, where you will be informed about the arrangements for this coming week?'

'Yes, I'll be only too pleased to attend,' I answered uneasily.

This interim time would have been an absolutely perfect opportunity for me to unpack my trunk. I have to admit though, at this early and highly unsettled stage, I was quite unable to force myself to unpack my clothing, especially my beautiful, sumptuous ball dresses. No, I simply could not do it. Instead, I began to invent a multitude of excuses for not doing so.

There was no point and I may be requiring my dresses to wear at the banquet to be held in my honour back at Riversdale on Friday evening – hence, there was no point in unpacking, only to repack the very same items a few days later.

At four-thirty, I began to quietly wend my way down the grand winding staircase, quite uncertain and totally unprepared for what might await me on the floor below. There were other women already assembled, and a buzz of general excitement appeared to prevail in the hall.

'Good evening, ladies!' The plump woman eventually proclaimed, 'And welcome to Leeds! I hope your stay in Leeds will be both a happy and productive one!

A few nervous laughs and anxious coughs ensued.

'I am Betty Davies, and the housekeeper responsible for the nursing accommodation block. Now, breakfast is from eight a.m. to eight-thirty, you will be expected to find your own lunch and the evening meal will be from seven p.m. until quarter to eight. Does anyone have any questions or queries, so far?'

There was silence for a couple of minutes, until at last a small girl with auburn hair, asked in rather frightened tones, 'Mrs Davies, are we permitted out in the evening?'

'Well, for special occasions you can obtain a pass, but on the whole, we really do like our lady probationers back in the evening for half-past ten. After all, I am attempting to run a decent, respectable establishment.'

'And what happens tomorrow?' asked someone else.

'Now, let me see...' said Mrs Davies, in what I suspected to be a purposely vague tone, 'All you new lady probationers are expected to assemble in the nurse education block at nine-thirty in the general lecture theatre. The next three months of your time here will be fully spent on entirely theoretical matters, at the end of which time, you will sit a written examination. The pass grade required to pass this test is forty-five percent. Once you have passed your written examinations, you will begin your practical work allocations, for which you will be provided later with your staff work cards... And now, young ladies, we do have some small refreshments on offer which consist of cheese nibbles and some wine, and everyone is extremely welcome to partake of them!'

It now seemed like a long time since I had consumed my roast meal at the Central Dining Rooms, but I was feeling both mentally and physically drained, I firmly believe that emotional trauma all too frequently adversely affects the nerves and muscles of my stomach, and often renders me unable to eat when traumatised. Instead, I uneasily sipped my wine and managed to casually converse with some of my would-be colleagues. After this rather impromptu inauguration, we were free for a further hour, at the end of which another meal of sorts would be served. Oh, my goodness! Please do not speak to me about food as long as I live, since it is rapidly becoming poison and a complete and total penance to me!

An hour later, I presented myself for the meal, I believe it was some sort of casserole, but I was only able to consume approximately half of my helping. No, I did not enjoy it in the least, and later that evening, the inevitable occurred. My evening meal saw the light of day for the second time, and this was to become a regular occurrence during those difficult first few weeks in Leeds. I am sorry to say that I was sick almost every night those first three weeks in Leeds.

I was feeling in a singularly feeble, empty, post-vomiting and highly delicate frame of both mind and body when I was roused from a state of semi-collapse, by a persistent knocking on my door.

'Oh, hello!' the disembodied voice shouted.

'Hello!' I responded, 'Please come in! I was a little unwell almost an hour ago, but I'm feeling better now. At least, I think I am.'

'Well, get yourself down the corridor… We're sitting in my friend Caroline's room… Oh, my name's Audrey, by the way, and I'm from York.'

'I'm Gertrude, and I come from Ripon.'

'Ripon, eh? Posh place, 'aint it?' Audrey queried. 'Well, we're sitting down in Caroline's room; that's room 7, further down the corridor and you're extremely welcome to join us!' I decided that this chance presented the perfect excuse for me to go and attempt to introduce myself to some of the others. Hence, I duly followed Audrey down the corridor.

'You must miss your mama if this is your first time away from home,' Audrey told me, 'So is it your first time away from home?'

'Yes, it is… I only have a step-mother, who to be honest I don't get on particularly well with at all. But I do miss my papa, terribly, in fact.'

'Oh, you'll soon get used to it here, just give yourself a few weeks,' answered Audrey confidently.

She seemed an extrovert, cheerful sort of girl, utterly uncomplicated and I found myself taking an instant liking to her.

At the end of the corridor, we eventually reached Caroline's room. Caroline's room looked very similar to that of my own; the single bed pushed against the wall, long Georgian window now obscured by a dark blue velvet curtain and two chairs, by way of additional furnishings. Caroline herself was a girl with dark, shoulder-length hair, a rather pallid colouring and blue eyes, who was at present comfortably occupied sitting on her bed.

Audrey by contrast, had a long, fair, slightly untidy head of wavy tresses, grey eyes and a pink, healthy colouring.

'Welcome to my room,' said Caroline, 'Everybody says the first night is always the worst, but after that it becomes easier. Now you sit yourself down, and please make yourself comfortable.'

'…Well, I sincerely hope it becomes easier,' I responded, and with that I began to settle myself in the hard study chair at the writing desk, 'Oh, er, and incidentally, my name's Gertrude and I'm from Ripon.'

'Do you know?' laughed my friend, Audrey, 'I think they're going to give us yet more rules in the morning, at least, that's what I suspect! Yes, rules, rules and yet more rules!'

'Oh, really?' I asked.

'Yes, I think so.'

'Excuse me, did you say you were from Ripon?' Caroline suddenly enquired.

'Yes. Well, about two miles south of Ripon to be completely honest. Riversdale Hall.'

'Oh, so you're our posh friend?' asked Audrey.

'Not really. No, not at all in fact… Father wants me to make something of my life, and I feel the same way myself.'

'It's alright! Your secret's safe with both of us!' Audrey and Caroline laughingly answered, almost in unison.

I also laughed and answered by saying, 'I'm relieved to hear it!' If truth be known, I was beginning to feel better, brighter and far more positive by the moment.

'Would you like a glass of our wine?'

Touched by their welcoming attitude and innate generosity, I answered that I would love a glass.

'I had to ask Mrs Davies specially for these glasses,' Audrey began to elaborate by way of explanation, 'And that was like trying to squeeze blood out of the proverbial stone!

Eventually, she relented because I said I needed to fit in and find friends when we were all so new, and I couldn't do that if I was unfriendly!' She began to pour out the deep red liquid, and added, 'Now I can't testify as to the quality of this, but let's hope it's at least drinkable!' She then proceeded to pass a glass across to both Caroline and myself.

'Well, here's to us and to friendship!' and with that, Audrey took a large mouthful.

Surprisingly, the wine was not half as bad as I had envisaged that it might be, although I can freely state quite clearly and categorically that it was not by any means a great vintage.

'To us and to friendship!' We all simultaneously repeated the toast.

Fortified by the liquid refreshment and the hospitality of the other two girls, I began to feel noticeably better and just over an hour later, I retraced my steps back to my bedroom, setting my alarm for the unearthly hour of eight o'clock, the next morning.

At this point, Izzy was approximately half-way back to Liverchester, when she was abruptly interrupted and brought back to reality by her 'phone suddenly deciding to ring out. She reached into her trouser pocket to answer it. It was James.

'Hello, dear!' He said in a strangely gushing tone.

'Hello, James.'

'So how did your visit to your papa's go?'

'Oh, not too badly,' answered Izzy dismissively.

'Well, I shall want to hear all about it,' said James persistently in response.

'And you will hear… All in good time!'

'Oh, er, Izzy?'

'Yes?'

'Could you do me a favour?'

'Yes, if I can. What is it?'

'Would I be able to meet you at the station? I, well, er, I would very much like to.'

'Yes, I would be pleased if you would.'

'Good,' answered James in his characteristic tones.

Almost the moment Izzy stepped off the Leeds train at platform seven at Liverchester Lime Street Station, she was approached by James, beaming from ear to ear and offering to take her luggage.

'Oh, thank you, James!'

'Not at all. Not at all. It's yourself… Why, you are doing me the pleasure of being my young lady.'

Izzy and James returned to the Percy Street flat to drop off Izzy's baggage, from where they paid a visit to Hannah's Bar.

Izzy began to elaborate on the recent acts of her half siblings, '…As far as I'm aware, Christopher is still employed three days per week as a shop assistant for a photographic company and Gwyneth… Well, er, Gwyneth's still out of work and she has been for the past three or four months now, trying to establish her own business.'

'Oh, my goodness!' answered James sympathetically, 'At any rate, dear,' he continued, 'You're home now, and best of all, we can start to plan our short break away to North Wales.'

'Yes, we can, can't we?'

'Oh, and I have something very special to ask you, dear.'

'Do you feel so inclined to ask me now?'

'No, because the timing is not quite right,' James answered, but then surprisingly added, 'This has to be asked all in good time, and most vital of all, only when the timing is right; and that's all I can say at present.'

'Well, I'll make no bones about this, it feels so good to be back in Liverchester.'

'I'm so pleased you feel that way, dear. Incidentally, darling, could we go to the Viva Brazil restaurant up by the Town Hall – not the Hanover Street restaurant this time; say, Wednesday evening, I'll arrive at your flat at say, eight-thirty and I'll reserve a table for nine?'

'Yes, I would love to, James.'

Izzy returned to Cumbria the next day, which just happened to be Friday and spent a further two days resting, relaxing and generally de-stressing. In the interim time, she began to become increasingly dependent upon Lady Gertrude's diary entries, which fast appeared to be becoming a rapid compulsion.

Thursday, 9th April, 1887. After an extremely rushed and hurried breakfast, I'm rather ashamed to say that I again felt rather anxious to say the least; and all I was able to manage to eat at breakfast, was three slices of toast, (the third slice of which was heavily burned!) and two mugs of tea, after consumption of which, I directed my steps over to the nurse education building and obediently lined up in the queue for the general lecture theatre. I have to admit, I was so eager to begin the theoretical aspect of my nurse training that I came to the lecture armed with two writing pads and five pens! I would be by no means short of writing equipment!

We then sat waiting for our lecture to start, and somehow I have the innate feeling that I will love the theoretical aspect of the nurse training program. The nursing sister who led the lecture introduced us to yet a few more, basic, rudimentary rules and told us that henceforth, we needed to call her 'Sister-

Tutor,' and Sister-Tutor would guide and be responsible for our written work and theoretical progress throughout our two years' time in the school of nursing. She then produced a set of notes for us to copy up, which began with the title, 'The Epidermis.' A deathly silence prevailed as we all sat there assiduously copying down the vital information. This then in turn led onto information relating to preservation of skin integrity, the prevention of pressure damage and the basic need to promote patient mobility, if at all physically possible.

We had a short coffee break and I talked briefly to the girl I sat next to during the lecture, but finding her company rather limited and superficial, I later absented myself to the school of nursing library in order to find further reading to supplement my written work. The school of nursing library is exactly opposite the general lecture theatre, so extra convenient to nip into after a session in the lecture theatre. I repeated this the next day when we had morning lectures and the morning after.

The next day (Thursday), we were divided into smaller seminar groups, where we covered further initial rules and began to focus on our written work. After our afternoon session, a slightly older woman in her late twenties, very out-going, friendly and chatty introduced herself to me.

'Oh, hello! You seem to be in my seminar group. I've seen you in the library. Incidentally, my name's Maria.'

'And I'm Gertrude. I'm from Ripon. I live in the accommodation block and I'm still in the process of settling in.'

'Oh, really?'

'Well, I'll be wending my way home now, but I'll see you tomorrow in the lecture theatre and hopefully, we can sit together. If we don't meet up in the lecture theatre, we'll certainly meet up in the afternoon session!' Henceforth Maria and I became good friends.

Monday and Tuesday passed without incident for Izzy and James did not reappear in chambers until Wednesday, since he was working from home for the first two days of the week. On Wednesday, Izzy went to work as usual, the bulk of the day being occupied with further requisitions, together with last minute examinations and checks of client proofs of evidence. She was certainly ready to leave chambers that afternoon at ten past five.

'Darling, I'll see you at eight-thirty at the Percy Street flat!' James shouted from his inner office.

'You certainly shall!' Izzy shouted back cheerily in response.

After a brief and unsuccessful wander round the shops on Church Street and Liverchester One, Izzy began to make her way back to Percy Street. Once back, she selected her clothing for her evening rendezvous with James. The black, relaxed fitted, embroidered jeans, her orange, strappy sandals and the new yellow and white checked M & S blouse were selected.

Alison's flat ring on her right hand and the two new ethnic bracelets comprised her jewellery. Entirely and totally appropriate, thought Izzy to herself. Izzy had a brief shower and then donned the new chosen clothing.

Did she have time to visit Gertrude's diary? Probably not. No, she would pass that pleasure up this evening; after all, she did not wish to be seen deeply engrossed in its' reading when James called round.

All too soon, eight-thirty arrived. True to form, James was his usual, punctual self.

'Would you like a little aperitif, dear?' Izzy greeted James with, when he arrived.

'Don't mind if I do!' was James's response.

Izzy led the way back upstairs to her first floor flat.

'So, James, would you like your usual strong Belgian lager?'

'Oh, yes please… I'll not say no.'

Izzy vanished to the veritable cocktail cabinet on her kitchen worktop. She then presently reappeared with James's lager, a glass and a bottle opener. She then vanished and reappeared again complete with the flavoured gin, a glass and a full bottle of tonic water.

'Just think, dear,' said James, 'We've been an 'item' dare I say it, for almost two months now? And we get on so well, though you'd not always believe it!'

'Too true,' Izzy responded, and then suddenly realised that this phrase was one so often used by James himself. Two months was far too short a time to fully evaluate the chances of success for their relationship, although no angry or exasperated words had passed between the two, nor had any serious fallings out or irritation arisen between the two.

'Well, here's to us!' said James and promptly raised his glass after a brief silence.

'Yes, to us!' answered Izzy and took a sip of the gin. It tasted excellent, and somehow, all the more special in the aftermath of two nights' abstinence from the liquid. True to form, James assumed his usual left hand on Izzy's right knee sitting position; and with a secret twinkle in his eye, he cast a brief glance around the lounge-cum-sitting room, taking in some of the fittings and furnishings.

'You really have got this place nice, you know.'

'Well, I hope so. Of course, when I took over the tenancy the flat was described as partly furnished, and so I've added a few little touches of my own, like the carriage clock.'

'Yes, it's beautiful… You see, my Izzy always has impeccable taste.'

Izzy blushed and felt acutely embarrassed for a minute. Was James building up to something? Furthermore, what was it that he wanted to ask her? She took another sip of the gin and once again, it tasted like nectar and sure enough, consumption of the said liquid was slowly beginning to relax her.

'So how are matters with your papa?' ventured James.

'Well, O.K. so far, but you know, like everything else in this life, it's uncertain.'

James was silent for a minute or so, and then his response summed up the situation in a nutshell.

'Well, Izzy, for goodness sake, don't let him push or boss you about.'

Izzy laughed and she took another mouthful of the flavoured gin, the warmth of which by now seemed to be seeping into and permeating her system and she managed to answer by saying, 'James, you're absolutely right.'

James glanced at his watch, 'Not of course, that I thought a charming and highly independent young lady like yourself would be in any danger of doing that, but, er, well, you know full well what I mean.'

'So true.'

'And now, young lady, I think it's probably best that we start to make tracks to Viva Brazil.'

The Brazilian restaurant on Castle Street was entirely new to Izzy and she was captivated by it. After much deliberation in conjunction with Izzy over the wine list, James chose a sweet Italian red wine.

Once the waiter had filled both their glasses and left them alone, James presently uttered with a strange, newly acquired jaunty confidence, 'Well, here's to us, let's hope we enjoy many more times like this!'

'Too true!' Izzy answered. My goodness! There she was again! Yet again, she later that evening recollected, that must have been the James effect, exerting its all-powerful influence over her, since she was now beginning to use some of his vocabulary and phrases.

After raising her glass, she took a mouthful of the Italian wine, briefly savoured it and thought how excellent it tasted.

'And also to our future together,' James added as an afterthought.

Izzy scrutinised the menu; even though she was in no hurry to order. Steaks, pasta, burgers, fish and seafood and griddle lamb chops, etc, amongst numerous other items were comprised in the evening menu; and yes, it was so special, precious and civilised sitting here in the late October evening drinking wine with James, her supervisor, here in her spiritual home of Liverchester. She took another mouthful of the Italian vintage and fully savoured its' delicate, piquant aroma.

'This is such a beautiful restaurant, James, and thank you for bringing me here.'

James pushed his glasses further up his nose with his middle finger and replied by saying, 'Not at all. Remember, it's my Izzy who's doing me the favour of being my young lady.'

Izzy laughed and found that her face was rapidly growing a delicate shade of puce.

'Oh, er…' James continued, this time a little uncertainly, 'and that reminds me of something else…'

'Yes, and what is that?'

'Well, you know, I think we're both of us long past the time of casual, fleeting, generally unsatisfactory relationships… I believe we've both reached the age and time in our lives when we're ready to progress to the, er, the next stage.' Izzy quickly took another mouthful of her wine, so was James building up to asking her something and was this what he had previously alluded to before the visit she paid to her papa's home?

'Well, er,' answered James, a little diffidently, 'there comes a time in a man's life, and that can occur at any age, be it from twenty-five to sixty-five, or for that matter, any age in between, when he suddenly feels as though the time is right.'

'For?' Izzy tried to prompt him. To be absolutely honest, she had a vague inkling of what was or might be coming next. Once again, she took another mouthful of the Italian vintage wine.

James took both her hands in his, and said in response, 'I know it's early in our relationship, but, Miss Jackson-Talbot, will you marry me?'

Somewhere in the background, Izzy heard her grandmother once again speaking to her, '…Take him, for goodness' sake Izzy, love, take him! And just think, in twelve to eighteen months' time you could be having babies!'

'Yes,' answered Izzy, 'with pleasure.'

James smiled, once again with gratitude and relief.

'Marvellous. I feel almost like a new man. Now we need to do some serious shopping over the next few days to find the ring of my Izzy's dreams.'

Chapter 14.

F *riday, 12th April, 1887. Well, Leeds has become a little easier, but I still miss Ripon and my Riversdale base quite sorely. I still classify the degree of alienation, unfamiliarity and hostility which I am subject to, as at least as high as 90%. I am forced to admit that I left the metropolis of Leeds with a, 'song in my heart,' so to speak, by means of the five fifteen post-chaise service. But I am only leaving temporarily, and I shall be back in Leeds on Sunday evening. As I said before, I have put my hand to the plough; and I wish to see this through if at all possible. I sent a telegram to papa at lunchtime, informing him of my impending arrival; and he was absolutely delighted to hear from me, why, the response I received was almost akin to the return of the prodigal, the prodigal daughter of course, this time. Papa and our cook are in the process of preparing a sumptuous banquet in my honour when I reach home. He is such a marvellous papa!*

The moment we were free of Leeds and its' dismal, urban sprawl, I began to notice the initial burgeoning's of spring, fresh, green and timeless, as always. 'Twill be still more beautiful when we reach Riversdale and the estate!

At any rate, I am home for two days to complete my private study and preparation work and I fully intend to complete it to the absolute best of my ability. So for now, I shall sit back, relax here and enjoy the carriage ride.

On Friday afternoon, 25th October, 2017, James and Izzy also managed to successfully complete the first rung on the ladder towards marital bliss. Nor was it exorbitantly expensive. A delicate, eighteen carat, yellow gold solitaire, priced at £3,550, from the new, unused stock at Miltons' the Pawnbrokers matched Izzy's needs down to a tee.

'Now we need to go about setting a date and time for our big day,' said James casually, as he ran Izzy to Lime Street station for her return to Cumbria on Friday night, 'I personally favour late May of next year.'

'That sounds good to me.'

'Or mid June. Whatever.'

They eventually settled on mid-June. Needless to say, there were also innumerable other wedding-related issues to be dealt with. Additionally, there was one key factor concerning which Izzy was entirely resolute, fixed and immutably decided upon. She wanted a low-key, quiet, small event with the magical number of thirty-five guests. Further fuel was added to her unconventional plans by Edith, who told her of the manager of the local Chinese take-away restaurant who had himself succeeded in marrying on the local Cumbrian beach, three years earlier. What a marvellous way in which to save money!

At this stage, Izzy also made a mental note to order a pretty, floaty, white dress with three-quarter length sleeves over the internet, priced at £156.00, to serve the purpose of her wedding dress. It was all that she was prepared to spend, at any rate. And of course, their wedding would not be complete without the services of Izzy's local parish priest; so at some stage Izzy would need to contact Father Albert Palmer concerning when he would be available and able to perform the honours.

Oh, and the guest list! What an absolute bad dream! Izzy began to roughly compile the guest list in her head – had she forgotten anyone? Her uncle John and his wife, Marion, their two adult children and their respective spouses, Rachel and Martin, Matt, Emma and their two little girls, Izzy's uncle Richard, her uncle William, uncle Colin, Oscar, cousins, Lawrence and Virginia, her mum, Edith, her papa, Agnieska, Gwyneth (if, and only if, she would deign to grace them with her presence), Christopher, whom Izzy hoped might provide the happy couple with some cut-price photography, Izzy's half-sister, Laura, whom she had not yet met and a few miscellaneous friends. By contrast, the groom's guests were relatively few in number simply comprising Martina, two unmarried cousins, a man named Bernard Sanders, a friend, business colleague and associate of James who James wanted as his best man and Benjamin and Lilian Watson. And no, we shall not bother with an evening function, the money could be better saved or spent on their honeymoon or a house deposit, thought Izzy to herself. Then of course, an outside caterer or local hotel needed to be contacted concerning the food; my goodness the organisation alone appeared to require planning with military precision and as Izzy casually commented to James on the 'phone a few nights later, it would be considerably easier and rather less stressful to simply, 'live in sin!'

After her conversation with James, Izzy again took refuge in the sanity of Lady Gertrude's diary.

Sunday, 14th April, 1887. I completed an extremely profitable weekend of private study after the marvellous, sumptuous banquet provided in my honour by my brilliant and exemplary papa, who was clearly so very pleased to see me.

After such fortification, I then departed on the Sunday afternoon post-chaise service and arrived in Leeds at about half-past seven. Do you know? This town still strikes me as alien and strange, but quite clearly and categorically not as unfriendly or hostile as it was last week. Maybe I am a little more acclimatized. I really do hope so.

Oh, and now I need to tell you a little secret! My Lord Ernest has made contact with me from the Italian Alps. He tells me that every morning he opens his curtains on Lake Lugano and says quite freely what a beautiful, special and precious place the Italian Alps are. He is staying a few more days before progressing on to Venice.

I will take a further three or four days to mull over in my mind exactly what I intend to say in response to Lord Ernest. In fact, I am already roughly framing a response in my mind as I currently write in my diary.

I am now safely back in the nursing accommodation block, complete with my suitcase.

Again, I see no reason to unpack and I've so far only unpacked my overnight essentials which simply comprises basic overnight essential items – i.e. my nightdress, hairbrush, toothbrush, carbolic soap and night-cream. 'Tis a pity I am unable to wear my jewellery but I would be highly likely to lose or damage it if I attempted to wear it in Leeds; no, my jewellery is far safer kept securely back at Riversdale Hall.

Once again, tomorrow will be taken up with a series of lectures, and I have to admit that I am quite looking forward to them. I do so enjoy the mental stimulation of critical, theoretical and practical reasoning!

I wandered down the corridor and spent quite a pleasant three-quarters of an hour talking to my other two friends, Caroline and Audrey and yet more glasses of wine were enjoyed.

Then, envisaging my early morning start I decided to 'call it an evening,' bade them both goodnight and returned to my bedroom for a good few hours' sleep. To my complete and utter surprise, I slept extremely well, but then as I began to regain consciousness a strange black cloud of depression began to once again settle over myself. I was far away from home in an alien, hostile town where I am forced to fend for and look after myself! Will I ever get used and acclimatized to this regime? At present, I fear I will not. And then, those precious and haunting three lines flashed across my brain…

'…God grant me the equanimity to accept the things I cannot change, Bravery and fortitude to change the things I can, and wisdom to know the difference.'

And here was I baulking at a new town! Go on, Gertrude, I told myself rather sharply, you WILL settle in here, and over in the general lecture theatre your friend, Maria will be waiting for you! No, you are not going to let anyone down!

At this point, Izzy was abruptly snatched from her scrutiny by the bleeping of the 'phone.

Either James or her papa, no doubt.

'Hello! Is that a certain person? At least, I hope it's a person… Or, the ghost of a person, at the very least?'

'Well, I really do hope so!' Surprise, surprise… It was her papa.

'And I believe congratulations are in order. Both Agnieska and myself are really happy for you. Of course, I shall need to meet

James, and soon; I know we've talked once on the 'phone already but don't you think it's time you were introducing him to your old dad?'

'Er, well, yes… I'm sure there'll be plenty of chances soon.'

'Good. I'm pleased to hear it.'

'Papa…….' Izzy ventured a little diffidently, 'I'm going to require your services when I actually do tie the knot… You're going to be needed to take me down the aisle.' But was there going to be an aisle at all, if she and James were having a beach wedding on the sands? Despite the fact that there would be no aisle, she would still require her father to preside in the role of 'Father of The Bride!'

'Oh, I'm sorry dear, but that's just not going to be possible… Why, I shall be busy attending to the musical arrangements!'

Izzy sensed that further trouble was about to erupt, besides, if they were going to marry on the sands, the amount of music required would be minimal. Why, oh why, was arranging and planning her wedding turning out to be so fraught with difficulty and major obstacles?

'Well, actually, papa, we're just thinking of a quiet, low-key event on the sands.'

'Oh, really? You see, with music being my forte, I would like to focus on the musical side of the service.'

Izzy felt furious. Why was her papa never there for her when she needed him?

'Well, you think over your role, you've still got plenty of time, after all, we're not doing it until mid-June of next year.'

'I'll have to go now,' said her papa rather dismissively and abruptly, 'I think your step-mother's calling me.'

'Goodbye, papa.'

'Goodbye, dear, and lorry loads of love.'

Izzy was still feeling irate as she replaced the receiver. Furthermore, to make matters worse, she was utterly at a loss in the face of her father's refusal to perform the honours, due to the fact that the music provision was his major and primary concern, of who to ask.

Her uncle William? No, he just would not do it. Her uncle Richard? Her half-brother, Christopher? Well, possibly, but he was in all probability likely to be fully occupied with the photographic matters.

Her uncle Colin? No. He too was altogether inappropriate! Her cousin Lawrence? Possibly. Her cousin Oscar? No, another one who fell into the category of 'never in a million years!' Absolutely not. The way things were looking at present, Izzy might well be making her own way across the beach.

Blanking out once again Izzy returned to Lady Gertrude's diary.

Monday morning, 15th April, 1887. I got myself up, washed and dressed and, after a rushed breakfast of coffee and toast, made my way across to the lecture theatre in the adjacent block. Already the lecture theatre is beginning to fill up and my friend Maria was waiting for me, I am so pleased! Our first lecture that morning was safe lifting and handling techniques, followed by prevention and management of patient incontinence. Maria and I are getting on especially well. We had lunch together and then attended our afternoon group session together. At the end of the afternoon session, Maria and I exchanged goodbyes and I made my brief way back to my accommodation. Yes, Leeds still feels strange, hostile and alien, but at least it is a little more familiar and welcoming than it was last week; yes, the hostile, alien and unfamiliar element now appears to have fallen to eighty percent. I shall continue to persevere.

After the evening meal, I sat in my room and completed some further background reading, furthermore, I noted down some items to tell Lord Ernest about, for example, my move to Leeds, my new friends and how much I currently missed Riversdale Hall and Ripon.

Suddenly, quite without warning, that famous prayer flitted once again through my consciousness.

'God grant me the equanimity to accept the things I cannot change… etc,' Yes, Gertrude you should, I told myself; which of course may also mean that if Lord Ernest feels we can ultimately have no future together and he finds another woman whose company he prefers, then this will have to be accepted with dignity. We shall have to see what transpires.

Tuesday, 16th April, 1887. Today was another profitable day and I enjoyed our lectures yet again.

Wednesday, 17th April, 1887. We were given clean sheets in order to remake our beds. As I changed my bed linen, an acute wave of sadness for Riversdale swept over me; I was simply not acclimatized or in any way used to changing bed sheets. How will I ever get used to this regime? Today, we were given an afternoon off lectures and group work, so I wandered into town, being careful to note the names of streets in order to be able to retrace my steps back to the hospital accommodation and took in the impressive architecture of the town hall, the flamboyant style of the Wool Exchange where papa frequently has business matters to attend to and the railway station. As I walked back to my accommodation, since I will not call it home, at least not yet at any rate, I felt a desperate pang to need to be on the train, the train departing for Ripon and my beautiful pastoral idyll of Riversdale, but remember Gertrude, you will be heading home in two days' time so try to make the best of your time in Leeds!

I am ashamed and disgusted with myself to admit that I was sick again this evening, and then flopped onto my bed feeling drained and fragile. This is not at all like me, since under normal circumstances I eat like a horse and usually enjoy my food without difficulty. When I was feeling a little more human and my stomach had had time to settle I began to pen a response to Lord Ernest. I completed the letter and put it to one side on my desk; it can be posted tomorrow.

I was just addressing the envelope when I was interrupted by a knock at my door. I shouted to the person to come in, which she did. It was Audrey. She and Caroline were sitting in another girl's room and would I like to join them? According to Audrey, she had knocked repeatedly earlier on and been unable to obtain a response. I apologized and told her that I had been unwell *a little earlier on and had fallen asleep due to sheer exhaustion, but yes, I would love to sit with them. I got up and followed her down the corridor.*

'My goodness!' Caroline was saying to one of the other girls, 'being here really makes me appreciate my home! I shall never take my home for granted ever again!'

'Too true!' I responded, 'And at present, I simply can't seem to get used to the food!'

'Oh, now I find the food quite good!' someone else commented.

How I wish I could say the same, I thought to myself that night.

Friday, 19th April, 1887. 'Tis Friday afternoon and I am now in the happy position of beginning to wend my way home by means of the quarter past five post-chaise service back to Ripon. I duly posted my communication to Lord Ernest which went into the five p.m. post. Hopefully, he will receive it early next week.

I am still not a devotee of Leeds, although this week has been slightly easier than the previous week.

I then enjoyed the carriage ride home. As we began to descend into the natural bowl of hills that encircles Riversdale Estate, I began to feel really excited. It felt so good to be going home! The estate looks so fresh, green and verdant and spring appears to have well and truly sprung! Another two days of private study await me.

Outside our home on the front terrace, my marvellous papa stood awaiting me with my step-mother, which I have to admit was a somewhat dubious pleasure!

'Welcome home, dear! You've been badly missed!' I did not stand on ceremony, but flung myself into his outstretched, welcoming arms. And I'm so happy to see you and have you here!

'Once back in Riversdale, Scamp could scarcely contain his excitement and sheer joy at seeing me again.

Izzy decided it was time to go to Hannah's Bar possibly for a couple of cocktails, so she disconnected the laptop and picked up her jacket from the hook behind the dining room door.

Izzy loved Hannah's Bar and over the years it had continually been her convenient little 'bolt hole.'

Well, such was it tonight. Furthermore, she was still at a loss for who to ask to perform her wedding honours. In fact, she was just preparing for bed when the 'phone began to ring out. Izzy went to answer it. It was James.

'Hello, dear!'

'Hello, James! Something rather unfortunate occurred this evening,' Izzy began pouring out her heart quite unreservedly to James.

'What transpired?'

'Well, I asked my papa if he would do the honours and take me down the aisle or across the beach and guess what? He refused! He said as music was his particular forte he would be focusing on the musical provisions and almost everyone else there seems to be a problem with!'

'I know the very person!'

'Who?'

'How about my business partner, friend and colleague, Benjamin Samuel Thomas Watson?'

Why hadn't Izzy thought of him before? Ben seemed just the man to fill the void.

'Try him tomorrow afternoon after work. I strongly suspect he'll be only too pleased to oblige. Goodnight, dear.'

And on that note, Izzy went to bed and slept soundly.

To Izzy's enormous relief, Ben was only too happy to oblige.

'Let's face it, I'd have felt insulted if you'd asked anyone else!'

Izzy gave him a hug. Another problem solved, for the time being at any rate. Thank goodness.

Once again, that night Izzy took refuge in Lady G's diary.

Monday, 22nd April, 1887. I'm just beginning my third week in the great urban metropolis of Leeds. Quite frankly, it is often a mystery to myself that I have lasted as long as I have, since at times, it has proved extremely difficult and a real struggle! Yet again, when I changed my bed linen at lunchtime, I wondered whether I would ever become used to it, and strongly suspected that I would not. Then later that evening, a few of us enjoyed further laughter and wine consumption in a colleague's bedroom and for the first real time in three weeks, I went to bed happy and under the impression at least that a good time had been enjoyed by us all. Personally, I still cannot yet warm to the town of Leeds entirely, although it is considerably easier, less strange and alien than it was last week and 'light years,' so to speak easier compared to the week before that. I would now rate my intrinsic degree of 'unsettlement,' at 70%. Once again, I took refuge at Riversdale from early Friday evening through to early Sunday evening and was again royally entertained by my wonderful papa.

Monday, 29th April, 1887. A strange, subtle, almost imperceptible change appears to have enveloped me. It is hard to believe, and I struggle to believe this myself, but I have been resident in Leeds for almost a month now and I am beginning to feel happy, settled and fulfilled. I really can scarcely believe it.

I have also received a reply from Lord Ernest. It must be borne in mind that I was extremely unsettled and new to the city when I penned my last missive. He thanked me profusely for my epistle and told me to persevere and not under any circumstances to give up, however tempted I might feel to do so. Do not worry, Lord Ernest, I am made of stronger stuff than that! To be completely honest, I am now beginning to enjoy solitary time in my room when I am entirely free and at liberty to do exactly as I please. Obviously, I spend a substantial amount of my time working, but my leisure time is equally precious and valuable.

On Thursday evening I packed my trunk, admittedly, three-quarters of my suitcase was still already packed but as I added my basic overnight essentials, I felt really happy! A vital turning point or crossroads seems to have been reached by myself.

We had two early afternoon lectures after a rather hurried lunch, and from there I began to retrace my steps over to the nurse education block, hopefully to meet up with Maria; I had walked but a few steps when I heard my friend, Audrey calling me.

'Gerty! Are you going over to the lecture block? Let's walk across together!'

'What an excellent idea!'

Audrey caught me up. She seemed friendly, outgoing and certainly keen to start a conversation with me.

'I can't believe it,' Audrey began, '…Just think, we've been here almost a month, it's quite frightening isn't it?'

'So true!' I answered. And furthermore, this is a fact. Yes, we have lived here for almost a month and here I am only able to speak for myself, but this week I have felt no sense of not belonging, unsettledness, depression, undue anxiety or alienation; my normal hearty, healthy appetite has returned and no vomiting sessions have occurred whatsoever. In fact, I have almost forgotten that I ever possessed those negative feelings. I do not think that I could have chosen a better town to study in.

I proceeded to sit happily in lectures and telegraphed my papa to inform him of my arrival at Riversdale early this evening. I have an essay to write, so I shall spend the bulk of the weekend in its' writing and composition. I also need to reply to Lord Ernest's letter, but I shall have to tell him of my newfound good fortune and how well matters are now progressing in Leeds. I do so love it, I feel now as though you could almost say that this is 'my city!'

Once again, this evening we enjoyed an excellent banquet and even my step-mother commented that I was looking far more like my old self.

Izzy passed a singularly unremarkable day in chambers, the bulk of the afternoon being largely occupied by a couple of client interviews, both extremely keen to clarify the provisions of their aunt Mildred's will. Just as Izzy was about to leave chambers at ten past five, who should appear but James armed with a new slightly later dated will relating to the same clients: a codicil had been added to the foot of the later will. As such, the clients now stood to inherit nothing from Aunt Mildred.

'Have you noticed this here codicil, dear? I'm extremely relieved to learn that those two money-grubbing creeps will now be inheriting precisely nothing from their Aunt Mildred!'

'Good.'

'My feelings entirely. Oh, I was also going to remind you dear, that now you've got your visit to your papa's home behind you, of course, we can now start to plan our short break to North Wales.'

'Sounds good to me.'

'It does, doesn't it?' And at that point, James smiled indulgently.

'Well, James, I'll leave that in your capable, competent hands. And now, James, I have matters requiring my attention at home, so I shall have to be making tracks.'

'Oh, really?' James appeared not entirely convinced by this excuse. 'Did you know mother would like to entertain us both for a special meal tomorrow, just think it will be our first meal with mother since we became engaged!'

That of course was true. Isabel could not help but show a brief flicker of irritation fleetingly cross her face; why ever had James not informed her earlier on during the week? Why had he left announcement of the proposed, impending rendezvous with Mrs Brodie until the last minute?

At this, James started to quickly try to smooth over matters, insisting, 'Now you know mother loves you! Why, in fact, she's desperate to meet you again?'

'Are you sure?' Izzy answered suspiciously, now unable to hide her innate irritation with James.

'Of course I am.'

At this point, Ben appeared from his own adjoining back office and asked tentatively, 'Oh, am I interfering in or interrupting something?'

'No, not at all,' answered Izzy, although in reality this was quite obviously not the case, 'in fact, I think it's time that I was getting myself home. I'll leave our short break in North Wales organization to yourself, James. In fact, you can start that tonight. Goodnight, gentlemen!'

Izzy stepped out into the hustle and bustle of Dale Street and was still quietly fuming when she arrived back at Percy Street. Why could James not have given her a little more warning, if only to allow Izzy time to mentally prepare herself, if nothing else? Once again, safely settled in the first floor flat, she resorted again to Lady Gertrude's diary entries.

Wednesday, 1ˢᵗ May, 1887. I feel so happy! Yes, happy and excited! Leeds has turned out to be all I ever imagined and envisaged, AND MORE! Additionally, I managed to write to Lord Ernest, and he himself is so very happy that I have settled in. He is now enjoying the wonders of Venice! They say it is a veritable wonder of the world!

We have examinations to prepare for in three weeks' time, so I have already begun my revision. This is a basic anatomy and physiology test, which I am quite sure I can easily cope with, provided I complete some thorough revision and preparation beforehand. Personally, I revise slowly, so it is best if I begin my revision early.

Strangely enough, Mrs Brodie's dinner party went surprisingly well, and Martina even produced a decent quality bottle of champagne to toast James and Izzy's future together.

Later that evening, as James and Izzy sat in Percy Street with their night caps, James told Izzy of his current attempts to organise and arrange their short break to North Wales.

'Well, I 'phoned round a few hotels, but was not too impressed with any of them, quite frankly. I'm certain I can find somewhere better to wine and dine my Izzy! Oh, er, and I'm sorry I placed my fiancée under a lot of pressure yesterday; that was not exactly the done thing. I really do apologize.'

'No, it's quite alright.' That was not entirely true. It had not really been acceptable, not by any means.

'And mother's not a bad old stick, either. Not when you get to know her.'

'I actually do really like your mother.'

'Good. I'm pleased to hear it. So, my fiancée really likes her future mother-in-law. I'm so very pleased about that. My fiancée… I've still not fully taken it in.'

Once again, James and Izzy bade goodnight at the Percy Street flat front door, James caught a taxi and wended his way back to his luxurious home in Woolton, Mrs Brodie and his strange dog.

On Monday evening of next week, Izzy was again disrupted in her reading of Lady G's diary by the 'phone. Once again, it was James.

'Now then, young Izzy! Don't you think that the time may well be right for us to start possibly looking round for a house to move into? After all, in mid-June of next year we will be a married couple!'

Why did the prospect of marrying James in seven months' time suddenly fill Izzy with a strange, deep-seated, inexplicable sense of panic and dread? Wasn't this a little too rushed? At this point, a phrase from Shakespeare's Romeo and Juliet coursed through her brain:

'Tis too rushed, too sudden, too unadvised…

Too much like the lightening, that doth cease to be, 'ere one can say it lightens.'

Bearing in mind the age gap, was this a wise move? Yes, Izzy and James worked well together, but that was not automatically a reason for Izzy to spend the rest of her life with him? No, most certainly not.

'You're very quiet,' James seemed slightly annoyed, and then he proceeded to add, 'Why, I at least think that we ought to start to look round.'

'Well, er, yes. Whereabouts in Liverchester?'

'Oh, I was thinking of Woolton again. Or at least, somewhere in that vicinity!'

Not Woolton, thought Izzy to herself, it was somehow so suburban! Whatever was wrong with a nice, decent house in Crosby or possibly even Falkner Square or Falkner Street?

'No, I need to be near Woolton,' James persisted, 'besides, I need, er, well I have to be within easy reach of mother… After all, she's not as young as she once was!'

Izzy thought of Mossley Hill; that was a green, verdant and well-heeled area, plus it was so convenient for the rest of town and the shops.

'Well, er, Mossley Hill's nice and so is Allerton!'

'Oh, never in a million years!' said James dismissively. He was completely persistent and seemed to refuse to take 'no' for an answer. Furthermore, every possible alternative place Izzy suggested, James promptly threw an obstacle in its' path.

'Well, for the time being we shall have to agree to disagree,' James said at last, in his characteristically heavy-handed manner.

'How sensible,' answered Izzy flatly. She felt almost beyond trying to further argue and reason. But as Izzy later looked back on the events of that evening, that night marked a momentous turning point in a decline in her relations with James, and Izzy began to realise that she still knew relatively little about James; doubts concerning the future and viability of their relationship began to henceforth sprout through the cracks were once only stability, trust and love had reigned supreme, and above all, was there a purpose or any point in James and Izzy as a couple?

A few days later, Izzy and James did spend some after work hours searching for a possible property, but then came to the conclusion that it might be best to call it a day for the time being, at any rate, since their taste in properties appeared to be so radically different. The next day at work passed unremarkably, with James absent, since he was once again working from home. To be absolutely honest, Izzy found she was not missing him, not in the slightest, in fact, matters seemed ultimately more straightforward and far less complicated in James's absence.

As Izzy made her way home past Sainsbury's, the bombed-out church and Hannah's Bar, she briefly reflected on how well the day had progressed. The moment she had set foot in the elegant, decorous, first-floor flat, she poured herself a glass of red wine feeling in need of a little liquid sustenance and then headed straight for her laptop wondering what pearls of innate wisdom were likely to spill from either the mouth or pen of her nineteenth century idol.

Thursday, 2ⁿᵈ May, 1887. Another highly profitable and extremely worthwhile day. I further consolidated all the revision I had so far completed.

At that point, Izzy was again abruptly interrupted by the front doorbell. She switched off the laptop and nipped down the stairs to answer it. Who awaited Izzy on the other side of the elegant Georgian door case? None other than James armed with an enormous bouquet of red roses.

'These, darling, are for yourself. I just wanted to say I was sorry for, er, being a little dictatorial.'

'Oh, James, that really doesn't matter at all. You'd better come in. Please come in and make yourself comfortable.'

'Oh, thank you, young lady,' answered James a little sheepishly.

Once again, they climbed the rickety staircase up to the first floor.

'Thank you, James. They're absolutely beautiful.' Izzy managed to find a large vase in the kitchen, which she filled up with tap water and carefully began to arrange them in the vase.

When she had completed their careful arrangement, she asked James, 'Now, darling, would you like your usual? Or anything else from my drink's cabinet?'

James beamed. 'I'll have my usual please, if I may. The strong Belgian lager.'

'Consider it done.' Izzy promptly vanished to the kitchen and reappeared with a bottle, a glass and an opener. Then she vanished and reappeared again with the pink gin bottle, a glass and a bottle of Schweppes tonic water.

'Well, what are we drinking to tonight?' asked Izzy, as she poured herself a glass of the gin.

'How about, 'To us finding a house which we both find acceptable!' James suggested.

'Yes, I'll drink to that!' answered Izzy emphatically.

'And also, to our future!' James added as an afterthought.

'Yes, to our future!'

They raised their glasses, and both took mouthfuls.

'I'm sure we'll find somewhere that we'll both be proud to call our own,' James said presently.

'Well, of course we will,' Izzy assented.

'Now, I wanted to come round for two reasons,' James began, rather pompously, 'one was to say I was sorry for being so impossible, and the second was to make some further arrangements and plans for our wedding next year; yes, our wedding on the sands!'

'Just imagine,' said Izzy a little uncertainly, 'bearing in mind how close I live to the beach, we're not even going to need any taxis! Why, we can just walk down from my house! We might need wedding cars to get to the hotel, but we could always contact a caterers and have the food at my house, or alternatively, out in the garden!'

'Sounds good to me,' James answered, 'and of course, that means we'll save some more money.'

'And I can have a bouquet of pink roses and white carnations, James.'

'Of course you may,' answered James as he quietly sipped his Belgian lager.

Izzy took another mouthful of her gin and carefully savoured its' pungent taste before it made its' way down her throat.

'And we can have our honeymoon in Sicily and Sardinia, or Grand Canaria or wherever.'

'Well, somewhere like that,' James answered, smiling indulgently once again.

'Yes, James,' answered Izzy, quite confidently at the time, although a little later on, looking back in retrospect she wondered whether in reality it had simply been bravado, 'In June of next year, I shall be only to pleased to take thee, James Dominic Martin Brodie to be my lawful wedded husband… To love, honour, cherish and obey… Till death do us part… You see, I'm an old-fashioned girl at heart, and yes, I will obey you!'

'I always knew you would! And I'm greatly relieved to hear it!' James laughed and took a further sip of his lager. Yet again, he placed his left hand on Izzy's right knee and after a couple of minutes silence, eventually uttered the words, 'So, once we find a decent house in a decent area, we'll be good to go. Somehow, I have this feeling we're going to be really happy.'

That evening in the Percy Street flat, an aura of 'calm after the storm,' peace, accord and happiness seemed to prevail. Izzy continued to sip her gin and after about a minute's silence, she managed to say in response, 'Yes. I think so too.'

James's next casual comment was music to her ears.

'Well, our wedding preparations are almost complete, with, er, one exception.'

'And what is that James?' Izzy queried.

'I am not, under any circumstances prepared to wear a wedding ring. No, I'm perfectly happy with my signet ring; in fact, next to my wristwatch it's all the jewellery I want and need.'

'How sensible.'

'I'm like my business partner, colleague and good friend, Benjamin Watson, remember, we're both ringless and furthermore, intend to remain that way!'

'Good. My feelings entirely. Incidentally, would you like another Belgian lager?'

'Don't mind if I do, young lady.'

Izzy went into the kitchen to retrieve the lager and they spent a further happy three-quarters of an hour in general conversation, before James announced that he believed it was now time for him to leave.

'Now then, our Izzy… I, er, don't wish to outstay my welcome, so I think that it's probably time I loved and left you.'

'Well, I was just about to make my way to bed, at any rate,' Izzy answered.

'Don't bother to come down, young lady… Now I may be working from home tomorrow, so you may well not see me in chambers, but I shall certainly be in the day after.'

'Well, I'll see you whenever, James.'

James held Izzy close to him for a few minutes, after which he made his way out to Percy Street and hailed a passing taxi.

Izzy proceeded to get her head down and then slept soundly and comfortably.

The next day was a singularly uneventful and unremarkable day in chambers with the usual range of tasks to be completed. Once again, that evening, Izzy took refuge in Lady Gertrude's diary entries.

Thursday, 2ⁿᵈ May, 1887. I still feel really happy and believe I have chosen the right path.

I am still attending all my lectures and classes, and on the whole, really enjoy them. Dare I say it? One afternoon, we were given a tour of the mortuary would you believe it? This was not by any means one of our better hospital experiences, and I am pleased it is now well and truly behind me! What a relief!

There was now no further diary entry until Monday 6ᵗʰ May, 1887.

Monday, 6ᵗʰ May, 1887. I sat happily in my morning lectures, studiously writing down the nursing notes. Oh, yes, and I have a small secret to share with you now! I have received a reply from Lord Ernest, who is now as we speak, thoroughly enjoying the delights of Venice.

He loves to lose himself on the canals and many back streets of Venice, admire the marvellous architecture of Venice's plethora of churches and sip his morning coffee in St Mark's square in the sunlight. Simultaneously, he is delighted I have settled in Leeds, made a few good friends, and am entirely committed to my nursing studies. Furthermore, he also highly recommends the Venetian aperitifs which he enjoys nightly before his evening meal.

I believe these comprise a measure of Pernod, white wine and lemonade, termed a 'spritzer!'

In fact, of his own admission, he even thoroughly enjoys to sip one comfortably sitting in the back of a gondola after a meal!

He believes he may next progress down to the Bay of Naples, Herculaneum and Pompeii, since he finds Roman ruins and remains fascinating, but this will not be for a good few days, since he is still entranced by the glories of Venice and wishes to see as much of the town as is physically possible in the given timespan. Like myself, he is similarly intrigued by the history of Venice and by the many poets, authors and artists who lived within its' confines and who possessed real, genuine talent and natural ability, yet who never managed to sell or profit from a single work and who ended their days in absolute penury in the upper rooms of Venice's many decaying, rotting tenements.

I believe if I possessed Italian nationality, Venice would be extremely special to me, in fact, you might almost say it would be the equivalent of what Leeds is to me now as a nineteenth century Englishwoman, who now really loves her home from home!

Friday, 10th May, 1887. When I returned to Ripon and Riversdale this evening, papa and I went for an early evening walk on the estate. It was a beautiful early summer evening, with all plant life bursting into flower and foliage, the weather was warm and calm, and a general overall sense of positivity and well-being seemed to prevail. I told papa how happy I now was in Leeds and I was certain I had made the right choice in my move to the great metropolis. Papa told me how pleased he was that I was now happy and told me he was a little worried about my older brother, Harry, who is now heavily embroiled in his final year examinations. As I have already said, I am also facing examinations in the not too distant future, but I have a little longer to prepare for them and the subject under examination is considerably easier.

We then returned happily to the hall in order to await our now customary Friday evening banquet, held in my honour. Needless to say, the food was excellent and I believe a good time was had by all.

Saturday, 11th May, 1887. This morning I sorted out my nursing notes, made a little more progress with my revision and successfully completed yet further background reading. I then ate a brief lunch and then resumed my studies until early evening when papa called me downstairs and told me that I had to rest and call it an evening for tonight. He was absolutely right. After attending church on Sunday morning, I returned to my studies feeling refreshed and greatly regenerated. I shall be all ready and prepared to face my lectures tomorrow morning. Just think, this will be my sixth week! It has quite simply flown past!

Monday, 13th May, 1887. We wrote several pages of notes today. At the end of our session at four-thirty my right hand quite ached with writing, but I do feel as though I have learned a lot and greatly increased my knowledge! It has been yet another profitable and productive day.

Tuesday, 14th May, 1887. Of my own admission, I thoroughly enjoyed my breakfast this morning. I happily consumed two rashers of bacon and a generous helping of scrambled egg, all rinsed down with two mugs of strong coffee. Thank goodness my normal, hearty, healthy appetite has returned. Of course, it now goes without saying that I easily and with no difficulty whatsoever kept my breakfast down.

Another day of heavy note-taking awaited us. And again, I am happy to say that I really enjoyed it. After my evening meal, I completed further revision and preparation for my forthcoming examination.

Much to Izzy's surprise, there were no detailed diary entries now until the end of May, 1887. Gertrude next put pen to paper on Wednesday, 28th May, 1887 and simply describes the last two weeks as, '…Filled with study, revision and general preparation.'

Thursday, 29th May, 1887. I sat my first examination. I do not wish to tempt fate, but I think it went reasonably well and I believe I tackled it fairly competently.

Friday, 30th May, 1887. I had another examination to sit this morning. No tempting of fate will occur, but I feel as though my response to the paper was reasonably satisfactory. I hope so, at any rate. The examination was over by lunchtime. I am pleased to say that in the aftermath of the examination, we were given the rest of the day off; so after a small amount of shopping in the city centre, I packed my suitcase and caught an early post-chaise service home.

I wish to stress at this juncture, that I certainly did not spend an excessive amount of money at the shops. No, I bought a medium-sized bottle of perfume which had been reduced in price, due to the fact that it comprised old stock and two tablets of delicately perfumed, luxury soap, which will be a welcome relief from the cheap tablet of carbolic with which my step-mother dispatched me from Riversdale, one month previously.

What a blessed relief! Happiness is having got my two examinations out of the way! My goodness, it is almost worth sitting examinations, almost like 'hitting one's head against the proverbial brick wall, yes, almost worth doing, since it is so nice when one stops!' Switch off now, Gertrude and try to relax. Of course, we have further examinations to revise and prepare for, but not just yet; these will occur later on during the year and there are several scheduled for next year, but obviously, I shall not worry about these yet, at any rate.

Do you know? My marvellous papa was again so very pleased to see me, so was Scamp, my wayward dog and even my step-mother appeared happy to see me. Best of all, I received further communication from Lord Ernest. He is delighted about my new-found happiness in Leeds, and is continuing to reside in Venice which he loves for only a further week; from where he is now proposing to progress to Florence (this is a slight change of plan, since he originally intended to progress from Venice straight down to Pompeii, Herculaneum and the Bay of Naples), so his grand tour will take a little longer.

He is now attempting to see all the churches of Venice which he has not viewed so far, as he actually tells me there are a hundred and twenty churches in Venice in total! I feel as though I am with him in spirit. I will reply in a few days' time.

Much to Izzy's surprise, there were no diary entries whatsoever for the next week. In fact, the next one was dated:

Friday, 13th June, 1887. At coffee break time, I received some marvellous news! I actually managed to pass both my examinations with fifty-three percent and forty-eight percent. I feel so happy and relieved! We will start our ward allocations in early September. I then immediately telegraphed papa with my good news and told him that I would be arriving on the early evening post-chaise service back at Riversdale.

Furthermore, papa had additional good news for me, so it was good news all round! My dear older brother did extremely well in his third-year examinations and obtained an average of 74%; in other words, first-class honours! Papa is so pleased with both of us!

I am pleased to say that I received a further epistle from the enigmatic Lord Ernest. He has now safely arrived in Florence three days ago, and is absolutely enchanted by the architecture. Again, he has found a place to sip his morning coffee in the sunlight. The ducal palace, the art gallery, the churches, what a place! He is spending ten days in Florence before progressing on to Rome, Rome, the eternal city! I am sure Lord Ernest will find plenty to interest him there!

Chapter 15.

When Izzy arrived at work the next morning, she was faced with a scenario she had encountered once before and was only too familiar with. James and Ben were having a row.

Angry raised voices seemed to be spilling from the confines of James's inner office. Izzy and Tanya cast each other anxious looks for a few moments, and eventually, Izzy not wishing to give the impression that she was eavesdropping on either partner, took refuge in her own room.

Matters appeared to reach a climax, when a furious Ben Watson stormed out, angrily shouting, '…Of course, it has absolutely nothing to do with me, but you know what they say, 'There's no fool like an old fool! I hope when I next hear from you again, you'll be in a slightly more amenable frame of mind! I'm going to Hill Foster's… Until further notice!'

So fifty-eight year old Ben Watson was leaving and lending his services to Hill Foster's?

Needless to say, three-quarters of an hour later, James called a crisis meeting.

'Er, you see, Ben and I have had a slight, er… Altercation and Ben has left chambers… For the time being, at any rate.'

'So did you two get each other's goats then?' asked Tanya.

'Well, in a nutshell, yes. Of course, in a partnership, this sort of thing inevitably sometimes happens,' James explained, 'but it beats me why he wants to go to those beggars; you mark my words, if our Ben stays any length of time with them, in a couple of months he'll be begging to come back to these humble old chambers – of that I am absolutely certain!'

'I wouldn't worry too much if I were you, James!' answered Tanya confidently and shuffled back to her desk on her sky-scraper heels.

Izzy felt as though her only option was to try to stay out of the way. Ten minutes later, James brought some tasks in and she set to work to complete them.

'So now of course, I'm a sole practitioner.'

'Well, er, yes, I believe so.'

'Somehow, I never thought our partnership would end in this way. It feels like the end of an era.'

The next few weeks passed uneventfully and James and Izzy continued to see each other, enjoying romantic candlelit meals, visits to wine bars and public houses. As the trainee, it fell to Izzy to calculate Ben's share of the profits, his earnings for November and his capital contribution towards the partnership needed to be returned to him in accordance with the partnership agreement from the appropriation account. Maths and basic accounts had never been either Izzy or James's natural fortes, but James checked the calculations through once Izzy had completed the exercise; then asked Mr Quinn from Stanley Street chambers to oversee the final figure of forty-three and a half thousand pounds, a cheque for which was duly forwarded to Benjamin.

'It's just not the same without Mr Watson,' Tanya commented sadly that afternoon, 'he was such good fun, I'd give anything to have him back. Always smiling and cheerful, he was!'

Izzy felt a little embarrassed, and now she felt the need to defend James, so she answered laughingly,

'You mean Mr Brodie's not?'

'Of course he is! I didn't mean it like that, Mr Brodie's a real gentleman; they were two gentlemen together, but Mr Watson was… er, a good laugh!' What Tanya really intended to say, Izzy strongly suspected, was that Benjamin Watson was a bit more fun than James Brodie, but did not wish to appear too derogatory or contemptuous of Mr Brodie in front of his fiancée.

'Yes, 'tis a real pity!' Tanya added. 'Right, I'll see you in the morning, Izzy!'

Retracing her steps back along Dale Street and North John Street, Izzy knew exactly what Tanya was meaning. In fact, she found it quite difficult to believe herself – James and Ben, now going their separate ways! The partners who had worked so well for so many years, combining their strengths and skills to form an extremely successful double act were now no longer a partnership. Their combined years of practical experience exceeding fifty years was now dissolved! And did Ben know anything about Hill Foster's? Izzy had to admit she knew nothing about them herself, but she felt a deep-seated sense of intrinsic dread and distinctly negative 'vibes!' She stopped at Clintons in Liverchester One shopping centre and bought a 'Good Luck in Your New Job,' card. She would drop it off at Hill Foster's tomorrow afternoon after she had finished work.

But meanwhile, Lady Gertrude's diary was again calling.

Saturday, 14ᵗʰ June, 1887. The entire estate looks so fresh, green and beautiful, as I take Scamp for his morning run. Furthermore, some of the gardeners, servants and workmen have commented on how healthy and happy I look. I am now in the happy position of not having to revise or prepare for an examination, having easily passed the previous two. That said, I shall start to prepare for my next term back in Leeds but that does not take place until early September, so I shall award myself the luxury of a few days 'breathing space,' before I begin my new preparation for next term.

Oh, and I have heard from Lord Ernest. He is now in Rome and this time he is enjoying the architectural delights and treasures of the eternal city. He loves the churches, catacombs and colloseum and thoroughly enjoys to wander round this city soaking up its' atmosphere and history. I will answer his missive in a few days, and inform him of my good news in passing the two examinations which I sat.

Ernest also commented that all this travelling was considerably broadening his mind, and it would seem extremely provincial to have to return to Bolton, (where his ancestral home is), and his workplace of Leeds in eighteen months' time! Do not be selfish, Gerty. If you two really do have a future together, this absence might make your union ultimately all the stronger and also when Lord Ernest does eventually return, you will have plenty to talk about! Alternatively, if you have no future together, it is probably best if we establish that fact now. At any rate, I feel so happy and lucky to now have a home from home which I love so much! As I said before, Leeds is most certainly, 'my city!'

Because I am now fully aware of a life beyond Riversdale Hall and Ripon, I am altogether now happier and far more satisfied with my life, when I am back resident at Riversdale. But that said, I shall be more than happy to return to Leeds in early September to start our practical work allocations. But until then, I shall enjoy every moment of Riversdale!

Izzy spent an uneventful evening in the flat and curled up early in her bed, bearing in mind that she needed to get a reasonable night's sleep in order to be ready for work the next morning. Her day at work was equally unremarkable and furthermore, chambers seemed so terribly quiet without Ben. Unnaturally so. Before Izzy left work at ten past five, she wrote and signed Ben's card from herself, bade goodnight to James and Tanya and began to make her way in the general direction of Hill Fosters' chambers.

Nothing could have prepared Izzy for the shock that assaulted her senses at these chambers. In fact, the chambers made a deep impression on Izzy and not a favourable one either. Harsh, glaring overhead lighting occupied most of the ceiling space and some rather tasteless piped music filled the anonymous, impersonal, far too large waiting and reception area. Had Ben seriously known what he was doing in deciding to move here? Something seemed definitely not quite right. As Izzy recalled a few weeks later, 'There was something somehow about those chambers which made my flesh crawl!' Izzy took her envelope over to the expressionless receptionist who Izzy noticed, possessed neat, immaculately manicured nails painted a harsh shade of bright red, and said quietly and calmly, 'I'd like this card to go to Benjamin Watson, please.' 'Benjamin Watson?' No signs of recognition whatsoever appeared on the receptionist's face. Then she routinely scanned the list of partners.

'Ah, Ben or Benjamin Watson! He's in our property department. It can go in the internal post.'

Izzy thankfully beat a hasty retreat. So, Ben had gone to the property department! But he hated that branch of law! Somehow, old-fashioned, dusty, 'Dickensian gloom' filled 79, Dale Street complete with the slightly bumbling James and the scatty Tanya seemed ultimately preferable and completely light years away! In fact, Izzy would only too happily kiss the floor of the front office when she returned next week! Izzy could not envisage Ben lasting long at Hill Fosters'. Not in that purpose-built, impersonal, anonymous, modern environment, where Izzy suspected, employees were not in the least valued; there, employees were exploited, resigned from sheer frustration, desperation or were fired and were then unceremoniously promptly replaced. At this point, Izzy remembered James's immortal words, 'Why, we couldn't run these chambers without you!' Yes, Brodie, the now sole practitioner, where employees were valued, appreciated and sensitively dealt with.

Izzy returned to Cumbria that evening where she spent a couple of days de-stressing. She loved her Cumbrian weekends, but she was more than ready to return to Liverchester on Sunday evening. No need to bother with Hannah's Bar tonight, Izzy thought she would prefer to save her money, besides, Lady Gertrude's diary was calling.

There were now no further diary entries until Sunday 3rd September, 1887. Again, a captivated Izzy read on.

Sunday, 3rd September, 1887. I returned on the half-past four post-chaise service back to Leeds. I have thoroughly enjoyed my sojourn back at Riversdale and Ripon, but I am now really happy to be back in Leeds.

Somehow, I feel as though the Rivers family (Junior) will be associated with the city of Leeds for quite a few years to come, since my dear older brother Harry begins his P.hD studies, again in the noble and urban delights of this Yorkshire city in early October and I still have another eighteen months left of my nurse training to complete; not only that, but I feel tempted to stay on to work here once I am fully trained. Oh, well! I shall have plenty of chances to sample different ward environments when we are notified of the exact venue of our ward allocations. We have been given specific instructions to present ourselves in the lecture theatre of the nurse education block tomorrow morning at nine thirty. The rest of Monday is to be a normal day of lectures, ending at four-thirty in the afternoon, when we will then be informed of the wards we will be sent to. I now feel really quite excited!

I prepared my clothes for the morning and went to bed quite early in order to get a full and decent night's sleep. Back at Riversdale, papa and Harry will doubtless be supping the port for some time to come! Let them! I am more than happy to go to sleep tonight at an early hour!

By quarter past nine of the morning after, I was retracing my steps along the path leading to the nurse education building. Once I arrived, I met my good friend, Maria, who seemed so very pleased to see me after our summer recess. We were given an essay to prepare, entitled, 'How to promote quality patient care,' which is due for submission just before Christmas. Henceforth, for the duration of this term, which lasts until just before Christmas, we will have what is known as one 'study day' per week, beginning at nine-thirty each Monday morning and is devoted to a series of lectures; with the remaining four days being given over to clinical practice in the hospital.

Maria and I ate lunch together and then went back to sit and enjoy our lecture whilst carefully taking down the notes. The lecturer also advised us not to attempt to start work on our essays until we had completed at least half the term's study days, since we would not yet possess enough adequate information to hope to complete writing our essays satisfactorily. We also had a session on how to take blood pressure readings, safely use the equipment and accurately record our findings, since this is a task all too often allocated to probationer nurses, which of course is what we are.

Last of all, we were notified of the venues for our first ward allocations.

'Gertrude Rivers, you will be sent to ward 3B, the geriatric ward.' We were then advised to visit the wards to which we were to be sent to in order to inform the ward staff that we would be arriving the next day and the shifts we would be required to attend.

Once our class had dispersed, and Maria and I had gone our separate ways, I walked back to my accommodation by way of the hospital, paying a rapid visit to ward 3B; which incidentally looks very nice and civilised and the staff seem both agreeable and helpful. I have been given two late shifts and two early day shifts. I am to work on the late shift tomorrow. I will be able to explain a little bit more after tomorrow is over!

Tuesday, 5th September, 1887. Of my own admission, I lay in bed rather longer than I should have done this morning. I missed breakfast, needless to say, so instead I ate a really early lunch and changed into my delightful pink probationer nurse's dress, complete with the dovetailed frilled cap, precariously balanced on my head with my long black hair brushed back and held in a large central slide with supporting small combs at either side. The afternoon shift begins in approximately fifteen minutes time.

I should not have worried. The staff on this ward are delightful and really are only too pleased for their trainees to learn and furthermore, to make their probationers' experience a positive and pleasurable experience. I introduced myself to the old ladies on our ward and informed them that I would be responsible for their care over the next few weeks.

Yes, Lord Ernest and I have again exchanged epistles. He stayed two months in Rome, due to the fact that there was so much to look at. He is now enjoying the flesh pots of the Bay of Naples, Pompeii and Herculaneum. Again, there is much to see. I shall pen a reply in a few days' time and when I have had sufficient time to be able to compose an appropriate response.

Wednesday, 6th September, 1887. The early day shift begins at quarter past seven in the morning. A horrible, unearthly hour, since I am not, certainly not a morning person. But it is a necessary evil and has to be done!

I have stated earlier, I introduced myself to the old ladies yesterday; and this morning, I assisted some of them to wash and change their nightwear. Much to my surprise, the vast majority really liked me and this afternoon, a singularly memorable event occurred! The newly trained staff nurse thought that it would be good experience for me to attend the 'ward round,' which I was quite keen to do myself. This basically comprises a brief inspection of the patients by the medical staff and a general conversation between the medical and nursing staff regarding patient progress. As the ward round party left the end bed in the left hand corner, the occupant, a Jewish woman in her early eighties became extremely agitated.

'What's wrong, Judith?' asked Martin, the registrar.

'Gerty! Gerty! I want Gerty!'

'Gerty will come back and see you when we've finished the ward round!'

'Good. I need her.'

There was no entry for 7th September, 1887.

Friday, 8th September, 1887. I again got up for the early day shift. No, the getting up so early is not too pleasant.

Anyone who believes that this is a glamorous job is absolutely wrong! This morning alone I emptied three stinking bed pans. My goodness, after the third one I almost heaved myself, right down the sluice!

There was now no further diary entry until 15th November, 1887.

Friday, 15th November, 1887. Today is the last day of my allocation to this ward, and I actually feel quite sorry to leave it! Guess what? And I really am so pleased about this.

Madeleine, the staff nurse who completed my clinical allocation work card told me and also wrote what amounted to this on my card:

'Gertrude! You've done really well. You are so very kind to the patients on the ward and they really do appreciate and value you for it. You have also adapted and coped extremely well with the distasteful aspects of the job. At the same time, you're also extremely popular with the ward staff. We wish you all the very best with your future ward allocations.'

She then proceeded to tick all the clinical competencies which I had attained.

At that point, Izzy was brought sharply back to reality by her 'phone ringing out. She leaned across to answer it.

'Hello, Liverchester, 707 4396!'

'Oh, is that Izzy?'

'Yes.'

'Oh, hello, Izzy. It's Ben Watson.'

'Oh, hello, Ben!'

'Er, Izzy, I've 'phoned for a couple of reasons. The first is to thank you for your delightful card. The second is, er, the new job…'

'Oh, how's that going?'

'To put it bluntly, and I won't mince my words, it's absolutely ghastly!'

'Do you know, Ben? When I went round there, at just after five on Friday, I had distinctly bad vibes.'

'Yes, I should imagine you might. Some of the powers that be have been making nasty, snide comments saying that they believe I'm too old to work for them, they prefer younger men in their twenties and thirties because they have a longer working life ahead of them, plus Lilian's told me I'm no longer the man she married – I'm apparently moody, irritable, unreasonable and foul tempered and if I don't resign, she'll leave me. Would you be able to put in some good words for me with James, I really would do anything to go back to 79, Dale Street?'

'Yes, with pleasure,' Izzy answered.

'My goodness! That place, you could write a book about it!'

'Oh, really?'

'Oh, for certain! Now James and I had a slight altercation, er, for reasons best known to ourselves, but at least James is a man of principle.'

'Oh, he's certainly that.' Izzy suspected what the subject of the altercation concerned, but she decided not to probe too far into that particular subject.

'Having a shower and then changing your clothing, sleeping in the office, amongst other things; I've done enough of that in a month to last me a lifetime. Work folders to be completed for every matter you work on, I'm just not used to that sort of thing.'

'Ben, leave it to me. Consider it done.'

Ben laughed at the other end of the 'phone. If you manage it, Izzy dear, you've saved my life and I'd be eternally grateful to you!'

'Don't worry, Ben, I shall work on James.'

'Somehow, I think you will. At any rate, I will have to leave you now and I shall start to write my resignation.'

'You know, Benjamin, I shall tell you what me old grandma used to say…'

'And what's that?'

'Don't let the bastards grind you down!'

'And that's precisely what some of them are!'

'Yes, I can imagine.'

'Just think, James will be a little surprised, old Tom Doolittle going back to Brodie's!'

'Doolittle? What do you mean?'

'Oh, it was a barrister's chambers that I once happened to drive past in Banbury in Oxfordshire, years ago. The name of the chambers was Doolittle and Dally and I was tickled by the name, you ask James about old D and D's!'

'Yes, I will.'

'I'm feeling quite a lot better already,' said Ben, 'at any rate, I shall have to go now, I think Lil's calling me! Goodbye, Izzy!'

'Goodbye, Ben!'

Izzy replaced the receiver on the 'phone. So one unhappy Ben, desperate to come back to 79, Dale Street. Yet again, Izzy's reflections were shattered by the 'phone ringing out. Izzy again reached over to answer it.

'Hello, Liverchester 707 4396!'

'Oh hello, Izzy, dear,' it was James, 'at last your 'phone becomes free; I've been 'phoning, phoning, phoning! Or at least, attempting to 'phone.'

'That was Ben on the other end of the 'phone… You know, Ben whom you used to work with. Well, it just so happens that he's really unhappy in his new job.'

'And does he want me to do something?'

'Well, in a nutshell, yes. He says he'd do just about practically anything to get back to our dusty old chambers.'

'And suppose James will not allow that?' James then broke into a sudden laugh, '…Get away! He can always have his job back, the door is always open at 79, Dale Street, to be absolutely honest, I'd be only too pleased to have him back, it's rather lonely being employed as a sole practitioner, our chambers have just not been the same without him!'

'So true,' Izzy answered.

'Now, dear, I telephoned because I wondered if you would like to eat at that quaint little below ground level restaurant, you know, the 'Olive Press,' I've eaten there once before and it was excellent.'

'Yes, oh, James, you know I would love to.'

'Say, tomorrow night; if I call at the flat at the usual time, say, eight-thirty?'

'Sounds good to me!'

'I knew it! Somehow, I just knew it! I knew Ben would dislike Hill Foster's, thank goodness we didn't destroy any of the partnership notepaper!'

'No, that was rather lucky,' Izzy assented.

'Just think,' ventured James, 'When Ben does arrive back we could have a little welcome back 'do', nothing expensive, we all just pay for ourselves, you know, in the back room at Rigby's.'

The prospect of the welcome back function made Izzy feel quite excited and she told James that she thought it was an excellent idea.

'Of course, I will pay for your good self. I think it's high time I got away from my image of being, 'the last of the big spenders!'

'Oh, I wouldn't worry about that if I were you, James, to my mind at least, you're an extremely warm and generous man.'

'Good. Well, you know I do try to be,' answered James, in his characteristically true to form manner of speaking, 'I'll next give Ben a call to inform him that his abrupt 'down tools' in a fit of pique has been well and truly forgiven and forgotten! Furthermore, both the senior partner and the trainee are highly pleased and relieved to have him back on board, just as soon as he's worked out his notice at Hill Foster's!'

'Oh, marvellous!'

'And you, young lady, how are you spending the rest of the evening?'

At this unanticipated question, Izzy felt a little embarrassed and 'put on the spot.' She had envisaged that she might continue to read Lady Gertrude's diary for a few further pages and then progress to Hannah's Bar for a couple of cocktails.

'I'm just reading something I found on the internet, and then I thought I might progress to Hannah's Bar for a cocktail. Then, I shall need to sort out my clothes for tomorrow night, if we're going to be wining and dining!'

'That sounds good to me,' answered James a little stiffly.

Izzy then remembered what Ben had said concerning the barrister's chambers in Banbury, especially Messrs Doolittle and Dally.

'Oh, James, Ben was saying something about Tom Doolittle, oh, and er, Mr Dally. He told me to ask yourself when I next see or speak to you.'

James laughed knowingly, 'Oh, that was our secret code name! I'll tell you a bit more when I see you tomorrow night.'

'Well, that will be a treat in store,' answered Izzy.

'I had better go now,' said James, 'I believe mother's calling me!'

'I'll let you go,' Izzy responded, 'and goodnight, James!'

'Goodnight, dear!'

Izzy replaced the receiver on the 'phone.

Feeling in need of a change from reading the diary entries, Izzy picked up her jacket, the novel she was currently in the process of reading and wandered down to Hannah's Bar.

Hannah's was its usual noisy, crowded self and Izzy had to pick her way through the crowds.

She consumed her two cocktails and then began to quietly walk back home. Needless to say, Lady G's diary was drawing her back.

Monday, 18th November, 1887. Well, we have a further month of lectures designed to supplement our clinical practice and I have to admit the theoretical element of our studies really does have its' compensations! No early morning get ups! Yes, I have to admit, there is a vast difference between getting up at half-past six in the morning for the early day shift and getting up at half-past eight in the morning for a day of lectures, starting at nine-thirty!

At the weekend, I received a further missive from Lord Ernest. As I have already stated, he has arrived in Pompeii and has been resident there for at least three or four days. On the day of his arrival, he reached Pompeii at lunchtime, just in time for a lemon cello, in short, a special Neapolitan aperitif. Ernest freely admits that he is fascinated by Roman remains and intends to see the entire remaining complex; the forum, the bath house complex, the floor and wall mosaics and the corpses of humans, yes, he is absolutely intrigued by it and by all things Roman!

At this point, Izzy began to feel the effects of the Tierra del Fuego cocktails beginning to work through her system. She then nipped to the bathroom. Whilst using the bathroom, she heard the 'phone ring out again. Oh well, the answerphone could pick up the call! Once she returned to the lounge-cum-dining room, Izzy replayed the answerphone message.

'Izzy? Oh, it's Ben Watson! Thank you! Thank you! You're an absolute marvel! I've just heard the good news! James has just told me that I can have my old job back! James! What a star of a man he is! At any rate, you're obviously out, so we'll speak again soon. Goodbye!'

So now one extremely happy Ben! Both James and herself were popular. All was well and truly well that ended well! For now, Izzy felt as though she needed her bed. She would resume reading Lady Gertrude's diary writings when she had time tomorrow after work, but for now she needed her sleep. After disconnecting the laptop, she got herself into bed and slept soundly.

Izzy passed another profitable, yet uneventful day in chambers. When all the day's business was successfully concluded, she bade goodnight to James and Tanya and left the building at just after five, after exhortations from James not to forget their rendezvous at eight-thirty for nine o'clock.

Once back at the Percy Street flat, Izzy had a quick wash and general freshen up and began to select her clothing for her meeting with James. She chose her black, relaxed fitted, embroidered M and S jeans and the bright pink linen blouse. Yes, thought Izzy to herself, that would be appropriate. Did she have time to visit Lady G's diary? Yes, she had. Izzy selected her jewellery. Her two ethnic bracelets would do very nicely, Alison's flat wedding ring on her right hand and the purple dropper earrings she had bought from the Bold Street jewellers a few months ago. Izzy wanted her jewellery to be both tasteful and understated.

Almost instinctively, she reached for her laptop. There was no entry whatsoever for Tuesday, 19th November, 1887. The next entry was the day after, Wednesday, 20th November, 1887.

Wednesday, 20th November, 1887. Of my own admission, I feel as though I am now really struggling to think of something to write to the dashing, gallant Lord Ernest. Is this a subtle hint or intimation that we have no future together? I fear it may be. Do you know? When I first met Ernest twelve months ago, I would never have believed we would still be in this strange, 'half relationship!' I would have believed we might have gone our separate ways, or possibly have married by now, but never, ever in a million years be in a position such as this! I feel strongly as though we really are drifting apart, inexorably. But not to worry, Gertrude! You are twenty years old and still have slightly over half of your nurse training still to complete! You still have plenty of living and maturing left to do, and best of all, you are based in a city which you now love!

I am still busy with my background reading. According to the probationer nurse allocation rota, I am to be sent to another medical ward for my next clinical allocation; and yes, I managed to pass the previous one all thanks to Staff Nurse Madeleine Rushton's kind and sensitive comments. What a delightful sweetie she was!

Ah, well! Now I shall sit back and enjoy my lectures! I believe the subject under discussion this morning is effective dressings application and the aseptic technique.

I sat in my study bedroom this evening and read through all the notes that I had made during the day. I also completed some further background reading in order to assist me with the next clinical experience.

Eventually, I managed to pen Lord Ernest a reply. Well, it was essentially a chatty little note, largely informing him of how happy and fully settled I was in my new urban environment.

Furthermore, I told him of how delightful autumn was on the Riversdale estate; how the woods and fields were a veritable blaze of mellow gold and brown. Quite beautiful in its' own way. Of course, I now regard myself as half a city dweller now, at least.

At this point, the doorbell sounded. James, without doubt. Quickly, Izzy disconnected the laptop and descended the stairs to answer the front door.

'Good evening, dear!' James greeted Izzy with rather stiffly.

'Would you like a little aperitif here?' asked Izzy.

'Well, er, don't mind if I do! I'll have my usual please, darling.'

'Consider it done.'

They retraced their steps up the well-trodden rickety staircase, and James chose his usual armchair. Izzy momentarily vanished to get the bottles, glasses and an opener. James appeared to cast a careful scrutiny over the lounge, for a few minutes he looked intently across at the disconnected blank screen of the laptop; then he suddenly looked away again.

'Well, well, well,' said James at last, 'well, we seem to now have one happy Ben, and of course, happy partners make happy chambers!'

'So true!'

'Yes,' answered James absently, taking a sip of his strong lager, 'I'm sure we could arrange a welcome back 'do' for a certain young sir when he makes his reappearance!'

'Yes, that sounds good!' Izzy took a mouthful of her gin, and added for emphasis, 'it certainly does!' Once again, James resumed the hand on Izzy's knee stance. Silence for a couple of minutes. Then James abruptly broke the silence by saying, 'Do you know, Izzy love? The first time I met you, I had this feeling that our futures would be somehow connected.'

'Oh, really?'

'Actually, I didn't just think, I knew… Well, my Izzy was a long time coming, but express it this way, she was well worth the wait.'

'Good. I'm pleased to hear it.'

At nine-fifteen, they were comfortably settling in at the Olive Press restaurant, awaiting the arrival of the wine which James had selected.

'So what's all this Doolittle and Dally business then?' Izzy asked James.

At this question, James threw back his head and laughed.

'Oh, that was largely Ben! He was absolutely tickled by the name, in fact, at times it became our secret code name when first we established the partnership. Ben called himself 'Old Tom Doolittle,' although he was only in his late thirties then, and I, I was Martin Dally!

Ben chose Tom because he has Thomas as one of his second names and I chose Martin for the very reason that I have Martin as one of my second names!'

'Oh, you two! You really are both such characters!'

James took a mouthful of the wine and answered quite confidently, 'Well, it would be a boring world without us!'

'Exactly so!' Izzy smiled back at him. That was an endearing quality which they both possessed. Neither partner cared the proverbial monkeys about the impression he made on others, both simply did his own thing. Izzy felt deeply relieved that the famous, off-beat, intrinsically idiosyncratic partnership was once again restored.

'And now, dear,' James began, 'we have plenty to talk about... Oh, and of course, plenty to plan!'

'Well, yes, we have,' Izzy assented.

'Now today, young lady, I did actually manage to do some 'phoning round for possible sources of accommodation in North Wales. There is a very nice place, two star, I think it is, named the 'Cross Inn,' on the road out of Conway. In actual fact, mother and I have stayed there once, oh, er, I think about five years ago and both of us found it very good!'

'Yes, that sounds like my sort of place.'

'Shall I give them a call sometime this week, then?'

'What an excellent idea!' Izzy took another mouthful from her wine glass. The wine tasted excellent.

'And how's your strange cousin? Now, er, what's his name?.......Oscar?'

'That's right, Oscar. Would you believe it? He's now intending to get married on a Greek island in late November. Furthermore, only very close family are invited!'

'Does that include yourself?' James asked.

'No, of course not! I wouldn't have wanted to go anyway; besides, I wanted to save the money for our big day next year.'

James took a sip from his glass and answered by saying, 'Now that sounds altogether much better!'

'My feelings entirely.'

'There'll be no job at Brodie and Watson's, otherwise known as Doolittle and Dally for loud-mouthed, irritating Oscar Talbot, I'm highly delighted and pleased to say!'

'Well, just imagine, I'm sure, no, I'm absolutely certain he would say, 'I'm not applying to Brodie and Watson, they're far too provincial and low key for me! I can do far better than them!' Yes, my strange cousin who has no idea of his own limitations!'

'Well,' laughed James, 'Remember, some people are just like that!'

'So true.'

Izzy idly picked up the menu and scrutinised the meals on offer: various steaks, fish, spaghetti carbonara, roasted belly pork and lamb chops cooked on the gridle, seemed to feature amongst other food items. Izzy quite favoured pasta in the shape of the spaghetti carbonara, but she was not yet ready to order, and for that matter, neither was James.

'Like yourself,' James said, 'I simply hate ordering immediately... You see, you and I, we have so much in common, in fact, we're almost like two peas in a pod!'

Izzy laughed. 'Come to think of it, yes we are!'

James took another sip from his wine glass and added, 'And so you see that's why I believe we have such a marvellous future ahead of us!' At which he reached out and gave Izzy's free hand a little squeeze. Somewhere, in the depths of Izzy's brain, she once again heard her grandma speaking to her '...I'm so pleased you saw sense and decided to take James! You two have a lot to look forward to!' Izzy took another sip from her glass. In seven months' time, she, Isabel Jane would be taking James Dominic Martin to be her lawful wedded husband; to have and to hold, in sickness and in health, so long as ye both shall live...etc. At this juncture, James, as if he could read her mind said, 'Isabel Brodie has such a nice ring to it!'

'Yes, it does.'

'Oh, and as I said last month, I really would like you to sit in on Barry's court case when it eventually reaches trial.'

'Now you know that I would very much like to.'

'And of course,' James added as an afterthought, 'It would be excellent experience for you as the trainee.'

'Well, yes.'

'And I can give you a specific, fixed date just as soon as I hear back from Queen's Square Courts,' answered James, as he pushed his glasses further up his nose with the middle finger of his left hand. 'Poor Barry, treated abysmally, he was, I'm so pleased he's managing to stay safely at his sister's house in Crosby!'

'Oh, so he's still living there then?' asked Izzy.

'Yes, as far as I'm aware Barry will be staying there until further notice; but he gets on well with his younger sister and she's going through a stressful divorce case, so Barry will be a bit of welcome company for her!'

James picked up the menu and began to scrutinise it intently. After a substantial amount of debate, he eventually again chose the roasted belly pork. James took another sip from his wine glass and dropping his voice a tone, repeated, 'You see, darling, as I said before, 'We're just like two peas in a pod!'

'Which can only be good!'

'Of course it's good!' was James's response.

Half an hour later, they ordered the food and James ordered a further bottle. The evening passed extremely well and the meals were excellent. At the end of the evening, James paid the bill which came to forty-two pounds, sixty pence. If truth be known both Izzy and James were both feeling a little the worse for intoxication, so James thought it sense to get back home for a reasonably early night, and besides, he had matters to attend to in the morning, hence, there would be no cosy return to the flat for night caps that night. Izzy slept soundly that night and into the hours of the next morning, until she was rudely interrupted by the strident chimes of her alarm clock, noisily proclaiming that it was quarter to eight. As she made herself a morning cup of tea, a sobering thought began to haunt Izzy. In mid-June, she, Isabel Jane Jackson-Talbot would take James Dominic Martin Brodie to be her lawful, wedded husband… Forsaking all others… To love, honour, cherish and obey… In sickness and in health… As long as ye both shall live… Until death do us part… And when Izzy was forty-five, James would be almost seventy; sixty-nine, in fact! Panic swept over Izzy very much akin to an abrupt, extremely rapid, incoming tide, and she then remembered the words of a problem page magazine which she had read years ago, '…If in doubt, get out!' based on the minefield subject of relationships. No, she simply couldn't do it! Izzy felt herself baulking at the prospect of marital wedded 'bliss' with James. In the event that she broke off her relationship with James, he might then refuse to sign off her articles contract?

Despite her brain descending into a strange, emotional turmoil, Izzy got herself up, washed and dressed and into work as normal. She would say nothing, for the time being at any rate.

Once in work, there were some client proofs of evidence to take down in another personal injury matter, and Ben, now in the happy position of serving his notice at Hill Foster's had returned his share of the contributed capital back to Brodie and Watson, the recording of which needed to be entered in the appropriation account; a task which as the trainee, fell to Izzy.

It was eleven-thirty when Izzy returned the newly amended appropriation account to James for final, last-minute checks. On later reflection, Izzy remembered James looked a little drained, pallid and slightly 'under the weather,' or maybe he was a little 'hungover' after the liquid excesses they had both enjoyed the night before.

'That was a most agreeable evening, wasn't it, young lady?'

'Yes, it was,' answered Izzy, 'I'll leave the new up-dated and amended appropriation account for you to check through.'

'Er, Izzy?'

'Yes?'

'Well, er… I'm feeling a little peculiar… I'm sure it will pass in goodtime!'

'Do you think you ought to go home? Or can I get you a glass of water or coffee or something?'

'No, thank you. I'm sure it will pass,' answered James in his usual stiff and heavy-handed tone.

Izzy had never seen James like this before and she began to feel quite worried. If he got back home, without doubt, his mother would fuss and minister to him until he was feeling a little more like his old self.

'…James, I think you should go home!'

'Why am I suddenly classified as an invalid? In actual fact, young lady, I'm perfectly well!'

James peremptorily snapped at her. Izzy was shocked; she had never witnessed James in this frame of mind before; nor was she in any way prepared for what next transpired. The next moment, James flopped face forward over his desk; he seemed to find breathing extremely difficult and let out a few frenzied gasping and gagging sounds. Izzy tried to get him to a chair, but she found his plump, portly frame especially hard to move.

'Tanya!' Izzy shouted, 'Mr Brodie's not very well! I think he's had a heart attack! Can you 'phone for an ambulance for him?'

Tanya shuffled back to the front office and duly 'phoned for an ambulance. Ten minutes later, the paramedics were swarming over the back office.

'Come on, just relax Jim. We're going to give you some oxygen. That should last you until you get to hospital,' Izzy heard one of them say. Izzy also further explained to the ambulance staff that she thought her fiancé looked unwell and ought to have gone home that morning, a fact which he refused to acknowledge and as a result, simply became irritable with her. The next minute, he collapsed face downwards over his desk and was scarcely able to breathe.

'And you, will you go with him?'

'Well, yes, of course. I'm James's young lady, you see we work together. Obviously, I need to be with him.'

'Just talk to him as though nothing's happened; all's well and good and he's perfectly normal.'

'Yes, I certainly shall.'

James was conveyed into the ambulance. In shock, Izzy climbed in after him.

'James, you're going to be O.K. You've not been too well this morning, but the hospital will sort you out.'

James seemed a little better. Right at that particular moment, he seemed more perturbed about the tone in which he had just addressed Izzy rather than his suspected heart attack; although Izzy took pains to tell him she did not mind in the slightest. Once safely in Liverchester University Hospital, James was taken straight to A and E Majors department.

Izzy sat anxiously on a seat outside in the waiting area for about an hour and a half, at the end of which, a male nurse came out to tell her that James had been stabilised for the time being, at any rate, and was about to be transferred up to ward 7A, the heart ward; at any minute. Izzy thought she had better telephone Mrs Brodie, as James's next-of-kin to inform her of his illness and hospital admission that morning, furthermore, to explain that the hospital had managed to stabilise him and his imminent admission to 7A, the heart ward.

Ten minutes later, Izzy also 'phoned Ben at Hill Foster's to inform him of the morning's developments.

'Poor soul!' commented Ben, 'I'll come round after work one night and see him.'

'Oh, thank you, Ben. Yes, I think James would greatly appreciate that.'

'You see, he just can't manage and nor can the chambers without old Tom Doolittle!' Ben exclaimed.

'Oh, Ben! I'll have to go now! James is on his way up to 7A. Goodbye!'

'Goodbye, Izzy!'

Izzy walked with the porters escorting the trolley on which James was lying, up to 7A. The ward staff were extremely good and allowed Izzy to sit at James's bedside, as he settled into his new accommodation. Once James was comfortable in bed, Izzy took one look at him and said laughingly, 'Your mother won't like to see you in those hospital regulation pyjamas! I did tell her you might need some new pairs bringing in.'

'I might have known! Yes, that sounds fairly typical of mother.'

'At any rate, your mother's coming in to see you this evening. I did tell her they had managed to stabilise you; and she didn't need to worry too much.'

'Izzy, you're an angel! And I'm sorry I shouted at you this morning.'

'Oh, James, it really doesn't matter. What you need to do now is to try to avoid stressful situations.'

'If only!' answered James.

'Oh, and Ben's going to come in some time after work to see you.'

'Marvellous man! A tower of strength is my business partner.'

'Yes, he is rather.'

'No,' repeated James, 'I couldn't manage without him, and nor can the chambers. My goodness, I've really struggled this last month.'

'Now James, love, why don't you get some sleep, and I'll come back and see you this evening?'

'Why, yes young lady, that sounds very tempting… And you've had a highly stressful morning, so you go home and try to get some rest. Don't bother going back to chambers, besides there's no-one to give you any work to do, Tanya can hold the fort for the rest of the day.'

After the stresses and tension of the morning, a return to 8, Percy Street seemed like a very attractive prospect, and of course, Lady Gertrude's diary entries were once again calling.

Izzy left both her mobile and landline numbers with the ward staff in order that she could be kept informed of any change in James's condition. James's present condition was classed as 'comfortable,' by the nursing staff of the ward and there was no more that Izzy could do for the time being.

Izzy walked back alone through the hustle and bustle of the hospital. She herself had once been admitted to hospital, due to overwork for some law examinations; but it was not the same hospital. She had to admit she was not overly keen on hospitals, but if you had to be an inpatient, this hospital was not a bad one to be in. She was three quarters of the way back along Rodney Street when her mobile sounded.

'Oh, hello, Izzy! It's Tanya!'

'Hello, Tanya!'

'Wasn't it awful what happened to poor Mr Brodie this morning! Why, he didn't look much longer for this world! What's he like now?'

'A and E managed to get him stabilised and he's been taken up to ward 7A, the heart ward. The nursing staff say he's in a comfortable condition now, but he has to avoid stressful situations.'

'Awww! I'll go and see him some evening.'

'Oh, thank you, Tanya. Can you man the office for the rest of the day?'

'I think I can manage to do that.'

'Good. We would all appreciate that.'

'Not at all! It's the least I can do! After all, Mr Brodie's been very good to me!'

'I might not be in tomorrow, either.'

'Oh, don't worry, Izzy! I'll keep the chambers going.'

How effective Tanya's management of chambers was going to prove was extremely suspect, Izzy thought to herself, yet Tanya was quite a good sort and it was good of her to offer to keep the business in operation in both partners' absence.

'I'm getting myself home for a rest, Tanya. I might even sleep for a few hours.'

'How sensible.'

'I'd better go now, Tanya! But thank you for calling. I'll speak again very soon. Goodbye!'

'Goodbye, Izzy!'

Once back at 8 Percy Street, Izzy flopped on the settee. What an eventful, traumatic morning it had been! Izzy made herself a strong mug of coffee and then switched on her laptop.

There was no entry for Thursday, 21st November, 1887. The next diary entry referred to was Friday, 22nd November, 1887.

Friday, 22nd November, 1887. We are now, once again, well and truly on the build-up to Christmas. I can scarcely believe it, Christmas has come round so fast. I am pleased to say that we have a Christmas break of a month, but that has not yet begun. We still have a further three weeks of lectures and two essays to write and submit. I am busy working on my essays at present and fully intend to spend the bulk of this weekend in their writing.

'Tis so good to be back at Riversdale! And do you know? Now that I am aware of a life beyond Riversdale and Ripon, I am far happier with my lot here at home. That said, I shall be pleased and ready to return to my spiritual home of Leeds on Sunday afternoon.

Saturday, 23ʳᵈ November, 1887. This morning I received further communication from Lord Ernest. He currently appears to be fascinated by the churches and back streets of Naples though I cannot imagine why, not for the life of me, since I have been informed that Naples is not too pleasant a town!

He has also paid a visit to Herculaneum, where he was intrigued by the wall and floor paintings. He informs me that he is next scheduled to travel round the coast to Sorrento, famed for its' restaurants and fine liquors.

To be absolutely honest, I am quite at a loss as to what to write to him! Our paths now seem to be diverging to such a degree. I am now more certain than ever that he simply regards me as a silly, immature girl who needs to experience her share of human life's triumphs and hardships, stresses and strains. You might possibly be well advised to look for another man, Gertrude, so that you cannot be hurt by Ernest. There, I have called him merely 'Ernest,' this time, and yes, this may be a sign that his intrinsic popularity with me is on a sharply descending spiral.

At this stage, Izzy found her eyes drooping. She, like James, needed further sleep, so she had a quick wash and slipped on her nightie, setting the alarm for four-thirty in the afternoon. She would have an early evening meal and then go out to see James. After the traumas of this morning, it felt like absolute bliss to sleep. In fact, the current situation was summarised by the quote of Mr Shakespeare, in Macbeth:

'Sleep that knits up the ravelled sleeve of care!'

Izzy woke up three hours later, without the help of the alarm. Probably the battery need replacing. She would attend to that when she returned from visiting James. Izzy realised she had been quite hard and fast asleep. There were two missed calls on her mobile. Both from James. Izzy duly called him back.

'Oh, hello, James!'

'Oh, hello, dear!'

'And how are you feeling now?'

'Much, much better, dear!'

'Good. I'm so pleased to hear it. Did you manage to sleep and rest at all?' asked Izzy.

'Yes, dear, I did. You get a bit more rest and recuperation, and I'll see you at visitor's time, which incidentally, is quarter past seven until quarter to nine.'

'I'll get myself there for about seven-thirty then.'

Izzy flopped on her bed for another hour. The events of that morning had really taken their toll on Izzy and she felt drained and exhausted. Even Lady Gertrude's diary entries would need to wait.

When Izzy managed to reach James on ward 7A, much to her surprise, Tanya was sitting with him; he was wearing a change of pyjamas, sitting up in bed and laughing and joking.

'Well, mother's been in to see me earlier on. Of course, she brought tons of pairs of new pyjamas in with her, bless her! She just couldn't bear to see me in hospital NHS regulation jamas!'

Izzy and Tanya sniggered simultaneously.

'Well, why?' Izzy asked.

'Oh, it's just a little fetish of mother's,' answered James airily, 'Oh, and Izzy dear, mother sends her love!'

'Oh, that was nice of her.'

'Er, Mr Brodie, when you had your mishap this morning, er, how did it feel?' asked Tanya.

'Oh, please call me James. How did it feel? If you really want to know, absolutely terrifying! As though someone was tightening a strong leather belt round my upper chest area; and I felt scarcely able to breathe! I did have heart problems years ago when I was in my late thirties, so I am fully aware that I have a health problem,' James proceeded to explain, 'and just luckily they managed to sort me out, and hopefully they will again!'

At this point, they were interrupted by a staff nurse who told James he had another visitor.

'James, there's a gentleman wishing to see you!'

'Please show him in then! My goodness, I now seem to have become extremely popular!'

Two minutes later, who should walk across to bed three in the men's bay and looking like something brought back from the dead himself, came Ben. Usually such a smart, well-turned out, natty dresser, the only adjectives which could currently be employed to describe his physical appearance and which immediately sprang to Izzy's mind were 'dishevelled', 'down-at-heel' and almost a 'shadow of his former self,' his usual healthy colouring replaced by a strange, ashen look, despite which he was cheerful and still making jokes. It then abruptly occurred to Izzy that Ben looked in a far worse physical condition than James, and James had suffered a major heart attack that morning.

'Hello, young sir! It's old Tom Doolittle come to see you!'

'Oh, hello, Ben!' answered James, a little stiffly, 'Or should I more accurately say, 'Oh, hello Thomas?''

'Well, as you can see, Hill Foster's have knocked me around a little, been through the mangle with them, you might say.' Izzy noticed he held a Tesco carrier bag, which at this point he handed over to James. It contained a bouquet of mixed pink and white flowers, a small box of dark chocolates and a carton of black and red grapes.

'I thought you might enjoy these little presents,' Ben explained.

'Oh, thank you, young sir!' answered James and then added, 'Much appreciated! My goodness, I've been really spoiled since I was hospitalised!'

'Not at all,' Ben insisted, 'Why, it was the absolute least I could do. Just remember, we're once again partners.'

'Well, I shall well and truly be pleased to have you back, Mr Watson!' Tanya said presently, and also added, 'Why, it simply wasn't the same without you!'

'No, it wasn't!' Izzy assented.

'And now James, I shall have to love and leave you! And you ladies and gentlemen, well, er, lady and gentlemen I ought to say, don't worry about not coming into chambers for the rest of the week since I shall hold the fort!' Tanya ventured.

'Well,' said James beaming, 'That's the chambers of Brodie and Watson, we look after each other!'

'James, Ben, Izzy! I shall have to go now, me da will wonder what's happened to me, but I'll come back in a few days' time and we'll put the world to rights again. Goodbye, everyone!'

With that, Tanya shuffled off on her high-rise heels.

'…And have you two been putting the world to rights?' Izzy asked James.

'No, not really. After all, bear in mind that Tanya's a little challenged in the intellectual department.'

Izzy was loathe to comment since she did not wish to sound too harsh on Tanya. Izzy also noticed Ben made no answer either.

'Now, James,' Ben asked, 'Would you like me to smuggle in some liquid sustenance for you?'

'Well, if I can have it,' answered James in his usual heavy-handed tone, 'but it all depends on what the ward staff say, and of course, remember, I'm on huge doses of medication!'

'Oh surely the odd glass can't do any harm!' Ben persisted.

'You, Benjamin, lead my James into bad ways!' Izzy laughed.

'Well, someone has to!' Ben countered with.

Both James and Izzy laughed at this comment. There was silence for about a minute or so, which James eventually broke by saying, 'And there's one person we shall not under any circumstances be employing!'

'And who is that person?' asked Ben.

'Guess who? Oscar 'Boasting' Talbot, Izzy's cousin!'

'Thank goodness!' answered Izzy.

'Is he really as bad as you two make out?'

'Well, in a manner of speaking, yes. Somehow, I can't imagine him wanting to be employed at our chambers.......He hates northerners, for a start!'

'Oh, really?'

'Well, I strongly suspect so! Added to which, he'll think we're far too 'back street' and provincial for the likes of him!'

'Silly boy!' laughed James again, 'Just imagine, in the unlikely event that we ever did employ him, he might find himself catching the rough edge of my tongue quite frequently; and I'm not in the habit of shouting or 'losing my cool,' so to speak.'

'I haven't incurred your wrath, have I, James?' Izzy asked, rather anxiously.

'No, of course not, dear; why, you are far too good at your work to do that... This young lady is probably the best trainee we've ever had!'

'And so say all of us!' answered Ben.

Izzy blushed and said quietly, 'Well, thank you, gentlemen.'

Ben glanced down at his wristwatch and presently told them both, 'It's probably time that I was making tracks... At any rate, young sir, don't let the bastards grind you down, oh, and incidentally, I did mean what I said about the liquid refreshment.'

'Yes, I'm sure you did!' James replied laughingly, and then added as an afterthought, 'And thank you for coming, Ben.'

'Not at all,' his partner answered, 'and I'll see you two again, very soon. Goodbye!'

That left Izzy once again with James.

'Marvellous man is Ben,' James muttered, 'always prepared to go the extra mile, he is.'

'Yes,' answered Izzy, 'and it was good of Tanya to come and see you too.'

'Too true! Oh, and I've just remembered, young lady, that when I come out of here, we have so much to plan, like our North Wales short break, and also our Cumbrian wedding scheduled for next year!'

With all the trauma caused by the sudden, unexpected turn of that morning's events, Izzy had to admit she had clean forgotten about both. Visiting time now appeared to be drawing to a close and yet again, Izzy was feeling the strange subtle magnetism of Lady Gertrude's writing.

'Will you be coming back tomorrow evening, dear?' James asked a little uncertainly.

'Yes, of course I shall,' answered Izzy, as she smoothed back James's hair and gave his forehead a little kiss.

'Good. Then I shall greatly look forward to it.'

Once safely back at home, Izzy reached straight for the laptop. She did not have to be in work tomorrow; so she was in the happy position of being able to get up late.

Sunday, 24th November, 1887. After much deliberation, I eventually managed to pen what I believed to be an appropriate response to Lord Ernest. I told him how well my work and studies were progressing in Leeds metropolis and also how much I enjoyed both the content and challenge of the lectures!

He, in turn told me that he is not returning to his ancestral home just north of Manchester for Christmas, but this year is returning to Venice for a real, authentic, Venetian Christmas.

Apparently, he is captivated by the prospect of masked balls and parties! Ernest, I believe it would probably be in both our best interests if we went our separate ways NOW; and you found yourself another woman. If you cared anything at all for me, you would not talk this way about the 'high life' of Venice. Besides, if I were there with you I would simply doubtless prove an embarrassment to you – a stupid, immature little girl, from boring, provincial old Ripon, now living in equally provincial Leeds most of the time; and furthermore, I have told him as much in my latest piece of communication. In short, I have ended what relationship ever existed between us. In fact, my exact words were:

'At present, at least, our paths appear to have diverged so much and also due to the fact that I believe your intentions towards me are not in any shape or form honourable, I believe it best for us both to say that our relationship is now at an end.

Yours sincerely,
Gertrude.'

I will post this tomorrow afternoon in Leeds, at the end of my afternoon lectures. Just think, Gerty, this will be the first day of the rest of your life without Ernest!

There were now no further diary entries until Wednesday, 3rd December, 1887.

Wednesday, 3rd December, 1887. We had another day of lectures, at the end of which I submitted the essays on which I had been working and then, as we sat at our evening meals in the nursing accommodation block, someone made reference to a party and 'smoking concert' tonight in the student's union of the university. I feel so excited! 'Tis the party season, after all! I might also add that after a few glasses of champagne, we were all in a highly merry frame of mind!

I simply could not miss the 'smoking concert!' What good fun and excellent entertainment this is! This 'smoking concert' basically comprises a large majority of the medical staff and faculty producing a crazy show-cum-play and consists of such items as simulating an operation only to pull out rubber ducks and other miscellaneous items from a pretend patient's innards, horrendous drinking competitions between the different years of medical students, which can only lead to extremely 'thick heads' by morning and a take-off on a Shakespeare play. If you want my honest opinion, 'twas all really good fun and highly entertaining!

Close to the end of the evening, I heard an only too familiar voice, very close to myself sharply reprimanding me, 'And you, Gertrude Rivers should be ashamed of yourself!'

'Why?' I turned round. It was none other than my older brother, Harry Rivers, now a P.hD student at the University of Leeds.

'How dare you make an idiot of yourself and our entire family!........Don't push me too far young lady!'

But Harry's wrath moved me not a whit, and only too defiantly, I answered, 'Tis the party and Christmas season! And I am here for the very same reason as yourself, to enjoy matters!'

There was very little he could say in response and I could detect quite clearly that he had been drinking heavily, and at last he muttered in slurred tones, 'I have no time… No time for intoxicated… Women whatsoever!' At which point, he was led away by a friend and I realigned myself to the friends and colleagues I had come out for the evening to party with. No, I believe that was entirely unreasonable of my older brother and I still to this day, believe that I did nothing wrong.

Thursday, 4th December, 1887. I got up as normal the morning after, strangely enough feeling healthy, happy and not half as bad as I expected to feel. In reality, I had consumed very little, only a couple of glasses of champagne to celebrate approaching the end of term and three glasses of wine, so, all in all, not an excessive amount!

I made my way across to the nursing lecture theatre, and once again, thoroughly enjoyed my lectures.

Friday, 5th December, 1887. Our lectures were very much the same as yesterday. When I returned to Riversdale Hall early that evening, I received the following communication from Ernest.

My dear Gertrude,

I was extremely saddened to receive your latest missive, which, in short, ends our relationship. I fully and freely admit that in many ways I have been stupid, selfish and shallow intent only on my own pleasure… That I should have been so very lucky to enjoy the favours of a girl as charming, delightful and idealistic as yourself!

I felt partly as though we both needed further time and space to mature and develop as individuals and to carve out our own sense of identity and through my European travels this was a means of allowing me to do just that… Yes, I was saddened to receive your letter, but even that I shall treasure, since it came from my beloved, bright Gertrude, my veritable jewel amongst the whole of womanhood!

Maybe you could give yourself a little further time to establish yourself in Leeds, and I am well aware of how you now love the town; and at the end of which, we could possibly re-evaluate matters. Incidentally, I shall leave this matter entirely to yourself and to you own discretion.

It simply remains for me to again say what a stupid, stupid man I have been and I sincerely hope that you will not think of me too harshly.

Your ever-loving and devoted servant,

Ernest.

So, an unhappy Ernest! Intrigued, Izzy read on.

Friday, 12th December, 1887. Well, the festive season is not too distant an event now! My beloved papa came to pick me up at my accommodation about mid-morning and my luggage has gone on ahead of me and back to Riversdale Hall.

Once again, we dined royally at the Central Dining Rooms, and guess who joined us? My brother, Harry! He gave me a few initial black, disgusted looks and then proceeded to become the life and soul of our lunch party! No more was said about my appearance at the smoking concert, I am highly pleased to say. We all dined excellently on ribs of topside of beef, Yorkshire pudding with fresh vegetables and chocolate and orange sponge, all rinsed down with an excellent quality claret and strong coffees to end our meals. I still feel so happy and fulfilled!

Before we left the great city of Leeds, papa yet again made an extremely generous donation to the poor and destitute of Leeds welfare fund. According to my marvellous, quite exemplary papa; the amount in question was a hundred and fifty pounds. My goodness, Gerty, you really are such a daddy's girl!

That evening, Izzy met her friend Francoise for cocktails at Hannah's Bar. Then she wound her solitary way back to Percy Street and her double bed where, after the traumas of the morning, she slept comfortably and soundly, secure in the knowledge that no early morning get-up was required.

Chapter 16.

Sunday, 11ᵗʰ January, 1888. Christmas at Riversdale was its' usual, delightful and happy self. Just imagine, when we reach the end of February, I shall turn twenty-one. In short, I shall attain my majority. Furthermore, in April, I shall be transmuted into a second year Lady Probationer nurse. Yes, I am quite looking forward to it!

We are due to start on our clinical practice again tomorrow morning and by tomorrow evening I will be able to tell you in a little more detail about the new ward which I find myself on. I do hope it is as good as the previous one.

Monday, 12ᵗʰ January, 1888. Well, I have a supervisor named Charlotte who seems to be extremely nice and civilised. Yes, the ward environment seems to be civilised and extremely positive, and the staff appear to be keen to teach me a range of new nursing tasks and skills, although I do not think it is quite as nice as the geriatric ward which I was placed on before Christmas! Once again, I am intent to do my absolute best and give it everything I have.

It was ten thirty-five a.m. at the Percy Street flat, when once again, Izzy was interrupted and brought sharply back to reality from her reading, by the persistent ring tones from her mobile. Probably James. In fact, it was.

'Oh, hello dear!' he said brightly.

'And how's yourself, James?'

'Feeling considerably better,' James answered, 'and are you going to be able to come to see me, early this evening?'

'Yes, of course I shall.'

'That, young lady, is what I like to hear!'

'Good!'

'Well, you take it easy today!'

'Oh, don't worry, I shall, only too easily!' replied Izzy.

'We've got the medical staff's ward round, any moment now, so I shall now be forced to love and leave you… Goodbye, Izzy!'

'Goodbye, James!'

Izzy returned to her study of Lady Gertrude's diary; and if truth be known, it was not without a secret sense of relief. Nor was it the first time she had felt and sensed relief.

Were James and herself going to be like Lord Ernest and Lady Gertrude and not end their days as a couple? But no, there Izzy reminded herself she was quite wrong, since hadn't Lord Ernest hidden all Lady Gertrude's jewellery in those magical hills in North Yorkshire fairly not long after she had departed this life? Furthermore, she also remembered the farm hand talking freely about Lady Gertrude and her husband Ernest. But Izzy's proposed marriage to James? To be absolutely honest, the prospect of her intended marriage to James was still filling Izzy with a deeply entrenched, firmly ingrained sense of dread and panic. In fact, nothing had changed from those negative feelings which had abruptly engulfed and enveloped her yesterday morning immediately before James suffered his heart attack. No, she couldn't do it!

Once again, she resorted to Lady Gertrude's diary, which appeared to Izzy herself to be fast becoming a sane and sensible refuge; a haven in a crazy and chaotic world.

*Tuesday, 13th January, 1888. At last, I managed to write a brief and to the point reply to the last letter I received from Ernest. And brief it was! So, he wishes to re-evaluate our relationship, if you can even call it a relationship in twelve months' time? Well, Ernest, I was initially flattered by your attentions as a young and immature nineteen year old, but now bearing in mind your generally cavalier attitude towards me, I shall under **NO** circumstances carry a torch or candle to yourself, as you yourself advised me not to, on that very first night when you announced you had been offered the chance to undertake the 'grand tour,' of Europe. Who knows, I might even find a husband in Leeds!*

I did not actually write in my latest letter anything too condemnatory of Ernest, otherwise the door to him would be forever and eternally closed to me. But I have to admit, much of my writing consisted of what I can only describe as slight 'modifications' of the truth. Yes, I was so happy and pleased he was still enjoying his European tour and I hoped he thoroughly enjoyed his Venetian Christmas and was remaining in contact with his parents and two sisters. I then proceeded to inform him of how well my nursing studies were progressing and also that I was thoroughly enjoying the challenge of it. I also stressed how happy and at home I now felt in Leeds. Yes, overall, I believe I gave the impression that I was doing, 'very well, thank you,' and in no way whatsoever, pining or sickening for the wayward Ernest.

Friday, 28ᵗʰ February, 1888. Today is, of course, a very special day. The birthday when I turn twenty-one years of age and officially attain my majority. Emma, my maidservant, told me that since I had transferred to Leeds and become fully settled and acclimatised there, I had blossomed into quite the young lady!

And yes, I feel so very much better than I did twelve months ago! That night in question, happened to be the night when Ernest casually informed me that he was departing Leeds in order to complete an extensive tour of Europe, but I am highly delighted to relate to my readers that the metamorphosis or healing and recovery process which has taken place somewhere within me is complete, total and not unlike the quote from the New Testament, '…If I prune the vine… It will grow up strong again!'

I also remember reading the writings of a famous philosopher a few years ago and you will never be able to guess what he said! Everything that happens to a person occurs for a reason or specific purpose. Hence, it cannot be altogether bad! I myself have debated over and wondered about this concept for years. Furthermore, I now have the classic example in my life! No prizes for guessing what that is. No, I tell a lie. I now have two classic examples.

The first is that I chose to undertake my nursing studies in the great city of Leeds; the second is that I have made a full and total recovery from Ernest's rejection of my affections. Yes, I have certainly lived to tell the tale, and that can only be good!

At this particular stage, Izzy decided it was once again time for a change. If truth be known, she was still feeling exhausted and drained, so she returned to her bed for a further hour and a half of sound sleep, waking up feeling singularly restored and refreshed at almost lunch time. Izzy got up in a leisurely way and then made her way down to the shopping centre for a small amount of retail therapy. This time, Izzy was successful in her shopping mission, and she purchased a few items, including a silver ring from Pandora Jewellery shop.

On her way back home, she stopped off at the Turkish restaurant for a mixed meat omelette and a glass of wine. Of course, one glass of red wine led to another, at the end of which, Izzy was ready to return to the Percy Street flat. On her way back, she also managed to buy a 'get well' card and a carton of red grapes, both for James. The card of course, would need to be signed before she left for the hospital this evening. Izzy then flopped on the two-seater settee. Liverchester was a hilly town and on returning from the centre of town, she was frequently happy to rest her legs for a while. Needless to say, Lady Gertrude's diary was for the umpteenth time exerting its magnetic effect upon her. Ten minutes later, Izzy reached across for her laptop.

Saturday, 29th February, 1888. All in all I have enjoyed a quite magical and precious birthday, and received some beautiful presents and all largely due to my marvellous, special and highly exemplary papa. In fact, it is now a double celebration; I have turned twenty-one and I passed my previous clinical practice allocation. Another allocation safely in the bag!

We are now back to a further month of lectures and theory and that can only be good news for me, since I am never at my best in the early morning! Of my own admission, I can only say that I am not the proverbial, 'morning person!' No, not at all, furthermore, I suspect I never shall be.

We have to sit an examination and have an essay to write and submit, but have been advised by the lecturing staff not to attempt to start our revision or write an essay until we have had the bulk of the month's lectures. Provided we pass this written work, we are then able to progress to our second year. This is where our examinations become more frequent, but not until later in the year. I shall not worry about these yet.

Izzy glanced at her wristwatch. Three-thirty in the afternoon. Strangely enough, Izzy still felt the need to sleep. Once again, she collapsed into bed and slept soundly for another hour.

When Izzy eventually surfaced, it was twenty-five to five. She completed a brief tidy and clean-up of the lounge and bedroom. Once again, after a brief 'flick around' on the internet and a brief catch-up with some friends on Facebook, Izzy went inevitably back to Lady Gertrude's diary entries. Surprisingly, there was no further entry until Monday 6th April, 1888.

Monday, 6th April, 1888. What a momentous day it has been! Both my good friend, Maria and myself are now second year Lady Probationer Nurses. It is exactly one year to the day since I started the nurse training, and do you know? It has gone so fast, especially after those first very difficult three weeks!

Additionally, I have further good news for all my nearest and dearest! I passed my physiology examination with fifty-seven percent and my essay with forty-six percent. I have to admit that I found the essay difficult and believe it to be quite a wonder that I passed it at all, since I found the subject matter quite boring and heavy-going; in short, it was a patient-focused essay which I quite struggled to write, since I did not spend long enough on the ward in question to become fully cognisant and conversant enough with the subject of my writing and general composition. At any rate, it is passed and another hurdle is behind me.

We have another three weeks of lectures and general theory with some afternoon sessions focussing on 'skills' practice and which can comprise anything from general bed-making and bed linen changing to the assembling of intravenous drips and dressing of wounds; it is quite extensive!

According to some of my nursing colleagues, the vast majority of us are to be next allocated to surgical wards, in order to gain general surgical nursing skills. Surgical wards are entirely 'uncharted water,' to me. I should imagine surgical nursing skills would comprise attaining competence in the use of dressings, use of the aseptic technique, removal of stitches, general observations and strict recording of observations, for example, blood pressure readings, temperatures and pulse rates and the provision of general assistance with patient personal hygiene, which Gertrude, I am sure you are ready, willing and easily able to effect! Once again, Gerty, try not to get too worried!

I do so enjoy my lectures and skills practice; and I now feel quite at home sitting in the lecture theatre in the nurse education block and I freely admit, I have said this more than once before.

Again, there was now no entry until Monday 26th April, so Izzy imagined all had been progressing reasonably satisfactorily.

Monday, 26th April, 1888. Well, I have spent my first day on ward 8X, and I cannot really say that I am overly enamoured. There is something about this ward that I do not like, although it should be good experience for me! The fast-paced hustle and bustle of this ward is quite simply not for me!

Let's face it, I do not really like surgical nursing. Nor does my confidante and good friend, Maria. Oh well, that said, I will get my head down, do it, and see it through.

Izzy glanced at her wristwatch. Quarter to seven. It was almost time she was going to see James. She switched off the laptop and picked up her jacket. With her flat keys securely in one hand, Izzy locked the flat and made her way downstairs and out onto Percy Street.

From there, she walked down Lower Canning Street, to Myrtle Street and then up Prescott Street. When she arrived in the men's bay on 7A, James seemed really pleased to see her. He was equally pleased with the card and grapes.

'I'm so pleased to see you, dear!'

'Not half as happy as I am to see yourself!' answered Izzy, giving James a hug.

'I'm feeling quite a lot better,' said James airily, 'And mother's been in to see me again; she came for afternoon visiting time today and brought all my shaving equipment in, bless her, so now I've no excuse for not having a good shave!'

Izzy laughed. 'I'm happy to hear it. James, you've now no excuse for designer stubble!'

'No, none whatsoever.'

'And so how are you feeling now, James?'

'Oh, much better. Remember, when I come out of hospital we've so much to plan and arrange.'

'Well yes, but don't you worry about that now. Just focus on getting better.'

'Oh, I shall, I shall.'

'I wonder how Tanya went on today with running and managing chambers?' Izzy asked.

'I can't imagine!' James winced at the thought. 'Although I can guess she might say something along the lines of, 'I ran chambers for a few days in the absence of both James and Ben… Why, it was such good management experience! She really is a one!'

'Well, yes.' Izzy assented; a quiet smile crossing her lips.

'Do you know? I've been getting a little restless since I started to feel a bit better, so I've been wandering over to the window. I love the views. On clear days you can see right across to the hills of North Wales, where we shall soon be spending some quality time!'

'Well, yes.'

'And thank you, once again, dear, for coming to see me in my hour of need. You really are the most attentive of lovers.'

'Oh, James! It was the least I could do!'

They continued to make general conversation until visiting time approached an end. Izzy gave James another hug and said, 'So provided you're feeling better, which I sincerely hope you are, I shall now be forced to leave you.'

'And with a bit of luck, I shall be feeling better still by tomorrow.'

'Yes, I'll have everything crossed for you.'

'Goodbye, dear!'

'Goodbye, James!'

With that, Izzy left the heart ward and the hospital. Once again, she was feeling the need for her bed and only too ready to sleep for several hours, the prospect of which appeared extremely enticing.

Izzy watched television for an hour and a half and then duly collapsed into bed. With both partners currently absent from chambers, Izzy's services were not required, so no early morning get-up was needed and again, slept soundly and securely. As Friday morning dawned, Izzy continued to sleep soundly. In fact, Izzy was only roused from her slumbers by the ringtone of her mobile phone. Still feeling half asleep, she reached for her 'phone.

'Hello!'

'Oh, hello, dear!' It was James.

'How are you feeling this morning?'

'Well, between you and I, not quite as good or improved as I felt yesterday,' answered James anxiously. 'I was getting washed this morning and I suddenly started to feel all tight and had real trouble breathing again!'

'Oh, my goodness! Shall I come in this afternoon, in view of the fact that's the earliest time I can see you?'

'Yes, if you would like. What it seems to ultimately boil down to is that I seem to be having an adverse reaction to the heart medication that I'm currently on.'

'Well then, your medication will need to be changed or adapted in some way.'

'Too true.'

'James, I will come in at half-past two. Come on, let's face this together.'

'That's right, young lady. You work your own particular brand of magic.'

'Now you focus on resting, relaxing and, as has been said before, avoid all stressful situations.'

'Yes, I shall try.'

For the rest of the morning, Izzy occupied herself with reading her nineteenth century idol's diary entries. Lady G appeared so sane and sensible.

Friday, 1ˢᵗ June, 1888. Well, this is to be my last day on this ward and very happy am I to be in that blissful position! I shall not be sorry in the least to leave and relegate it firmly to the past.

Quite frankly, on the whole, I find the staff here unhelpful and uncooperative. I well remember Nursing Sister Sloane from the geriatric ward uttering the immortal and precisely to the point phrase that she had detected over the years from her experience, that there was 'a certain type of surgical tidiness,' that she was unable to cope with. And now, from bitter experience I know precisely what she means. All that I can say is I hope my next surgical experience is a bit more positive. I later discovered, strange though it may seem, that I actually managed to pass that ward allocation. Perhaps the strange staff wanted me to end on something at least approaching a positive note.

I am back home tonight, back to Riversdale and Ripon and I shall be pleased to reach home. Of course, we are being sent home with two essays to write and an examination to prepare for, but the essays are not due for submission, nor is the examination due to be sat until early September, so I have plenty of time to write them and complete examination preparation. There is no point in worrying about these tasks just yet.

Izzy glanced at her watch. Quarter to two. She had best be making tracks back to see James.

When Izzy arrived at two o'clock in time for afternoon visitors' time, she was shocked to see James looking quite a few degrees worse. Izzy immediately gave him a hug.

'Now how are you feeling darling?'

'Well, I'm sorry to say, not too clever!'

'I suspect it's your medication, James.'

'Well, quite possibly.'

'And how are they treating you?'

'Oh, very well. No, seriously, the staff are very nice. They simply seem to have a few problems sorting out my medication.'

'Don't worry, James. I'll speak to a member of staff when I leave. I fully realise it's not very nice for you, being crammed full of tablets!'

'No, it's not really, but let's face it, I don't really have any alternative!'

'Too true!' Izzy answered. 'Too true!' Izzy reflected to herself on the strange irony of now having spent large amounts of time with James, she was even beginning to use the same words and phrases that he himself used.

'And remember, you know dear, we have so very much to plan and arrange… When, of course, I finally manage to get myself out of here!'

'Yes, we have.'

'And do you know, dear, I'm really looking forward to our North Wales short break, why, even the planning is making me feel excited! Of course, I would have got it all sorted and in hand a few days ago, had I not been so rudely interrupted by my heart problems!'

Izzy gave James's hand a little squeeze and she answered by saying, 'Look, dear, that's just one of those things – we can always easily re-arrange and re-schedule our short break for some time next year.'

'Oh, and Izzy?'

'Yes?'

'Izzy, I have something to tell you… All I was going to say was, if something does happen to me, please, please don't carry a torch for me… Ben's coming back to chambers in the next couple of weeks, get him to take you to Liverchester Law Society events; why, he knows all the crowd from Hill Foster's… Get him to introduce you, I'm absolutely certain he'll oblige!'

Izzy flushed puce and she answered, at that stage truthfully, 'You know, James, he will need to be a very special man to replace yourself!'

James laughed, 'I'm not so sure about that!'

They continued to converse for a further half hour. By the time the further half hour had elapsed, visiting time had reached an end, and it was time for Izzy to depart. Izzy remembered that she needed to speak to a member of the ward staff. As Izzy left, she poked her head round the nurse's station, only to encounter Senior Staff Nurse, Susan Hillman.

'Erm, Staff Nurse?'

'Can I help you?'

'Yes, I'm a bit worried about James Brodie on the men's bay… Why, he doesn't seem to be improving!'

'No, he does seem to have had an adverse reaction to his tablets,' answered the staff nurse vaguely.

'Well, I'm not entirely happy about this,' Izzy replied.

'Now there is a new tablet we would like to try James on…' answered Staff Nurse Hillman.

Izzy looked visibly shocked and eventually she managed to say in response, '…Try? …Try? Well, that means you're simply experimenting with my fiancé?'

'Yes, in a manner of speaking!' came Staff Nurse Hillman's reply.

'Whether he'll take his tablets is entirely up to himself, but I am not entirely happy, not by any means!' Izzy answered tartly. Various individuals, among them, Edith, had commented on Izzy's newfound aggression in stressful situations and also, how they were not entirely pleasant to be on the receiving end of.

Looking singularly intimidated and cowed, Staff Nurse Hillman managed to respond by saying, 'I'll pass the message on to Mr Griffiths; we'll need to see what he has to say about it!' At that point, Izzy stormed off, and bearing in mind her anxiety and stress levels she was entirely oblivious to the import of the Staff Nurse's reference to Mr Griffiths.

Izzy was still fuming as she retraced her steps back down Prescott Street, the university precinct and back along Rodney Street. If truth be known, she was still unsure whether she could have a future with James, but that said, nor did she wish him to die! Once back within the safety and security of the Percy Street flat, she resorted to the sanity and wisdom of Lady Gertrude's diary. There were now no further entries until Tuesday, 6th September, 1888.

Tuesday, 6th September, 1888. I took an examination yesterday morning which went tolerably well and after the examination I submitted my completed essays. I spent quite a lot of time and trouble writing my essays, so I sincerely hope that they will both obtain a pass grade. Oh well, we shall have to wait and see! Once again, we are due to go out into clinical practice in two weeks' time and do you know? This time I have good vibes concerning where I shall be sent to! After all, it could not be much worse than the ghastly ward 8X. Gerty, put that straight from your mind!

Wednesday, 7ᵗʰ September, 1888. We had a day of lectures and I sat there happily in my new home from home. I have now spent just over a year in Leeds and the time has just flown past! How I remember the difficulty of those first three weeks which have now all but fallen into oblivion! Of course, in those early days I was still in regular contact with Ernest, but that too, is now firmly in the past and that is a fact, concerning which, I have no regrets whatsoever. There will never be any way back for us. No, I veritably believe he has fallen into a category of phases that I have outgrown. Dare I say it? I feel considerably better without him! I have my friends, my work in Leeds and a beautiful, secure and comfortable base out at Riversdale and Ripon, oh, and this is not to speak of my many hobbies, my writing, love of classical music, passion for local history, opera and burgeoning interest in, now what do they call it, photography, I think the word is!

So no, Ernest, I am not in any way regretting your departure from my life… I am at last now in the happy position of being able to say, 'CURED,' and I have written this word in capital letters and duly underlined it for emphasis; I am certain he will no longer dare show his face again at Riversdale!

Izzy glanced at her watch. Quarter to four in the afternoon. Once again, she felt drained.

Dare she show her face on ward 7A again in view of her display of irritation and frustration at the management or possibly mismanagement of James's medication? She would have to.

James was sick and he needed her.

The next morning, Izzy herself was unwell, a fact which she put down to general nerves, anxiety and becoming generally over-stressed concerning James. James called Izzy on her mobile to say that he was feeling a little better and Izzy told him that she would come for evening visitors' time at the usual time.

'I shall greatly look forward to that,' James told her, and then added, 'You know, Izzy, you are such a dear!'

Izzy laughed at the other end of the 'phone and managed to say in reply, 'Well, I'm not so sure about that, but I do try to be!'

'Well, you know, you do seem to manage it!'

When Izzy called round that evening, James did indeed seem a little better. Furthermore, he told Izzy that Ben had dropped in to see him last night and cheered him up no end.

Izzy felt completely drained and the heat in the hospital was beginning to take its' toll on her.

'You know what they say?' James suddenly asked Izzy.

'No, what do they say?'

'You don't value your health until you lose it!'

'No, precisely.'

'My goodness, you and I, we make a right pair!'

'James, if you'll just excuse me, I'm going out to get some air!'

A few minutes later, still feeling groggy, Izzy was standing outside Accident and Emergency attempting to get some clean, fresh air into her lungs. Eventually, she 'phoned James on her mobile to wish him goodnight and tell him she would come back to see him tomorrow evening.

'Oh, Izzy!' James expostulated, 'You're too good to me! You really are the most attentive of girlfriends! Right, now you get yourself home and spoil yourself!'

'Yes, I will, don't worry! Goodnight, James!'

'And I'll try to get some sleep, goodnight, Izzy dear!'

Given the state of Izzy's current health, in addition to the fact that the way back to Percy Street entailed the need to walk down narrow, dimly lit streets, probably unsafe at this time of night, she caught a taxi back to the Percy Street flat. Yet again, Izzy felt absolutely exhausted. She helped herself to two small glasses of red wine and collapsed into bed.

Needless to say, she slept soundly.

Twelve hours later, Izzy began to surface from her long sleep, disturbed by the sound of the cathedral bells. Much to her surprise, her physical health seemed greatly improved. If she got up now, she could wend her way over to the cathedral and still be in time for the eleven o'clock church service.

As Izzy sat comfortably in the eleven o'clock service, she somehow sensed that someone was attempting to speak to her. She felt certain it was once again, without doubt, her grandma… 'Do you know? When I passed away, I still felt the need to protect you, Izzy, love…' And that in turn reminded Izzy of when the Talbot family had lived at the other house, right out in the middle of the Ribble Valley and a happy memory suddenly coursed through her brain… A baking hot afternoon and she was ten years old, sitting out in the back garden, happily reading a book, being approached by her then hale and hearty grandma who asked her, 'Now, Izzy love, would you like to watch your television?'

'Your television!' Izzy loved that phrase, as though the television somehow belonged especially to her alone. Izzy then remembered her response, 'No thank you, grandma. I'm quite happy reading my book.'

'Izzy…' she thought she heard the person again say, '…Try to stop getting so het up! You need to steer clear of stressful situations… Why, it does your health no good at all!'

Like James, Izzy thought to herself. Then as Izzy re-focussed her attention on the mid-morning Sunday service, she felt an abrupt sense of peace and calm envelop her; an intrinsic sense that ultimately positivity would prevail. When the service ended, Izzy left the cathedral feeling mentally stronger and far more optimistic and she also remembered a quote she had read years ago, '…You will not be tested beyond the limit of your strength!'

Well, that had been true; and of course, that in turn reminded Izzy of that singularly unfortunate, extremely unpleasant interlude which lasted eight months and she had been employed in Chester, now frequently referred to by both Izzy and Edith as Izzy's 'durance vile!'

Izzy walked back through the town currently basking in the early December morning sunlight. She did so love this city, probably about as much as Lady Gertrude, who was now so deeply attached to Leeds. Yes, Liverchester, a true and veritable town for all seasons.

As Izzy made her way back through central Liverchester, the same phrase resounded in her brain, '…You will not be tested beyond the limit of your strength!' And Chester had well and truly almost exceeded the limits of her strength and endurance. Izzy vividly remembered how she had had her life made a misery by two colleagues, as a result of which, bearing in mind the extremely hostile and unpleasant work environment and atmosphere to which she had been subjected, she was eventually faced with no viable alternative other than to resign. Izzy's mind was then brought sharply back to reality and the present day – she needed to switch on her 'phone. In fact, Izzy was just rummaging in her jacket pocket for her key, when her 'phone began to blast it's persistent chimes out into the street.

'Hello, dear!' It was James.

'Now how are you feeling at present?'

'Well, better, but still not entirely right.'

'Oh, well that's something, at least.'

'And did you do as I said last night? Did you spoil yourself as I advised you so to do?'

'Yes, of course I did. Sleep, eh, it works wonders!'

'Of course it does. So, will you, young lady be gracing me with the pleasure of your company tonight?'

'Yes, you know I will. Right, I shall be making myself something to eat and then I shall continue to spoil myself for a few hours before I come to see you at visiting time.'

'Good,' answered James pompously.

'Well, we'll speak soon. Goodbye, James!'

'Goodbye, dear!' answered James, a little stiffly.

Izzy turned the key in the lock. With a rusty creak the lock gave way, she stepped in and made her way upstairs.

Yes, Izzy had been relieved to leave Chester. To Izzy, all Chester had comprised had been isolation, loneliness and a deeply ingrained sense of 'alienation' and 'hostility', the latter two negative emotions being very similar to those feelings once suffered by both Izzy initially in Liverchester and Gertrude, during those first few weeks of her sojourn in Leeds.

'So often, when things look at their absolute worst, a person can frequently be saved, right at the last minute or eleventh hour…' Izzy remembered this clearly from the priest's homily this morning, and of course, such had been the case with her durance vile in Chester.

On that note, she made herself a strong mug of coffee and once it had been consumed, she crawled once again, gratefully back into bed for another few hours' sleep.

Once again, Izzy woke up feeling considerably better. Needless to say, she simply could not keep away from Lady Gertrude's diary entries.

Friday, 9th September, 1888. I am back at Riversdale this evening as I sit and write this section of my diary. We have enjoyed a week of lectures which were undoubtedly a source of pleasure to me. If truth be known, I am so happy to be back at Riversdale and Ripon this weekend. Of course, true to form, my marvellous papa is planning his Friday night banquet in honour of my return to Riversdale.

Speaking of my work, we have a further week given over to lectures and then we are back out into clinical practice again. I had better pay ward 5Y a visit towards the end of next week to introduce myself and ascertain when I need to first present myself for work.

Friday, 16th September, 1888. Well, I have largely good news for everyone! I passed my examination with fifty-four percent and one of my essays *with fifty percent. With regard to the other essay, I was not so fortunate and only managed a miserly forty-two percent. It will need to be re-written and re-structured later on in the term! Oh, and the other reason for my good news! I paid a quick visit to ward 5Y, and I am pleased to say it looks very nice, best of all, the staff look reasonably civilised and I believe my initial sense of positivity was only too correct this time.*

Well, I am once again back at Riversdale and extremely pleased to be so! Enjoy your time in your pastoral and rural idyll, Gerty for you will soon be back deep in the thick of the urban sprawl again!

Monday, 19ᵗʰ September, 1888. I have completed my first day on ward 5Y, gastroenterology. So, a medically based ward, which I am greatly pleased about. To my mind, it is so much better and eminently more preferable to a surgical environment! Cold, clinical, exact, fast-paced and impersonal! These are the adjectives which spring to mind when describing the typical surgical ward!

Although Izzy was feeling better, she still had a persistent feeling, as James had so accurately described it – that of being, 'still not quite right,' in short, she felt drained, weak and still lacking in energy. What had happened to her? This time, even the fascination of Lady Gertrude's diary could not glue her to the laptop. This felt like a peculiar form of sleeping sickness and again, Izzy crawled back into the inviting depths of her bed to sleep for another two hours, setting her alarm for six o'clock this time.

She was woken up at just after six by the chimes of her alarm, filling the bedroom. In a leisurely way, Izzy got dressed, she was not by any means accustomed to spending her weekend days in Liverchester, since Edith was usually only too pleased to see her Friday evening until early Sunday; plus spending her weekends back in South Lakeland was a habit Izzy had acquired and developed from her earliest student days in Liverchester. But now, with James in this fragile state she would need to stay with him, at least until he was out of danger.

Once again, Izzy put her clothes on, applied a small, minimal amount of make-up, a rapid brush of her hair and she was ready to depart. When she arrived at the hospital ten minutes later by taxi and had got herself up to ward 7a, a small knot of visitors was already starting to build up in the corridor outside. Izzy managed to pick out Tanya, who had obviously arrived to see James.

'Oh, hello, Tanya!' Izzy greeted her with.

'Oh, hello there, Izzy! Why, Izzy, you don't look too good yourself! You look ever so pale!'

'Well, to be honest, that's how I feel!'

'Oh, is it now?'

When the ward swing doors were eventually opened and the visiting crowds swarmed in, Tanya and Izzy made their way to James's bedside. James looked better than he had yesterday, but clearly still needed to make substantial progress in the rest and recuperation departments. In fact, he looked very white and drawn. Nevertheless, he was pleased to see them both.

'Oh, James!' simpered Tanya, 'You've got two adoring women on either side of you! In fact, you remind me of our special needs teacher when I was at school, Mr Wilson, I think his name was, he often used to say, 'I know I've a way with women!'

'Not so sure whether I have!' James laughed rather feebly.

'Oh, you're much nicer than him!' Tanya added, 'In fact, I think he was one of the laziest men in Litherland!'

'And was he?' asked Izzy.

'I wouldn't have been surprised! He was always telling us the story of his life, he was! He told us with great glee that one morning he was sitting in the kitchen at his mother's house, eating his breakfast before he went to work and Mrs Wilson said to him, 'When are you going to be a man, Robin, and leave home?'

'And what was his response?' Izzy further queried.

'Guess what he said? Well, you know, mother, I might actually get married! After all, three years ago I became engaged. Admittedly, Susan and I broke it off, but you never know; if I meet the right woman next time, I might actually go the entire hog and make it down the aisle, you never know! Then Muriel Wilson roundly told him, 'Marry you?' 'Marry you? Who in their right mind's going to want to marry you? Well, you mark my words, he wasn't very attractive! He had this ghastly pock-marked face!'

At this point, Izzy thought she might try to steer the conversation away from Robin Wilson; after all, had Tanya been managing to keep the chambers ticking over in both partners' absence?

'How are you managing in chambers, Tanya?' asked Izzy.

'Hey, I'm not doing so badly!' answered Tanya breezily. 'Just imagine, this humble old typist-cum-receptionist is actually managing to hold these old chambers together – what good experience to be able to put down on her CV!'

The conversation continued in a similar vein for a further three-quarters of an hour, and then Izzy began to again find herself feeling distinctly unwell. She could leave Tanya talking to James for the remaining half hour of visitors' time.

'Well, James and Tanya, I'd better get myself home, so I'd best depart now!'

'You be certain to get a taxi, young lady!' answered James, 'And I'll see you tomorrow evening. I hope you'll be feeling a bit better by then!'

'Oh, I surely will do!'

Izzy bade goodbye to both James and Tanya. She made her way through the hospital and out to the waiting taxi rank and ten minutes later she was back home, back to her warm, clean, comfortable flat, the eminently enticing double bed and Lady Gertrude's diary entries. That night, Izzy slept soundly, securely and comfortably. Surprise! Surprise!

Izzy was woken up again the morning after by her mobile 'phone ring tones shattering the peace and calm of her bedroom and the sleep and rest she desperately needed.

'Oh, hello, dear!' It was James, making his by now customary morning call.

'So how are you feeling?'

'I think I'm feeling rather better today.'

'Good! I'm so relieved to hear that. Remember, you've had a big shock to your system! It will take time.'

'And how do you find yourself this morning, dear?' asked James in his customary tone, 'Feeling a bit better, I hope?'

Much to Izzy herself's surprise, she was feeling quite considerably better, and she answered truthfully, 'Much better, thank you!' As Izzy suspected, possibly all her health problems were all due to one singularly unfortunate factor of modern-day living, stress.

'Well, I do hope you'll be able to come to see me this evening. As I said yesterday, you really are the most attentive of girlfriends, Izzy Jackson-Talbot.'

'You know I try to be!'

'And you most certainly manage it, dear!'

Izzy laughed. 'Well, I'll come and see you at my usual time this evening! Goodbye, James!'

'I shall greatly look forward to that treat! Goodbye, darling!' With that, James 'phoned off.

Izzy went back to sleep for another hour and then made herself two strong mugs of coffee.

What was happening with Lady Gertrude and her new medical ward? Once again, Izzy needed to find out.

Tuesday, 20th September 1888. Since we are now out once again in clinical practice our lectures and the theoretical element of the nursing course is limited to one day per week, termed our study day. I always enjoy the study days. I will also admit that so far I am thoroughly enjoying ward 5Y which seems to be a very civilised, decent environment. I am absolutely certain that my natural forte lies within medical nursing, which appears to be so much more varied and diverse compared to simply caring for patients before and after operations. No, surgical nursing is simply not my 'tasse de the'.

Friday, 11th November, 1888. My last day on the gastroenterology and liver ward, and I am really sorry to leave it! Again, the good news is that I managed to pass the ward allocation.

Sister Evans thought I was extremely good and possessed the innate capacity to ultimately become a nursing sister! Yes, my nursing studies are progressing very well. I also re-wrote and re-submitted the essay which I failed to pass; and overall, I am still very much enjoying the challenge of my studies.

I have had no contact whatsoever with Ernest for quite some considerable time, and, if truth be made known, I am not in the least missing or regretting his absence. After all, I do have other things to occupy my time!

'Tis now mid-November, and the year has gone so fast! We are fast on the build-up to Christmas, again! I can scarcely believe it! We now have a month of lectures combined with some afternoon skills sessions, i.e. injection techniques, correct use of intravenous drips, that sort of thing. We also have some tests to sit, although not until right at the end of term.

Izzy glanced at her watch. Eleven-thirty. She would make herself another mug of strong coffee and then wend her way down into the town centre, for possibly a small amount of retail therapy. Then she would have lunch out somewhere and then work her way back for a few more hours rest, before going to see James in the early evening.

Yet again, there were no entries in Lady G's diary until Monday and Tuesday, 1st and 2nd December, 1888.

Monday and Tuesday, 1st and 2nd December, 1888. We had two written examinations to complete on both these days; both of which were morning *examinations and both of which for me, progressed tolerably well. Nevertheless, what a relief to get them out of the way, for the time being at least! Incidentally, I passed my re-written, re-submitted essay with forty-nine percent, which is not brilliant, by any means but is a decent, clear pass grade. I shall hope to score better in future.*

We are due to officially end the term for Christmas on Friday 15th December, 1888. Yes, the festive season will once again, soon be upon us! I am forced to admit that yes, I am quite excited about the prospect of Christmas. In fact, our noble old pile of a house and home really lends itself to Christmas!

Time for Izzy to be in town. She quickly switched off her laptop and made her way down into Liverchester One. Izzy loved this town and she had now loved it for many years.

After all this time, I am still quite unable to get enough of it, Izzy reminded herself, sounding almost exactly like her nineteenth century role model, Lady Gertrude. Feeling in need of a few treats herself, Izzy bought herself a new blouse from M & S and two small items from the Pandora jewellery shop. She then had lunch at a city wine bar and after a general wander round, then began to retrace her steps back towards the Percy Street flat. Once again, Lady Gertrude's writings were calling Izzy.

Thursday, 10th December, 1888. Well, I have reasons to believe a, 'good time was had by all,' last night. We consumed rather too much red and white wine and other generally intoxicating liquors than was altogether good for any of us; and here, I am referring to me myself and a few of my nursing colleagues. After a few glasses, toasting the end of term and the joys of the forthcoming festive season we eventually got ourselves once again, to the 'medical smoking concert,' termed and abbreviated in common parlance to, 'the smoker.'

It was all enormously good fun and helped to get me right in the mood for Christmas and this time I was lucky enough not to meet Harry, who would doubtless have publicly chastised and berated me.

Friday, 11ᵗʰ December, 1888. It is early evening and I am happy to be back at my country seat of Riversdale Hall, near Ripon, in the county of North Yorkshire. Once again, my marvellous papa came to pick me up in Leeds and sent my luggage on ahead of me.

Needless to say, we wined and dined sumptuously on first-rate Yorkshire fare, washed down with two bottles of Claret and furthermore, my older sibling, Harry was not present this time due to the fact that his postgraduate term ended on Friday of last week – a fact which I am forced to admit was a bit of a secret relief! Papa yet again, made an extremely generous donation to the poor and destitute of Leeds benevolent fund, I believe that this time it was in the region of a hundred and seventy-five pounds! What a man he is!

Well, we are about to start our celebratory dinner, which papa always holds every Friday night in my honour – he really is a papa in a million and I, I might add, have plenty to do in the morning; in fact, I might even go back to Leeds, only for the day though, in order to complete my Christmas shopping.

Looking back, I am so very pleased I managed to make the transition from Riversdale to the urban fleshpots of the city, for, with the exception of the first three weeks, my life has become so much wider and fuller and as I stated before, I am happier as a whole with the time I spend back at Riversdale and Ripon.

I am due to return to Leeds on 7ᵗʰ January, 1889, when we will have a further month of lectures, followed by six weeks of clinical practice. Medical or surgical ward? I sincerely hope I will be given a medical allocation. At any rate, I shall not stress about that at this point, I shall now relax and enjoy the evening ahead of me.

There was again no further entry until Monday 8ᵗʰ January, 1889.

Monday, 8ᵗʰ January, 1889. Well now, I am once again back in the city which I love so very much and I have had the results of my recently completed examinations. 'Tis good and bad news! I managed to pass the first examination with sixty-six percent, but narrowly missed the second, only by four percent, I wish to note! It really does not matter, I shall re-take it.

At any rate, I have half-proved myself and intend to continue to prove myself to the absolute best of my ability!

Christmas at Riversdale was its' usual magical, charming self and I thoroughly enjoyed every minute of it.

At this point, Izzy decided she would take some time out in order to rest and relax further before nipping across to the hospital to see James at evening visitors' time.

When Izzy got herself up to James and ward 7a that evening, James appeared to be greatly improved and he was in good spirits, in fact, full of plans and arrangements for their next date. Izzy, her own health considerably better and greatly relieved to see an improved James, stayed until the end of visiting time and then made her way home, taking in Hannah's Bar where she consumed two Tierra del Fuego cocktails before eventually returning to Percy Street, where she slept well and soundly until she was woken by James's morning call at ten-thirty the next a.m.

True to form, as always, after her morning conversation with James, Izzy resorted once again to Lady Gertrude's writing.

Wednesday, 18th February, 1889. I hate this present ward; I have to admit it and am quite ashamed to say that I hate it! It is a medical ward, which I am naturally good at, but the staff, I am sorry to say I find quite objectionable! My goodness, a ward simply stands or falls by its' staff! I really am ticking off the days as I complete them. Ending my singularly unpleasant sojourn on this ward, ward 12 at Leeds Cottage Hospital simply cannot happen fast enough for me! I believe many of the staff regard me as 'posh' and 'upper crust,' and that is the sole reason for my unpopularity. Strangely enough, I later discovered that I actually managed to pass this allocation which really is a complete 'turn up for the book,' as they say, but I will not mince my words, I thoroughly disliked it! In fact, I will go so far as to say that the stress of being in an alien, highly hostile environment is causing my health to break down. My health is not half as good as it once was before this horrible experience!

Forget it, Gertrude!

Well, Ernest has been gone on his travels for twelve months now and quite frankly, he may stay on them as far as I am concerned! In fact, terminating all communication with him has been one of the best acts I ever committed!

Again, there was no further recorded entry until Monday, 4th March, 1889.

Monday, 4th March, 1889. Well, strangely enough, I now have two events to celebrate. I have re-sat my second examination and have managed to pass it at the second attempt with a very respectable fifty-two percent and I even managed to pass the clinical allocation on ward 12 at Leeds Cottage Hospital, good Heavens! Wonders will never cease! I will make no bones about the fact, I found the entire experience of ward 12 intensely unpleasant, yes, that and the surly staff! Perhaps my success was largely due to the fact that I managed to impress some of those unpleasant characters with my extensive array of theoretical nursing knowledge! At any rate, that is another successful ward allocation safely relegated to the bag!

Furthermore, I might also add that I have turned twenty-two, or, as my maid-servant, Emma at Riversdale describes me, I have become, 'quite the young lady about town!' And of course, this is the image which I like to project.

Well, we are now in the happy position of having three weeks' holiday over the Easter season and I shall be so pleased and happy to rest my weary limbs and also to sleep soundly and securely in my bed, safe in the knowledge that no early morning get up is required of me! There is no doubt about it, I shall enjoy my Easter break!

Wednesday, 6th March, 1889. Papa and I dined quite sumptuously at the Northern Hotel, Harrogate. This, I admit is not really in the spirit of Lent, but papa was so pleased with my excellent progress in my nursing studies so far, that he wanted to treat me! He also gave me some further money for new dress material. My dressmaker, who is herself based in Harrogate, took my dress measurements this morning and I left the selected material in her competent and capable hands. The dresses, the designs of which comprise a beautiful lilac ball dress of watered silk with a dipping neckline and a russet, red velvet day dress will be made up and completed by early April. 'Twill be a nice Easter present for me!

Once again, I feel happy and I have so much to be grateful and thankful for!

Izzy made herself another mug of strong coffee. She would spend a further hour studying Lady Gertrude's diary and then pay a brief visit to town, just as she had yesterday.

Thursday, 7th March, 1889. I thoroughly enjoyed the visit which papa and I paid to Harrogate! 'Tis an extremely pleasant town and was recommended to me by my dear friend and colleague from my nursing course, Caroline, whose own home is Harrogate, when she is not resident in Leeds. There are so many tempting, inviting restaurants and hotels in which to wine and dine and why, the choice of shops closely rivals the great city of Leeds!

Yes, there is absolutely no doubt about it whatsoever, I am intensely proud of being a Yorkshire woman and a plain-speaking, no hidden agenda woman at that! A white rose woman in every sense of the word! In fact, if I were to attempt to accurately describe and generally sum myself up, I would say that Gerty Rivers is very much a, 'what you see, is what you get,' type of woman, or, alternatively, you could say, 'Take me as you find me!'

Papa made a further donation to the Leeds Homeless and Destitute fund by means of a cheque paid into the bank in Harrogate, and true to form, it was a very liberal amount; a hundred and ten pounds, to be precise.

Well, my sibling, Harry, is returning to Riversdale estate for his Easter break tomorrow evening and he and papa will doubtless enjoy many a spring evening putting the world to rights over the port!

It was at this juncture that Izzy was sharply reminded of how alike Lady Gertrude and herself were; simply plain-speaking, strong women who made no attempts to impress others and most vital of all, possessed no hidden agenda whatsoever. Lady Gertrude of the white rose of Yorkshire was so closely reflected by her twenty-first century equivalent in Isabel Jackson-Talbot of the red rose of Lancashire, with the exception that Lady Gertrude was dark haired and Izzy was fair haired.

Izzy glanced at her watch. Quarter to twelve and time that she was getting herself into town for a little more retail therapy. She rinsed her empty coffee mug and left it on the draining board, then picking up her jacket, she made her way back into the town. A rapid wander round Liverchester One and the shops on Church Street, followed by lunch at quarter to two in the Turkish restaurant on Leece Street. This time, Izzy bought nothing.

From there, Izzy walked back to the Percy Street flat. With all the trauma and worry of James's sudden illness and hospitalisation, Izzy was still feeling the need for further sleep, so as soon as she got back to the flat she pulled on a nightie and once again collapsed into bed, sleeping soundly for the next three hours. When Izzy eventually surfaced from her sleep, it was five-thirty and again, Lady G was calling.

Friday, 8th March, 1889. 'Tis so good to be back at home at Riversdale and Ripon for a while.

How I love to take Scamp for his mid-morning run on the estate parkland and then out he goes again mid-afternoon. On his return he consumes his meal, I play with him, he plays and cavorts at my feet after our supper and then either one of the footmen or the butler will take him for one last early evening run. For much of the interim time, he sleeps on the silken cushions which I bought for his basket a few years ago and which Harry strongly disapproves of, nuzzles up to my feet or relaxes on the rug infront of the roaring log fire in our hallway. He really is one of the most spoiled dogs to ever walk the face of the earth!

Early this evening, papa let me in on a little secret. Once again, he had business to attend to during the day, this time in Harrogate again, but he did not take me with him this time, since I was rather busy myself, having some private study to work through and complete, hence I remained at home. At any rate, papa told me he had seen a beautiful silver dress ring set with a quite dazzling sapphire in a leading jewellers in Harrogate. My brilliant and very generous papa has ordered one for me, which he says will arrive just in time for Easter.

'And could you describe it in a bit more detail, papa?' I asked.

'No, of course not! Why, that's for you to find out in due course!' he smartly replied.

'Thank you, papa… You really are one in a million!' I answered and gave him a hug.

Papa has his peculiar little ways, but I do love him for it! Papa, thank you for being the best father that ever was!

Izzy switched off the laptop. It was time she was getting dressed and getting herself over to see James. She rummaged in her wardrobe. Eventually, she decided on the new green M and S linen blouse and the black relaxed fitted embroidered jeans, a very light touch of make-up, quick brush of her hair, a rapid shot of perfume behind each ear and on each wrist and she was ready to go.

When Izzy arrived at ward 7a, she was a little surprised and taken aback to see James looking miraculously much improved.

'Well, you, young sir, look an absolute load better, incidentally, the staff nurse told me you were eating better too!' And with that, Izzy gave James a hug.

'And I'm feeling much better!' answered James emphatically.

'Good! That's absolute music to my ears!'

'And remember, we, young lady, have so much to plan and look forward to… Our short break and, why, our wedding next year!' As he uttered these words, James took Izzy's left hand and gave it a little squeeze.

'Too true.' There! Izzy had said it again!

They continued to talk in this sort of vein until visiting time eventually drew to a close.

'Well, I'm off home now, but I shall be back tomorrow to keep you company!'

'You know, dear, you really are an exemplary girlfriend, and what's more, something tells me you'll make a still more exemplary wife!' answered James, as Izzy prepared to leave.

'Well, I'm not so sure about that!' Izzy laughed sceptically, 'At any rate, goodnight, darling!'

'Goodnight, my angel!' answered James.

As Izzy was leaving ward 7A, she noticed Senior Staff Nurse Susan Hillman sitting in the nurse's station, busy writing up patient care plans.

'Staff Nurse Hillman?' Izzy asked, 'could I have a brief word?'

Staff Nurse Hillman looked up from the desk looking quite clearly intimidated with a frightened look on her face.

'Yes!' she answered feebly.

'I'm really sorry I exploded at you a few days ago, it seems to have become a habit I've developed over the last few months when I'm under stress and pressure; I was just so worried about James!'

'Not at all, Miss Jackson-Talbot! That's what we're here for.'

'No, seriously, if I've caused any offence, I am sorry. 'Goodnight, Staff Nurse!' And with that, Izzy walked away.

Once again, Izzy did not relish the prospect of walking down narrow side streets at that time of night, so she caught a taxi outside the hospital.

Ten minutes later, she was back on beautiful, elegant Percy Street, Izzy was still feeling tired and drained and most of all she needed her sleep. Yes, even Lady Gertrude's diary entries would need to wait until another day. Ten minutes later, Izzy was once again asleep.

At half past ten the next morning, Izzy's sleep was again rudely disrupted by the persistent chimes of her mobile 'phone ring tone. She extended an arm to answer it. James, doubtless.

'Hello!'

'Hello, Miss Jackson-Talbot. It's Susan Hillman, the staff nurse from 7A. Could you come to Ward 7a as soon as possible, please?'

Izzy was filled with dread and she could tell by the serious note of the staff nurse's voice that the news was not going to be good.

'Yes, I'll come straightaway!'

Izzy threw on her clothes, her mind racing. She managed to hail a taxi at the end of Percy Street and gratefully piled into it; James had seemed almost larger than life last night and at one point, he had even been laughing, joking and confidently saying that he believed he would live to fight a few more battles!

When Izzy reached ward 7A, she was met by Benjamin Watson looking grim and haggard, Staff Nurse Hillman looking harassed and a white coated, fair-haired man in his mid-forties of average height, who introduced himself as Charles Griffiths. They were shown into Mr Griffiths's office and asked to sit down.

'Miss Jackson-Talbot, I'm so very sorry… James Brodie passed away at nine-fifteen this morning,' Mr Griffiths informed Izzy flatly.

Izzy remembered the events of a few years ago and the sudden, almost abrupt, totally unanticipated passing away of her grandma and through the shock and grief of her loss, she recalled steeling herself for attending her grandmother's funeral that grim August morning which had so irrevocably and inevitably heralded the end of an era and telling herself, '…Izzy Jackson, you will bear this and conduct yourself with stoicism and dignity!'

Somehow, she had managed. At this point, Izzy felt once again, plunged into shock.

'Of course, and I'm sorry to say this,' continued Mr Griffiths, 'one of you will have to identify him…'

At which Ben leaned forward touching Izzy's right arm lightly and answered quietly, 'It's alright, Izzy! I will do it!'

Ben, the man for the hour who could always be counted and depended on to hold things together, even at moments of crisis like this!

'…Didn't you at least try to restart his heart for three-quarters of an hour?' Izzy asked Mr Griffiths rather critically.

'We certainly did. We tried everything.'

'And what exactly happened? I do need to know.'

'James was getting washed this morning, and I'm sorry to say, he suffered a massive heart attack. We strongly suspect he may have suffered some natural defect present in the heart's electrical firing system… Some individuals who die as a result of heart attacks are naturally prone to it.'

Izzy studied Mr Griffiths's face, his fair hair and fairly regular features; he actually looked vaguely familiar from somewhere, but due to the state of shock and trauma Izzy was currently in, she lacked the basic mental energy and effort to even attempt to refresh her memory regarding exactly where she had previously encountered him.

'You'll have a few other things to see to. Would you like half an hour's privacy to talk things over?' asked the staff nurse.

'Yes, we would,' Ben answered.

Mr Griffiths and Staff Nurse Hillman duly vacated the room.

'Have you told everyone connected with James?'

Izzy asked Ben anxiously, 'Have… Have you told Mrs Brodie?'

'Yes,' answered Ben wisely, 'I tried to do it in as gentle and kindly a way as possible, but poor soul, she went into such a state of shock that she had to be admitted to hospital herself; she's now under heavy sedation and not expected to live for very much longer.'

'And how about the poor old dog, you know, Manc, who James loved so much?'

'Oh, him! He's the least of your worries! He's now living temporarily at our house; he might well even be staying permanently.'

'Thank goodness!'

Izzy recalled the first few days in the aftermath of Ben's somewhat abrupt departure from the partnership. '…After all these years, I've now become a sole practitioner!' Now of course, that was all reversed; Ben was now the sole practitioner, unless he took another partner.

Ben gave Izzy's hand a little squeeze and then he said quietly, 'Izzy, James was a good, decent, hard-working man – a man of principle. I believe in life after death, and he's up there now praying for you, even as we speak. I think we will appoint another partner, but it won't be for at least twelve months as a mark of respect to James, my business partner and above all, my valued friend. Now you've had enough stress and trauma for today; leave the funeral, division of the estate and assets to me, I will sort them.'

'Oh, thank you, Ben.'

At that point, they were interrupted by a knock on the door and Susan Hillman popped her head round the door.

'Oh, I've got an envelope with some of James's possessions in it; as one of his next-of-kin you are entitled to them, Miss Jackson-Talbot.'

Izzy opened the small brown paper envelope. It contained James's wristwatch, a half-used blue bic pen, two credit cards, sixty-five pounds and fifty pence in cash, one set of keys to chambers, a small solitary key and James's signet ring.'

'This seems so strange…' Izzy said, '…The isolated fragments of a life.'

'Yes, precisely. At any rate, you get yourself home, Izzy love… I'll 'phone or even call round in person later to check on how you are… Try to get some decent sleep and rest.'

'What an excellent idea. Right, I had better leave, and thank you, thank you, Ben for all you've done so far and continue to do!'

'Nonsense! I've known James and been both his business partner and friend for a long time. It was the absolute least I could do, given the circumstances. Oh, and I think we can arrange James's funeral for, say, the end of next week and we'll try not to be too morbid about it; instead, we'll celebrate the life of a good, decent man!'

'Yes, my feelings entirely. Right now, I'll go and thank 7a for all they did for James, and then I'll get myself on my way. Goodbye, Ben!'

Isabel wandered back to the nurse's station. Back in the nurse's station, Mr Griffiths was sitting at the desk intently completing some paperwork; furthermore, a handful of nurses were milling about, among whom was Susan Hillman who kept repeatedly rather furtively eyeing up and looking across at Mr Griffiths's profile as though she secretly rather fancied him.

'I just wanted to thank you for all you did for James!'

Mr Griffiths looked up casually from the desk and answered breezily, 'Not at all! He was a real character and we enjoyed looking after him!'

'Yes, he was a bit of a character!' Izzy laughed uneasily and shot Mr Griffiths a rather shy smile, after which she walked quickly to the ward doors and left to walk out into the corridor between 7a and the neighbouring ward. In the outside, connecting area between the two, she again met Ben, at that stage, just leaving Mr. Griffiths's office.

'Oh, hello, Izzy! We have to stop meeting like this, eh? Well, I'd better get myself home, as I've got quite a lot to do and arrange! And you, young lady, get yourself home and rest, I'd also advise you to have a few drinks at Hannah's on the way home if you feel you need them!'

'Do you know? I might just do that!' Right now, the prospect of Hannah's Bar appeared rather attractive and they opened at one o'clock. Izzy wandered down Prescott Street, back through the university precinct, halfway along Hope Street and down onto Leece Street. Strangely enough, if Izzy admitted it to herself, she suddenly felt far less stressed and anxious, added to which the sense of panic which had totally submerged her at the prospect of her forthcoming marriage to James was now resolved, O.K. thought Izzy to herself, she had never envisaged it would be concluded so dramatically, but then she recalled the eleven o'clock service in the cathedral and the priest's words whilst giving the homily to his flock, '…Sometimes, when things appear at their most black and hopeless, one is often miraculously saved, quite frequently at the last moment.' So true! Somehow, Izzy could almost feel the spirit of James very close to her and one of their final conversations flashed upon her consciousness, 'Izzy, if something does happen to me, don't hold a candle or torch to me!' and Izzy had responded by saying, 'It would take a very special man to replace yourself, James!'

There was Hannah's Bar, a little further down the hill on the opposite side of the street, and with Izzy now feeling slightly improved, it looked like quite an enticing prospect. This is the girl who does not consume cocktails on a regular basis, but I think in view of the morning she's been subjected to, I think on this occasion, it will be permitted! My goodness, she was becoming almost as pompous as James! With that, Izzy ordered a Tierra del Fuego rum cocktail. After she had consumed this one, she would have one more and then begin to make her way back to Percy

Street, where the prospect of a sleep in her double bed was an offer she was in no position to refuse.

Izzy sipped her cocktail, feeling the slightly burning rush of the rum at the top of her throat as she swallowed it. Over the years she had so often sat here, watching the traffic sweep past and the world go by in her spiritual home, by far quite the best town in the world, or city, to be more precise! Izzy took another sip and another. Gradually, the cocktail began to relax and steady her fraught, yet slowly recovering nerves and without feeling guilty, she ordered another.

Yes, James had been treated well on 7a, thought Izzy to herself. She would need to buy the staff some chocolates and a 'thank you' card.

'…He was a real character and we enjoyed looking after him!' Izzy remembered Mr Griffiths utter as she had prepared to leave the ward. Why did the image of Mr Griffiths's face suddenly and entirely without warning present itself in Izzy's mind's eye, and also again on the opening page of her newly purchased novel? Charles was his name. Then it presently dawned on Izzy; Charles, with whom she had enjoyed one casual date within the booming, strobe-lit depths of the Blue Angel, that glitzy, romantic night at the height of the party season. Their relationship if it could have been termed a relationship - brief, transitory and unresolved. That very first momentous, memorable life demarcation point; all of nineteen years ago. At any rate, thought Izzy to herself, instantly dismissing the memories to the back of her consciousness, she was in no mood for a new relationship, no mood whatsoever. No, she would focus for the time being at least, on getting the rest of her life back into some semblance of order and normality.

After the second cocktail, Izzy retraced her steps back to Percy Street. In no time at all, she had put on her night clothes, had a thorough wash, applied her night cream and after placing James's envelope of belongings in her top clothes drawer, crawled gratefully into bed. She lost consciousness almost instantly.

Izzy surfaced from sleep three hours later. Once again and true to form, Lady Gertrude's diary was exerting its' magnetic, irresistible charms. Feeling considerably refreshed and renewed, she switched on her laptop.

Easter Sunday, 24th March, 1889. What a special, precious day this is! Spring is well and truly burgeoning all over the estate, the first daffodils, their shoots all fresh and green are beginning to burst through the ancient earth, symbolising growth, new life, repair and innate positivity. I have another week remaining of my Easter break, then we have a further three or four weeks of lectures before we are to go out into clinical practice again, but I shall not think about that just yet! Besides, I shall enjoy spring at Riversdale until then, since it really is quite exquisite!

Incidentally, after we had attended the morning church service, my glorious papa gave me such a beautiful present! The silver and sapphire dress ring, fresh from the Harrogate jewellers. What a beautiful ring it is! I really will treasure it! Sapphire and silver in an elegant square setting... And rather a good combination they make!

Sunday, 31st March, 1889. It was so good to meet up with my friends once again after our Easter break, and I have to admit I am looking forward to our month of general lectures. No early morning get ups for a start, and this is something I am really relieved about! Well, I shall turn in now for an early night, since we are due in the lecture theatre tomorrow at nine a.m. and I need to be able to sleep while I can. At any rate, I am back in my home from home of Leeds, and it feels extremely good!

Monday, 1st April, 1889. Someone on our corridor put around the myth that there was to be no breakfast laid on this morning, and of course, it turned out to be nothing more than an April fool! My goodness! Needless to say, our breakfast food arrived as usual! And I will not mince my words, I needed a decent breakfast of sorts if I was to face a day of solid lectures!

Yes, I consumed my two rashers of bacon and generous helping of scrambled egg, all rinsed down with two strong mugs of coffee.

From there, I made my way over to the general lecture theatre, armed with a writing pad and pens to meet up and sit with my good friend, Maria, who seemed equally pleased to see myself. The lecture in question was general physiology, which again, I thoroughly enjoyed.

Do you know? Something springs instantly to mind in my study of human physiology, as far as I have progressed with it to date. The key word here is, 'HOMEOSTASIS,' which means, quite literally, balance and stability. All is designed in the human body to maintain balanced, even conditions for the natural lifespan of the individual for seventy or eighty years or so.

Just at that point, Izzy was brought sharply back to reality by the persistent ring tones of her landline 'phone. She leaned across to answer it.

'Hello, Liverchester, 707 4396!'

'Hello, Izzy! It's Ben! Now, love, how are you feeling?'

What an excellent man Ben was, thought Izzy to herself.

'Oh thank you for calling! Strangely enough, I'm actually much improved from the shock of this morning. Oh, er, and incidentally, I did exactly as you yourself advised, why, I went to Hannah's Bar, just as you suggested.'

'Good. Well, of course, that's my job, providing advice, 'aint it now?'

'Well, yes.'

'I did all that was required this morning and I have the funeral in hand for next Thursday morning, eleven o'clock at St. Thomas's in Woolton. Once that's completed, we can start to get back to some semblance of normality!'

'Too true!' There, Izzy had said it again!

'At any rate, I'm so pleased you're improving. Don't be too hard on yourself, just give yourself time, you probably don't feel like this now, but time, the great healer, really does work wonders.'

'Yes, I know.'

'And I will be officially coming back to chambers on December 16th so ten days' henceforth.'

That, of course, begged the enormous yawning question of exactly when Izzy herself was going to return to work. Izzy certainly wanted to do some work, so she told Ben in response that she thought she might be best to return to work part-time and to gradually build up her employment hours.

'That sounds excellent. Now you probably need to get a bit more rest and quality relaxation time, Izzy dear. I'll need to leave you now, but I can only repeat 'DON'T BE TOO HARD ON YOURSELF, and GIVE YOURSELF TIME, and incidentally, if things get too much for you I'm only a 'phone call away, just get on the 'phone again and call me!'

'Thank you, Ben! Goodnight!'

'Goodnight, Izzy!'

Izzy replaced the 'phone. She also decided it was time she made herself a meal, which she duly did and poured herself a glass of red wine as an early evening small treat. Since Izzy was not required at work this week, she caught a late afternoon train back to Cumbria, where she remained until Wednesday.

When Izzy returned to Liverpool, she had only quite literally just set foot in her first floor flat when she heard her landline answerphone bleeping.

'Izzy, it's Ben Watson… There'll be a car provided to take you to St Thomas's in Woolton tomorrow morning. It's one of those traditional black cars, I wanted to conduct James's funeral decently; you know afford him some dignity in death… The car will arrive at your flat for ten fifteen tomorrow morning. I've made all the requisite arrangements so you've nothing to worry about. I'm still in the process of sorting out James's will.'

The next morning, Izzy got herself to James's funeral. Along with Ben Watson and Tanya, Izzy herself was the principal mourner. Needless to say, the general overarching theme of

James's obsequy, was James, the man of integrity, principle and fair play, who like every other mortal on this earth, '…Sprang up in the morning like a flower, and then the wind changes direction and he is blown away…' And human life, 'being changed, not ended at death…' Surprisingly, the church was absolutely packed, which seemed to be visible proof of James's inherent popularity and the priest concluded the proceedings by stressing that this was, 'merely a temporary parting' of the ways. As Izzy sat in the pew, idle thoughts flitted in and out of her brain… How could she have managed without Ben over the past few days? Ben, the man for the hour, who could always be counted on to step in during a crisis… He had identified James, picked up the death certificate, arranged the mechanics of James's funeral, chosen appropriate music, organised the transport, flowers and catering… And suddenly, Izzy sensed James was still present, somewhere deep within the recesses of her consciousness, Izzy was absolutely certain she heard James utter his so often used phrase, '…Too true!'

Izzy put in an appearance at the event after the funeral, although it proved difficult for her since she was entirely unfamiliar and unacquainted with the vast majority of the mourners, having never met them before in her life, but Ben's initial idea of celebrating the life of James rather than mourning his death was highly sensible and as a whole, successful.

As Izzy climbed into bed that night, she folded the silver embossed funeral card into the envelope containing James's possessions, it read: 'Funeral and Celebration of the Life of James Dominic Martin Brodie, 15th March, 1955 to 6th December, 2017.'

'…Thank you, James Brodie, for all the good and happy times we enjoyed together. You were such an exemplary supervisor, and I shall look forward to seeing you again in a few years,' thought Izzy to herself.

Somewhere, somehow, Izzy was certain that she heard James mutter his customary assent, in recognition, '…Too true.'

Chapter 17.

Next week, Izzy returned to part-time work at the chambers, starting on Wednesday morning at nine o'clock. For the first few days, chambers seemed really peculiar in the obvious absence of James, but over the next few days Izzy rapidly acclimatised, and, if truth be known, if she admitted it fully to herself, her day's work was far easier, straightforward and less complicated without him. After all, Izzy reminded herself, I never even wanted a work-based relationship! Somehow, it seemed too close to home, a fact which she had heard others say.

As Izzy retraced her steps back along Dale Street, she reminded herself that she needed to sort out the remainder of James's possessions, such as they were and in particular, those which still occupied the desk in his inner office. Ben was currently in the process of sorting out James's will, according to Ben, James had prepared a replacement will, bearing in mind his forthcoming marriage to Isabel, but in view of the fact that James had departed this life before their wedding had occurred, the later will never took effect. James's earlier will left all his property to his mother who had herself died two days before James's funeral, but Ben had managed to trace two cousins in Burscough, so it was envisaged that the bulk of James's property, for example, the Woolton house, the car, James's savings and the house furniture would pass to them. Izzy would receive nothing, but it was not a matter which unduly peturbed her, since she was earning enough money to be comfortable and eventually she would receive Edith's money. She had no need for further.

But right now, for the time being, Lady Gertrude's diary was calling Izzy. Once she got back to the Percy Street flat, Izzy headed straight for her laptop. There was now no further entry until Sunday, 2nd May, 1889.

Sunday, 2ⁿᵈ May, 1889. We have a study day tomorrow, once again in the general lecture theatre, and I am unsure of what the subject of the lecture is. I am certain all will be revealed in due course and a ten o'clock start seems ultimately preferable to a quarter past seven early day shift start!

On Tuesday morning, I am due to start my clinical practice experience on ward 27 at the dreaded Leeds Cottage Hospital again! I will make absolutely no bones about it, I have extremely negative 'vibes' concerning this hospital! No, I certainly do not like it! I thoroughly enjoyed my study day, but the dread of Tuesday morning cast an ever-present, black shadow or blight over it. I shall doubtless feel better when Tuesday is over and firmly relegated to the past.

Tuesday, 4ᵗʰ May, 1889. Well, this ward is not exactly my ideal or my dream ward, but 'tis just about tolerable. I will further enlighten you when I have had further time to settle in and acclimatise to the environment.

Friday, 7ᵗʰ May, 1889. My initial instinct was absolutely correct, regarding this ward, I hate it! I absolutely hate it! Already, I am ticking off each day as I complete it.

'Cheer up, Gerty! Everyone gets one grotty, ghastly clinical allocation!' various colleagues have told me.

As you can gather, I have greatly revised my individual views and opinions from Tuesday of this week, when I last put pen to paper! I am in full accordance with Susan from Armley[12] who was sent there when I completed my happy, carefree allocation on Ward 5Y… Oh, What happy, halcyon days! For the most part, the staff are, once again, surly and un-cooperative, (in fact, very similar to those of ward 12, at the same hospital!) Sure enough, they regard me as, 'posh' and 'upper-crust,' and I am expected to conduct myself as a Senior Staff Nurse, i.e. a fully trained nurse with at least three or four years' experience, which obviously I am quite unable to do. The staff are completely objectionable, I am well and truly sick of being stared at with distaste as though I were a specimen in a bell jar to be critically examined and found deficient and furthermore, this is a veritable hell!

---

[12] Armley, in North Leeds.

This lunchtime I was attending to a patient's dressing, when I received a telegram from would you believe it? My stepmother! Papa has had a heart attack! I am now so worried, to add to my many other existent woes! Can my problems become any worse? As a result, I asked to be immediately released from the ward in question, a request which, of course, some unpleasant members of staff were extremely loathe to honour! Surprise! Surprise!

Eventually, I was at last granted permission to do so! Thank Heavens! What a relief! I caught an early post-chaise service home, my goodness, it was absolute bliss and almost, 'heaven on earth' to leave that ward! To be blunt, I disliked the previous ward, but ward 27 is three hundred thousand times worse! To cap it all, it is a surgical ward – orthopaedic surgery, which ought to be a good and positive learning environment for a trainee, but sadly it is not!

At this point, Izzy took some time out from the diary entries, since she needed to make herself an evening meal. As she waited for her supper to heat up, Izzy opened a bottle of red wine and gradually began to sip it, whilst making a mental list of what she needed to do in the morning. Top of her list of tasks was opening James's desk to remove the contents, it would need to be emptied out and cleared before the new incoming partner arrived, in any case. Yes, that had to be done and preferably, as soon as possible. Izzy needed to remember the envelope containing the keys tomorrow morning.

The next day in chambers passed quite uneventfully, and Izzy was busy preparing to leave at ten to five, when she presently remembered the solitary key stuffed into the Jiffy bag with a few of James's possessions. Now was as good a time as any to do it. Izzy rummaged in the bag, picking up James's keys to chambers in the process, no, these would not open the desk, at least… But the solitary key… Holding the solitary key in one hand and the Jiffy bag in the other, Izzy went through into James's office. There stood the impressive, black oak, green leather topped desk, just as James had left it; and strangely enough, the desk itself looked almost as though it were simply waiting for James to return. Izzy inserted and turned the key in the lock, slid open the top drawer. It contained three half-used blue bic pens, a freshly sharpened pencil and a framed photograph of a fair, wavy-haired girl, her golden tresses tied securely back, with piercing blue eyes, clad in barrister's robes. Izzy assumed it was Alison. Well, nothing whatsoever unusual about that. That said, nothing prepared Izzy whatsoever for the shock she encountered in her investigation of the contents of the second drawer. A transparent, polythene bag had been hastily stuffed into the drawer. Furthermore, the bag seemed to be crammed full of letters and notes. Izzy stuck her hand into the bag and pulled out the top one. If truth be known, Izzy was not quite sure whether she really did want to read the contents, but a horrible compulsion and fascination held her in thrall. What she read shook Izzy to her core. On official headed notepaper, but handwritten, was the following missive:

Jones, Mills and Ellis,
Consulting Architects,
27, Water Street,
LIVERCHESTER,
L1 3BH
16th May, 1985.

My darling James,
    I can scarcely believe it! It is three days, i.e. seventy-two hours since I have seen your handsome face! I sit here alone in the drawing office picturing your face in my imagination, and quite frankly, I simply can't get enough of it!
    What a magical few days we spent in North Wales! Do you know? That was my first time, and I am highly delighted to say that you were absolutely marvellous with me, so loving, patient and caring. Why, I enjoyed every minute of it! With a little bit of practice, I will surely be

able to perfect my technique. You really are, to express it in Shakespearian terms, 'The Master of My Passions!'

It is a pity I am unable to address my correspondence to your home address, but I fully understand there may always be the possibility of your mother intercepting our communication, which is a little unfair, since we are two consenting adult males. You, my darling are thirty and I am twenty-five, so we are both perfectly old enough to know our own minds!

I am so pleased that silly Alison girl is no longer part of your life! Whatever sort of life would you have had with her! I mean I am not pleased about the nature of her death and how it occurred, but somehow, yourself and Alison never, can I say it, 'sat right' as a couple! Not with me, at any rate!

Where do you propose we go for our next date? I, personally, would very much like to try the bars on Stanley Street, or sometime, we could even go to Manchester for a meal, you know, they have the thriving gay quarter over there, and I for one would love to try it! In fact, I feel excited at the very thought!

Perhaps you could reply to this letter at your earliest convenience, or give me a call in the Water Street office. My direct line in the drawing office is 051-736-7669. I have a few things to do right now, so I shall sign off for now.

All my love,
Your ever-loving and devoted sodomite,
Tony XXX

And James had been proposing to take Izzy on a short break to North Wales! Had he intended to take her to the same accommodation as he had taken his boyfriend? At that moment, the concept raised in the church homily coursed frenziedly through Izzy's brain, 'Often, when things look at their absolute blackest and most hopeless, one is quite often saved… Or the matter is removed from one's hands!' Izzy's relationship with James now seemed like the classic example of this! Now, the matter had been entirely removed from Izzy's hands. Izzy also lately remembered her sense of dread and foreboding at the thought of her forthcoming marriage to James; but suddenly that all slipped into oblivion and was no longer her problem. Furthermore, James appeared to have led an almost Jackyll and Hide like, double existence – to the outside world, he was the quiet, shy, impeccably-mannered, gentlemanly partner solicitor and commissioner for oaths, still quietly mourning the death of his barrister fiancée in his own way; the other was a rampant homosexual who enjoyed dipping into the most certainly seamier sides of the life of the town… To cap it all, Alison and herself had fallen hook, line and sinker for the charade. '…Everything that happens to a person, occurs for a reason, so therefore it cannot be entirely bad.' Yes, Tony's letter, at one stroke had removed all Izzy's feelings, illusions and perceptions of how she had initially imagined James. Izzy idly picked up another from the mound of letters and notes.

Bergsons and Partners,
28, Old Hall Street,
LIVERCHESTER,
Merseyside
L3 8NH

28ᵗʰ October, 1989.

My darling Jimbo,

This is just a short note comprising a few lines, I largely simply wanted to tell you how happy I am to have you in my life!

*I have a little secret which remains strictly between you and I…
And here it comes, you, my darling, lovely laddo are my 'raison d'etre,'
to put it bluntly, you're at the back of everything! The reason I go to
work in the morning, the reason I sit at a table and eat a meal or even
drink a glass of wine… Why, in fact, if anything happened to yourself,
there would simply be no further point in my life! It would be a mere
existence!*

*I simply cannot wait to see you again, and am eagerly awaiting your
reply. I am even on the point of telling my parents about us as a couple,
and if a ton of trouble erupts as a result of my disclosure, I shall tell both
my parents that you, my darling, are thirty-four years of age and I am
twenty-eight years of age – both of us have lived long enough in this world
to know what will make us happy!*

I remain your admirer and devoted lover, All my love,

Phil XX

The bag was crammed full of similar letters from other male
lovers and admirers all in a similar vane. And what sort of life
would Izzy have faced had she married James? At one stage, Izzy
had believed that there was no guile or deviousness to James – well,
she couldn't have been more wrong, she thought to herself! Thank
goodness that was no longer an issue! Izzy remembered a work
colleague of her grandpa, whose daughter, when in her late twenties
or early thirties had married a homosexual, or supposedly, reformed
homosexual.

Of course, needless to say, the marriage had been an absolute
catastrophe!

Still in a sense of shock, Izzy knocked on Ben's door and
showed him the two epistles. Ben read them both, his eyes
widening in absolute horror until his face bore a close likeness to

an alarmed owl. Eventually, he put them down and gave Izzy a hug.

'Oh, Izzy, I'm so sorry! I had no idea!'

'No, nor did I!'

'Oh, my goodness! You are most certainly best off out!'

Izzy's brain slowly began to make sense of the information she had so far gleaned. She vaguely remembered James once telling her of the time he had spent in his early twenties, the time he had devoted to his priestly studies in Durham and which he had been unable to complete. Furthermore, there was something else she remembered hearing from years ago on that most delicate subject of priestly training 'If a man's vocation shows the slightest trace of homosexuality, he will NOT be permitted to be ordained.' This was doubtless the reason why James had abandoned the idea.

'Are you feeling a bit better?' Ben asked.

'Considerably.' Izzy answered.

'Let me dispose of all these on my way home!' Ben said, and further added, 'And you, Izzy dear, you get yourself home!' Once again, the man for the hour had stepped in.

Thankfully, Izzy stepped out into the daylight and sanity of Dale Street. Sure enough, Lady Gertrude's diary was once again calling her, but due to the fact that she was both mentally and physically so very much stronger and far more positive, she stopped off again at Hannah's Bar for an early evening cocktail. Well, well, well! James's guilty secret which he had kept well and truly hidden from most individuals who knew him! Ben had known nothing of it, Mrs Brodie obviously knew nothing and had no inkling of it, without doubt, Bernard, James's father when he was still living, had had no suspicions, Alison had probably never suspected anything and nor for that matter had Izzy, until she was forced to face up to the evidence of her own senses.

'I've not seen you in here for a while!' The barman said to Izzy when she ordered her cocktail.

'No, I've not really had time... A person who was once very dear to me became unwell, and I needed to sit with him in hospital... He's er... Now passed away!'

'Oh, I'm sorry!'

'Thank you. But I've just finished work and I thought I would celebrate his life.'

'That's the spirit, love, and incidentally, please have it on the house, seeing as you've suffered a bereavement.'

'That's very kind of you, thank you.'

'Not at all, love. That's my treat. And when you need the next one, don't feel too embarrassed to ask for a refill – also on the house, which goes without saying.'

Of course, one cocktail inevitably led to two, but when Izzy had consumed the second one, she felt as though she had consumed her fill of cocktails, for the time being, at any rate. In addition, her nineteenth century idol was again exerting her magnetic hold over Izzy. She thanked the barman and left.

Friday, 14ᵗʰ May, 1889. I hate this ward! I hate it! And I do not say such things lightly. I had to force myself to go into work this morning; somehow, I feel as though the atmosphere is so hostile to trainees, and hostile to me in particular. Once again, I can feel my health beginning to deteriorate, added to the fact that I am so worried about my papa!

*How is my papa, you may ask? Well, our doctor managed to stabilise him, but told us that he must rest and take things far easier in the aftermath of his heart attack. At present, I am so disillusioned with nursing that I feel like taking some time out, **R I G H T N O W** to look after and tend to my papa. After all, once I left the tutelage of my governess, I carried out large amounts of basic, rather unskilled nursing tasks for some of the elderly and ageing estate employees, assisting with personal hygiene, helping them to dress, bed-making, serving of meals and drinks, that sort of thing.*

I left a note with the School of Nursing stating that I really was so very unhappy on ward 27 (and this is not at all like me, under normal circumstances! No, not at all!!!), asking if in view of the extremely difficult circumstances on ward 27, I would like to be released and allocated to an alternative ward. I do not really wish to describe this ward in greater detail, since it is so very unpleasant, all I can say is that I find many of the staff completely obnoxious and I do not feel as though I have been treated fairly, nor do I feel that I am in any way to blame!

Surprise, surprise!! I failed the only half-completed ward allocation and I am now sitting by my papa, as I write in my diary, tending and ministering to his every need! What bliss to escape the unpleasant hellhole of ward 27, where my name is quite literally mud! At any rate, the good news is papa is almost restored to full health again. In fact, he appears to be improving with almost every passing day. What excellent news!

The School of Nursing have asked me to return in early September, where I shall be re-deployed to another ward. But what a beautiful country seat I have to return to; summer is just about to blossom on the estate, or it will in a few weeks' time, yes, our pink, white, red and yellow roses, the bluebells and violets in the woods and celandines out on the estate parkland, yes, my rural and pastoral idyll will be a veritable riot of colour and a true delight to walk through.

So, Lord Roger had also suffered heart problems. Intrigued, Izzy read on. There was now no entry until Monday, 28th May, 1889, which simply specified that Lord Roger was now out of danger and had made a full recovery. Lady Gertrude, needless to say, was highly delighted and relieved.

There was now no further entry until Monday, 3rd September, 1889.

Monday, 3rd September, 1889. We had another study day entitled, Nutrition and Maintenance of Adequate Hydration in patients. Again, I thoroughly enjoyed it. I also paid a rapid visit to my next clinical practice area both to formally introduce myself and ascertain which shifts I was required to present myself for. I am needed for tomorrow morning, the early day shift. Oh, horrors! Despite this, the news is quite good. Ward 6X looks perfectly decent and so do the staff. I will be able to further explain when I have completed tomorrow. Thank goodness my ghastly, highly unpleasant ordeal is behind me!

Tuesday, 4ᵗʰ September, 1889. Well, what a nice, decent ward! I simply have one matter to currently bring to your attention! My basic problem now seems to be that civilised though this ward is, I am not quite able to function at my absolute optimum level due to the fact that I have lost a great deal of my confidence, and this is doubtless the fault of that disgusting ward 27. What a horrible environment that was! In fact, I shall go so far as to say that no trainee should be subjected to and be forced to suffer what I had to face up to on ward 27.

Friday, 15ᵗʰ October, 1889. Well, our work allocation cards are marked in sections of twelve.

For ward 6X, I managed to obtain ten grades of excellent and two of satisfactory, but I am certain that had I not been forced to endure that foul, unpleasant environment that calls itself ward 27 at Leeds Cottage Hospital, I would have easily obtained a full complement of excellent grades. I submitted my work allocation card to the School of Nursing, and highly relieved I was for it to leave my possession.

Monday, 10ᵗʰ November, 1889. The School of Nursing have informed me that I am advised to take the next six months out and then return to complete a further two ward allocations.

Obviously, I will not be re-deployed on the two on which I came an untimely cropper! If truth be known, I am only too happy to do this, yes, take some time out and return refreshed in a few months' time!

There was now no further recorded diary entry until the year after, and that was well into summer.

Friday, 14ᵗʰ July, 1890. What a pleasant ward 4Y has been, an extremely positive learning experience and lastly, I shall add that I shall be really sorry to leave it. I am so very pleased to inform you that I obtained a pass-grade!

Tuesday, 5ᵗʰ September, 1890 to Friday, 16ᵗʰ October, 1890. My time has expired on ward 9Y, but again, it was constructive and highly positive. Once again, I obtained a decent pass grade!

Monday, 3ʳᵈ December, 1890. Well, well, well! I am twenty-three years old, and now I am pleased to say that I am in the happy position of being able to call myself a Staff Nurse! I did need to visit Leeds in any case, since I needed to collect my Staff Nurse uniforms. But you will never guess what transpired! After I had obtained my uniforms, I began to retrace my steps towards the Central Dining Rooms to meet papa, when who should I see walking in the opposite direction on the same side of the street as myself, and furthermore, to cap it all, he had seen me, was Ernest! Yes, Ernest, just about the last person I either wanted or needed to see!

'Well, well, young lady and good morning to you!'

'Good morning, Ernest!' I answered tartly, 'And don't think you can suddenly and quite miraculously worm your way back into my attentions!'

'Excuse me! I was not attempting to!' Ernest answered, rather indignantly.

'Did you know I have now become a Staff Nurse?'

'No, I was not aware.'

'Well, I have!'

'Forgive me, young lady… No, I really do mean it… I have been an extremely stupid, shallow and selfish man. I've returned from my travels and exquisite though they were, they would have been all the better with you, young lady at my side!'

'Well, you've left it a little late for that!' I responded rather sharply.

'Why, do I sense I have a rival? Have you had your head turned by a member of the medical profession?'

'No, but you, quite frankly, are far more trouble than you happen to be worth!'

'Well, I'm truly sorry you feel like that. Yes, I fully admit you have every right to be annoyed and angry with me, but could I possibly write to you in a few days' time?'

'Well, yes, you can, but do not assume that means that you are once again flavour of the month with me! Now, if you will excuse me, I'm due to meet my papa at the Central Dining Rooms for lunch, in ten minutes time! Good afternoon, Ernest!' And with that, I walked rapidly in the opposite direction towards the Wool Exchange and Central Dining Rooms. I said nothing whatsoever to papa concerning the subject of my unanticipated rendezvous with Ernest.

Monday, 10th December, 1890. My goodness! This year has simply flown past! We are, yet again on the build-up to another Christmas! We have spent the bulk of today doing the usual estate visiting, giving out the Christmas foods and parcels to the estate employees.

Guess what? I received a brief missive from that, 'wolf in sheep's clothing,' Ernest, and that, I feel is what he is. I have not yet thought of or had time to construct an appropriate response. Just give me time.

There was now no entry until Monday, 12th January, 1891.

Monday, 12th January, 1891. Well, I am settling in well on my new ward, 4X, which is the respiratory ward, and a medical ward, I am highly pleased to relate. Furthermore, I am Staff Nurse, Gertrude Rivers now.

I eventually managed to pen a response to Ernest. I told him I hoped he was settling in back in Leeds, and that business was flourishing (I believe he is something connected to the woollen trade) and that I was greatly enjoying the challenge of my new post here on the respiratory ward. But let me stress here that there were no passionate declarations of undying love and nor will there ever be.

Friday, 16th January, 1891. (Early evening) Guess what occurred this evening? A large bouquet of out of season, 'Christmas' roses arrived for Miss G.E.J. Rivers (Gertrude Emily Jane) is my full name, now placed in a vase of fresh water; according to my stepmother they arrived in the middle of the *afternoon. The flowers arrived with a small card, which was duly inscribed, 'My darling Gertie, expect a surprise next week! All my love and best wishes, E.*

XXX.'

Izzy was still feeling drained and still needing her sleep. She would return to Lady Gertrude's diary tomorrow after her day's work, besides, it suddenly occurred to Izzy that she had not yet investigated the other side of James's desk which certainly needed to be cleared out in time for the arrival of the new partner. She switched off the laptop, had a quick wash and brush of her teeth, pulled on her nightwear and crawled into the inviting depths of her bed. She was asleep almost instantly.

The next day passed equally uneventfully, until half-past four. As good a time to do it as any. Clear and tidy the desk out… Yes, it had to be done. Once again, she went through to James's inner office, slid the solitary key in the lock and firmly pulled the top drawer out.

The top drawer yielded a blue and black bic pen and three rubber bands. What did the next drawer hold in store? It was far easier to open the second drawer on this side, since Izzy suspected she knew what might await her.

Another polythene bag stuffed full of notes and letters greeted Izzy on its' opening. Again, Izzy picked one out at random. It read:

Imperial Chambers,
Barristers-at-Law,
28, Dale Street,
LIVERCHESTER,
L3 5CG

15th April, 2001

My dear James,

What a lover you are! Have you been taking lessons over the years? Maybe you are like a rare, unique vintage wine which simply matures and improves with age! At any rate, keep on with what you do, since it obviously comes naturally.

At any rate, I'm sitting here writing this poor beggar's defence and all I can think of is you, my marvellous, delightful, sexy Jimbo! I really can't wait to see you again, in fact, I'm counting the hours, I so long to see your handsome face again.

I could not help but overhear from the Head of Chambers this morning, that at one stage, (going back to the early eighties), you once conducted a romantic dalliance with a lady barrister, Alison Maitland, who was actually employed by these chambers; come on, admit it, Jimbo, you far prefer men, you fit in far better with the gay fraternity!

I still am quite unable to believe my luck in having met up at my age (I'm thirty-four), with such a marvellous man as yourself. Well, I had better sign off now, since this defence will not write itself.

All my love, my darling, handsome, sexy Jimbo… There is someone here who loves you dearly and totally without question…

I remain, your ever-loving and very devoted sodomite,

Stephen W
XXX

Never, ever in a million years, or by any stretch of the imagination would Izzy ever have classed James as handsome, but according to the writings of some of James's boyfriends, the gay fraternity certainly regarded him as fulfilling that criteria and falling without doubt into that category! For all these years, James had lived a lie! As Izzy suspected, the only purposes served by Alison and Izzy herself, were to act as decoys; and to present an impression of seeming normality to the outside world. No, she was far best off out!

Izzy, acclimatized by now to the trauma, casually picked out another. It read:

> *Reed and Nelson,*
> *Dental Surgeons,*
> *15, Princes Parade,*
> *Toxteth,*
> *LIVERCHESTER,*
> *L8 3ND*
>
> *16th October, 1998*
>
> *My dear James,*
>
> *I just can't get you out of my head! The image of your face continues to materialise in the dental filling material, the handle of the electric drill which I use and your very voice is quite simply music to my ears.*
>
> *I need to see you again, there is no doubt about it, in fact, I shall not mince my words, I SHALL COUNT THE HOURS UNTIL I SEE YOU AGAIN…….*
>
> *All my love,*
> *Dave*
> *XX*

(P.S. I so enjoy the attentions of an older man!)

Izzy picked up another. This one was a really old epistle and looked to be written by James himself.

Minskills and Partners,

14, Castle Street,

LIVERCHESTER,

Merseyside,

L1 3BH

28th October, 1981

My dear Brian,

I can scarcely believe it! It is a week since I have last seen you. Please finish your conference and return to me, since I feel I really do have much to still learn from you. (In more ways than one!!!)

Of course, I shall soon be leaving Minskills Partnership, since my articles'/work contract is almost completed, and the chances are I will be moving to Pearson and Foster, just round the corner, almost at the top of Dale Street. Now don't feel unhappy, since I shall not be far away; we will still be able to maintain regular contact and meet up at Rigby's after work for food and drink.

My new 'phone number at Pearson and Foster is 051-706-3989.

All my love, my darling Bri,

Your ever-loving and very devoted sodomite,

James XX

(P.S. I have not yet told my parents of my sexual predilections, but if this does for any reason leak out, I shall tell them I am a twenty-six year old man, and you, in turn are twenty-nine, in fact you turn thirty at the beginning of next month; hence, we are both fully able to know our own minds!!!)

So Minskills was where James had completed his articles. Additionally, Pearson and Foster's number was the same as Brodie and Watson, Izzy could not help but notice. Not surprisingly, Izzy had no wish to see any further communication. Once again, Izzy took them through to a shell-shocked Ben, who told her he would again dispose of the bag. Anxious to steer the conversation away from James's sexual proclivities and leaning against the front of his desk with his arms folded, Ben said casually, 'Well, we gave the old sodomite a decent send off at least!'

'Too true.' Too true! My goodness, Izzy had said it again!

'But you know what I say, 'There but for the grace of the Almighty go I…' And, '…Hate the sin, but love the sinner…' In so many other ways he was such a good, decent man and a fair employer…'

The memory of James's funeral requiem flashed through Izzy's consciousness.

'…And remember the funeral words, '…And forgive any sins he may have committed in the folly of human weakness!' Ben continued.

Izzy remembered a queue of practising believers lining up to take communion and distantly remembered Ben Watson among them.

'Are you also an R.C., Ben?' asked Izzy.

'Well, I'm a convert. I came from an agnostic family in Warrington; but Lil's a very sincere and committed R.C. When I started seeing her, her father, Frank was quite unhappy about my religious beliefs, or rather, the lack of them – he kept quite repeatedly saying, 'Honestly, our Lil, you'd be far better off with a man of your own faith…!!! It's far better when like sticks to like!' Eventually, after much debate, since I felt as though it was only right to convert if I felt committed enough, I decided to go, now what do they call it? Under 'instruction?' Is that the word? …Poor old Father MacKenzie… I drove him absolutely screwy due to the fact that I queried, questioned and challenged everything, but here I am now, more Catholic almost than the Pope himself! Guess who was my sponsor?'

'I've no idea!'

'Our devoted sodomite, James!'

Izzy could not help but laugh. There was also something that Izzy had noticed in the missives from James's boyfriends, a strange pattern had begun to emerge. With the exception of the extremely old one from October, 1981, they were all written by much younger men. Presently Ben himself made reference to that fact.

'Izzy, in so many other ways he was such a good man, a man of principle. I'm sure he's up there, praying for us now, or at least, well on his way there. If James really did possess those sexual proclivities which I think he may, that was his misfortune and he had committed no crime, but what I do not approve of and really do deplore is corruption of younger men. Furthermore, his so-called romantic dalliances with both yourself and Alison! Well, to my mind, both those acts of misbehaviour were completely beyond the pale!'

'So true. My feelings entirely.'

'Oh, incidentally, Manc, you know, James's dog, loves his new home. He was a little unsettled the first two nights, but neither of us had the heart to return him to the Animal Rescue Centre… He loves his evening runs through Sefton Park!'

'Good! I'm so pleased to hear it.'

'Now you get yourself home, young lady, and, as I said before, take it easy and spoil yourself!'

'Oh, don't worry, Ben. That's exactly what I intend to do.'

Izzy happily left chambers, once again, Hannah's Bar and Lady Gertrude were calling her and the latter, in particular, was exerting its compulsive, all-powerful effect upon her. There was now no entry in Lady Gertrude's diary until Monday, 18th January, 1891.

Monday, 18th January, 1891. Well, I completed the late shift and then withdrew to my bed, which I sorely need to, since I need my sleep; and I am due to work the early day shift tomorrow morning. What is all this about Ernest and his surprise? To me, the man is a total enigma and I have no surprise yet. He really does blow hot and cold!

I will now need to write and thank him for his very generous gift of the beautiful flowers, and I will do this when I have the time.

There was no entry recorded for Tuesday, 19th January, 1891.

Wednesday, 20th January, 1891. I have been once again allocated to the late shift. For the most part, the late shift passed smoothly, but unremarkably, and that is all I can really say about it; until ten minutes before the end of my day, i.e. five past nine at night, when I returned to the nurse's station, having been attending to a breathless patient for a few minutes; lo and behold, another beautiful bouquet of pink carnations and white freesias had materialised, together with a small card which read, 'To Staff Nurse, Lady G Rivers… Sorry to have missed you, I will make contact over the next few days… All my love to my most exemplary lady…….Love, Ern XX.'

In other words, Ernest! What a character he is! And I believe Ernest is now being a little presumptuous! How after all this time has elapsed, does he now believe that I am still 'his' lady?

Thursday, 21st January, 1891. Well, I was once again completing all my tasks when I was informed by the nursing sister that there was a gentleman wishing to see me. No! There will be no prizes for guessing who the gentleman in question is. As I stepped out of the ward swing doors, I knew him only too clearly! There in his frock-coat, shapely top-hat, which, of course, he had carefully removed and was holding, elegant waist-coat of lime green watered silk, impeccable, navy-blue breeches and immaculate crisp, white lawn shirt, he looked very much the country gentleman.

'Gertie, I must speak with you!' He told me.

'Hello, Ernest,' I answered in reply, still managing to maintain a manner of singularly detached neutrality; at which, of course, the nursing sister left us alone.

'Gerty, you drive me insane!'

'Oh, do I now? And incidentally, I need to thank you for your exquisite floral tributes, they were both quite beautiful.'

'Not at all. Gerty… My dear Gerty, would you come with me next week to a lecture? In fact you would do me the greatest honour if you would grace me with your presence. The lecture is given by the 'Leeds Homeless, Poor and Destitute Benevolent Fund,' and concerns how we can generally improve their lot.'

'Well that,' I answered, 'Is a subject extremely close to my heart. Sometimes, Ernest Watkins, I will go almost as far as to say that I half like you. Yes, I shall be only too pleased to attend.'

'Well you, young lady have made me an extremely happy man! Thank you, my dear!' And with that he vanished.

Friday, 22nd January, 1891. Well, I am now happily writing my diary from our family seat of Riversdale, close to Ripon. I have told neither my papa nor my step-mother of my renewed friendship with Lord Ernest, since I have to admit, it is still very much in its' infancy and I am still quite unsure of how it will develop. But I have until next week, Wednesday night, in fact, to look forward to and await it.

I have for long thought of and worried about the fate of those less fortunate than myself. As a nurse, I could employ my nursing skills to assist in a clinic, to help those less fortunate than myself, free of charge of course. In fact, I would love to do this! I really am happy in my nursing role and to be completely honest, I regard this as my life's work! Retrospectively, when I cared for the elderly and infirm estate cottagers, they seemed to largely really appreciate my attempts…

'Oh, Gerty… I'm so pleased and happy that you were able to attend to me!' and someone else passed the comment, '…Some of these attendants, why, they can be so abrupt, but you, Gerty, are totally different!' And another, '…Oh, Gerty! In times of crisis, you can always be counted on to save the day and help us out!'

For tonight, I shall simply enjoy the Friday night festivities; I shall be back to my normal urban environment Sunday evening!

There was no now further diary entry until Wednesday, 27th January, 1891.

Wednesday, 27th January, 1891. My dear Ernest! I have to admit, I am once again, quite enamoured of him! I thoroughly enjoyed the lecture which Ernest invited me to attend. A little later, as we enjoyed an evening meal together, I told him of my still very basic plan, still existing in embryonic form only at present, of the free clinic, which I would be fully prepared to devote some spare time to.

Yes, as I said earlier, I feel as though I am quite enamoured… You know what they say, or, at any rate, I am certain I have read this in one of Mr Hardy's[13] novels of, '…A passion truly ignited, can never really die!' Well, I suppose that all really depends on the recipient!

There was now no further diary entry until Friday 5th July, 1892.

Friday, 5th July, 1892. Well, well, well! I have been asked after only eighteen months of, as they term it, 'staffing,' as St. James's hospital in Leeds to fill the newly arisen vacancy of nursing sister! I never believed I would ever have been capable of it!

---

[13] Thomas Hardy, the Victorian writer.

Both papa and Ernest are highly delighted. I am now twenty-five years of age and reasonably well-established in my career.

Monday, 7th July, 1892. I am pleased to relate to you that we opened our clinic, and this is all largely due to the exemplary endeavours of both my marvellous papa and Lord Ernest, who both donated substantial sums of money. I think the clinic will progress nicely, and I have definite plans to add on a homeless refuge centre to the clinic; I am absolutely certain that both papa and Ernest will support me in this venture.

There was now no further entry until Thursday, 26th October, 1892.

Today was not so good. I have overworked lately, tried to take on too much and more than I was able to cope with, both with my ward-based job and the establishment of the clinic and refuge centre. Hence, this is largely my own fault. I collapsed in the nurse's station and went clean out, I am ashamed to say. I then eventually came round, feeling roasting hot with a horrendous, persistent cough, which required the use of my handkerchief. On removal of the handkerchief, it was stained bright red.

Seeing me in such a horrendous way, one member of staff sent a telegram to my papa, who is sending a carriage to pick me up and return me to Riversdale.

'Staff Nurse Rivers, I fear you may be in the early stages of consumption, but like any other disease, if caught early, as it has been, you stand a good chance of recovery,' the junior doctor told me. 'You must now get yourself home, bedroom windows wide open, plenty of bed rest and your bed needs to be warm, comfortable, piled high with blankets and we need to kill the disease.'

My legs felt so very weak that they seemed to have almost forgotten their basic function of holding me upright. I had to be carried down to the carriage and placed on the interior seat by two hospital porters.

Again, there was now no further entry until 3rd December, 1892. Poor Lady Gertrude!

Wednesday, 3rd December, 1892. I am pleased to say that I am feeling so very much better!

Papa has been so worried about me. In fact, the entire family have rallied round me, even my wayward brother, Harry has come to see me to check on my progress a few times and still more surprisingly, my step-mother, who has spent many hours sitting by my sick bed!!!

I sent a telegram to Lord Ernest telling him of my recent recovery. I have also told him that when we reach the new year, my new year's resolution would be to try to be a better person. He, of course promptly telegraphed back to say that there was no need for that, I was already a good person! Well, be that as it may, I am certain there is still room for improvement, but I shall not think about the new year yet. I shall enjoy regaining my strength and look forward to the Christmas festivities at Riversdale, which will now of course, be a double celebration as I am feeling better and of course, 'tis Christmas!

Sunday and Monday, 15th and 16th January, 1893. I am now fit to work once again and have just returned to Leeds this evening. I am due to start work again tomorrow afternoon and 'twill be my very first shift as a nursing sister.

There was again no entry until Monday 3rd March, 1893.

Monday, 3rd March, 1893. I am twenty-six years of age, in fact, I turned twenty-six at the end of February, and what a celebration that was! At any rate, I am highly pleased to tell you that we have opened the refuge centre, as of today!

Again, there was now no entry whatsoever until 30th March of the year after.

Thursday, 30th March, 1894. What a special day! I am twenty-seven years old and Lord Ernest and myself have become an officially engaged couple!

I really am so happy! And Lord Ernest was absolutely right! We both needed to establish ourselves and our own sense of independent identity before we formalised our relationship. In fact, we sealed our commitment this morning, courtesy of the exemplary Mr Summers of Leeds – a gleaming, delicate solitaire, set in eighteen carat yellow gold! We shall return to Mr Summers later on in the year for purchase of my wedding ring. Since I am twenty-seven years old and Ernest is about to turn thirty-three, no-one can say that we are too young, or have rushed into it; after all we have known each other almost eight years and we are certainly no longer children!

Thursday, 16th October, 1894. I married my dear Lord Ernest! As I write these notes, we are currently honeymooning in Venice! Venice is absolutely magical and we absolutely love wandering about its' back streets and savouring the decaying grandeur! We also love sipping our morning coffee in St Marks' Square, I might add.

Thursday, 30th October, 1894. I am sorry to have to tell you I had another bout of coughing this morning. The result of my expectorations was once again, an ominous red stain on my handkerchief. I feel extremely weak and once again, I am running a raging temperature.

Monday 3rd November, 1894 was obviously added to conclude the writings.

Monday, 3rd November, 1894. With her characteristic cheer, positivity and great dignity, Lady Gertrude departed this earthly life, so in the manner of those poets, artists and authors of Venice who met singularly untimely ends.

The devastated Lord Ernest returned Lady Gertrude's mortal remains to Riversdale where she was interred in the family chapel. He himself died in total penury, in Whitby, North Yorkshire, five months later, a sad and broken man due to the collapse of his business. The entire estate, with the exception of the extremely infirm turned out to mourn Lady G and follow the funeral cortege. Lord Roger himself, was so crippled by grief due to the death of his much-loved daughter, that he only outlived Gertrude by a further eighteen months; it was believed he himself contracted consumption from Gerty. Yet again, at his death, almost the entire estate turned out to mourn his passing. In the aftermath of Lord Roger's death, Lady Alice Rivers fled to live in obscurity in Leeds, where she eventually married a much older man. Harry Rivers, who on the death of his father became the next Lord Rivers, successfully completed his P.hD studies but died of alcohol-related complications at the untimely age of only thirty-two. He was unmarried. Riversdale Hall remained empty and uninhabited for at least ten years, until Lord Edward Rivers and his sister, Lady Rachel Rivers returned to live there, and the ancient, noble pile was once again, restored to its' former glory.

Izzy was brought sharply back to reality at this point. All those deaths towards the end of the story, but then, Izzy reminded herself, death from consumption would have been in those days an only too common occurrence. Pity, thought Izzy to herself; she would have loved Lady G to have enjoyed a happily married life with two children… Yes, two, thought Izzy to herself; a small mini Gertrude, followed by a boy, two years or eighteen months later.

Twelve months passed. Izzy had only a few months of her articles contract left to complete, and she was not altogether sorry, not by any means. Incidentally, no-one had replaced James in Izzy's life, and if Izzy admitted it to herself, she was not looking too hard. Strangely enough, Izzy found herself still captivated by the memory of Lady Gertrude and her untimely death at the extremely young age of twenty-seven. That evening, she was idly dipping back into the Lady Gertrude Rivers' website, when she was interrupted by the persistent chimes of the ring-tone of her mobile 'phone. She reached into her trouser pocket to answer it.

'Hello!'

'Hello, there! Er…, it's Charles Griffiths, and how do I find Izzy Jackson this evening?'

Izzy had to think hard before she was able to remember who Charles Griffiths was. Oh yes, the heart specialist who had cared for James in the last few weeks of his life.

'Well, it's not been easy, but I'm coping.'

'Er, the reason for my call, is, er… Well, I wondered whether you could make… An old man really happy… In short, could you meet me for a curry next week?'

Well, this was a little out of the blue and totally unanticipated. At this point, Izzy reflected that their hour of glory had simply comprised a few all too short but magical, precious hours in the depths of the Blue Angel, after which he had vanished from her life. So no… That had been left unfinished… Unresolved… Nor had he become an item with Senior Staff Nurse, Susan Hillman… Sometimes, as Izzy reflected to herself, personal and private life were far best kept separate and apart from the work environment, a fact she had so firmly enshrined herself, until her encounter with James. Izzy had nothing whatsoever to lose.

'Yes, I would be only too pleased!'

'Excellent! Say, next Wednesday evening at, what? Say ninefifteen?'

'I shall greatly look forward to it.'

A warm glow enveloped Izzy. This was suddenly all very exciting! 'Could you make an old man really happy?' resounded in her brain for a few hours after their telephone conversation.

'Well, I shall have to go now, I have work calling me, but if it's alright, could I call you over the weekend?'

'Yes, gladly, Charles. I'd be only too pleased to talk to you.'

'Good, so I'll say goodbye for now, but we'll speak again soon!'

'Goodnight, Charles!'

'Goodnight, Izzy!'

Izzy spent an ordinary, average sort of day in chambers the next day, and the day after, Friday, was equally average. During the past week or so, various individuals had passed in and out of chambers since Ben was now interviewing for the vacant post of partner and he appeared to be singularly unimpressed so far, with the majority of the applicants which he had received.

Much to Izzy's surprise, at quarter past four, when she was providing Tanya with instructions for the production of a piece of buyer's property information, Ben suddenly arrived in the front office and announced, 'Well, ladies, I'm highly pleased to inform you both that after all this time we've eventually found a new partner.'

'Is this another dissident from Hill Foster's?' asked Izzy uncertainly.

'Well… In a manner of speaking, yes. I think you could say he was my only friend in the property department at Hill Foster's… Yes, Hill Foster's, the partnership from Hell! When you reach a certain age, they no longer want to know you. Well, this gentleman's decided to leap before he gets pushed. Brian Edwards, his name is… Very, very nice. Incidentally, we should have a good time with him, just think, Rigby's Bar awaits!'

Half an hour later, Izzy had a further piece of completed work to check through with Ben, so she went through to the privacy of Ben's inner office, which he duly scrutinised and gave his seal of approval to.

'I think you'll like the new partner, Izzy,' said Ben confidently. 'Just think, Watson and Edwards has rather a good ring to it. When James passed away, in so many ways it seemed like the end of an era – the end of the partnership. Now, it seems like the beginning of a new, different, quite exciting phase. I'm also thinking in a few years, but, of course, only if you want and need it. Well, in two years or so, it could well be 'Watson, Edwards and Jackson-Talbot or alternatively, Edwards, Watson and Jackson-Talbot, whatever sounds best! Oh, and Brian's a bit of a party animal, so expect plenty of bonding sessions and Rigby's back-bar events, and furthermore, as far as I'm aware, my friend, Brian is currently single and unattached!'

Just at that moment, Izzy's mobile 'phone began to ring out.

'Hello!'

'Oh, hello, darling. It's Charles!'

'Oh, hello Charles!'

'I just wanted to hear your voice. I'll give you a call over the weekend, and then we're due to meet up next week for our curry night.'

'Yes, it's so exciting!'

'Well, I'll love and leave you for now, I'm in work all this weekend. My goodness, you know what they say, 'No rest for the wicked,' eh? We'll speak soon... Goodbye, love!'

'Goodbye, Charles.' With that Izzy ended the call.

Ben looked up from the desk, looking slightly puzzled.

'Am I missing something? Oh, I'm sorry, please forgive me. Obviously, not my business!'

'It's the new man in my life, Charles. I think you may have met him when James passed away. Charles Griffiths, the heart specialist.'

'Oh, him!' Ben's face broke into a deep beam as he realised who Izzy was referring to.

'Seriously, Izzy, I never really did altogether totally approve of the James and Izzy liaison. The age gap for a start, in fact, it was the reason that I had those two altercations with him... You were far too much of a bubbly, outgoing livewire for James, not to speak of his guilty little secret which he kept closely guarded and hidden all those years! I hope it does work out with this Charles, I really do, but if for any reason it comes to nothing, there's always my new partner, Brian – who I suspect will probably be ready, willing, able and interested in our Izzy! But at any rate, old Tom Doolittle wants to meet Charles soon, but this time, he wants to meet him under happier circumstances!'

THE END.

About the Author

Estelle Jane Kennedy was born in East Lancashire and went on to study English and Philosophy at the University of Liverpool. She trained in nursing and later in Law and is presently in the process of completing her legal studies. Fairytale Caverns is Estelle Kennedy's first book. Estelle lives in Liverpool and divides her time between her Merseyside and East Lancashire homes.

This rough idea for this book was originally triggered when I was about nine years old, on a Sunday afternoon visit to North Yorkshire, and which had lain idle in the depths of my brain for years. Similarly, no specific plan for the book materialised for many years.

Ultimately, the basic themes for the book comprise respect and in turn enjoyment of nature and the natural world and the value of personal relationships with others.

BV - #0004 - 161222 - C0 - 210/148/24 - PB - 9781913839604 - Gloss Lamination